She supposed a person ought to say something; everybody did when they won something. She pulled her beret down more over her ears.

"It wasn't us," she said in her hoarse, carrying voice. "Jist luck, I guess. I got it at the Penny Novelty when I took the kids to the clinic last spring. So I guess it was just luck—an'—an' goat manoor." She made out the faces of Mrs. Tregillis and Mrs. Fitzgerald; the whole St. Aidan's Church Ladies' Auxiliary would be down there. "An' the Lord," she amended quickly. "I don't know what makes anything beautiful," she said almost helplessly," unless it's luck, the Lord, an' goat manoor."

And Canon Midford, as shocked as anyone else when the award had been announced, thought that if the philosophy of salvation must rest upon basic simplicities, then luck and the Lord and goat manure would do as well as any. Mame Napoleon was right. She could have written Ecclesiastes with her wonderfully steady sense of the ways of the Universe and of prize-winning roses.

ROSES ARE DIFFICULT HERE

A novel by

W. O. MITCHELL

SEAL BOOKS
McClelland-Bantam, Inc.
Toronto

*This edition contains the complete text
of the original hardcover edition.*
NOT ONE WORD HAS BEEN OMITTED.

ROSES ARE DIFFICULT HERE

*A Seal Book / published by arrangement with
McClelland & Stewart, Inc.*

PRINTING HISTORY
McClelland & Stewart edition published 1990
Seal edition / November 1991

ISBN 0-770-42496-1

*Seal Books are published by McClelland-Bantam, Inc. Its trademark, consisting of
the words "Seal Books" and the portrayal of a seal, is the property of McClelland-
Bantam, Inc., 105 Bond Street, Toronto, Ontario M5B 1Y3, Canada. This trademark
has been duly registered in the Trademark Office of Canada. The trademark
consisting of the words "Bantam Books" and the portrayal of a rooster is the property
of and is used with the consent of Bantam Books, 666 Fifth Avenue, New York, New
York 10103. This trademark has been duly registered in the Trademark Office of
Canada and elsewhere.*

PRINTED IN CANADA
COVER PRINTED IN U.S.A.

UNI   0 9 8 7 6 5 4 3 2

To Hughena McCorquodale,
editor of *The High River Times*

CHAPTER 1

HE TILTED BACK IN THE DESK CHAIR, STARED UP TO THE framed blow-up of the masthead hung above the filing cabinets. Cloud arched over the jagged outline of the Rockies; across the soft wells of the foothills in upper case was printed: SHELBY CHINOOK, PUBLISHER AND EDITOR, BENJAMIN J. TROTTER. The letters slanted to starboard as though blown by wind, or else Benjamin J. Trotter had gone several times too often to the silver flask in the right-hand top drawer of this desk when he had designed the masthead for his weekly back in 1902.

"Chinook . . . 5.(lc) a warm, dry wind which blows at intervals down the eastern slopes of the Rocky Mountains." It was a wind of forgiveness, pardoning plants, insects, animals, and humans with reprieve from winter punishment, breathing over the Pacific, off the Japanese current, and then gusting high above the Rockies and down the eastern slopes with gathering speed and power to clear grey skies, honey-comb ice, melt and shrink the snowdrifts. At forty, fifty, sixty miles an hour it came, so thermometers soared to San Francisco high, holding up there for as long as ten days at a stretch.

Praise the Lord! Born-again Spring!

Beside the masthead photo was the first Pulitzer Prize

ever won outside the United States, awarded to: "BENJAMIN
JAMES TROTTER, EDITOR AND PUBLISHER OF THE SHELBY
CHINOOK, FOR DEFENSE OF FREEDOM OF THE PRESS." That had
happened in 1935, when the new provincial government
had brought down censorship legislation forbidding criti-
cism of government policy, either in print or on radio. Ben
Trotter broke that law, attacking it editorially with rage and
satire, smiting it again and again, hip, thigh, and shinbone,
all the way to the provincial Supreme Court, where it was
declared *ultra vires*. If it hadn't been, he would have
shinnied on up to the federal Supreme Court. Way to go,
Uncle Ben!

Very early in childhood he had come to know his
mother's brother well through the annual visits down East,
made for publishing-business reasons, his uncle always
said, but more likely to make sure the boy and his mother
were doing all right since his father's death. Each time
Uncle Ben would stay with them at least a week in their East
York house. His earliest remembrance of Ben Trotter was
the fruity smell of chewing tobacco, and the bouquet of
printer's ink that came with the man across almost a
continent. Also, at times, there would breathe from him
another aroma, sweet and heady and yeasty, that had
something to do with the skinny silver flask snugged in his
hip pocket, curved from his sitting on it so much. He loved
the guy, and he knew his uncle loved him too. He would
always keep an after-image of the little bearded man with
the wild hair and the wild eye, who had an endless store of
funny and exciting anecdotes. And who also swore a lot.

Uncle Ben had died an untimely death New Year's Eve,
1948, frozen in the snowdrifts behind the Ranchmen's
Club, with an empty sterling silver flask in his buffalo coat
pocket. He would have achieved eighty-seven on February
11. Now the masthead read: "SHELBY CHINOOK, EDITOR AND
PUBLISHER, MATTHEW B. STANLEY," since Uncle Ben had
willed the weekly to the nephew whom he had also printed
well. Hard act to follow.

Well, Uncle Ben, for almost six years now I've done my
best. Hasn't been easy with you looking over my shoulder.
Spent many hours of solitary confinement in here, looking
up at your goddam Pulitzer Prize. Six years of setting type,

proofreading, making or missing Thursday deadlines; six times fifty-two makes three hundred and twelve of them. What a far cry from my daily days on the *Star*, salvaging time from who, what, when, where, how, and the odd colour story in order to do another piece that might make it into the *Atlantic Monthly* or *Esquire* or the *New York Times* or a least *Liberty*. Done just a handful of failed short stories, and quit promising to some day do the Great New World Novel. Instead:

SHELBY ROUND-UP

Mrs. Dodds announces the opening of classes in voice and piano May 12. For particulars phone 379.

Charles Wendle of Retlaw, a recent visitor in Shelby to see his sister, Mrs. R. J. Dooley, who has been receiving treatment at the Holy Cross. Charles says Retlaw spells Walter backwards.

John Barnes' arm, so badly mangled in the feed chopper last month, thanks to the surgical skill of Dr. Fitzgerald has made such a remarkable recovery he is again able to drive his tractor in time for Spring seeding.

Richard Harold (Dick) Milligan, aged seventy-two years, of Shelby, passed away April 17 following an illness of nine months.

Roosters four months old, three to five pounds—thirty-five cents a pound live weight. Apply Calvin Mooney—RR3 Khartoum.

For six years he had followed a policy of considerate omission in reporting Shelby life. Almost from the first he had known that rural intimacy dictated greater restraint than a city reporter used in writing the news of metropolitan lives. He knew that he did not report and editorialize alone; what he did not present to public attention, many others did eagerly without press or paper, ink or mailing list. With the quick swallow, the clucking tongue, the lifted eyebrow, they coloured and they embellished, distorting not so much out of malice as from relish in a story better told.

In the pages of the *Shelby Chinook* the people of the town and district lived blameless lives. They neither raped nor were raped. They were heterosexual. They held rodeos and church suppers, ran curling bonspiels, turkey shoots, community bingo games, bridge and whist parties; they paraded and observed three minutes of silence on Remembrance Day, and danced at Thanksgiving, Hallowe'en, New Year's, and Valentine's Day. They became engaged, married, went into hospital, and were born always in wedlock, died of old age, accident, or sickness, but never of suicide or murder. From railways, chartered banks, implement firms, the civil service, and grain elevator and lumber companies they were transferred or retired; they did not embezzle, nor were they ever debauched, disrobed, or defrocked. Their children played Little League baseball, Pee-Wee and Bantam or Midget or Juvenile hockey, fattened purebred calves that took Four-H Club Championships, won Governor General's Medals, Activarian Club Oratorical Contests, and the honour of travelling to Ottawa to look into the parliamentary face of Democracy. They passed Toronto Conservatory of Music exams, and they braved frogs, skunks, snakes, nettles and mosquitoes and horseflies for ten days each July at Piney Dell, the Girl Guide and Boy Scout (alternating) camp up the Spray in Paradise Valley; as nurses they won their caps, or as teachers their schools, or as nuns their veils, or as typists their business-school proficiency certificates. Shelby names did not appear on police blotters for child abuse, contributing to juvenile delinquency, forgery, or breaking and entering, for stealing cars, siphoning gas, or for drinking beer along the river road or at country dances.

If he reflected only the best of all possible Shelbys in his paper, it was because he felt he had come to call the town his own, had never regretted till now the six years in Shelby—three of them with Ruth, three with Sarah.

As it always did when he thought of his child, a dark and diminutive Ruth, his heart gave a small lurch. It was wonderful to love your wife and to have a daughter who echoed her mother; compared baby pictures proved that. He had always suspected that Ruth must have been a little girl like Sarah, compounded of equal parts of loving warmth and terrifying will-power.

Now he was seeing her in his mind: the good little Sarah, the cruel little Sarah with thin pigtails standing out stiff. Was there anything more moving than the fragile, ploughed nape of a little girl's neck! She was an always feminine Sarah, at one moment tearing his heart with the lilting plaint of "Nobody loves me"; the next, "You go 'way." How many Sarahs were there? At night, pray God, it was the true Sarah, who came out after her bath in a nightgown soft and yellow as chicks. That was the clinging Sarah, the thousand-kisses Sarah, the water-drinking Sarah murmuring, "Where's the little boy looks after the sheep! Under the hiccup fas' sleep!" The wistful Sarah with wide, intent eyes, the promising Sarah. "Sarah won't undress onna street, Daddy. Any more." It had been a promise of true sacrifice.

Yes, he had liked his years as publisher and editor of the *Shelby Chinook*, had liked Shelby itself and most of its people.

He turned his chair toward the window. The spring chinook lied to him softly through the window screen. It was still too early in the year for angling the Spray; the water too high and too swift for rainbow or cut-throat to be deceived. He looked over toward the coat-rack by the door, at the wicker creel and the net and the rod there. Like the *Shelby Chinook* they'd all been Uncle Ben's once. That was a signed, hand-crafted bamboo Hardy.

Perhaps Ruth was right when she said that he didn't care if he caught anything—that fishing was simply an escape for him. From what?

From:

The eye specialist, H. N. Miller, will be at Oliver's Trading Company Store Wednesday, April 12, from 2 P.M. till 6 P.M. . . .

Notice—since Lucy May Hilton has left my bed and board I will not be responsible for any debts incurred in my name.

Notice—since Everett David Hilton never give me no

bed nor board worth putting up with living with the
likes of him, I will not be responsible for anything he
says or does. Lucy May Hilton.

And three weeks ago his front-page story:

SHELBY ATTRACTS NATIONAL ATTENTION: SOCIOLOGIST TO DO SURVEY.

Among the newcomers to Shelby last week was Dr. J.
L. Melquist, now staying at the Cayley Block. Dr.
Melquist has come all the way from Ontario to spend
the next few months with us. A sociologist, Dr.
Melquist proposes to do a survey of Shelby and district
as a typical foothills Western community and her stay
is for the purpose of gathering material about Shelby
people and Shelby ways. Dr. Melquist is a native
easterner, who has taken sabbatical leave from University work made possible by the Chandler Bureau of
Social Science Research. We are sure that Dr. Melquist
will find all the co-operation needed for this work. We
might suggest that all skeletons be kept out of sight in
cupboards for the rest of her stay with us.

Just as he had anticipated, more than the usual number
of callers had dropped in to the *Chinook* the day after
release of the story. The first was Clem Derrigan.

"She ain't very short-coupled—is she," Clem had said
that day in the office.

"I guess not, Clem."

"Leans some toward a line-back, don't she."

"She's tall, but she's a woman, Clem—not a Hereford
heifer."

"I noticed. Just what is she doin' here in Shelby, Matt?"

"Looking us over."

"What for?"

"She's—ah—she's a sociologist."

"What the hell's that?"

"Tell you the truth, Clem, I'm not too clear about that
myself. Sociology is a—type of science—or, ah, study."

"What of?"

"Humans. Functioning of human society—fundamental laws of human relationships."

Clem had taken a Golden Grain tobacco sack and papers out of his shirt pocket to roll one. "Just what the hell has all that got to do with us?"

"She intends to do a study of Shelby and Shelby district. Our life-style—our relationships with each other in our community—what it's like living togeth—"

"Shee-yit!" Clem had stopped in the middle of licking his cigarette. "Sounds just like Flannel Mouth Florence!"

"Oh come on, Clem. She is an objective scientist doing a sociological paper—treatise—profile of our town. Dr. Melquist—"

"She's a doctor!"

"Ph.D."

"Oh. Sure. One of them kind of doctors don't do you any good."

"If you want to put it that way, Clem. I can tell you one thing—she runs across many like you while she's doing her research and interviews, she isn't going to have an easy job of it."

"I'm out of matches."

"Corner the desk."

After Clem had lit up he said, "Tell me somethin', Matt. These here scientists—like of her—studyin' the way folks get along together. Is there any of 'em specializes in bees or wasps or ants—mountain goats—or sheep?"

"May very well be, Clem, but she specializes in humans. I suspect the others find their work a lot easier than she does."

"Mmmmmh. Understand she's boardin' with Aunt Fan."

"Yes. After she checked out of the Arlington Arms."

After Clem there had been a procession of others. Mayor Oliver of Oliver's Trading Company, Sadie Tregillis, whose husband was the Royal Bank manager, Rory Napoleon, Malleable Jack Brown, even Sam Barnes from his ranch west of Mable Ridge. Sam had lingered a little awkwardly at the counter, a shaggy badger of a man in a faded denim smock with the light winking from its brass buttons.

"Matt."

"Yes, Sam." Matt handed him his receipt. "That takes care of it for another year."

Sam folded and refolded the receipt; he spoke without lifting his head. "I was wonderin'. Noticed your piece in the *Chinook* . . ."

"Yes?"

"This doctor comin' from the East here. He . . ."

"She, Sam."

Sam's head snapped up; his raised eyes were cold with disbelief. "She!"

"She's a woman."

"Oh." There was neither approval nor disapproval.

"She'll be here for about six months, Sam."

"Gonna do a book? Gettin' material for a book about Shelby?"

"An academic paper, Sam. She's stayin' at Aunt Fan's."

"That's nice."

"Sociologist," Matt said.

"Well now, Matt—that's what I was wonderin' . . . I was wonderin' what that's like."

"It means that she's a scientist, Sam. Her science is sociology. She studies institutions—the—habits of communities."

"Oh."

"She's going to make a study of ours."

Sam nodded. "That's what this . . ."

"That's right—Shelby and Shelby people."

As Sam contemplatively rubbed a cheek, Matt could hear the rasp of calloused palm over whisker. He turned away slightly, then looked back at Matt. His face was quite bland as he said, "Gonna measure heads?"

For a moment Matt was not sure of himself; that was the worst of not being born and raised in the foothills like Ruth, who would have known her ground instantly. He had no way of knowing whether this shrewd and prosperous rancher was serious or not. If he were, and he gave him a flippant answer, it would offend him; if he were joking and he gave him a solemn answer, it was distasteful to seem a fool.

"Not mine, Sam."

The weathered face cracked in a slow grin, but with the smile Matt felt uneasiness trickle through him, almost guilt. He was compelled to add, "She's a nice woman, Sam. What she's here for is—it's important—it's just as important as your calf crop."

"Sure," Sam said generously. "I guess it is."

Some of the smile still lingered in his eyes. "How's Ruth? The Senator?"

"Just fine, Sam."

And after Sam there had been others: Harry Fitzgerald, Charlie Tait, Grace Norton. All brought up Dr. Melquist's project, and with each of them Matt found himself making a sort of atonement for his earlier lightness with Sam Barnes.

Then it had been Ruth. "I think you'll like her," he said. He saw what he called Ruth's *wry* look come over her face. "I guess I've said that before."

"Several times, dear. Perhaps I will. We'll see. When I meet her."

"She's—she's nice, Ruth." He added a little unfairly, "Even if she comes from down East."

"All us cowgirls don't hate easterners," she said. "I ought to know. I married one."

Aw, to hell with it; the chinook through the window now carried a faint scent of wolf willow. He got up, headed for the coat-rack and the creel and net and rod.

"Goin' fishing again, Mr. Stanley?" That was Millie hunched over her desk in the outer office.

"Just taking a break. Back before lunch, Millie."

The only escape he needed was from Millie—little self-effacing Millie, press-day-smudged Millie, cripple-grammared, misspelling Millie, reading her *True Love* or *Ranch Romances* or *I Confess* between subscribers and advertisers and stationery buyers, but neat and tidy Millie all the same, keeping files and office and accounts in meticulous order. He must remember that he was lucky to have Millie; he mustn't forget that she could be making half as much again as he paid her, in her old job as telephone operator. Always the way it was with Millie: annoyance and impatience with her, then shame for being uncharitable with one who so obviously had every right to sympathy and charity. Perhaps that was the annoying thing about her, that simply by breathing and being Millie Clocker she achieved a sort of meek demand for sympathy, a mild and never-failing plea for understanding and affection which he simply did not have in him—for Millie Clocker.

He had taken the back door and gone down the alley rather than the street in front of the *Chinook* building. Wouldn't do for people to see the publisher and editor of the *Shelby Chinook* early in a working day, with rod and reel and creel, heading for the Spray. Especially this hopelessly early in the season.

As he turned the lumber-yard corner, a smell of full organic decay travelled to meet him: shit. Rory Napoleon, halfway down the street. As the town nuisance wagon rolled past him, the driver, standing high upon it with legs apart, raised an arm in nonchalant salute. Matt waved back to him. No need to worry what Rory might think of his goofing off work early in the morning to go fishing.

Years ago the Senator, Ruth's father, had sketched the Napoleon genealogy for Matt. In Rory's veins flowed the blood of Brittany, tinted, the Senator thought, with Basque and mingling with one-quarter Peigan contributed by his maternal grandfather, Chief Baseball, who had signed the Blackfoot Crossing Treaty in 1878. These genes had been given Rory by his French half-breed mother, who had met and loved under lodgepole pines a remittance cowhand in 1908, so that Rory also boasted the proud blood of the clan MacCrimmon, composers of pibroch and pipers to the chiefs of Scotland. He had been raised on Paradise Reserve by his mother and was still, academically speaking, a ward of the government, though he had not been on a reserve or taken treaty money since the age of fifteen.

Mame Napoleon, his common-law wife, was ten years younger than Rory, but looked ten years older; like Ontario Cheddar she was pure Canadian.

Their offspring—Byron, Buster, Avalon, Evelyn, Esther, Elvira, living, and Violet, Herbert, Calvin, and Clarence, who had died at birth or in infanthood—carried, with the exception of Buster, the Breton-Basque-Peigan-Scotch blood. Buster was a different mixture, with Galician blood contributed by a section-hand one week before Christmas on the straw of the old Stettler livery barn, when Mame needed two dollars and ninety-eight cents for the purchase of a box of Winesap apples from the Red and White, as a holiday treat for Buster's living sisters and brothers.

Between Rory and the Royal Bank manager's wife, Sadie Tregillis, a sort of guerrilla warfare went on tirelessly. Matt had heard Rory's own version of the feud.

"I dug her cesspool for her eight years ago," Rory said. "She's on the rise goes past the school an' Harper's corner. Jist about the highest point there is in town. Good ten foot before you hit gravel—only there's a fault there, an' that first gravel ain't water level at all. There's a layer of clay there, an' after you get through that, then there's five more foot till you do hit water. I told her all that, but you can't tell her nothin'. When I hit gravel first she said that was it. I told her it wasn't it, that we had to go deeper. She said it was it, an' she told me to go ahead an' crib her in. I said I wouldn't, an' she went straight to Mayor Oliver, an' he said go ahead an' I did. Eight years now I pumped her out an' pumped her out—spring—summer—fall—even winter. Mrs. Tregillis ain't got any goddam seepage—she fills up an' she fills up an' she fills up with Tregillis shit an' piss. Then she goes yellin' to Oliver an' he makes me go pump her out agin!"

A slight, dark man with a rather wild eye, Rory could be seen daily in the Post Office just before mail time. He usually wore a faded blue jacket, its breast pockets lined with a battery of pens and pencils. He would take up his usual position, leaning against the wall near the door, under the WANTED posters and the civil service examination notices. He had no mailbox, so that when Mr. Fry lifted the frosted window and swung in the brass grill, Rory took his place in line with those lesser individuals whose mail came in a lump under the initial letter of their surnames in General Delivery.

Mr. Fry regularly handed out to Rory the *Shelby Chinook*, both city dailies, *Nor-West Prairie Farm Review*, *The Country Gentleman*, *The Star Weekly*, *The Saturday Evening Post*, and Dr. Winesinger's *Calendar Almanac*. "I see by the paper today" was Rory's unfailing gangplank to conversation. He was unable to read or write.

Both of the Napoleons had become a familiar sight to Matt as they rolled down the streets in the honey-wagon, since Mame accompanied Rory whenever he had the team hitched to the human-sewage tank and pump. It was Mame who had painted the woodland scene upon the rounded sides; Matt supposed one could call it the only ambulatory mural in North America, with jack pine and spruce spearing up to white clouds against brilliant blue sky, yellow wheat sheaves stooked in the foreground. Initially, it had been as fine a work of art as the does and bucks and fawns drinking around the walls of the Arlington Arms Beer Parlour, though the painters of that art had been afforded a more stable medium. The honey-wagon did slop and spill, so that after the first few rounds in the spring Mame's landscape changed from romantic representational to impressionistic, to ultimate abstract: in an esoteric sense anyway, more pure.

He turned up Lafayette, a residential street. In shaded places the walk still held dark patches where the dampness of last night's rain lingered. As he turned the Oliver corner, a bit of canary yellow darted low into the hedge. He looked up to the clear April sky, then to trees that misted the end of the block with spring green, and beyond that to the Rockies so distinct it was hard to believe they were thirty-five miles distant. In his six Shelby years he had not yet got over the lift he got at each new sight of the Rockies, and doubted that he ever would; he seldom entered the newspaper office without a last glance in their direction, and many mornings he went to the door simply to look out at them. It was not so much the first ridge of the foothills and its shadowed darkness that appealed, but the more remote range, snow-covered summer and winter, checked with dark draws, its purity complete reflection of all light.

CHAPTER 2

FREE OF THE TOWN NOW, HE CROSSED THE ROAD, MADE IT
over a barbed-wire fence and into pasture fragrant with
clover and loud with bees. Cows lifted their heads and
stared at him with gently moving jaws. A red and white calf
went rocking off with tail high. At the fence on the far side
of the pasture, a partridge startled from the long grass made
him catch his breath at the unwinding whir of its wings.
God, it was wonderful to get out and along the river in
spring. Or summer. Or fall.

He came to the overgrown ruts of the river road winding
through cottonwood, willow, and saskatoon; the coolness of
shade closed round him. For a moment he stood still,
striving to catch the hoarse pulse of the river. He heard it
faintly; with a quick thrill of anticipation he walked on,
holding the rod tip out ahead.

The sound of the river was full in his ears now as he
crossed open grass to the shale and rock of the river bank.
The water *was* high, and though it was not so murky as he
had thought it might be, he knew that a dry fly would be
useless. Above him the stream, frothing deep through rock,
fell with a thumping roar into the spreading pool below,
where foam and spray anguish ended abruptly in slick water
slowly eddying.

Perhaps he ought to try that small pearl spinner with the
red dot like a drop of blood in the centre—and a worm.
Ruth's father said that a worm was the only thing early in
the year. Still, it would be nice to try a silver doctor wet a
couple of times. Then, if they weren't taking that, sink a
worm. Strange that the Senator should be a worm fisher.
But trout fishing was all things to all men. To the Senator it
must mean stillness and contemplation warmed and lulled
by sun and the sound of the wind in leaves and grass—
serenity only deepened by an occasional strike.

Yet he had never come to understand quite what it meant
to himself. Certainly not peace. He fished the whole stream,
never long at a riffled run or a pool, always looking ahead
to an up- or down-stream curve, a new and likely smooth-
ness under an overhanging bank, the next promising fallen
log. It might be a lot like the lure of strange flesh. Another
conquest—that was it; never so wonderful in reality as in
anticipation. In consummation, when the catch gleamed
silver and curving limp in the net—that *was* it—the post-
coital feeling! Perhaps Ruth's father had once been a fly
fisherman after all, and it was age that brought a man to
worms and the back against a tree.

The blue and silver of the wet fly were brilliant between
his fingers as he tied the lure to the end of the leader. After
several false casts he dropped the fly across the pool and
downstream slightly, letting it sink and drift. He retrieved
the line, cast again, this time up toward the end of a fallen
tree that lay half submerged on the other side. When the
current had carried the line fully out, he laid the rod down
on the bank. As he sat, small crumbs of shale rolled from
under his feet and pocked the surface of the pool. He lit a
cigarette.

He almost laughed to himself; he must tell Ruth. "Ruth,
it isn't a constitutional weakness inherited from Uncle Ben
that drives me to fishing and sends me on dawn and evening
hunting bats. It's not escape from anything—it's a sublima-
tion of the Stanley sex drive. Consider yourself lucky when
I come back home late for supper. Better trout in the creel
than women in the bed. Better a weakness for rainbow than
redheads—better German browns than blondes."

And Ruth would know it was just smart-ass talk they

could both recognize quickly and easily. Humans took themselves too seriously, explained their behaviour much too pompously, creating formal terminologies without poetry or humour to explain simple-as-breathing things like a man's delight in spring in having a rod in his hand and his back against a rock. That explained the mild feud he had carried on with the *Mable Ridge News* for the past two years.

The issue had grown out of a long-standing rivalry between Mable Ridge and Shelby, had come to a head in early March when one evening late in the *Chinook* office he had written the First Gopher of Spring piece.

Yesterday half a mile west of the Hamilton place young Byron Napoleon on his way home from Little Bow School spied one of the harbingers of Spring. The furry, tawny little fellow was flirting at the lip of a hole dug "just below the rise of what used to be the old Olsen gravel pit," Byron says. He sat up (the gopher did) with his little paws held before his chest, looking out of black button eyes, his rodent nose twitching. The gopher dropped to all fours to gambol about over the frozen prairie for several long moments. Finally with a flirt of his bushy tail he disappeared down his hole.

This is the earliest in the year that a gopher has ever been sighted in the Shelby district or the entire West. The previous record was held by Grandma Lucy Meynell, who came West from Huron County in nineteen-one. In the diary she kept of her homesteading days she records a Spring appearance for a gopher in nineteen-four as early only as March eleventh of that year.

The *Mable Ridge News* had accepted the challenge, for barely a week after the First Gopher of Spring in Shelby district, it ran an answering story:

It was a pioneer butterfly that spread its wings and fluttered through the chill March air two miles west of town last Thursday. This brilliant bit of colour fluttered

across the Melanchuk yard as Bridget Melanchuk was
hanging out the wash. She stood transfixed with a
clothespin in her mouth, unable to believe her startled
eyes as the hardy little insect disappeared beyond the
Melanchuk chop house. Many will remember Bridget's
essay, "Sooner or Later Our Own Canadian Flag,"
which received honourable mention in the Wheat Pool
All-Canadian Essay Contest and which was printed on
the pages of the *Mable Ridge News* last fall.

"I don't believe it," Ruth said firmly when she had read
the butterfly story.

"That she saw a butterfly in . . ."

"That Bridget Melanchuk got honourable mention in the
Wheat Pool Essay Contest."

"Whose side are you on?" he asked her.

"You mean in regard to whether spring came first to
Mable Ridge or spring came first to Shelby this year?"

"Mmmh."

"Well, I have divided loyalties—Mable Ridge was our
shipping-point when we were on the ranch."

"I know, I know."

"And it was the Napoleon boy who reported your first
gopher of spring."

"What's that got to do with it?"

"He's pretty well known for telling whoppers—awful
little liar. You should have verified his gopher before you
wrote it up."

"Now, just a minute . . ."

"And Mable Ridge does get chinooks that we don't get.
I—I believe in their butterfly."

"But not in our gopher."

"Not in Byron Napoleon."

The next year it had been the Mable Ridge paper that
reported the first gopher of spring the last week in March.

"I believe *that* gopher," Ruth said to him. "Sam Barnes
rode for Dad, and if Sam says he saw a gopher he saw a
gopher."

"Mm-mmmh." Matt shook his head. "They're cheating."

"Cheating! You question Sam . . ."

"Oh, he saw a gopher all right—I imagine there was a gopher."

"If there was a gopher, then how can you accuse them of cheating?"

"Mable Ridge's first-gopher-of-spring gopher. Somebody raises them in a basement cage all winter just to be able to turn them loose early in March and claim the first-gopher-of-spring gopher."

"Oh, Matt!"

"Anyway, the *Shelby Chinook* has an answer to it. Just read that." He held out to her the proof copy he'd brought home to lunch with him.

Ruth looked up from it. "Matt! That's not true—a bluebird!"

"In the hedge at the Oliver corner."

"It couldn't be. This early!"

"Several people saw it. Reported it—came in—phoned in."

"Who?"

"Mrs. Oliver for one—Aunt Fan—you've got to accept it."

"But a bluebird! I don't remember seeing a bluebird in town at any time of year, let alone . . ." She broke off, staring down at the paper. "Matt."

"Yes?"

"Classified ads here—'Lost and Found.' "

"Oh."

Lost in the vicinity of Third and Macleod streets a budgie bird answering to the name of Twinkie. Blue. Get in touch with Mrs. Nelligan—Phone 392— Reward.

"She got it back."

"Before or after the bluebird had been sighted by several people in the Oliver corner half a block away?"

Matt shrugged.

"Before or after?" she persisted.

"After, I guess." Matt grinned.

•   •   •

It had been fun; right from the start the light rivalry had
been a warming thing of amusement and delight.

Dimly he could see the jagged outline where the river
had cut its way through sandstone depths till the eye was
lost in a dark and underwater cavern inaccessible to man.
Twig and leaf debris rose slowly, drifted almost to the
surface, then circled and withdrew, sucked from sight. A
shorter, thicker length of branch—no, a trout—lifted casually to hang languidly with tilted front fins moving slowly,
holding in there against the current. Reluctantly it returned
down into the marine darkness from which it had appeared.

To hell with proving his angling skill! He took out the
can from his creel and began to retrieve his line. He did not
change the silver doctor, just baited it with a writhing worm;
he bit a piece of shot into the leader, then carefully lowered
the line into the pool.

All he had to do now was to wait with patience. Senator
fishing. Old-man angling. Just the right sort of fishing for a
man who—

"Matt! Hey, Matt!"

He looked up- and then down-stream to see the bulky
figure in the shallow tail of the pool.

"Harry!" he called to him.

"Any action?"

"No."

The man waded across the river, then upstream. Before
he had reached Matt he had made seven casts, laying his
line out over the water, leaving it barely a few seconds,
ripping it off and sending it rolling out again without a
single drying false cast. It was as though the man fished
impatiently against time. When he had stopped by Matt he
laid his rod against a bush there, took off his shapeless khaki
hat to wipe the perspiration from a face already vivid with
sunburn that flamed against his white forehead.

"Too early—way too early," he said as he sat down,
"but it's nice to get out. Hersch is just upstream."

He spoke of the Anglican Church minister, Herschell
Midford, and Matt was thinking that with himself and Dr.
Harry Fitzgerald, the three men in Shelby most likely to be

rushing the angling season were now accounted for. "What are you using?" he asked.

"Streamer—big marabou thing Hersch tied. Looks like a powder puff dry and a minnow when it's wet. Tried to get me to use a little muskrat fur nymph with a red tag on a number ten hook." The doctor's eyes strayed to Matt's rod, then from the tip along the line dropping deep into the water.

"Worm," Matt said.

"Probably the only way to get anything this early. Might have tried it myself—only with Hersch . . ." His voice trailed off and there was no need for further explanation; in many things there could be no compromise for Canon Midford, and angling only with a wet or dry fly was the first of these. "He'll show up in a while," said Fitzgerald as he took a cigar from his breast pocket. He exhaled the first deep puff with a sigh and leaned back against the slope of the rock. "Nice."

Matt nodded.

"Gets the winter out of a man."

Matt nodded again. The sound of the river seemed almost to have become part of him, like the pulse of his own blood in his ears; it dulled self-awareness, erased all tension. In the roaring heart of the falls, half articulations chuckled and broke off just short of communication, both hoarse and shrill conversations only dimly heard.

Now, if Ruth had accused Harry Fitzgerald of using fishing and hunting as an escape, she would have been right. Escape from Nettie. Defeat or escape: there could be nothing else with such a woman. It had been a long time since Harry had won a victory, and it was a hell of a way to run a marriage, having to make flaming stands or retreats. Obviously the major engagements were coming less and less frequently, now that the campaign had died down with time and age to occasional border incidents and brief encounters, kept alive by sporadic outbursts and the odd ricocheting shot from long range.

Matt sat up; the willow and birch on the opposite river bank drifted and wavered and ran before his eyes, now used to the race and swirl of the stream.

"Matt! Matt—your line!" Harry's voice was tight with excitement.

Matt saw then that the line was wandering slowly and pulling out the loose coils on the bank beside him; it changed direction and moved up against the current. He picked up the rod, and, as he did, he felt a fierce, impatient tug. He did not have to set the hook, for he was fast. Taut and alive, the line sliced back and forth and out. No more uncertainty, no more waiting! Here was ultimate communication! And then he was pulling limp line, frantic and clumsy with apprehension that a taut, shared faith might be forever lost.

The fish broke the water. Matt took in line, his heart constricting with fear that an angry tail might free the hook. There was ineffable relief as the line went tight again, electric with running, deep-boring life. Slowly he gained, till now and again below him he could see the flash of silver side, which was gone but returned again as closer and closer to the river bank the line moved over the smooth surface with the idle abandon of a child's pencil scrawling. And in the clear water he could see the spent fish slowly glide to one side, then swiftly turn back again in the pendulum movement of all caught wild things.

"Five pounds—he'll go five sure as hell!" Harry on his knees reached out with the net. "Bring him closer!"

One last rise and then, as he brought the fish to the net, the slattering, slapping fury to escape before Harry lifted it out silver and violet and raspberry in the sunlight.

Matt felt the breath of relief leave his body of its own accord.

"God, what a darling!" Harry said.

Matt stared down at the silver doctor beautiful in the rim of cartilage at the corner of the mouth, and at the fluted gills opening and closing to the rhythm of his own heart's pound.

Harry, seated on the rock again, watched him as he cleaned it, then pulled sparse spring grass to line his creel.

"You giving up?" he asked as Matt began to disjoint his rod.

"Due back at the office. Then Ruth'll have lunch ready."

"You're not doing it right, Matt. You can be two kinds

of late—annoying and irritating late, or you can stay out till she's gibbering with anxiety and fear. About an hour and a half should give her imagination time to work, then when you do show up she'll be welcoming you from a watery grave. Works during hunting season, too—a whole man, instead of bits blown over the stubble by shot-gun blast."

Matt laughed. "You're not talking about my wife, Harry."

"No," Harry said, "I guess not. She's tough." He reflected a moment. "No reason a woman can't be tough the right way." He looked out over the river. "Enough of them are tough the wrong way." Without turning back to Matt he said, "That woman—your Melquist woman—she's tough too, Matt. I think she's hard as nails."

"She's not my woman." Matt felt his face warm in spite of himself. It flushed more as he saw Harry staring at him. "I don't think she is tough."

"What's the matter?"

"Nothing. I just don't think Dr. Melquist is—is hard as nails, as you put it." Mostly now he was annoyed with himself for being irritated so easily.

"Now, hold on. I didn't mean it in a disparaging way. I meant she's a woman with character. I'd say she had the talent for not letting sentiment stand in the way of whatever she had to do. That's how she struck me the first time."

"Harry, Matt."

Canon Midford had come up from behind them. Even as he spoke, his eye caught the silver glint of Matt's magnificent catch in the open creel. "What a beautiful rainbow!"

"Matt's," Harry said. "Caught him on a dry bucktail in the tail of the pool."

"He did not!" Canon Midford contradicted. "Perhaps a streamer—bucktail streamer wet—or a nymph . . ."

"Dry," said Harry.

"No way on a dry fly."

"Now there's a snap judgment," said Harry.

"It's too early for dry fly." The minister looked down to Matt. "Spinner?"

"No," Matt said honestly.

"Salted minnow?"

"He didn't use a salted minnow," Harry said.

"Raw beef."

"No—I . . ." began Matt.

"How can a man be so cynical?" Harry was shaking his head. "So little faith in a friend's honest report on how he caught . . ."

"Look, Harry, there's a point at which angling faith enters, and in this case she simply has to wait until there are insect hatches alighting on the water. What did you use, Matt?"

"Silver doctor."

"And?"

"Worm."

"Oh." Canon Midford set his rod carefully up against the willow, unslung his creel, and took out a pipe. As he did, Harry seemed suddenly to remember.

"Matt—about the Melquist woman, I meant that she struck me as a hard woman but an honest one. An exact woman." He turned to the minister. "Dr. Melquist, Hersch. Don't you think—wouldn't you call her that?"

"I don't know. I haven't had the time or the opportunity . . ."

"Competent," said the doctor. "Maybe that's what I should have said. How exactly does she work, Matt?"

"Interviews mostly."

"Whom has she interviewed so far?"

"I think she started close to home—Aunt Fan where she's staying—she's just getting started, Harry. Give her a chance."

"What does she ask about?"

"How do I know," Matt said a little shortly. "She hasn't interviewed me. I think she has some kind of questionnaires—a pattern of questions—form interviews."

"I don't think our people fit very well into forms or patterns," Canon Midford said.

"They just facilitate things for her," Matt explained, "help her to keep from going off too much at a tangent."

"Most things worthwhile are generally the result of someone's going off at a tangent, aren't they?" Hersch said. "I'm not very fond of forms. I hate generalities."

Matt smiled down at him. "That's nice. You get a dandy

one off your chest just before you say you hate generalities. I've got to go."

"You'll be an hour before your dinner time," Harry warned him.

"Got to drop by the office. I need about an hour. Get a bit of work out of the way."

"Do more of that light stuff—First Gopher of Spring, First Crocus," Harry said.

"More serious. The dog-poisoning's started again."

"No!" Harry jerked upright. "I didn't know that!"

"The Chivers cocker, and I've got to do a few notes on an editorial. The poison was in wieners this time. A child could have picked one up. I want to appeal directly to him, but I don't know whom to appeal to."

"Well, I've got to tie Prince up," Harry said. "Damn it, every spring. Happens every single spring!"

For the past three years there had been many poison deaths among the canine population of Shelby, and just yesterday morning Corporal McCready over coffee at the Palm Café had told Matt about the Chivers cocker spaniel. Tough problem, the Corporal had explained, a lot like arson, almost impossible to track down the culprit and even then almost impossible to gain a conviction.

After Matt left, Canon Hersch had gone upstream; Harry Fitzgerald went down to the tail of the pool, began to lay out his fly, and thought how terrible it would be if anything were to happen to Prince. Should have brought him along even though it was a cruel thing to bring a Chesapeake out and *not* let him into the river. No more Prince. No more Willis for angling company.

It had been seven years since the last time Willis had come out with his tenth-birthday-present rod and reel; Harry had carried him in his arms back to the car after Willis had slipped on treacherous shale. There had been no more fishing trips that summer, for after the six weeks Willis's leg had been in the cast, the boy had been too busy catching up on the piano lessons he had missed in preparation for his Toronto Conservatory Grade Four examinations. The next year Nettie had taken Willis East with her for the summer.

Harry had given up the following year; Willis by that time was not interested in fishing.

Ah well; retreat had been the only strategy left. He must save just himself from Nettie. He sought peace in reverie, closed the doors of willing attention, welcomed night calls, spent evening after evening at the office over histories and books, and his off afternoons in the field or along the stream. It had been a long and almost happy retreat until it had ended in Harry's tragic discovery that she had carried their son, Willis, hostage into her camp. She had sent the boy away to St. John's boarding-school at eleven. Now, at seventeen, Willis would be writing his Grade Twelve examinations in June. He would fail, for he had neither the scholarship nor the character to become the doctor Harry wanted him to be.

He really wished that he had brought Prince along. Willis wasn't the slightest bit interested in coming with him. It was not true, as Nettie thought, that he had wanted to make the boy an extrovert barbarian; all he had wanted to do was to share his delight along the river and in the goose pit with his son. But he never had, for he had never successfully challenged Nettie's assured conviction that the raising of a child was exclusively a woman's mission.

For all he knew, she'd let Prince out of the yard again to wander through back alleys all over town.

Strychnine probably—it had been the other years. What kind of person poisoned dogs! Had to be the same one for all of them. If every eccentric in Shelby poisoned dogs, the town would be up to its pelvis in carcasses. It wasn't that the dogs were poisoned out of spite, he was sure, as a result of a specific quarrel between two individuals—nothing retaliatory about it. Serial killing. Whoever it was had done away with over a hundred of them, at least. It was hard to believe that anybody in Shelby hated that many people— had it in for everyone so indiscriminately.

He began to reel in his line. Matt had got the only trout biting today. Looking upstream he saw that Hersch was sitting where Matt had caught his fish. Obviously through and waiting to accompany him back to town.

Town was lucky to have a man like Matt and a paper like the *Chinook* every Friday.

As he walked along the bank towards the minister, he supposed he'd been a little blunt about Dr. Melquist. If Matt accepted her, it should be good enough for him—even if she was a social scientist, a sociologist. Hell, for all he knew it was possible that it *was* a science. Along with chiropractics!

"Tell me, Hersch," he said as he came up to the minister, "you think this Dr. Melquist might be a good speaker for our Rotary service committee?"

"She might."

"You want to ask her or shall I?"

"I'd suggest Matt."

"Mmmh. I think I'll head home—little worried about Prince."

"I thought you would be," the minister said as he got up. "Let's go."

CHAPTER 3

MATT RE-ENTERED THE TOWN BY FOLLOWING THE RIVER PAST the swimming-hole where the children had put up their slant diving-board. Often he had watched them bottoming it, running along the board to hang briefly in mid-air like half-opened jack-knives before they cut the water. Like angling, still too early in the year for that. Under light and shade he walked on till he came to the CPR bridge.

Why was it that he found himself on the defensive whenever June's name came up? And with Harry of all people, who should be one of the first to accept her, take her and her work seriously! Harry was too intelligent a man to make snap judgments of people, to distrust automatically anything he was unfamiliar with. She was a pretty nice girl, and on that score alone they should accept her as he had ever since her arrival in Shelby.

She had hit town this year in March. He had arrived in early October six years ago. Except for the seasonal difference, their initial impressions of Shelby must have been quite similar. For him the foothills air had the wild tang that first frost gives to apples, turnips, and to children playing Red Light under corner street lights. For her it would have been the year's *final* frost touch. As the train rolled into town, he had seen men and boys with elbows on the rails of the CPR bridge, angling for the fall grayling run. Cottonwood trees along residential streets had turned to amber so luminous in the October sun that walking under them a person felt he was seeing their colour through his forehead. When she registered at the Arlington Arms Hotel, nine leathery old gentlemen in nine leathery old lobby chairs would have been watching her with bland interest; all would be wearing high-heeled boots. Outside on Main Street men with the same look of distance in their eyes would be stilting toward the Beer Parlour, the Palm Café, Barfoot's Leather Goods, Finlay's Vulcanizing, Dirty Bill's Blacksmith Shop, the Cameo Theatre. The high-heeled boots, spurs, faded blue Levi's, and Stetson hat were the uniform of their trade. They were cowmen, and you simply could not imagine them walking between barn and house in flat farm boots, with a foaming milk pail in each hand.

He guessed that she had called first of all on the *Chinook*. With the exception of Artie Buller, who had probably picked her up at the station—and Bill Johnston, who had just as probably been on the desk at the Arlington Arms Hotel when she registered—he guessed that he must have been the first of Shelby's citizens to meet her.

He had been alone in the front office, for it was Millie Clocker's afternoon off, when he heard the door open and looked up to see a tall woman, perhaps in her very early thirties, standing at the counter. It was one of the soft chinook days, and through the open window by his desk he could hear the steady reiteration of a dripping eave; he had looked up for long moments to a well-poised woman with very fair hair braided into a sort of crown which seemed quite in keeping with her erect slenderness.

Her name was Dr. June Melquist; she mentioned the Chandler Foundation Bureau of Social Science Research. For a moment he had flinched; he *had* work to do, and no time or patience for a long and oblique sales pitch for some expensive encyclopedia set that would he given to him free simply because he was a leading Shelby citizen. But no, she wasn't trying for another sucker. She would be living in Shelby for at least six months, she explained, while she conducted a survey of the community as typical of

many ranch villages. He had not really managed to accept
her mission and her profession even as he automatically
promised her any help he might be able to give her during
her stay in the town. With a directness that reminded him of
Ruth, she said that he could do something right now.

"I'm looking for somewhere to stay—the hotel is
temporary."

He looked down at the ad that he held in his hand on the
counter: "Spring is near—now's the time to clean up and
paint up."

"A light-housekeeping room—it doesn't matter much
where," she said.

"Then there's just one place for you," he told her.
"Aunt Fan. That's Miss Cayley," he qualified. "She has the
Cayley building between Finlay's Vulcanizing and the
Beauty Parlour. I understand one of the suites is vacant.
Aunt Fan has one for herself. Millie Clocker has one."
Under her steady gaze he felt compelled to go on. "Millie—
Miss Clocker—works for me—her afternoon off."

He was willing to bet that the woman was good at her
work—interviewing, observing people, whatever anthro-
pologists or sociologists did. It wasn't that she stared at a
person, so much as that her face held a steady and quite
impersonal candour that could not be soon or easily accepted. It was something you had to adjust to, as when
brilliant light has been thrown upon the pupils after a long
time in darkness. One thing it did: it told a man instantly
that he was a man and that she was a woman, and since that
impertinent difference had been disposed of, they could get
on with more important matters.

He left the office with her, crossed to the Post Office
side of the street, then past the Palm Café, Willie MacCrimmon's Shoe and Harness, to the Cayley or, as it was better
known, the Aunt Fan building. It was two storeys of
tan sandstone, tilting visibly on foundations that had been
sapped by year after year of floods. Tall, narrow, and
squeezed between Finlay's Vulcanizing and the Beauty
Parlour, it looked somehow a little like an elderly maiden
lady who had come upon distressing times and companions.
Aunt Fan Cayley had arrived from England thirty years
before with a young brother, Hubert. He had drunk up his

own and most of his sister's money, leaving her only the Cayley building, which he had won from Ollie Pringle in a game of Saskatchewan Show at the Ranchmen's Club over the Palm Café two years after his arrival in the district and one year before he had been barred from the club for the use of a deck of cards whose backs he had meticulously pricked with a needle.

Until Hubert's death the building had been steadily piling up tax arrears which continued to eat up most of the income Aunt Fan derived from the rent of its suites. She supplemented her rental income by the sale to friends of greeting-cards each Christmas, of seed packets in spring, and of magazine subscriptions the year round.

They stepped inside the Cayley building and met Aunt Fan at the foot of the stairs, evidently just on her way up from the garden, for she was wearing a liberally ribboned straw hat, and carried a small trowel in one work-gloved hand.

"Flower beds," she said. "Get them ready early. Our season's so short."

Matt introduced Dr. Melquist to Aunt Fan, who turned to the other woman with head up and almost archly held back, with a bright, tense smile that revealed quite clearly a chip out of the faded orange gum of her upper plate. Matt had never been able to come to any sure conclusion about Aunt Fan's age; he knew that she must be in her seventies, but he could not be certain, for her black eyes were the eyes of a much younger woman. Her hair was straight across her forehead in tight curls which, with the ribboned hat, the long nose, and the slight puffing around the mouth caused by badly fitted dentures, gave her the appearance of a prize ewe.

Upstairs she showed Dr. Melquist the available suite, accepted fifty dollars for the first month's rent, then added, with the sociologist's agreement, a dollar ninety-eight for three years of the *Nor-West Prairie Farm Review*. By this time Aunt Fan had donned her hearing-aid. In the years he had known her, Matt had never got used to the shrill British voice punching her speech with tiring regularity as it rolled along like a fast stream that ended often and without warning. Then she would stare at her listener with head

tilted expectantly, dark eyes intent. Dr. Melquist seemed
totally unprepared for the first of these pauses, and Matt
waited, knowing that she would be startled when Aunt Fan
took up the conversation again.

He knew there would be no obvious connection with
what Dr. Melquist had just said, or even with the words
Aunt Fan herself had spoken. It was as though Aunt Fan's
conversation had suddenly dipped and flowed on merrily
out of hearing, to burst forth with shocking ellipsis at an
entirely fresh point. She herself seemed to become aware of
this at times, for it was then that she would point to her
breast and the hearing-aid.

After he had left Dr. Melquist to Aunt Fan, he had
returned to the office, and found himself reluctant to get
back to work, aware of a lift of excitement within himself
that was hard to explain.

At the CPR bridge he stopped, undecided about his route
through town. Should he take the same one he had when
he'd gone out, avoiding running into . . . Hell no! Not
with this silver beauty in his creel. He took the fish out and
put it into the net. With that over one shoulder he'd go right
down Main Street, past Jackson's Buy-Rite Hardware, the
Royal Bank corner, the Arlington Arms, and the Cameo
Theatre. Maybe take a kink off to the west and pretend he
was just picking up his mail in the Post Office. It would be
past sorting-time now. Tell them he'd taken it on a wet
streamer. Neither Harry nor Hersch would squeal on him.

He turned in at the *Chinook* office. Millie Clocker
looked up as he entered, her eyes going immediately to the
creel and rod he carried.

"Millie—any calls for me?"

"Just Miss Melquist, an hour ago, Mr. Stanley, and
Corporal McCready."

"What did he want?"

"The dog-poisonings. They've found two more."

"Whose?" He unslung his creel, rested the rod against
the front counter.

"I don't know, and I don't know what she wanted
either."

"Who?"

"Miss Melquist. She didn't say. She said it could wait—she'd drop in later."

"All right." He started for the door of his office.

"That's fine." The petulant tone of her voice said it wasn't fine at all. She did not like it when he went fishing and left her alone in the office, or left her to spend Saturday afternoons at the outer office desk. He had to have a clear day for Ruth and Sarah and there had to be somebody there on farmers' and ranchers' day in town or they'd miss a lot of subscription and want-ad business. Couldn't be all that tough on Millie; she could read her goddam romance magazines just as well in the office as in her Aunt Fan suite—or wherever she wanted to spend her Saturday afternoons.

Before he could make it into his office he heard the front door open, looked back and saw Joe Manley.

"Matt."

"Joe." He went back to the counter, reaching it just as Millie did.

"Hold it, hold it, not all that important," Joe said. He laid a folded paper on the counter. "Pony League score—first game of the season. Mable Ridge took Shelby fourteen to seven last night. There's the line-up, and it would be nice if you could acknowledge George Wing's generosity in providing the new uniforms."

"Sure." Matt picked up the paper. "Come on into the office."

"Mr. Stanley."

He looked back to Millie's desk, saw that she was holding up his rod and the wicker creel. "It's dripping—*slime* all over the floor. "

"Oh, sorry, Millie. I'll take it into my office—keep the slime on my floor there."

"Don't tell me you caught something, Matt."

"A dandy. Just about the biggest rainbow I've ever taken out of the Spray."

Within his office, Joe commended him on the size of the trout, but his admiration was specious, for he did not fish, could hardly tell a pike from a cut-throat.

Joe Manley had started out a fervent and talented

teacher. But many years ago, before Matt had come to Shelby, he had ceased to look forward to term opening each September, or to welcome ordered days that began and ended with a peremptory bell. He supposed his discontent with his teaching lot in life had begun in some small and unnoticed way, like the story of Peter, the Brave Little Dutch Boy. Maybe he had discovered the hole in the dike of his interest years ago, in a sound-wave experiment in Physics II perhaps, or maybe Ovid and Horace and the ablative absolute the seventeenth time round. "Sohrab and Rustum" had always bored him almost as much as "The Highwayman" and most of Wordsworth. In time he had found it difficult to summon up honest enthusiasm for a discussion of how Galsworthy's "Quality," about the two shoe-making brothers, held within the story the entire industrial revolution. He had long forgotten the precise point in the past—as the fall days contracted and the lights had to be turned on for the last class of the afternoon—when the Magna Carta, the War of 1812, the Family Compact, the Selkirk Settlers, and Confederation had become dry as the dust of the schoolroom, making him breathe a little more deeply, as though to rid himself of a weight on his chest.

But this had not dulled his competence as a teacher, Matt felt. Over the past fifteen years the community had come to owe a great deal to Joe Manley. Matt had once estimated that roughly thirteen hundred children had filed by Joe while he kept his position in the educational reception line, handing out irregular verbs to them before they left to work on the farm or the ranch. In the years he had taught he had given them *Silas Marner* to prepare them for running a grain elevator, *The Cricket and the Hearth* for the barber shop, logarithms and *Lord Jim* for the lumber yard, the pool hall, the bowling alley. Balance equations and run the beauty parlour; solve by substituting before entering the surgery or the law office; translate at sight, then to the church, the hospital, the filling station, the freight shed.

"We haven't seen much of you," Matt said as Joe took a chair before the desk.

"End of the year—last push before departmental examinations. And you've been busy, I hear on all sides. Where are you hiding her?"

"Who?"

"Whom. I certainly don't mean Millie. Your Dr. Melquist."

Now that was the second time this morning she had been called *his* Dr. Melquist, and he didn't like it any better from Joe than he had from Harry Fitzgerald out fishing. Somehow it suggested patronizing amusement at what was a very young and quite shallow friendship with a newcomer to town. And if this was to be a general response toward her, quite likely she was going to need his friendship. "You'll meet her," he said a little shortly. "I haven't been hiding her."

"I haven't met her yet. Haven't even seen her."

"Not my fault," Matt said.

"How's her survey coming?"

"Haven't the slightest idea."

"You ought to. From what I hear you're driving her all over the country."

"Who's saying that!"

"My usual source of information. Mrs. Nelligan." Joe named his landlady. "I don't think she approved. She seemed to think that . . ."

"The hell with Flannel Mouth Florence." He had said it with a little more force than he intended.

"Oh, I told her there was no need to worry about you and Dr. Melquist. "

"Thanks. No more than you'd have to worry about talk concerning you two."

"What two?"

"You and Flannel Mouth Florence."

"Is there?"

"Is there what?"

"Talk about me and Mrs. Nelligan?"

"Not any more."

"That's nice. I guess they've had to give up on me." Then he added, "In that department, anyway."

Joe was making an oblique reference to his drinking, which worried Matt and Ruth a lot. Joe had not lost discretion to the point of sitting in the Arlington Arms Beer

Parlour, but unlike some teachers Joe had not the hypocrisy to delegate someone else to make his purchases for him in the government Liquor Board store. He had admitted to Matt that he had been undecided about his Scotch and rye buying policy: whether he should go to the vendors for a whole month's supply at a time and thereby risk being seen by a school board chairman with his arms full of the stuff—or whether he should buy it bottle by bottle and be seen often. Quantity or frequency; he took the first simply because it was more convenient.

Joe warmed himself at the hearth of Matt and Ruth, whom he loved, and had even come to accept Sarah's calling him Uncle Joe, though he still flinched within himself whenever Matt or Ruth did.

Matt had often wondered how many years before Joe had stopped including marriage in his dreams—or feminine companionship, even. Probably whenever he had understood that the hunger was no longer so sharp or urgent, and that celibacy was a matter of common sense and taste. Joe was too fastidious for brief alliances with a generous acquaintance or a part-time tart; occasional engagements could only waken and whet an appetite he hadn't a hope of satisfying with any regularity. A man simply had to remind himself to be a good Greek.

The telephone on the desk rang. Matt picked it up. It was Corporal McCready. The poison had been strychnine and they were trying to check for a purchase source, but that avenue was not likely to lead anywhere, for almost every farmer or rancher in the district had bought strychnine for gopher poison or coyote bait. Would Matt run a notice asking people to report anyone seen walking down the alleys, spending time in a part of town he did not usually frequent. The two new dogs poisoned had belonged to the Barkers and the Saunderses.

Just as Matt hung up, Millie appeared in the doorway.

"She's here." For just a moment Millie seemed startled at the bluntness of her own announcement. "Miss Melquist."

"All right, Millie. Just a moment, Joe."

Dr. Melquist waited before the counter. "Come on into my office. Somebody I'd like you to meet."

As they went into his office, Matt shut the door after them.

Millie Clocker did not pick up her copy of *Thrilling Confessions* immediately. Closing doors behind them, and they wouldn't be talking about any dog-poisoning either. Matt would be going to the filing cabinet and pulling out the bottom drawer and taking out the bottle there and getting glasses in the toilet off the office and getting Joe Manley started off so he'd have trouble getting sobered up in time to teach school tomorrow morning.

As far as the dog-poisoning went, she knew who was doing that. Dogs tipped over garbage cans, and if anybody was going to poison dogs it would be the person that had to handle the garbage cans and that was the Napoleons and they were just the sort of people to go around poisoning dogs.

She could tell Miss Melquist a few things about people in this town. *Miss* Melquist. Just like Sabra, Merton's wife in *My Sin Baby*. Sabra hadn't cared at all. Sabra hadn't even dreamed that Merton's love was on a higher, more spiritual plane. Sabra had done her best to drag it down to the level of the gutter!

And Aunt Fan had tried to tell her *Thrilling Confessions* and *I Confess* and *Alluring Love* were trash, and anything but true to life. A lot she knew! Come to think of it, Matt was exactly like Merton, too. Both Merton and Matt would have the selfsame identical scruples when faced with utter purity and innocence.

And Miss Melquist was probably anything but innocent— sitting in there behind a closed door and drinking with two men . . .

She turned her attention to *Thrilling Confessions*.

"After all, my life had been one long, carefree flirt. Then debonair Irvine came along. Here was a conquest that really mattered. We were both young. Too young to know the real meaning of love, but we were old enough to sin."

Within Matt's office there were no glasses, no filing-cabinet bottle of Scotch, simply an introduction of June and Joe

Manley, and a discussion of the dog-poisoning in which Joe had put forward the theory that the poisoner was a flower-lover who had reached the limit of his patience after years of putting up with ravaged flower beds, broken perennials, and defiled lawns.

"Just look for the most ardent gardener in town," said Joe, "and you have your man."

"Not that easy, Joe," Matt said. "Using that yardstick that would mean . . ."

"Mr. Oliver." Joe spoke of the town's mayor, proprietor of the Oliver Trading Company General Store; he served in the district as foreman whenever inquests were held, and was police magistrate for the town as well. Flowers were his passion, his roses having won the Colonel Irvine Cup in the Shelby Annual Perennial and Annual Flower Show for the past seven years.

"That's ridiculous," Matt said.

"He loves flowers enough to . . ."

"So does Aunt Fan."

"No—Aunt Fan's out . . ."

"You might as well accuse Nettie Fitzgerald."

"Well, now, there you've got something. Didn't think of her—Oliver, Nettie Fitzgerald—between those two," Joe said.

"He's not serious," Matt explained to June. "It's not often he is. Mrs. Fitzgerald and Mr. Oliver are the two most unlikely dog-poisoners in town."

"You may be right about Oliver," said Joe. "I'm not so sure about Nettie. All the years that Chesapeake of Harry's has been shedding over her house. No—she'd have poisoned Prince for her first."

"Harry would have been first on her list," corrected Matt. He turned to June. "I'm forgetting—Millie said you'd called earlier . . ."

"Nothing pressing," June said. "Just a little more help."

"How?"

"I wondered if there were somewhere—Miss Cayley's is a little small for me to work in *and* live in. I wondered if you might know where I might be able to rent a place where I won't have to clear the table of breakfast or lunch dishes to set up my typewriter and file cards, then take them off again to make supper."

Matt thought for a moment. "There'll be some place," he said. "Take a day or two to turn it up."

"No hurry," June said, "no concern of yours actually, but I thought you might know of a possibility."

"No trouble," Matt said. "See what I can do."

He knew as soon as she asked, but refrained from making his suggestion then. In front of Joe. There was satisfaction in seeing that she had scored with Joe right away, and it looked as though Joe was not so immune as he had thought he was.

The two left the office together.

It would be nice, he thought, if she were to move into Flannel Mouth Florence's; give people something to talk about during her stay in Shelby. Here he was arbitrarily pairing people off just like Ruth! Indulging in a feminine sort of wishful thinking. And he still hadn't done the dog-poisoning piece! He glanced at his watch: 12:30! He'd have to get to it after lunch!

He gathered up his creel, still stringing slime, and started from the office.

"Millie! I thought you'd gone home long ago. You didn't need to stay this late!"

She looked up from her magazine. "Oh, Mr. Stanley, I don't mind. I don't mind at all."

As he went out he was wondering why it was that he found her sweet compliance harder to take than the hurt sullenness that sometimes descended upon her.

CHAPTER 4

THE SAME DAY HE HAD INTRODUCED JOE TO JUNE, HE DECIDED they ought to have June over for dinner. Ruth had not responded to the suggestion with instant enthusiasm.

"Look Ruth, she's picked Shelby for her project with care. She says it's a typical community that's been living ever since the earliest days of the Canadian West, one that will personify all communities."

"Mmmmh."

"She thinks Shelby fills the bill. I agree with her. Now, who better to tell her all about Shelby's childhood than your dad? With a brandy in his hand he'll tell her all about the winter of ought-six and -seven, the early hivernanters, French and Métis, the cattle drives in the seventies and eighties coming up the trail from Wyoming and Montana . . ."

"Dad didn't ride up with them. He's from Prince Edward Island."

"I know, I know. But he knew the guys who did. He can tell her all about the wolfers, beaver trappers, whiskey traders, the earliest cattlemen like 'Nigger John' Ware, Livingstone, Ackers, and 'Liver-eating' Johnston. How about Tuesday?"

"My bridge night."

"Oh yeah, and Wednesday I got to wrap the paper up. Thursday's Rotary. How about Friday? Or Saturday?"

"I'll think about it."

"Aw come on, Ruth. By the way, she's already met Joe."

"Has she."

"He didn't have to take time to make up his mind about her."

"Really!"

"Yep. They hit it off fine."

That had been very clever of him. Ruth was a cowgirl yenta. She'd never give up trying to find a right mate for Joe.

"Saturday," she said. "And let's have Clem Derrigan, too."

"I don't know about . . ."

"I'll warn him to keep his language clean for a change. Best storyteller in the western hemisphere."

"Did he clean them up when you were a child?"

"Not always. You make sure Joe sticks to soda water."

"I'll try. What are you going to serve them?"

"Goose."

Mentally he computed the time since last November when he and Harry Fitzgerald had pitted in on Seeney's barley stubble. "Six months. Do you think it will be—you don't think it might be . . .?"

"We've eaten them after nine months in the freezer. It'll be fine. Pick it up at the locker on your way home Friday. It can be thawing and I can stuff it in the morning. Pineapple dressing."

"I'd better pick up a bottle of wine, too."

"That would be nice."

"Uh—white or red?"

"Whichever it's supposed to be."

"Well, that's just it. I'm not sure which it should be."

"White wine with fowl, isn't it?"

"But goose is *dark* meat."

"It flies. Don't bother with wine if it's going to be that complicated."

"I'll get both."

He also picked up a bottle of Cointreau which he knew Ruth's father always liked with his cigar after a meal.

He felt the evening had started out well enough with the first faint surprise he noted on June's face when she stepped into their home. He could tell instantly that she hadn't been prepared for the muscular evergreens of Emily Carr's print over the fireplace, or for the happy marriage Ruth had achieved with green, salmon, and tan in their living room.

Before dinner there was a little difficulty with Sarah, who fell instantly in love with June's clear plastic overshoes. The child brought them in from the front porch, smeared with mud, clutched passionately to her breast; she refused to give them up. When Matt took them by force she screamed; he arranged a compromise by letting her have one of them after it had been carefully washed and dried.

Before dinner the Senator sat quite still, bulking large and solid in his chair, his hands upon thick knees, his pale eyes on Dr. Melquist. The old man didn't have to make it quite so evident that he was taking his own deliberate time to size her up. Matt supposed it was the sight of the roast Canada goose that finally warmed the Senator. Conversation at dinner—in spite of Sarah's shrill interruptions and insistence on singing "Old Macdonald Had a Farm" seven times—took on a happy carelessness. Several times the Senator smiled at something that had nothing whatever to do with Sarah. Under their wild brows, his eyes gleamed when they moved to the living room and Matt brought out the square bottle of Cointreau; he sighed as he bit the end from a cigar and leaned back into his chair.

Only to the east, he told June, lay wheat farms; west of Shelby the ranches sprawled through the foothills to the forest reserve in the mountains beyond. Shelby was a cow town really, the Senator insisted. On festive Saturday nights, men in tight denim pants with copper rivets, a brilliant kerchief knotted in the hollow of the neck, teetered as they walked into the Arlington Arms Beer Parlour, the Cameo Theatre, or Willie MacCrimmon's Shoe and Harness Shop. They had weathered faces like farmers', but they were riding, not choring, men. They belonged to the softly swelling foothills under the Rockies, withdrawn and cool and abiding, not the billiard table to the east.

"Don't buy the celluloid myth, Dr. Melquist. Those shoot-out artists, Western bad men . . ."

"Yeah," Clem Derrigan said. "In the Arlington Arms—Yukon gold-rush days—Soapy Smith . . ."

"Shut up, Clem," Matt heard Ruth say. "Senator's got the floor."

Clem shut up.

"—hung out in saloons mostly—card cheats, pimps, bushwhackers. Always played with a stacked deck on or off the poker table."

The Senator brought back Shelby's younger days beautifully as he told how ladies used calling-cards and held afternoon musicals, and how there were formal balls such as the 1912 Polo Ball to welcome home the Shelby boys and ponies who had played off for the North American championship in Hawaii. At these affairs women swept the floor with their long gowns, carried fans in their kid-gloved hands, danced in patent-leather slippers. Ranchers rode into town, took their dinner jackets from a gunny sack hung on the saddle horn and changed before entering the hall.

He spoke highly and fondly of Uncle Ben and the *Shelby Chinook*, which had brought the community international recognition with the winning of the Pulitzer Prize.

The Senator stared down at the end of his cigar, touched it on the tray, to leave behind a cone of ash like a pygmy wasp's nest. After a sip of his liqueur, he wiped at his grey moustache with the back of his hand.

"Your turn now, Clem."

Startled, Matt looked sharply to Ruth. What the hell was she encouraging Clem for! Her eyes were innocently lowered to her brandy glass. Clem would sure as hell give a much different perspective than the Senator had. It would not be one of dignity and grace. For a start, Clem Derrigan was a name assumed when he'd crossed the border one jump ahead of the sheriff after handguns had been outlawed in Texas. He was one of many such immigrants leathering on both sides across the Forty-Ninth, looking for sanctuary in Canada. He'd found it on the Anchor T with Ruth's father. Never, Ruth had early warned Matt, ever ask a fellow what his real name was, because there were still a lot of Clem Derrigans in the foothills.

Clem leaned forward and there came the plastering slap of tobacco juice followed by a tuning-fork ring in the heart of the spittoon Ruth kept in the house only for her father's old foreman whenever he visited them.

"I never played no tiddlywinks on horses," Clem said. "I worked on 'em. Most the girls I run with didn't carry no fancy callin'-cards neither. Nor dance cards. I never wore no monkey suit, so I wouldn't know much about them polo players' big balls the ladies liked to hold."

Just about cancelled out the Senator's version of early Shelby.

He agreed with the Senator that Ackers and Johnston were the founding fathers of Blackfoot Crossing, which had become Shelby further downstream, but he added that they were both whiskey traders and that Ackers was usually called "Knackers," that Johnston had been an Indian-fighter in Wyoming and Idaho who was usually addressed as "Liver-eating." He was a self-confessed cannibal, boasting often of how he had eaten a Nez Percé liver, at first out of simple curiosity and on several later occasions for ritualistic reasons.

"Told me so hisself. Lotta times after he started up the Arlington Arms. 'Clem,' he'd say. 'First time I wasn't all that hungry. Spur the moment you might say. Surprised me—wasn't no gamy taste to it at all. Way ahead of porcupine belly or muskrat or beaver tail. Kind of looked forward to the next time. Always was fussy about fried liver.' "

Now Clem was going on about remittance men. He was not an anglophile:

"Lot of 'em started out as babies in ermine di'pers. Look at the Earl of Egmont out Pincher Creek way. He was a hired man married to a hired girl and they discover he's the last livin' Earl of Egmont. Ended up ownin' half of London. Country was lousy with 'em—dukes an' dukesses, lords an' ladies, earls an' earlasses. Got into trouble in the old country an' come up before the judge one time too many an' he knew their folks so he made a deal with 'em. Suspended sentence an' no time at all in the bucket if they got their ass out of Merry Old an' spent the rest of their life in South Africa or Australia or New Zealand or Canada. Folks sent 'em quarterly cheques."

As Matt was pretty sure she would, Miss Shackerly

came next. He'd already heard of her many times both from
Clem and from Ruth, whose childhood Clem had enlivened
with his stories.

"I rode a spell for her back in the early twenties, after
Ruthie's mother died an' the Senator figured he'd sell out
an' go back to Prince Edward Island. He changed his mind,
thank God."

Matt saw that Ruth nodded her head in agreement.

"Quite a woman, Shackerly was. Full-moon-nights kep'
wakin' me up in the bunkhouse. She howled all night long.
Me an' all the bedbugs. She always rode side-saddle. Never
forget when Lord an' Lady Minto come all the way from the
old country to visit her. Birch Jaw brought them out from
Shelby—Birch Jaw Heidigger run Heidigger Livery. Everybody called him Birch Jaw. Birch for short. See, he was
always losin' his dentures—once down Peterson's well,
another time Harve Davidson's privy. Then there was the
time he never thought to search for them in the Arlington
spittoon. Loose-fittin' I guess. Never wore 'em except
when he et or come into town. Carried 'em in his overhaul's
pocket. Not the hip. Might of bit hisself in the arse."

"Get on with it, Clem," Ruth said. "Miss Shackerly."

"Oh yeah, well, Birch got tired of losin' 'em, so he
carved hisself a set out of birch. Some said it was hickory
out of an old rocker he had, but then they'd of called him
Hickory or Hick. Said he never had so good a fit and the
price was right. Only fellow in whole Shelby district had
wood teeth. Anyways, he took Lord an' Lady Minto out to
Miss Shackerly's an' I saw 'em drive in an' they knocked on
the door an' she was havin' a bath in that big copper dish the
English use, and she come to the door and she was drippin'
suds an' water behind one them big English towels she was
holdin' up from under her chin and down her front.

" 'Well, well—if it isn't Dwight and Cessie,' she says.
'How lovely and thoughtful of you to call. Just give me a
moment to make myself presentable.'

"She turned right round an' back into the house, but she
didn't shift that towel from her front to her back. I knew
then why she always rode side-saddle. I never seen her bare
arse before that, and she had one on her like a tame bee.
Must of been why she rode side-saddle. Only way she could

get it into a saddle. Unless it was one of them English pancakes or maybe an Australian army sadd—"

June's clear and unrestrained outburst of laughter interrupted him. Up to then, Matt had noticed that Ruth had kept her gaze steadily upon June, a most unfeminine stare, naked and hard and non-committal as a horse gypsy's. It was not a look he remembered ever having seen before on his wife's face, though he had once seen it on her father's when the old man had been faulting a young sorrel mare in a community auction years before. He was certain now that Ruth had deliberately nudged Clem into taking part as some sort of test; he was just as certain that June had just met it.

"Clem," Ruth said, "get to the royalty part of it."

"Sure. She was descended straight down from the House of Hangover."

"House of *Hanover*," Matt said.

"I know that. It was Chuck Dolittle called it that first and then everybody else in Shelby district. Shackerly was a half-sister or a cousin of the Earl of Minto. Bastard daughter of Edward Eight or George somethin'."

"Not really!" That was June.

"Yeah. We all found out when the Prince of Wales bought his EP ranch. That was the brand he run. Everybody excited in Shelby district they were gettin' him for next-door neighbour. Next King of England. See, he bought the MacMillan spread out on Pekisko Creek. Called it the EP ranch. That was the brand he run. Edward Prince brand. Right up till then folks spent a lot of time laughin' at Miss Shackerly. Then they quit."

"Why?" That was June again.

"Well, Ralph Hoshal, he was postmaster at the Post Office. He found this card in her mail—you know how everybody in the Post Office reads all the postcards—and the dirty magazines people get prescriptions to. Well, Ralph, he sees this card to Miss Shackerly, and it was from Buckin'ham Palace, an' it said how he was lookin' forward to seein' her—and it was signed Edward. . . ."

Clem leaned forward and let one go at the spittoon. As always: bull's-eye. He wiped at his mouth with his bandanna, then delivered his punch line:

"It was addressed to: 'Dear Auntie'! First time anybody

ever took Miss Shackerly serious. From then on fallin' all over theirself, kissin' her arse to get her to introduce 'em to her nephew. Prince of Wales."

"What a marvellous story, Mr. Derrigan," June said. "Is it true?"

"Of course." Even when both listener and teller knew he was lying, nobody probably had ever asked Clem that question before.

"A while back—you said something about Soapy Smith."

"That's right."

"What happened with him?"

"*To* him," Clem said. "In Arlington bar on his way up to the Yukon—I give him the shit kickin' of his life. Later on he was up to his old tricks in the Klondike and a fellow shot him on the dock in Nome, Alaska." Both these statements were true, Matt knew. The Senator and Ruth had told him so.

He knew now that he had been unfairly apprehensive about the evening. Ruth knew what she was doing, and was choreographing the whole affair. She kept giving Joe Manley cues, but he was not taking them; simply sat in unusual silence, grimacing now and again as he took a sip of his soda water. His eyes seldom left June.

After a refill of Cointreau, the Senator described how Shelby had been a natural stopping-place for gold-seekers on their way north to the Yukon. He verified that Soapy Smith had indeed underestimated Clem in the Arlington bar. He came back often to Uncle Ben and the *Chinook*, told how Ben had written and printed the rules and regulations for "Liver-eating" to nail up in all the Arlington rooms:

1. Those upstairs shoot up. Those down, down.
2. No tobacco spit in the beds. We need the sheets for tablecloths during the day.
3. Access to rooms after nightfall by mothers, wives, sisters only. Private entrance to and exit from rooms for other ladies by ladder at rear.
4. Unwanted guests: pimps, card sharps, bushwhackers, rustlers, safe-crackers, politicians, and Bible salesmen.

5. In case of fire, exit by window. No evacuation on
   stairs.

The Senator said that employment notices in the Post
Office or store windows did frequently bear the caveat "No
Englishmen need apply." He told of how Hollywood had
discovered the scenic promise of the foothills. He recalled
the movie advance man who had led an international covey
of journalists up and down the Spray River, stopped, lifted
his arms wide with palms turned out, swivelled through 360
degrees, dropped his arms, and faced the assembly to say:
"I don't think you Canadian people actually know or
appreciate what you've got here. Terrific! You have got the
sexiest scenery on this whole North American continent!"

Ben stewed over that for several days, the Senator said,
then came up with his story entitled "The Sex Life of Old
Mount Rundle."

> Your editor had always thought the Three Sisters were
> virginal, never dreamed that Edith Cavell lay in close
> proximity under majestic Eisenhower for sexual rea-
> sons. We have difficulty with old Flat Top and Mount
> Hood, about as sexual as door-knobs. We have never
> understood till now that the fierceness of our chinooks
> was the panting of warm lust, that lodgepole and jack
> pine and spruce were simply arboreal erections.
>
> We have given the matter a lot of thought. We do agree
> that the union of life-giving rain from skies above,
> falling upon fertile mother earth, does bring forth
> increase, but surely our MGM informant did not have
> that in mind. It simply is not the Hollywood concept of
> sex.
>
> When the film, tentatively titled *North-West Stampede*,
> does hit cinemas from coast to coast, with Jack Oakie
> and James Craig in hot and lustful pursuit, tithering and
> tothering over the side-hill braes after Joan Leslie while
> the mountains and creeks and draws and buck brush are
> going at it hammer and tongs, what a sexy movie that
> will be! It will have to be branded R.

The piece had been reprinted in *PM* and in *Puck*, but "It
should have got Ben another Pulitzer," the Senator said.

All the dinner guests agreed.

"Tell them, Dad, about Frazier Hunt and the Prince of Wales and Helen Keller."

The Senator did.

A regular *Cosmopolitan* contributor, Frazier Hunt in the twenties had fallen in love with the Canadian foothills. He had bought a ranch high up the Spray River and across the ridge from the EP spread on Pekisko. This was handy, for in those days the Prince of Wales was frequently poured off his royal purple CPR coach in Shelby to take colonial sojourns from his royal duties, and Hunt was able to do his best-seller, *My Neighbour The Prince*. He also one summer had Helen Keller as a guest, stringing ropes so she could get out and around. Did a book on her as well. There were many other famous visitors: Peter B. Kyne, Buster Keaton, and Guy Weadick, who had once been with the Buffalo Bill Wild West Show, had performed with Will Rogers in Pantages vaudeville, had founded the Calgary Stampede, and had stayed on in the foothills with his guest ranch just down the trail from Frazier Hunt's place. Irvin S. Cobb was a summer regular.

"Just about the frog-ugliest man I've ever seen," the Senator said. "Always had a cigar over a foot long in his mouth under what must have been a twenty-gallon Stetson. He never wore Levi's though. Voluminous bloomers. Checkered. He called them plus-fours.

"Great poker parties Hunt used to throw. Prince of Wales never missed a one of them, which made it difficult for the rest of us devout poker players. The Prince preferred to shoot craps. As well as drink the liquor we all chipped in on. He didn't. Pocotello down the road from Guy Weadick's place did not like that at all. He went out back to get what was supposed to be the last jug, came back in with it, and in the other hand he was holding up a dead mouse. By the tail, of course. Said he'd found it floating belly-up inside the jug. Must have been the first time in his life the Prince ever turned down a free drink."

"I never got invited over to them Hunt parties," Clem said, "but I seen the Prince ridin' past the Anchor T now an' again. Know what he raised on the EP? Dartmoor ponies. Not beef! Dartmoor ponies! An' bluebottle flies. See, when he wasn't there, which was most the time them years, ranch house was empty an' nobody takin' care of it. Just when they knew he was comin', then they'd clean the place up—take down the spider webs an' wasp nests, get rid of the pack rats an' mice an' their turds. Out on the verandah so's he wouldn't be up to his royal arse with 'em they swep' up the horseflies an' bluebottle flies.

"Wall-eye, that Duchess his, she just came with him the once—his last time. She preferred London or Paris to the EP."

Why was she letting Clem go on like this! He caught her eye and knew right away that she could sense his annoyance. She gave him the impish smile he knew so well—abrupt as a light turned on and instantly off.

"Another, Matt." She was holding out her liqueur glass. "Please."

Senator's turn again: "Irvin S. Cobb was an unflagging talker. So was Guy Weadick. And your Uncle Ben. He and I made a secret bet. A case of whiskey. Well—we did let others in on it—and they agreed to shut up with us and let Weadick and Cobb go on and on till one of them finally shut up. Your Uncle Ben won the whiskey on the first to quit."

"Which one did he bet on?"

"Guy. Cobb kept right on rolling another two hours. Till daybreak, when he stubbed out his last cigar and headed for his bunk. The Prince had turned in early."

"He wasn't very swift, was he?" Clem said.

"Perhaps not," the Senator said.

"Even by English standards," Clem said.

"I see you're not a royalist," June said.

"God-damn rights I ain't. I'm a Texan."

The pine fire crackled and showered sparks upwards; Sarah kissed them all and finally permitted Matt to carry her to her bed. After three drinks of water, two teddys, Baby Jane, Lucy dolly, a cookie, one halting "Now I Lay Me Down," twelve "Don't leave me's," and a final rendition of "For the Bible tells me so," he returned to the living-room.

It was as though the Senator had done his bit for the

evening. He had fallen profoundly silent, sitting perfectly still in his chair. Looking at him, Matt was suddenly struck with the thought that were it not for the shallow rise and fall of his chest he was as still as he would be in death. And quite likely, he decided to himself, he would die like this, in consummate repose. No wasting would ever take him off; he could not die in bed helpless under sheets—hair ruffled, his teeth in water by the bedside, a young nurse professionally and patronizingly cheerful.

He had driven the Senator and Clem home; Joe had taken June. In retrospect he felt that the evening had gone well enough; June had definitely gotten a good taste of early Shelby, now knew the nature of frontier humour with its exaggeration and its acid edge. Quite often black. In the end it was a defence really, against blizzard and drought, grasshoppers and cutworms, low grain and beef prices, but particularly against loneliness.

When he had pulled the car into the boulevard in front of the house, he sat for a moment. There was moist coolness in the chinook breathing against his cheek and carrying the smell of damp earth. Halfway to the front door he stood with his hands in his pockets and looked up to the sky; it was dark and utterly starless, with all the moon to be seen a pale paring low in the river direction. Then he placed the sound swelling in shrill reiteration through the night from deep in the distance—frogs. Instantly he pictured bubbled white membrane rounding up and under the unwinking eyes of a bloated bullfrog, throat bag inflated as squat on leaf feet he laboured to bring forth his call.

Just the porch light was on; Ruth must have gone to bed in the time he had been taking the Senator and Clem home. On his way to their bedroom he looked in on the baby. She lay abandoned in sleep; the puff was down, her nightgown was rolled about her chin, and her arms were up and before her face on the pillow, her shoulder blades like the poke beginnings of young wings. He looked at the bare foot hanging down over the edge of the bed and he was shaken with fierce love for her.

Just as quickly he was moved by a feeling of helplessness; he looked down on the dark eyelashes lying across the fair cheeks and their slight flush of sleep. How could you possibly express what you felt for your child! How could you communicate such intensity of emotion any more than you could shout from Vancouver to Halifax—from one planet to another planet. You'd think a feeling this vivid would make it possible. Perhaps that was all emotion was—whatever it was—a bridge across which people walked to each other, a wonderful buoyance the better to hold the heaviness of communication.

Carefully closing Sarah's door, he felt almost as though he were floating. The elation had not diminished by the time he entered his own room, and saw the mound of Ruth's hip under the blankets, her head turned from him, deep in the pillow. He undressed in the dusk, slid carefully into the bed.

He lay still for a moment. Her body did not touch him at all. He could not hear the slightest stir of breathing, yet without touch or sight or sound he was aware of the warm intimacy of her at his side.

She turned to him. He felt the light brush of her hair over his cheek. He could hear the ringing pulse of his own blood, the beat of his own heart clubbing. The lifting suffocation at his chest and throat was almost unbearable as he felt the touching warmth of her against his thigh.

"Ruth." His voice was hoarse.

"Matt—oh, Matt." She turned to him. "Your Dr. Melquist left one of her overshoes—"

"Oh, shut up about overshoes. How can you talk about overshoes when I—"

"I love you too, Matt."

CHAPTER 5

THE SECOND MORNING AFTER THE CANADA GOOSE DINNER, June had stopped in at the *Chinook* office. She thanked him for the evening, said that the Senator and Clem had given her a most helpful glimpse of Shelby's early days.

"Great story-tellers. I enjoyed them. It was very nice of you and your wife—Ruth—to have me into your family. Sarah's a dear little thing."

"I agree with you."

"Oh—something you might do for me . . ."

"Yes? "

"My other overshoe. I think Sarah must still have it."

"I'll pick it up for you at lunch. I'll drop it off at Aunt Fan's."

"No. I—ah . . . When Joe drove me home last night, we stopped off at his place—Mrs. Nelligan's. She showed me a back light-housekeeping suite—well, not a suite exactly, but twice the size of Miss Cayley's."

"Hey, there's a coincidence for you. I thought of that last week when you and Joe were here. The one Jim Duncan had—until he . . . died just after Christmas. Taught with Joe."

"Yes. He told me. I'm moving in this morning. I'll drop by and pick up that overshoe this afternoon."

Just before she left she said, "Do you know a woman they call Arlington Agnes?"

"Everybody does."

"Is it true that her boyfriend dumped her last January and she turned off the gas and went to bed—planned suicide by freezing to death?"

"Mrs. Nelligan told you that?"

"Yes. Agnes couldn't stand the cold, so she got out of bed and turned the gas back on again. Dr. Fitzgerald had to treat her for severe frostbite, had to amputate three toes and a finger."

"June, I have to warn you about your new landlady. She is Shelby's champion gossip. She's in here all the time with stories she thinks I might like to print. As with most of them, the Arlington Agnes Suicide By Frost one is not true. Agnes does have a drinking problem and that night she just forgot to turn the gas on. It was *she* who dumped her boyfriend. Matter of fact Agnes has quite a few boyfriends. By the way, have you run across the nickname Mrs. Nelligan goes by in Shelby?"

"Yes."

"Flannel Mouth Florence. Quite apt. Nice alliteration and deadly accurate."

Sarah had taken an early nap after lunch, so the retrieval of the plastic overshoe had been no problem.

June dropped by shortly after four just as Byron Napoleon was picking up the *Chinook* copies he dropped off each week at all the downtown stores and offices. As usual he was dressed in old riding breeches of the English style, clinging tight to his thin calves; each time the laces would be hanging loose, with bare, dirty leg showing between the pant legs and the tops of his broken running-shoes, leaving the impression of a thin and uncompleted boy. On each of his visits the same younger brother, Buster, would be at his side, clinging to the fullness of the pants.

After they'd left with their wooden wagon loaded, June asked Matt about the Napoleon family. He explained that Rory had once been the World Champion bareback and saddle bronc rider; upon retiring from his rodeo career he had run the Shelby Livery Stables, but had lost them during the depression years and now worked for the town.

"I'd like to interview the Napoleons," she said.

"Why them?"

"Oh—they have an interesting significance."

"Such as?"

"Bottom of Shelby's social scale, wouldn't you say?"

"I suppose. Along with Arlington Agnes and Art Ulmer, the town drunk. Why start at the bottom of the scale? Why not the top—Harry Fitzgerald, Canon Midford, Mayor Oliver, Ollie Pringle, me?"

"Okay. You."

He hadn't been ready for that.

"How did you end up in Shelby?"

He pointed up to the Pulitzer Prize. "That guy was my uncle. He founded the *Chinook* in 1902. When he died six years ago he left it to me. You going to take notes?"

"No."

"Journalist's dream."

"How's that?"

"Oh, pay the rent, grocery bills, support a family—call your own shots without assignment handcuffs so you can salvage writing time for more important things."

"Such as?"

"Fiction maybe—short stories—a novel or two. North American dailies are loaded with people who are going to write the Great New World Novel."

"Have you?"

"Have I what?"

"Written the great—?"

"Of course not." Thank God she had dropped it there.

"Do you—have you missed the stimulation of living at the centre—"

"Not really. Being an urban ant isn't so much stimulating as distracting. Here I have a detachment I value. In the arts and cultural centres of the world you run across an awful lot of talker novelists and talker composers and talker painters."

"But how many novelists—or noted painters or playwrights—live in the Shelbys of North America?"

"Why don't you ask Hardy or Faulkner or Steinbeck or Eudora Welty or Sam Clemens or Willa Cather?"

"I didn't realize they lived in Shelby communities."

"In their childhood and their fictions they did."

"You have a point."

"In his youth Shakespeare got caught poaching a deer around Stratford district. Byron was a small-town boy clambering around the mountains in Scotland. You're pretty good at this."

"Thank you."

"Let's go back down to the bottom of the social scale. You're interested in the Napoleons."

"Yes."

"All right." He picked up the phone. "Art's Taxi will take us out there right now."

Anything to get her off a pretty touchy subject for him.

After Art had let them out in the Napoleon yard and left, they stood for a moment, looking at the house silvered by age and wind and sun, and at the goat standing on the back stoop. Even for a goat it was singularly un-beautiful, its squared body still retaining a shaggy winter coat that hung loose as a ragged blanket thrown over its back. Long and leaf-like ears hung down and forward. It was wall-eyed. The goat was returning their stare as it chewed thoughtfully, the shallow jaw metronomic under aristocratic nostrils, the goatee keeping perfect time.

Suddenly, with unpredictable grace and undulance, it—no, he—sailed from the stoop to the drunken fence that tilted close along the side of the house; no sooner had he touched it than with the same deft movement rippling through neck, shoulders, and body, he flew to the lean-to roof. With ballet delicacy he picked out a few steps there, then took flight again to the ridge of the house, where he rose to his hind feet with forefeet held loosely to his chest, balancing seemingly on the very tips of his hooves.

During the depression, Matt explained to June, Rory had lost most of his quarter section, and now had only ten gravelly acres left along the Spray River, barely able to support one cow, some chickens, a growing herd of goats, and the Napoleon family.

"Why, Mr. Stanley." Mame Napoleon had lifted the plum-coloured cloth that served as a door. She stood just inside, a slender birch of a woman with a face like an old apple; the rims of her eyes were red as though she had just come in out of the wind, had been crying gently, or was about to. A wisp of dun hair had escaped from the faded beret pulled down over both ears.

"Nice of you to call." Her voice was firm and loud with a touch of hoarseness.

"Mrs. Napoleon. I'd like you to meet Dr. Melquist."

"Pleased to meet you. Come on in." She lifted the faded curtain. "Ain't much better in than out but come on in." Inside she turned to June, indicated the rocker standing by a makeshift stove of firebricks over which rested a sheet of cast iron. "You set there, dear—it's the only one'll hold you. You take the edge of the bed, Matt."

Matt lowered himself to the rumpled blankets of the brass bed and as he did there came a thin bleating from behind the stove. Mame's face reddened. She snatched a broom from the wall. "Git! Outside!" The poking of the broom squirted a young white goat from behind the stove; it bounded through the curtain door. Mame Napoleon turned back to them.

"I guess there's some folks wouldn't take it the right way—seein' a goat in a person's house," she said almost apologetically to June.

"I guess not, Mame," Matt helped her out.

"Well, he ain't in by invitation. An' he's the only one of the whole forty that gets in the house," she assured June earnestly. "Person gets tired of puttin' him out all the time. Havin' that curtain for a door—not much I can do." She dippered water from the pail on the table and into the kettle. "He's come in ever since he was a kid. Buster brought him in late last fall when he was borned an' I thawed him out behind the stove." She set the kettle on the stove. "He's a smart goat."

"Is he?" June said.

"Oh sure. He's smart for a goat—smart for anything for that matter. Smartest goat we ever had, an' we had a lot of 'em. House-broke right from the first. Takes a real smart goat a person can house-break, wouldn't you think?"

"I'd think so, Mrs. Napoleon," June said.

Mame Napoleon had not returned the smile; there was

calculating directness in her eyes that did not shift from June's face; it was obvious that her mind had been only half on her talk of the goats.

"Dr. Melquist is a sociologist, Mame."

"That's nice."

"She—ah—she's doing a survey. The town—district."

"Uh-huh."

"She'll be talking to a lot of us in the next few months."

"Will she." There was still little warmth in the red-rimmed eyes. "What sort of stuff you tryin' to find out?"

"This is just a visit, Mrs. Napoleon." June smiled at her again. "A first visit. I'm not trying to find out anything."

"Uh-huh. Not this time."

"Pardon?"

"Next time you'll be diggin' for stuff."

"Perhaps." Now there was an edge of firmness to June's voice; she did not smile. Mame turned away, took down a brown teapot from the wooden board that formed a shelf over the stove. As she shook tea into it, she said:

"You're a doctor."

"That's right, Mrs. Napoleon." June's voice now was just as non-committal as Mame's.

"Operatin'?"

"No—I'm not a medical doctor . . ." Her voice warmed a little. "You might almost say I'm not really a doctor at all."

Some of the coldness seemed to have vanished from Mame's eyes. "Tell you the truth," she said, "I'm not too fussy about doctors—doctors," she emphasized, "an' social people." She had turned round full to June. "You're social," she accused without any real feeling.

"Well—perhaps," admitted June. "Some of us are. But I'm not, really, and quite honestly this is simply a visit, Mrs. Napoleon. Any time I call during my time here, it will be simply for a visit and to gather material—whomever I may call on."

Mame grinned. "Well now, that's interestin'—kind of takes some of the sting out of it."

"How's that, Mame?" said Matt.

"We're all in the same boat, you might say—first time for the town an' the first time for the Napoleons." She left the stove and sat down relaxed in the backless wooden chair by the table. "What you want to know about us, dear?"

"All sorts of things," said June. "How many children in the family?"

"That's easy," Mame interrupted. "There's three my kids in school—Byron an' Esther an' Avalon. I got three more at home—they're playin' now down by the river. Buster, Evelyn, an' Elvira. She's the baby. An' I'll tell you somethin' else"—she leaned forward confidentially—"I ain't likely to have any more. That's why I ain't fussy about doctors. After Elvira, Doc Fitzgerald—you met him yet?"

June shook her head.

"You will. He lost Mrs. Olsen her baby last summer. After Elvira, Doc Fitzgerald, he said I had appendiseedus an' I believed him. I got no way tellin' whether I got appendiseedus or not. So I said he could operate an' he got me up on the table an' he out with everything so I wouldn't have no more kids. I didn't have appendiseedus no more'n you have. He bin tellin' me long as I can remember I ought to. That's how he did it." She paused as though June might wish to express herself on the villainy of Dr. Fitzgerald. Beyond the interest on her face, June made no comment.

"It bothered me at first, thinkin' how I couldn't have no more kids, but I got over that. I guess he had his reasons. My kids ain't very smart. Them not bein' smart doesn't worry Rory an' me too much. They're good kids an' I don't care if they're smart, so long as they're happy. That's the main thing." This time June nodded agreement.

"An' Rory's happy too. Doc Fitzgerald should of tied off Rory's toobs whilst he was at it. It ain't me—it's Rory. Rory's treaty—not all, just quarter. Him I met whilst I was cookin' for the Rockin' E years ago an' he was one of the Paradise Valley fellahs used to give Sam Barnes a hand with hayin' an' fencin'. We moved into town but it's Rory is the reason my kids ain't so smart, an' that's because Byron an' Evelyn an' Avalon an' the others is part smoked. So they ain't as smart as other kids which ain't smoked."

During the last part of this, Mame had stood up to tip the boiling kettle into the teapot, and set out cups and saucers on the table. While they drank dark and bitter tea from the thick soiled cups and saucers, Mame Napoleon carried most of the conversation; Matt realized that he had been right in his first estimate of June in her work. She had flinched neither at the sight of her cup, nor at first taste of the tea; she was an excellent listener, drawing Mame's attention and remarks completely to herself. Here was a sort of confessional art that concealed art. He had at first decided that its salient quality was its impersonality, but had to revise this, for there was a subtle and gentle responding that had at first escaped him; with a look, with a slight gesture, with a word, she encouraged Mame to more deeply intimate confidence, to more generous garrulity.

There was the slightest lifting of the corners of her mouth when Mame said, "I'm the only psychiatric person in the whole Shelby district, an' it's a great gift I got through no will of my own. Goes right back, back to when I was a girl in Tiger Lily. Flor'nce," said Mame and paused to finish the tea in her cup. "Sister. We was all girls in our family. Flor'nce used to take petty fits." Again Mame stopped, but at June's nod she said, "Ruby."

"Ruby."

"My sister Ruby—between me an' Flor'nce."

Just a shadow of expression on June's face indicated that she understood Ruby's position between Mame and Florence.

"Ruby was."

"Yes."

"Flor'nce was the baby, then there was Ruby then me, an' Ruby never went out with the others to play volleyball. Blind staggers. Durin' the Physical Trainin' part in school, Miss Crosley, the school nurse, she said—to the teacher—to all Ruby's teachers—she said you just let Ruby Partridge—I was a Partridge before I married—well, before Rory an' me—you just let Ruby Partridge set in the schoolroom—at her desk—whilst the others play volleyball."

"Oh."

"An'," said Mame triumphantly, "she did." She turned to Matt. "More tea, Mr. Stanley?"

"No thanks, Mame." But she had hardly heard him, for her attention had returned to June.

"Just shows you."

"Yes."

"Shows what?" asked Matt.

"Runs in our family—Flor'nce an' Ruby an' me."

"Blind staggers?" he asked in spite of himself.

"No. We all must of had a touch of it. But I've got it the most. Seems like I'm fertile for the spirits. When I go into one of my trances, why they just pile up there—out there—waitin' to come through me like grey honkers whangin' down a coulee to a sixty-bushel barley field. It's a wonderful power I got that's given to only a few in this world. A natural-born medium. Tooned to the other world of the spirits."

It was a little as it was with a child daring another to do a dangerous or impudent act; it was as though June by some quiet magic created a state of imbalance so that a person was vaguely compelled before her patient and understanding attention to tell—to confide—to try for approval—to achieve balance again.

He thought about this as they walked back to town; in spite of the green blush of very young wheat in the fields, a meadowlark's brightness that startled again and again as though the same bird were following them, the April landscape seemed slightly out of focus to him, his attention turned within.

"You know," he said at length, "you did that well."

"Oh, what do you mean?"

"With Mame Napoleon—the way you drew her out."

"You make it sound rather calculated."

"No. Oh, no," he said quickly. "I didn't mean that. I meant—talking with her . . ." He broke off. What did he mean? That it had not seemed calculated at all. "I meant that it isn't easy to walk in—especially with a woman like Mame—without showing surprise or—or awkwardness—to put her at ease the way you did. I think she liked you."

"Do you? I liked her."

"Do you always?" She did not answer him immediately, seemed to be considering his question. "Do you always like the people you talk to—interview?"

"Of course not," she said. "It hasn't a great deal to do with it really."

"I'd think it would have."

"Not any more than in your work, I imagine. Do you write a better story because you like the person you're writing about? Or the thing?"

He didn't have to consider that. "Sure. It's easier if there's some emotion involved."

"In an editorial?"

He nodded.

"What sort of editorials or stories have you done that were easier that way?"

For a moment her directness startled him. He cast his mind back. For years he had urged the beautifying of the cemetery; he could hardly say there'd been great emotion involved in that, though—simply a matter of respect, no, pride. Pride involved emotion, didn't it? There had been his attempts to stir up interest in the costly project of artificial ice for the rink, the construction of an old folks' home. He supposed that meant that he liked children and old people, that he was in favour of the dead who couldn't transplant their own bedding-out plants, or mow their own grass.

"Offhand it's hard to recall," he said. Then there were the Social and Personal columns, the weekly Complaints of Cattle, Horses, and Poultry, all the fillers over the years. "Value of Canadian mineral production this year reached $890,215,856," and "The flying fish is believed to take to the air frequently to escape its enemies."

"Most of it's pretty minor-key stuff," he said.

"What sort of minor key?"

But she had persisted too far. Now her charm was suspect as he realized that he must be on guard himself. The knowledge saddened and disappointed him a little, as the tarnishing of innocence always saddens and disappoints. "Quite minor key," he said.

She seemed to sense that she had upset him and let it drop. From time to time there stole to him from her some pale and feminine scent reminding him in its fragility of the pastel fragrance of sweet peas. Hell—he supposed he'd been buried out here in the foothills so long, any talent he might have had for social communication had been blunted. And suddenly it was very important that she should not suspect at all how gauche he was feeling.

"I didn't do it so very well with you, did I?" The richness of her voice startled him; he had not realized till then that it possessed such relaxation, dropping easily into a vibrant lowness unusual in a woman's speech.

And suddenly he knew that she had not been doing it at all, or rather not deliberately. "That's all right," he said. "It's just that it's that way—minor key. You wouldn't believe what has been the longest-continuing issue in the *Shelby Chinook.*"

"Freight rates?" she said.

"No."

"Civic corruption? High tariffs?"

"Spring."

"Spring!"

With some diffidence he outlined briefly for her the course of the feud between Mable Ridge and Shelby over the issue of which town welcomed spring earliest. For the first time since he'd met her, he saw her smile, and the effect was quite disarming. He saw that in the blue of her eyes there were vivid ginger and brown flecks, and that her teeth were astonishingly perfect.

"How have your readers responded?" she asked him.

"Some were a little puzzled by all the fuss. I suppose some dismissed it as tomfoolery. About the same response as to the Rotary Club Fashion Show."

When he had dropped her off at Aunt Fan's and returned to the office, he sat in contemplation at his desk for some time. Then he got up and went into the outer office.

"Millie."

Millie looked up from *Appealing Stories.* "Was the last *Mable Ridge News* in the mail?"

"On the corner of your desk, Mr. Stanley."

Back in his office he opened the paper, his eye going straight to the story at mid-page:

Now Magnus Benson knows why our Western crocus wears its furry grey pants, for on the south side of his new barn, almost covered by the overnight fall of snow, he found one out in full bloom. Magnus reports it seemed almost to shiver there in its snowy coverlet of snow. This is the earliest crocus ever reported in the three prairie provinces during the past three decades. Magnus brought it into the *News* office this morning. .

He supposed he'd have to do something about that early crocus now. It was reassuring that the spring business amused her, as Mame Napoleon had. Now where would people like the Napoleons fit into sociological surveys? Didn't such works concern themselves with groups? Trends, norms, broad classifications of individuals? What possible generalization—social, moral, economic—could be balanced on the eccentricity of the Napoleons? The Napoleons were the Napoleons and only that. He must remember to ask her that next time.

His crocus rebuttal would necessitate a drive to Mable Ridge. He was unable to argue against the existence of the actual crocus, but he did call on Magnus Benson—a sheepish Magnus as it turned out, who rather unwillingly took Matt to the side of the barn where the crocus had been picked. On his return to Shelby, Matt wrote what was to be the final story of the year on the matter of spring.

> Your editor has just returned from a trip to the neighbouring town of Mable Ridge. While there he visited the offices of the *Mable Ridge News* to see for himself the crocus which that paper reported to be held in a saucer of water on the *News* editor's desk He saw the crocus. He also saw on this visit Tommy Briggs and Ernie Fowler, neighbours of Magnus Benson, on the south side of whose barn the flower was plucked a week ago. Mr. Fowler and Mr. Briggs have cleared up the mystery and confounded Mable Ridge's claim to the first crocus of Spring. The south side of Magnus Benson's new barn happens to be the location of his new cold frame. Small wonder that with glass drawing and concentrating the rays of the early April sun where the year before Mother Nature had sown a wild crocus, there should come forth a blossom well ahead of time.

> We cannot allow the Benson Crocus as a natural herald of hasty Spring to Mable Ridge District but as a man-forced freak—and we deplore the *Mable Ridge News'* partial attitude in withholding essential facts from the reading public in this matter.

CHAPTER 6

A FEW DAYS AFTER THE MAME NAPOLEON VISIT JUNE MELQUIST jumped to the top of her societal scale. He suggested to her that she drop into Wing's Palm Café on a regular morning-coffee basis, as did most of the town's business men.

"Wing's is Shelby's political forum. The male one."

"And the female one?"

"Over the back fence—the party line. By the way, while we're on the subject, how's it panning out for you at Mrs. Nelligan's?"

"All right. I could still use more space, though. To work in. I was wondering. You know of any—ah—corner there might be for me? Preferably downtown?"

"Possibly. Let's get that coffee at Wing's."

Wing had just given them their cups when they were joined by Harry Fitzgerald.

"See what I mean," Matt said. "Bring your coffee over."

"No thanks. Had it."

"Sit down anyway."

"Due at surgery. Not like these business fellows spending all their time drinking coffee or something stronger. I am glad to see you, Dr. Melquist. Been wanting to get in touch with you."

"Yes, Doctor?"

"Ah, don't want to impose on you—I mean, if you're working harder than these fellows." He indicated the café half full of coffee-drinkers. "If your time is—if your work is . . ."

"Oh, I've hardly started yet."

"I imagine a sociological survey is work. Any science. It is a science . . .?"

"Hold on, Harry," Matt said.

"Do you think it is, Dr. Fitzgerald?"

"Well"—Harry sat down on the stool next to her—"the social sciences bother me some."

"How?"

"My opinion is probably inaccurate and unfair."

"It often is," Matt said.

"I couldn't defend it. My reservations—an expert could knock holes in them—subjective, biased, personal. I have too much faith, where the study of humans is concerned, in common sense. You know what an inadequate armour that is. But let's say . . ."

"Harry," Matt interjected, "common sense isn't going to take out a gall bladder for you. It isn't going to . . ."

"I didn't say that. I said where the study of humans was concerned, there are territories a scientific stranger may enter with statistics and abstractions and techniques and emerge still a scientific stranger."

As the Doctor had been speaking, June had been looking down at her coffee, her spoon idly stirring; she looked up at him now. "So you're a little rough on psycho-analysts as well?"

"That's right," Harry said.

"Jurists? Your own profession?"

"I'm rough on anyone who says a human doesn't know as much about himself in certain regards as another human, however learned—however trained."

"What are these regards?"

"I'll just ask you this: what is it you're looking for in Shelby?"

The bluntness of his question seemed to catch her unprepared, Matt thought. "That's a little hard to answer, Doctor. I won't really know—not until I've finished . . ."

"But you know what you're looking for," Harry persisted. "You'd have to know that before you came here, wouldn't you?"

"A lot of my work was planned before I ever came here. But that doesn't mean I've come with preconceived conclusions. Rather, a framework of questions." She returned his level gaze.

There was no need, Matt was thinking, for Harry to be quite so brutal. He felt that he should intercede for her in some way, but at the same time he had the feeling that she was quite capable of handling herself, that anything he might say would quite possibly interfere with her own defence.

"Tell me," Harry was saying, "when you constructed your framework of questions, what did you do about pets?"

"Pets?"

"Well, specifically dogs. I've often wondered how Shelby's canine population compared with the national dog—ah—population."

"How do you think it would compare?"

"Offhand, about three-quarters of a dog for every man in Shelby district, though that might be a little high."

"You'd know that better than I would."

"Whatever it is, I think it's significant. Dog ownership ought to be some sort of index in any society. It's cardinal, and I'm not speaking sentimentally. In Shelby now, what breed would you say was predominant?"

"I have no idea."

"Labrador—outnumbers all other breeds ten to one. All the retrievers—Labrador, Chesapeake, rat-tail—probably closer to fifteen to one. Cockers, springers, the yappy little terrier breeds, smooth, wire-haired, Boston—farm and cattle dogs—make up the balance."

"Has it always been that way?"

"No, and that's my point. Ten, fifteen years ago it was setters and pointers. Why, there were five Llewellyns down my block alone."

"And you think this is significant?"

"Of course I do. Consider the situation fifteen years ago—mainly upland game then, with prairie chicken and partridge which could be worked by setting and pointing dogs. Not today. The prairie chicken has vanished. Look at that."

"I'm looking," she said.

"Population increases. Agricultural changes. More and more grazing lease disced and sown to crop with earlier and earlier maturing grain that can be harvested before the foothills' frosts. The prairie chicken had a trusting and conservative nature that couldn't stand up to civilization. We mourn the passing of the prairie chicken, and change from setters to retrievers for bringing the ducks out of the water. We're not a natural duck flyway, but with the end of the drought years, the creeks are higher, old lakes are full, and new ones have been born, so that the migratory birds take flyways further West along our foothills. Only one thing for a man to do: get rid of his setter since there are no prairie chicken or partridge to hunt, and get a retriever to handle the pintails and butterballs and mallards and green and blue winged teal. The dogs tell a story, Dr. Melquist, one of change in land use and major climate variation, the death of the threshing machine, the binder, crop-stooking, the coming of the combine, Asiatic immigration . . ."

"Asiatic immigration!"

"The Chinese ring-necked pheasant. Retriever versus setter has its influence on marriage—family life—business. You really shouldn't have omitted dogs from your plan of questioning."

"Perhaps not, Doctor."

"Days of the prairie chicken, the partridge, and the grouse are over. The men who hunted them were men who loved the ritual of the hunt. They went by the rules."

"Have the men changed as well?"

"Perhaps there are just as many with manners and restraint, but today for every hunter who went out with a double-barrel, there are possibly a hundred piling out of cars along the roadside with pump and automatic shotguns, blazing away in green feed where cattle graze, in wind-breaks close to farmers' dwellings, driving over swathes and shelling out grain, leaving gates open. The same is true of trout-fishing. You know what Sam Barnes did two years ago?"

"No, I don't."

"Fishermen up the Spray spooked five of his cows into the river. He lost two of them, and there'd been a third the month before. She'd stepped into a tin can. When he found her, the tin was still on her foot and he had to shoot her. Sam did what a lot of farmers and ranchers would like to do. He managed to get the car licence number. He looked up the owner in the city at the licence bureau there. Then he took his big truck and two horses, some deadfall, and six months' accumulation of ranch refuse and garbage. He drove to the address, picketed the horses on the lawn, built a blazing campfire and cooked his supper, dumped the garbage over the grounds. Fellow called the police. Sam was fined fifty dollars and costs, but he'll tell you it was worth it."

"Well, do you think there's a—feeling against urban people?"

"I think more people are hunting and fishing. More people since the depression have cars to transport them fifty or a hundred miles to good hunting and fishing. More people, after years of vicarious pleasure through fish and game magazines, now have money for guns and rods, shells and lures, so they're giving it a whirl for the first time. With more of them, there's more likelihood of the bad-mannered ones showing up here more often. And I'm afraid they do. So you can read your depression and prosperity rhythms in Shelby's stubble fields and along her streams."

Matt sensed that Harry had lost a lot of the brittle quality with which he had started his exchange with June. He knew now that he'd been right to let her handle it for herself. "Harry."

"Yes, Matt."

"I know you're a much busier man than most of us who sit and drink coffee all day in Wing's café, so it seems only fair to remind you that you said you had something you wanted June to . . ."

"Oh, yes—yes, actually something you should have done long ago, Matt."

"Me!"

"Your club service committee, nice if she'd address Rotary for us." He turned to June. "Would you?"

"Yes, Doctor."

"This Thursday?" Then, as he saw her questioning look, "I know, it's not very much notice, but then we never do seem to give speakers much better."

"I'd be glad to."

When Harry had left for his hospital appointment, Matt said, "Your work is really cut out for you if you get many like Harry."

She smiled. "Oh, I don't know."

"By the way, what do you do if people are uncooperative?"

She shrugged. "Then I don't ask my questions."

"Give them up as a bad job?"

"Oh, no. They can still reveal a lot about themselves without the questions having been formally asked." She was silent for a moment. "Matt, do you know this Sam Barnes?"

"Yes."

"Some time I'd like to talk with him."

"Sure. June—about that work space downtown. I think I have something for you."

"Great!"

"You can have a corner in my front office."

"Look—that wasn't why I asked . . ."

"I know it wasn't. There's lots of room there—you can have a desk by the press-room door . . ."

"I don't want to . . ."

"It's a good place for you to work from. Sooner or later everybody in Shelby comes to the *Chinook*. Like in the Palm. Or the Arlington Beer Parlour."

"That's awfully nice of you. I don't want to upset your office routine—Miss Clocker . . ."

"You won't bother Millie at all."

"If you're sure."

"I'm sure."

He explained to her that she could move in any time she was ready. As he left her and turned the Royal Bank corner and began walking up the block, he saw the Greyhound bus loading before the depot. At the end of the queue stood Mame Napoleon and most of her children. All had a gay and holiday air. On their way to the city, he guessed. He wondered if there was anyone else in Shelby who went more often.

The bus had not been crowded, so that they were able to get seats where they liked them best, right behind the driver. This was the monthly herding of Buster, Avalon, Esther, Evelyn, Elvira, and Byron to the city clinic, just to make sure they were A-one. To please the authorities of the Shelby Medical Health Unit, and to keep *their* mouths shut. When she told herself it was to keep *their* mouths shut, she always underlined "their" in her mind; also in her mind she bared her teeth. By *their* mouths she meant Mrs. Dr. Fitzgerald's mouth and Mrs. Oliver's mouth and Mrs. Tregillis's mouth; she meant the Ladies' Auxiliary mouths and the IODE mouths and the Book Club mouths; she was quite clear about the mouths, and she knew the mouths she did not mean. She didn't mean Matt Stanley's mouth, or Ruth's, or her father, the old Senator's, nor did she mean Aunt Fan Cayley's, but by God that just about covered all the mouths she *didn't* mean. Oh, and she also didn't mean that doctor's mouth that came to visit with Matt—the real pretty young woman doctor that said she wasn't a doctor really. Hell, you were either a doctor or you weren't a doctor, weren't you! Anyway, you could tell she was social. Smell it a mile off—not strong, but it was there all the same. She'd be the professional social—not the amateur social, the used-baby-clothes, hamper-whomping, tongue-clucking, nose-lifting social. And for any variety of social she was easy to take. Matter of fact, she kind of liked her.

The score would be perfect this time: no scabies, no head lice or crabs, Wassermann's negative. And after the doctors had done their stuff, they'd have their lunch: hot dogs, Orange Crush, and ice cream between waffles. Then they'd go to the Penny Novelty and do all the counters till the matinee would open at the Gaiety.

The last time it had been a dandy: all about this kind old man who had a shop where he fixed watches and he stopped this girl from throwing herself off the bridge and she told him it was a piano-player who was the father of her unborn child. The old man had taken her in and there was no funny stuff and they had this party with the champagne and the baby sitting up in the high chair when he married her because the neighbours had started in yapping just like they did with her and Rory and the kids. Then the guy who played the piano showed up when he was fixing this clock and he dropped this watch fob by mistake on the floor and he had been looking high and low for her all the time and didn't know anything about the baby and she remembered this watch fob from way back when she picked it up off of the floor later and she knew her husband the watch-maker was trying to keep it from her and that gave his ass the heartburn and his watch shop was going all to hell because he knew he wasn't doing the right thing at all keeping it from her even though she knew it all the time and wouldn't tell him she knew it and he died keeping it from her saving the little boy from getting burned up when the place caught fire so she was able to marry him after all and it worked out all right in the end even if it was a little rough on the old watch-maker. Had Anne of Green Gables skinned a mile!

When she had paid for Byron's tin horn and the rings for Evelyn and Elvira and Avalon, and for Buster's balloon, she found that besides her return bus fare and the money for the show, she had twenty-nine cents. It wasn't enough to buy them all another ice-cream sandwich. As she wondered idly what she could spend it for, her eye strayed over the store and to the counter beyond the toys; there the gardening supplies were displayed. Bundles were heaped high like dried faggots over which a girl leaned with elbows up and wide as she sprinkled them from a green watering can. She got all the children in front of her and headed for that counter. They waited till the clerk would finish sprinkling. She was about to ask for twenty-nine cents' worth of gladiola bulbs when she saw the little wooden marker wired to one of the bundles of bushes: "29¢ ea."

"Gimme one of them," she told the girl.

"Hybrid tea or floribunda, madam?"

"One of *them*," Mame said a little stubbornly; she liked it the way they called a person "madam," even though she knew it was automatic and carried no special respect toward her. "What are they?"

"Roses, madam. But which variety . . ."

"Well, gimme one of 'em then," she said again, opening her purse.

"Bush or tea?"

She looked up from her pursuit of the last penny to make the twenty-nine, stared at the salesgirl.

"I mean—isn't there—what kind of rose plant did you wish?"

"Don't make any difference."

"What *colour* then, madam?"

"Yellah."

"Did you wish them for cut flowers?"

"I wish them jist for roses," Mame explained patiently. "Yellah roses."

At the Gaiety she had left the thing behind and had to go back to the theatre for it; she would have forgotten it again on the bus seat if Byron hadn't picked it up and carried it home with him. There she dropped it by the back door on the south side of the house, intending to stick it into the ground somewhere or other the next morning.

When he had left June Melquist, Matt had every intention of getting right down to the editorial on the dog-poisoning; he had taken several runs at it, then given it up each time with a feeling of helplessness. It seemed that anything he might write could only be inadequate. He had already done the notice that Corporal McCready had requested, but it hardly seemed enough. Certainly a formal and hortatory piece on the dastardly nature of dog-poisoning would do no good; everybody but the poisoner was *against* dog-poisoning, and the poisoner would simply not be reached by an editorial. Perhaps he ought to limit himself to the special danger of the poisoned wieners. That was it—make vivid the danger to children and at least bring it to the poisoner's attention. Quite likely the poisoner had no desire whatever to poison children.

But before he had a chance to begin writing, Millie was bringing in Mr. Oliver, perhaps the most politically conscientious soul in Shelby. A short and bulbous man, he had lost an eye to a playmate's arrow early in his Sussex childhood; Ruth had once, with an unfeeling lightness untypical of her usually sympathetic nature, spoken of "King 'Arold 'o looked hup at the Battle of 'Astings an' got a h'eye full of h'arrah."

His mission was to ask Matt and Ruth to dinner Wednesday evening. Matt had difficulty in attending as Oliver explained that the dinner was actually to break the ice for Dr. Melquist, who was in a way honouring Shelby with her work here. It was only fitting that he and Mrs. Oliver should have this dinner for Dr. Melquist, since he was mayor of Shelby.

He was also the town's leading horticulturalist, Matt was thinking, unable to shake loose the irreverent burr earlier placed in his mind by Joe Manley about dog poisoners and garden lovers.

"Mr. Manley and Miss Cayley and Miss Clocker." Mr. Oliver was finishing up his list of guests.

"Millie?"

"Yes—she plays—and we felt that after dinner we'd have a musical evening."

Millie played, Matt knew, and of course it had been unnecessary for Mr. Oliver to say that Mrs. Oliver sang. This she did every Sunday in the St. Aidan's choir.

"We shall see you," Mr. Oliver said, "and perhaps you and Mrs. Stanley could bring Dr. Melquist with you."

"Yes," Matt said. It was utterly ridiculous, as he had told Joe, to suggest Mr. Oliver as a dog poisoner, even jokingly. The man was conscientious if unimaginative, priding himself on his fairness and justness. He was also sentimental. There was something touching, Ruth had once said to Matt, in the way the Olivers had brought back with them the wooden cross of their only son, Walter, when they had made the trip with other Battle of London bereaved to visit the war graves.

"And now"—Mr. Oliver looked pointedly at Matt's typewriter holding its blank sheet of paper—"I've held your work up quite long enough, I know."

"That's all right."

"And I must get over to the Express. The tenth, you know. Always like to get new bushes in by the first if weather permits."

Matt guessed that he had a shipment of rose bushes

waiting for him over at the Express office. Roses were Mr. Oliver's speciality, an unfortunate one for people in the foothills, yet perhaps it was the challenge that appealed most to his horticultural soul.

"It's the country," he was fond of saying, "—it's not friendly to roses. Early frosts and chinooks in winter coming the way they do—they catch a plant unawares. They raise the temperature as much as thirty degrees in two hours—start the sap rising. I've seen it happen that way in January. I have.

"Not like glad-eye-oh-lie or sweet peas," he would explain. "This is naturally glad-eye-oh-lie and sweet-pea country, but roses—hybrid, wild roots and tame bush—sooner or later they revert, you know. They do. Winter-kill and the roots take over. I know roses. They're what you might call my special forte. Roses are."

Matt found it difficult to get back to work after Mr. Oliver had left. It was true that an editorial stressing the danger of the poisoned wieners to children might cause the poisoner to change back to the cubes of raw meat he had used in past years, but surely there was something he could write that would get to the man. If he could only touch him in some way, communicate to him what the dogs had meant to their owners. After all, the loss of a dog to a child was just as tragic a loss as the death of a member of the family. All three of the Chivers, Barker, and Saunders dogs had been children's pets. Joe Chivers was only eight, and Matt remembered that Joe's father had told him that they had buried the dog under the tree in the backyard.

And then he had it! He had it! He had it!

His typewriter took up its quick stuttering tapping.

CHAPTER 7

THE DAY OF THE OLIVER DINNER WOULD HAVE TO BE A
Wednesday, Matt's day for calling on advertising accounts.
It was always the same, like a first plunge into cold water;
each store door meant tightening himself against the anticipated shock. Of course, it actually didn't come at all; either
he sold the space or he didn't sell the space, and in either
case he left with relief. He would always find it an
uncomfortable part of his work, looking upon it as a mild
form of blackmail, never quite convinced that he was giving
his customers their money's worth unless they were buying
a sale display or giving him an order for letterheads,
stationery, circulars, or posters. He'd once told Ruth about
it, saying that it would be nice if all he had to do were to
write the news and ads and set them up. It was all right,
she'd assured him, not an unusual reluctance at all; others
felt the same way about facing the dentist, the banker, the
year's income-tax returns, giving reports to their clubs.
Matt only wished his discomfort were annual, too—not a
weekly routine.

Sarah was not as usual waiting for him on the street
before the house; he found her in the bathroom, tiptoe on
the shoe polishing box she'd pulled out from under the
washbasin. He stood in the doorway while she examined

her interesting face in the medicine-cabinet mirror, opening
her mouth wide and studying her teeth, which seemed quite
satisfactory. She considered the unique tip of her tongue,
then, blowing out her cheeks, she turned her head from side
to side the better to catch another view of her fascinating
self.

Together they washed their hands, and after he had gone
round her face with the washcloth, he lifted her into his
arms.

"There you are—just as big as Daddy."

"Not now. You're holding up me."

"Well, some day you'll be just as big as Daddy."

"I don't want to be a daddy," she said as they went into
the kitchen.

"Of course you don't. You'll be a mommy."

"I don't want to be a mommy. I don't want to be
anything."

"Not anything, darling?"

"Just a horse."

"A horse."

"I'll be a horse with hair under my arms and a gun."

"That's nice. We'll put you in the Little Britches Rodeo
parade. You'll win a prize."

"You got a 'prize for me, Daddy?"

"Matter of fact I have, dear."

"What's the 'prize?"

"Not now. It's for after supper. When you go to bed."

"After."

"That's right."

"A sucker?"

"After supper, dear."

"After. 'Prize for Sarah after." She added sadly, "*After*
Sarah's all gone to bed."

The surprise was a colouring book, which meant that
she must take her crayons to bed with her. There was,
however, none of the usual evening argument about retirement.

"You spoil her terribly, Matt."

He had to agree with Ruth that he spoiled his daughter,
but not terribly. More than Ruth did, yes—but not too much
more. You couldn't expect the current of indulgence to pull

just as evenly through both parents. Husband and wife were not equally cursed or blessed with conscience, possessed of identical moral strength. It was always Ruth who remembered birthdays and anniversaries, answered their common letters, did the thank-you notes and Christmas cards.

Yet with June Melquist it seemed to him that Ruth had responded with less than her usual hospitality toward a newcomer to their town. Neither of the women could be called naturally effusive, but it should be clear to Ruth that a great deal of June's restraint was simply professional reserve. He knew that now, and he also knew that once you got past that you found charm. She had something new and fresh to bring them. Small-town life could go stale in time; the same faces day after similar day, the tyranny of daily trivia, could in time give a man geographical claustrophobia. June's friendship could give their lives a little more depth, a little more significance.

Though he was not too optimistic about it, he hoped that the evening at the Olivers' might bring his wife and June closer together. He would wait until the evening was over before he told her that June was moving into the office—or perhaps while they drove to pick up Aunt Fan and June. No—after.

There would have been little opportunity anyway during the drive, for Aunt Fan left few pauses in her account of the past Sunday's church services. Although he and Ruth had not attended, he knew that last Sunday had seen the initiation of the hearing-aids that had been fitted in two St. Aidan's pews for Aunt Fan and several other Anglicans whose hearing was afflicted. The sermon had turned out to be a rather stormy one for them, given by Bishop Wilton-Breigh, who had come down from the city to mark the hearing-aid installation.

"He shouted so. He doesn't scare me, but that's just what he was trying to do." Aunt Fan's lips came away from the words like those of a fastidious child taking bites at a slice of bread and jam. Matt could appreciate the assault of the Bishop's voice coming at her raw over the new hearing-aid after years of dimly heard sermons. "I shouldn't be surprised if he were high church. I'm so glad Canon Midford is not high."

Matt saw the quirk at the corners of Ruth's mouth and knew that she was recalling the Canon's fierce stand in the matter of relaxed liquor legislation and local-option plebi-scites which had already introduced cocktail bars into the province's major cities.

"It would be a shame if our community were high. I always say—go down the block to Father McNulty. Yes, I think it best that St. Aidan's stay low."

In a sense she would be a sort of sociological mother lode for anyone mining the community, he thought. She had unwittingly ticked off the Canon's puritanical stand for abstinence, and his intolerance for the whore of Rome, two personal attitudes that were in some degree reflected in a part of his congregation, and of others as well.

Mrs. Oliver met them at the door, pale, grey-eyed, with black hair that looped down like curtains on either side of an archway. When she spoke, it was with an Oxfordshire accent, in a soft and rather uncertain voice. Neuralgia down the left side of her neck and into one shoulder caused her to carry her head like a bird upon a lawn, tilted slightly to one side and down.

Within the Oliver living-room, Matt saw that Millie and Joe had already arrived. Mrs. Oliver moved into the dining-room, leaving the conversation to Aunt Fan, who had finished with the Bishop and moved overseas to the vicar of her girlhood, who had sired nine daughters.

Matt glanced toward June and noted that she was looking at the top of the burl-walnut cottage piano with its ornate brass candle-holders. Since she had sat down she seemed to be dividing her attention between two photo-graphs there: a robust and fiercely moustached gentleman, obviously a blacksmith, in leather apron, with tongs in his hands, standing in the shadow of a low, wide-roofed structure and against a line of anonymous horses' rumps. The other picture was a head-and-shoulders shot of a young man in uniform, with wide and staring eyes burning out from the cabinet photograph.

"That's our Woalter," explained Mr. Oliver.

"Nine daughters—fancy!" said Aunt Fan. "He said it was like having water on the brain!"

"Battle of London," said Mr. Oliver.

"They couldn't go into business," said Aunt Fan, "there wasn't anything they could do in those days. So it *was* a little like having water on the brain—wasn't it?"

"Our only son," said Mr. Oliver. "RAF. We lost him. The other is Cousin Rupert taken in Shanghai, I think."

". . . the boys were sent away to school, but there was a governess for the girls—it didn't matter so much with the girls. We went into the village for music, of course."

At dinner Mr. Oliver expertly carved a very large roast puddled in blood on the platter before him. As they were being served, Aunt Fan talked of the Pringle wedding that had taken place the week before, her eyes never leaving Mr. Oliver's end of the table, where steam wreathed from bowls of potatoes and beets. Her hands were below the table, her chin slightly out, thin shoulders forward.

"The trip to Montreal was just to buy them," she said. "The nightgown—there were twenty nightgowns—and a negligee for every one." She pronounced it to rhyme with glee. "Now what could a person possibly do with twenty—oh, thank you." Her gaze went down to her plate just placed before her as she waited for the others to be served.

"And how are you finding your new Mr. Sparrow?"

Matt saw Joe's attention flick to Mr. Oliver. "Fine—oh, he's fine."

"You'd know by now certainly—coming to the end of the school year, and science is important. Mr. Duncan, who left us," said Mr. Oliver, lifting a slice of roast between the tip of the carving knife and the fork, and turning slightly to June on his left, "was a very good science teacher." He looked to Joe as though for confirmation. Joe nodded.

"A very good disciplinarian and strict in the matter of regulations, which is a very good thing in a schoolmaster. I believe in them. I do."

"The Pringles hadn't intended putting out what it cost," said Aunt Fan.

"The Regulations of the School Act are the same as the lows of the country—both are there for a purpose, I say." With carving knife and fork held upright on the table Mr. Oliver stared at the roast. "Foalty kidneys."

Matt saw the brief surprise on June's face; probably for

one wild moment she thought Mr. Oliver was diagnosing the beef he had just carved.

"It was foalty kidneys did for Mr. Duncan—or rather, the operation on them. Just after the Christmas holidays."

"The mint just spreads everywhere, it goes where it pleases. Mother never ever cooked without mint. I always put a sprig in the frying pan whatever I'm cooking. Francie says Charles eats mint raw. Would you like some mint?" Aunt Fan had not turned her head, so that June did not realize she had been addressed.

"Yes—oh, yes, Miss Cayley."

"Then I shall give you some."

"Some of those young women—the older ones—Grade Twelve," said Mrs. Oliver, "must take some handling, Mr. Manley."

"Very snippy," said Mr. Oliver.

When they moved back to the living-room and Walter and Cousin Rupert for tea, Matt found himself sitting next to Millie. He realized then that she had said not a word throughout dinner. She was wearing some sort of sheer blouse under her brown two-piece suit; he could see quite clearly the lace line of her slip. He supposed that if she were to take the suit coat off, straps as well would show over her shoulders. And suddenly he felt a pang of contrition and what was almost sympathy; poor little Millie with her pale, transparent face—listening. June was a listener too, but in a different way. For the life of him he could not put his finger on the distinction; it was a surprisingly fine one.

He saw that there was no place for him to put down his empty teacup. He considered getting up and carrying it in to the dining-room table, but decided he ought not to interrupt Mr. Oliver. He wondered if he could lean over and set it on the floor by the chair, but that wouldn't do either. He continued to hold it on his knee while Mr. Oliver explained the nature of law and his magisterial duties. One of his favourite expressions was, "in the eye of the low."

"As a police magistrate, I believe things have to be done according to the low. The low is there for the protection of the people, and in the eye of the low we are all the same—equal." As he explained, his live eye sparkled. "I'm only a minion of the low—that's all. A minion of the low's higher authority. It's not for me to say whether the low's right or wrong; it's for me to carry it out, whatever my own personal feelings may be."

And that was the distinct yet common quality in the listening of June and Millie, it struck Matt. It was as though both were court listeners; but Millie listened in the prisoner's dock, June listened from the bench.

"Same thing with school regulations and the school," Mr. Oliver was saying, and now he spoke to Joe Manley. "Wouldn't you say?"

"Oh—yes," said Joe.

"Boys' and girls' toilets, for instance—the School Act says they must face in oapposite directions ten yards apart, and the girls' and boys' toilets do so. Whether or not I should like them to face in the same direction has nothing to do with the matter. It is written down in Section Eleven, paragraph seventeen, of the School Act that they shall face in oapposite directions. They do. Not," he added confidentially, "that I'd *want* them to face in the same direction. For I don't."

When they had done the dinner dishes, Aunt Fan and Mrs. Oliver rejoined the rest in the living-room. Mr. Oliver suggested a little music, asking June if she played the piano. When she said she didn't, he looked over to Mrs. Oliver and nodded toward the piano, where she and Millie Clocker took their places side by side on the bench. Elbows touching, peering intently ahead at the music, glancing frequently down to fingers romping gaily over the keys, now and again one of them breaking off to sit with stilled hands in her lap, while the other went tinkling on, they played "In an English Country Garden." Several marches followed, and then Millie played the accompaniment while Mrs. Oliver sang. At the first notes of the song, Matt saw June stir slightly in her chair; it was almost as though Mr. Oliver's wife had been successfully secreting a second voice, for a strong contralto filled the room, low and rich in contrast to the reedy and rather plaintive voice of her conversation. With a strong tremolo, she scooped her way unmercifully through "By the Waters of Minnetonka." The evening's music ended with another piano duet: "The Waterfall."

• • •

The guests had left at eleven. For some time after, Mr. Oliver sat in the dark living-room, his easy chair opposite the piano with its staring-eyed photograph of Walter and the other of Cousin Rupert in the act of shoeing a horse somewhere in the Orient—perhaps Shanghai. From the stand beside the chair he picked up the evening paper he hadn't had an opportunity to read because of their dinner party.

Mrs. Oliver stood hesitant in the archway to the dining-room as though she could not make up her mind to stay or to go to bed. Her husband lowered his paper. "Everything was nice," he said. "I think we did well by Dr. Melquist. Interesting young woman—sensible, I think." He picked up his paper again. "Tidy. I imagine she thinks tidy for a woman. We must help her all we can with her work." He was silent a moment, the paper in his hand, his gaze upon Mrs. Oliver in the archway. "Miss Cayley said the Yorkshire was particularly good—puffy. She had three helpings. I think she really appreciates having dinner with us."

"Besides being hungry."

"Oh—yes," said Mr. Oliver. "What, besides being . . ."

"She comes to eat, you know," Mrs. Oliver said.

Mr. Oliver weighed this. "Do you mean she's . . .?" His wife nodded.

"Hungry!"

Again Mrs. Oliver nodded. "Even if she makes it difficult—not hearing and upsetting the conversation, I don't mind having her so much. When you think . . ."

"But that's incredible!" Mr. Oliver let the paper slide to the floor at his side. "People don't go hungry!" Then he added: "These days! Do you really think . . .? She can't help her affliction. If that's the case, we must have her more often."

"She doesn't miss a Sunday," Mrs. Oliver said.

"I hope she doesn't if you're right. Whenever we—you bake, be sure to send her—be sure you give her some buns."

"I already do."

"And vegetables. We have more than enough. Next weekend I'll have Napoleon haul a sack of potatoes over to her. They'll just sprout." He picked up the paper again, but he was not reading it, his gaze lost before him. "We must plant the sweet peas tomorrow." He was silent again, the paper on his lap, unheeded. The chair would not seem to release him, to let him relax completely back into it. At length he said, "The days are getting longer now." Then, with an unusual abruptness that was almost impatience, "Couldn't we have more light in here?"

"Of course, Arthur. Only, you've asked to cut down on the electricity, and if the days are getting longer . . ."

"We can afford to have a little more light in here. Strain on the eyes. More light more sight." He picked up the paper again. "Nasty thing to be cut off from people like that—not hearing them, what they say." He put the paper down again. "My handkerchief."

"At your elbow," Mrs. Oliver said more fully. "At your right elbow."

Mr. Oliver turned almost completely round that he might bring his eye to bear on the handkerchief. "So it is." He picked it up, took out his glass eye, wiped at the socket briefly. "I'd have in another light," he said almost absently. "We'll put Woalter's cross out next week."

He picked up the newspaper with an air of finality. Mrs. Oliver turned in the archway and walked toward the stairs.

CHAPTER 8

HE WALKED THE FOUR BLOCKS THROUGH THE MAY NIGHT, HIS heels echoing down the empty streets, till he had come to his own entrance to the apartment on the third floor of Mrs. Nelligan's house, an enclosed stairway applied to the outside of the high and narrow frame building.

He supposed it was only fitting as Mrs. Nelligan's stylite that he had furnished his room with chaste bareness. Most anchorites would have approved of the linoleum on the floor; he had added bookshelves of board and brick along one side, a wine-coloured chesterfield, three ascetic kitchen chairs from the Shelby Hardware. In the centre of the room stood a fumed-oak table monastic in its square ugliness; on this he ate the meals he prepared for himself in the kitchenette end of the room; here he also corrected essays, laboratory reports, and examination papers, and made out term papers and income-tax returns. On the same table, during the early years when he had lived at the Arlington Arms, he had tried to write poetry. He no longer tried to write poetry, for he was a clear-minded man and his almost humble honesty had told him that the sprung rhythm and rhetorical strophe of his verse leaned more and more toward an unfortunate enumerative quality—as though the margin release of his typewriter had become stuck well over to the left.

In other ways the earlier years of the hotel-room period had been poetic years; not lyric perhaps over the boom and bung and banter of the Arlington Beer Parlour below, but enthusiastic. His Saturday nights had not been the conventional nights of a teacher in a foothills community. They had been exuberantly shared with other young men of the town: good talk, chow mein and chop suey at the Palm Café after the curling-rink jitney dances to the music of Sonny Sawyer and His Silvertone Seven, jugs of sweet catawba wine along the river road in spring and summer and fall. All but he had gone from the town long ago—the bank cashiers, the assorted clerks from the implement company offices, Oliver's Trading Company, and Johnston's Drugs, and Scotty McLeod, the violin and piano teacher. Scotty had not left Shelby by the usual route of head-office promotion, transfer, or loss of position through depression lay-off. Into his twelve-gauge Scotty had pumped a high-base goose-load Imperial shell, and shot himself.

The dinner at the Olivers' must have been an ordeal for her, he told himself as he walked through the darkness to the centre of the living-room and turned on the table lamp. He had always suffered dinner at the Olivers' with impatience, yet tonight he had been almost sorry when it was over.

What was it that set some women apart for him? Why did it happen with some and not with others? He could remember every one of them, it seemed, though there had been almost none in the last ten years. Betty his first year at university, with her small, deft face and invitational warmth. Joan, who had taught Primary in his first school. Allure had been too serious a word—not friendly enough for it. Often he had thought it was a matter of eyes and their expressiveness, or mouth, or a walk accompanied by the distant roll of toy drum and fife. There must have been many fragmentary clues to femininity: piquant hair at the nape of a neck; scent may have entered into it, the lift of a breast. Whatever it was, it was immediate as summer lightning, the flash of a bluejay's wing, the glint of sun along a spider web.

Obviously, he told himself, it was a pretty common

experience for all men, could be measured in terms of adrenalin, pulse rate, blood pressure, tumescence; it had not saddened him that as he had got older it had happened less often. Till now he had thought himself quite clear of it.

And he was not. She was thirty-odd to his fifty-one; he guessed that age would be an impertinence to her. And after all he was *just* fifty-one. Cool and lovely and herself. Fresh—God, she was fresh as a silver willow by a river bank! Rain after drought. Steady eyes, clear skin—her womanliness travelled from her and he was not such a good Greek at all! He was just one of the lonely and homeless ones, his only community the community of Aunt Fan and poor little Millie Clocker. No community at all—de la Mare's "host of phantom listeners."

That was what they truly were, he told himself as he took down the twenty-six of rye three-quarters full. Aunt Fan and Millie and himself. He poured his drink into the tumbler. Thronging the Shelby moonbeams, simply listeners. All the same—here's to you, June Melquist.

When he had sat beside her after dinner in the living-room, she had seen how he had looked at her—and stared. She was quite sure he had been staring at her a long while before that. She hadn't been imagining it. And she knew what he had been staring at; even though it was under the brown suit coat, it had almost lived up to the promise of the advertisement in the back of *Alluring Love:* "He'll be charmed by the allure of this expensive French triumph in skin-clinging sheer nylon." And the brassiere she had sent for at the same time, under the coat and the blouse and the gardenia-white slip—it, too, must have helped. "Up and out," it had been described in the magazine. "For you who have dreamed of Heaven-sent cleavage and youthful pointed uplift—but never found it."

She was reluctant to take them off now, to destroy the new individuality of her body, and put it within the folds of the cotton nightgown. Even if he hadn't looked at her like that, she was quite satisfied. They weren't a gyp like the Love Charm of the Rhine Maidens or the Secret Shell of India. Not that she'd been foolish enough ever to send for

that sort of thing, but in the interests of increased beauty she
had written away for the unique-formula Couchons-nous
Creme with its forty thousand units of government-
approved Estrogenic Hormones plus extra beneficial oils in
a plain wrapper. One jar had a sixty-day supply and you
rubbed it into what breasts you had. Three dollars a jar, but
she had taken advantage of the double offer and saved a
dollar. Well—as far as her bosom was concerned, two jars
of Couchons-nous Creme had left her still in a plain
wrapper. It was just a way to gouge money out of girls who
were helpless because they were girls and couldn't go up to
a man the way a man could go up to a girl, and invite him
to go to a dance or a movie or for a drive.

Men were so different and so removed and alien in their
maleness, and it wasn't fair that a girl couldn't take the
initiative. Men didn't even know that—most of them. It was
because of this that she knew for sure it was a woman—a
nasty woman—who stood behind things like Couchons-
nous Creme and the Love Charm of the Rhine Maidens and
the Secret Shell of India. Behind each of them there could
only be a woman who understood how it was for a girl who
wasn't beautiful and had never *been* beautiful even when
she was a baby or all through the time when she was a little
girl. Some woman figured things like that out. Some nasty
woman. Probably beautiful herself.

Like Miss Melquist!

She stood quite still in the centre of the room, her arms
upraised so that the nightgown would slide down. *She* had
ended up beautiful and desirable. Matt had looked a lot at
her during the evening, and Joe Manley had never taken his
eyes off her. And she hadn't even noticed it. She was used
to men looking at her all her life; they looked at her without
her even lifting a finger! She wasted it! She wasn't one
stitch better than Rheba in *I Was an Unmarried Bride*, she
told herself as she got into bed.

For a moment she lay, the light from the bed lamp
falling upon the pages of the opened *I Confess*.

It was probably wonderful. That cold, beautiful Miss
Melquist would know all about it; she'd done it, so she
didn't have to wonder what it was like. She'd done it a lot
of times with different men.

Not sure whether or not she felt better, Millie lifted *I Confess* before her pale little face.

I swallowed the bitter tears and tried to quench the bitter heart ache but there was no balm for the awful truth that stared me in the face now. Blinded by the yearning in my heart I had plunged madly down-hill to self-destruction from the very first night when I had agreed to ride with devil-may-care Arthur on the buddy seat of his new Harley-Davidson motor cycle. Had I only listened to the still, small voice within my heart and not been dazzled with the soaring happiness I foolishly thought could be mine . . .

It had been a nice dinner party; it was too bad it had to come near the end of the month—in another week when the rents came in she could have afforded new batteries. She had worn the dead hearing-aid only so they wouldn't think she couldn't afford the batteries, but they must have wondered sometimes. She'd been able to tell from their faces now and again; Miss Melquist had looked startled just before dessert, and Mr. Oliver too, but that might have been caused by her third helping of Yorkshire pudding. Which was just as bad, really.

A person flying blind through the conversation had no way of telling whether or not what she said sounded ludicrous to the listeners, or even indiscreet.

She dragged out the business of going to bed, turned out the light, and lay on her back, staring up into the darkness. The stillness had now taken unto itself absolute emptiness, as though all the sounds had been sucked from it finally and forever. She hoped she had not said anything she shouldn't have.

The crooked yet precise chatter of June Melquist's type-writer tapped for almost an hour after she came home. She typed nothing about the Oliver dinner, but rather:

ALTITUDE
3400 feet   Latitude 50/76   Longitude 113/51W

TEMPERATURE
Average summer   51.7F
Average winter   23.7 F
Average annual   38 F

RAINFALL
Average rainfall   11.42"
Average snowfall   72.50"
Average annual   18.67"
  precipitation
Note: The foregoing averages cover a period of 31 years.

GEOLOGY
The underlying rocks in the Shelby district are shales and sandstone which were deposited by streams in lakes and deltas. They are thus fresh water in origin and are several hundred feet thick in this area. This is the "Peskapoo" formation of an early Tertiary Age beginning some fifty million years ago.

When he and Ruth had returned after driving Millie and Aunt Fan home from the Oliver dinner, he had laid three logs in the fireplace. They were well ablaze by the time Ruth had paid Rowena for her baby-sitting and checked out Sarah. Ruth took her favourite stool at the right corner of the hearth.

He felt a little depressed, more than he might ordinarily expect after dinner at the Olivers'. And it wasn't fair really to credit the Olivers with any part of his vague dejection. That was a strong term for it, really—more like the let-down feeling of schoolboy days and getting back a composition on How I Spent My Summer Holidays measled with Miss Morse's red pencil and labelled with an only adequate B. Perhaps it was because the paper would be in the mail and on the counters tomorrow, and he was not so sure now about doing the dog-poisoning piece. It might offend and shock, but then what mattered was whom it offended or shocked. Certainly not Harry; or Hersch Midford.

Perhaps it had been an evening with an unusually subdued Joe. June and Joe; their response to each other was important to him. June and Joe.

"Ruth."

"Mmmmh." Chin in her hands, she did not take her eyes from the fire.

"Wouldn't it be nice—if . . . Don't you think it would be nice if Joe and June could—were to hit it off together?"

She did not answer him for a moment, did not move her attention from the fire. "Maybe."

Her non-committal tone startled him. He had been diffident about mentioning it to her, for in a way it was such a feminine suggestion that it would have come sooner or later from her. Joe was a very dear and important friend about whom she was concerned; the right woman was her simple answer to almost any male problem. It seemed strange that she . . .

The cry came twice—shrill and terrified. As he rose to his feet he heard the soft thud of bare feet on the floor, then the rustle of footsteps in panic down the hallway. In the darkness there he caught Sarah up into his arms and she clung to him, clung to him with her legs tight at his waist, her arms convulsive about his neck. He could feel her hot, moist cheek; her head turned from side to side in blind seeking movements, her eyes bewildered and unseeing under the damp ringlets of her hair.

"Just a nightmare," he said to Ruth as he carried the child to his chair before the fireplace. He held her closely, stroking her, soothing her, remembering the unbearable falling dreams of his boyhood. Or perhaps she had dreamed the chicken pox or measles fever dream in which the whole world became a tactual horror with the tongue harsh and frightful against the roof of the mouth.

A log shifted suddenly in the fire; sparks showered, the light expanded, pushed back the living-room darkness for a brief moment, then contracted again; the quinine pungency of burning willow strengthened on the air. With a last tickle of hair against the side of his chin, the baby was asleep again. "I'll just hold her here till we go to bed, Ruth." Leaning forward on her stool by the fire, her knees almost touching her chin, Ruth nodded.

It was evident that she didn't care to discuss a June-and-Joe relationship any further, perhaps thought it such an improbable match there was no point in talking about it. But he knew it was more than that really; she was not concerned about disparity in age, probability of mutual attraction—or even Joe's suitability as a husband and father. In some way June had failed to win her. And it had not been lack of opportunity that had prevented him from telling her that June would be moving into his office to work; it had been because he sensed Ruth's reservation.

He looked from his wife to the sleeping child. She would never have her mother's gypsy skin, but she'd have her same trim smallness. Already she had Ruth's way of lighting all inside candles at once—and putting them out just as quickly. The same brilliant listening look lay on her face when she held up her toy red phone to her ear, saying, "Oh, no—no!" and laughing delightedly just as she had heard her mother do.

She exalted him and frightened him at the same time, for she was so engrossed in being Sarah that it made her remote from him; it was as though all he possessed of her were countless stilled reflections of her. Fresh as dew from her bath, her hair tied back with a bit of store string, she was the Roman matron Sarah. He had the picture of the little mother Sarah denuding her anatomically impossible doll, then gravely wiping over the pink rubber with a soapy washcloth; the washer-woman Sarah with pinafore askew, jam-smeared face under hair wild and tangled; Florence Nightingale Sarah; Sarah, the cold-hearted bawd offering up her false kisses for cookies or candy.

But the one that made him most vulnerable of all; that was the Sarah wandering waist-deep in autumn grass, barely old enough to make it to the end of their street and to become lost then frantically found, covered with burrs and spear grass and thistle spines, a foxtail in her hair. Sarah, oh, Sarah—with tear stains on your cheeks and a foxtail in your hair, the refrain cried through his mind like a ballad line.

He wished that he had casually mentioned the arrangement with June in the office; he wished to hell he wasn't making such an important thing of it. He saw that Ruth's eyes were still lost on the fire, that she seemed quite unaware of him, the baby. It was as though she had deliberately removed herself from them, and for a moment he was swept by a feeling of sadness and inadequacy that he could no more help than he could the cooling of warmth from his cheek with the passing of cloud over the sun. And even as he told himself that it was unreasonable as Sarah's nightmare, Ruth had looked over to him; she smiled her quick smile and he knew that she had not been so far away after all. The smile said that she had never strayed from the unsteady umbrella of firelight where these three lived and loved; it was not a new smile but one that had quite probably been smiled in a cave mouth, a teepee, anywhere that firelight marked off a timeless part of earth from the night and the wildness around it.

When she had looked over to Matt with the sleeping baby in his arms, she had been hardly aware of the smile for them; nor could she remember what it was that she had been thinking with her eyes lost in the heart of the fire. Before the smile had quite died and as she saw the anxious look leave Matt's face, she was suddenly sure that this had happened before. These recurrent and ephemeral sensations of familiarity had interested and sometimes disturbed her all her life. They were gauzy illusions that everyone must have; they stirred; they escaped to return in an unguarded moment with such urgency that the mind cried out, "I was wrong— this isn't something from a forgotten dream! I'm sure I've been in just this situation—I was standing just like this— there was a book on the table—her face held just that expression—I've heard those words with that same intonation at another time!" All attempts at identification were in vain; she had never been able to pursue right to certainty.

Probably it was the faint bitterness of willow smoke—or some unimportant fragment of the whole—that recalled an occurrence in the past. It could have been that Matt with Sarah in his arms reminded her of something a week ago, a year, far back in her ranch childhood. She supposed that people whose formative years were spent in the isolation of the foothills had more than their share of mysticism. If that

were so, then hers must be a most generous allotment,
raised as she had been since the age of six, and the death of
her mother, by her father, Clem Derrigan, and Chan. Her
time away at St. Catherine's boarding-school had always
seemed like exile made bearable only by Easter and
Christmas and summer vacation.

She remembered her mother not at all; it had been Chan
who had coloured Easter eggs and Clem Derrigan who had
hidden them for her to discover in the foot of the straw stack
Easter morning. As a little girl she had been thankful that
her birthday came in July so that she could have it at home
and not in a boarding-school dormitory.

Her earliest memories seemed always of the ranch
kitchen and the smell of wood smoke and wet buckskin.
Often Howard and Mary Rolling-in-the-Mud called, and at
fencing and haying there might be Jonas and Maxine
Stud-horse, or Sadie and Willis Prairie Chicken. They sat
with Clem and her father and seemed to communicate
through long and stretching silences by the creak of a chair,
the scuff of a shoe or moccasin, a cough or a sigh. Now and
again broken bits of conversation were negligently dropped:
how was Lucy—fine—good grass year—yes. It was as
though each one lowered and lowered a bucket down into
the private darkness of his mind, tripped the rope, then
raised and raised only to find the lip of the pail had caught
very little. As a little girl she had tried too, but the bucket
had come up clanging hollowly against the walls of her own
well, and it had been impossible for her to pour out any
conversation for them.

Some years later, when she was sixteen or seventeen or
something, she had told her father that she was sure they
had all conversed with each other by telepathy. He had
laughed; she was still certain that most had been said by
eyelid, by light or soft breathing, or by the tilt or relaxation
of a shoulder. Perhaps that was the most important and
successful sort of communication between any humans. It
was with her and Matt: a voice shade, the touch of a hand,
a reticence, the quick lift of similar feeling, a perfect
anticipation, the same sort of thing that was real between
playing children engrossed in sunshine or the vibrant dusk
of a hayloft.

Her childhood stories had not been Goldilocks or Little Red Riding Hood on a mother's lap, but "One-and-a-half-Step" Bovey and "Nigger John" Ware, at Clem Derrigan's denimed knee. No Mother Goose for her; instead, Clem's nasal plaint and the sweet picking of his mandolin for:

"Let the kiyoot howl—let him howl,
Put his dog nose to the moon.
Let him howl for me;
Let him howl for you;
Let him howl for the Indian maid so true."

It was nice that Sarah should have Clem for her girlhood, too. He fascinated the child with his songs and stories, and she supposed that her father must have often experienced the surprised sensation of familiarity when he saw his granddaughter entranced on Clem's lap. Perhaps it was a fundamental human requirement, the need for heroes, just as cardinal as any of the body hungers; the heroes would be part of security. She knew that Clem and her father had possessed that quiet nobility that belongs to heroes. And Matt. Heroes must be simply made. She was certain that they were not loud and dramatic; surely the convincing legendary heroes had charmed much by their own unawareness of charm, through inadvertent magnetism. Others' eyes strayed to them for approval; they turned to Ulysses and said, "Don't you think so?" And a laconic Ulysses indicated that he thought so or he didn't think so. And if it were true, then her husband was a hero. She thought quite possibly that was what a marriage was for, to allow a man an opportunity to be a hero; to permit him to be one to himself at least, the illusion deliberately assisted by his wife and his children.

And perhaps that was why she could not see June Melquist as a possible woman for Joe. She could not see her assisting in any illusion—any at all. It involved a giving and a warmth, and so far she was not sure that June Melquist was good at these things. She guessed her to be capable and intelligent, possessed of strength of character—much more capable and much more intelligent than she herself was. And that might be why she could not feel completely at ease with her; it might also explain the feeling of inadequacy that descended upon her in June Melquist's presence. It might.

She looked over to Matt with the sleeping Sarah in his arms. She wondered, as she had ever since Millie had mentioned it to her at the Oliver dinner, why Matt had said nothing about June Melquist's moving into the front office.

CHAPTER 9

HE SHOULD NOT HAVE WORRIED ABOUT THE DOG STORIES AFTER all. There were no accusations of poor taste. There were many warm comments from people who stopped him on the street, spoke to him in the Post Office. "Good for you, Matt," Harry said to him. "Thanks, Matt," said Charlie Chivers. "If anything can appeal to the stony-hearted bastard, that will!" Laurence Saunders dropped in to pick up six extra copies.

He had not headed the column: "Obituaries," as he had first intended, but had simply run them under each other:

CHIVERS, BROWNIE

Funeral services were held yesterday for Brownie Chivers, who died on the corner of Lafayette Avenue and Third Street just in front of Little Bow School Saturday afternoon, April 23rd. He was six years old at the time of his death.

Brownie was an adopted dog. He had adopted Joe Chivers three years ago come August, the day he followed Joe home and after being fed under Joe's bed for only three days was discovered by Mrs. Chivers. Joe was in charge of arrangements in the back yard corner under the Manitoba Maple.

The second and longer obituary had run down and over into the next column:

SAUNDERS, FRECKLES

Freckles Saunders, pet of Jamie Saunders, died yesterday suddenly. He was seventeen years of age at the time of his death. An octogenarian among dogs, Freckles had raised two generations of Saunders under his practised and patient care, having been Jamie's father's dog when he was a boy. For all his great age, Freckles had been enjoying fine health till the day of his death, handicapped only slightly by rheumatic twinges in his hind quarters. A multiplicity of hobbies and interests filled his time to overflowing and kept him perennially youthful and in touch with the present.

Freckles was far from ready for retirement; in his older, later years he continued to give an enthusiastic and continuing support to the extermination of gophers and to keep up his keen interest in children, bones, lamp posts, mallards, prairie chicken. Many who were familiar with him on Shelby streets and around Shelby sloughs and stubble fields will miss his bright spirit.

The final death notice had been for the Barkers' dog:

BARKER, MAGGIE

Died—Maggie Barker—beloved dog of Tommy Barker. Besides Tommy she leaves to mourn her passing six puppies: Molly, Fibber, Pooch, Cooky, Rusty, Burke. Maggie Barker had a lovable spaniel nature, her democratic warmth winning for her a wide circle of friends of both sexes.

June's moving into the office just before noon added extra interest to the day as well. It did not involve much, for he had already moved a small desk over by the stationery shelves and set a typewriter there. She demurred, but he explained that the machine was a spare one hardly ever used and that she could keep her own in the suite for work during the evenings or the days that she didn't want to come down to the office. Then there was the embarrassment of settling a rental charge, until he agreed finally that she could pay fifteen dollars a month if she insisted. Millie was a pale little watcher at her own desk during this, saying nothing after her murmured greeting when June first came into the office.

At lunch he managed to mention to Ruth casually that June would be working in the office; he felt inordinately relieved afterwards, just a little irritated that he should be. June was at the desk when he returned to the office, busy with the typewriter.

"At work already?"

"Rotary talk tonight."

He had forgotten Harry's invitation in the Palm Café. "He should have given you more notice."

"That's all right. Sometimes I think I work better with pressure."

He worked better under pressure himself, he knew. Not that he had experienced much the past few years. It was still pretty short notice that Harry had given her; not too short, he hoped. It was quite important to him that her talk be successful—not like Dick Metherall's. He still remembered the engagement he'd made for Dick, the Eastern correspondent and old friend who had stopped off with them on his way to the coast. "Coldest and most forbidding bunch I ever talked to," he'd told Matt after. Dick had not spoken lightly, and Matt could see that he had been shaken by his experience. Nationally known as an expert on Canada's economic life, he had not realized when he decided to be funny that the Shelby Rotarians would take every single word he said seriously. They had believed him when he denied Matt's warm introduction of him as a great and literate Canadian. With politely stilled faces they had accepted his assurances that he was much prouder of his skill at taking beer-bottle caps off with his teeth, that he had successfully evaded the payment of income tax for the last twelve years, and that he was descended from a long line of deflowered shopgirls. Matt had not been too disappointed in his fellow Rotarians, for Dick had never really shone at being funny; his muscular wit had been patronizing. If it had taught him to stick to his economic last, it had been a worthwhile experience for him.

He cast his mind back over the recent speakers—there'd been Arley Adam's talk on The Rewards and Hazards of Raising Pearl-faced Foxes, and before that the inspirational address from Canon Midford. Hersch generally gave three of these in a year, not because the Rotarians were in *need* of inspiration but because sooner or later there was no speaker, local or out of town, *other* than Canon Midford. There'd been Jackie Mitchener with his coloured slides, returned from the Queen Scout Jamboree, and, by Judas, Metherall could have learned something about succinctness and enthusiasm from Jackie. The last talk had been given by a city Juvenile Court judge: God, Queen, Parliament, and Home— The Unbroken Chain of Love to Hold Delinquency at Bay.

If only Harry, this year's President of Rotary, had enough sense to cut business to a minimum!

Harry did so; he condensed the community singing to only "Juanita" and a rousing "Alouette." Matt was proud of his fellow Rotarians as they listened attentively to June's quiet, sure voice telling them of the good society and the part played in it by the church, the community schools, and business and service clubs like their own. It was quite evident that they understood her fully when she told them that the function of the social structure must be to fix the individual in a satisfying relationship to his society—that all must belong, and that they must be unhappy if they did not belong successfully.

She spoke briefly of good and evil and of right and wrong. As it always did, there came a rather awkward silence after Harry Fitzgerald had thanked her and asked for questions. Then Hersch Midford rose and cleared his throat.

"Dr. Melquist—when you speak of good and evil, right and wrong, is it possible that this, ah, realm of human conduct is accessible to the—to your scientific methods of measurement? Can a person *measure* right and wrong?"

She remained seated and silent for several contemplative moments, then lifted her head and answered him without rising.

"Our techniques are perhaps still somewhat faulty. There are many aspects of human behaviour we can't be sure of measuring."

"Then you lack Thomas Hobbes's confidence in his set of algebraic equations to explain ethics?" persisted Hersch, a little unfairly Matt thought.

June smiled. "I agree with Laurence Sterne," she said. "I don't think that the social sciences will ever plus or minus us to heaven or to hell—so that none but the expert mathematician would ever be able to settle his accounts with Saint Peter."

She was home free!

When they returned to the *Chinook* office after the Rotary luncheon in the Arlington dining-room, she said, "Matt, you know Canon Midford pretty well, don't you?"

"Oh yes. He's no exception. In Shelby you tend to know a lot of people. Maybe better than you care to. Hersch is a fine fellow."

"Quite interested in sports."

"Oh, he curls. Plays tennis. Badly. Well, mostly with Father McNulty. And he's a fine dry-fly man. Purist, actually."

"Rugby?"

"Probably played when he was younger, in the old country."

"I mean, he attended Rugby?"

"I believe so."

"Cambridge?"

"Mmmh."

"Fits into the community well, does he?"

"I'd say so. I think I see what you're getting at. He showed up here fifteen or so years before I did, and Shelby folks do not welcome outsiders with open arms. Until they've made up their minds. Especially Brits like Hersch, who might consider us Canadians still colonists, and who speak with unflawed upper-class accents, wear Homburg hats with earmuffs in winter instead of a toque, and spats and skinny rubbers instead of shoe packs or galoshes. I'd say Hersch smartened up his very first winter."

"Stopped treating them like colonists?"

"God no! Hersch would never have been guilty of that. He's been a fine and caring shepherd. His whole parish is right behind him."

"Scoutmaster."

"That's right. Wasn't a Scout troop in the district till he set one up. The boys would kill for him. Every one of them."

"Would you say he was—an emotional person?"

Now just how in hell did he answer that one? "Aren't most of us?"

"Of course. But—I mean—more so than the average?"

"He is a warm person." He had decided not to mention the time Hersch had decked Pete Wearmouth off the parsonage verandah rail and ass-over-beer-bottle into the spirea bushes for whaling young Chuck Wearmouth once too often.

"He carries his handkerchief in his sleeve cuff."

"Yep. We all giggle a bit about that. Except for Corporal McCready, head of the RCMP detachment. He carries his in his uniform cuff. I'm pretty sure Corporal McCready did not attend Rugby or Cambridge." Matter of fact he wasn't too sure Corporal McCready had managed junior or senior matriculation out of collegiate.

"So, unlike Canon Midford, the Corporal would not have gone through the usual English public school student roles of rugby, soccer player—paper-chaser."

"Just hockey, baseball, curling."

"Latin and Greek scholar," she said.

"Hersch? Sure. And later—Aramaic and Hebrew."

"At Cambridge."

"That's right. Doctorate. King's College. Something else about his past—he was an early Buchmanite."

"Pardon?"

"You know—Oxford Group."

"Oh yes."

"Sharing—group confession for divine guidance, dedication to absolute honesty, purity, love—unselfishness."

"I know."

"Today, I'd say Hersch was a devout existentialist. Low

church. Unlike his predecessor. To the discomfort of some
of his flock."

"Like who?"

"Oh, I don't know." He did of course know—Mr.
Oliver, to name one.

"So—Rugby, Cambridge, upper class."

"Yes."

"Fag, don. Strange he should end up here."

"How's that?"

"With all his qualifications—classics scholar, Cambridge degrees—I'd think he would be higher up in the
Anglican hierarchy, wouldn't you?"

"I don't know. That one's for him to answer. Ask him
about that."

"I intend to. You said you know him well, so I just
thought you might be able to . . ."

"Look. Better you should ask me why I'm here running
a weekly newspaper."

"Why are you?"

"By choice. Because I love the foothills and its people.
That simple for me. Ask Hersch. You may or you may not
get a similar answer. Ask him."

"I will."

She returned to questions about Hersch on numerous
occasions. Especially his Scouting and Sunday school
activities, which were much more than Bible lessons and
Morse code and tying knots. He told her how Hersch had
taught the boys to dap, to roll and back-cast, to read water,
how to tie flies. Wet or dry. Made them promise never to
use bait, live or dead. Scouts' honour.

"Before Shelby, ah, did he come straight to Shelby
when he came over from the old country?"

"Oh no. I believe he was in the East for a while—uh—
Peterborough—then West. Couple of years in Northern
Saskatchewan. There's an interesting thing about him, he
has a great understanding, rapport, with Indians."

"Does he?"

"Uh-huh. He really has two parishes you know—the
Shelby one and the Red one. Each Sunday afternoon he's

out to Paradise Valley and then back for evening services in town. Sometimes during the week, too—marriages, christenings, funerals."

"Busy fellow."

"Uh-huh. Mind you—there's great rainbow and cutthroat and bull-trout fishing on Paradise Reserve. I wouldn't be a bit surprised if Hersch didn't flog the Spray on the Sabbath now and again up there. Wait a minute. I don't believe I said that."

She stopped writing in her note pad. "Okay. Now you've mentioned the reserve, it reminds me of something. I understand he's taken his Scouts up there for camping trips quite often."

"Oh yes. Become a tradition. Summer, winter."

"Winter?"

"Mmh-hmh. They call it teepee time. December holidays. Sleeping under canvas in below-zero weather, eating beans and bannock and elk or deer or moose, just like the Indians do. Or did. Hard to say who learned more out of it, he or the boys. He told me once that they taught him a lot about roughing it—how to build a campfire a lot better than explained in the Boy Scout Manual, how to heat rocks in the coals and tuck them down in the sleeping-bag, and to cinch a rope around his middle to keep the body heat trapped under the windbreaker."

He went on to tell her about last Christmas Eve when he and Hersch had sat long in front of the fireplace after Ruth and Sarah had gone to bed. They had attended service at St. Aidan's earlier and the sound of the choir still lingered with him.

"Another brandy?"

"No thanks, Matt. I should be going."

"You're quite a guy, Hersch."

"Oh."

"Yep. That choir of yours."

"You liked it?"

"Everybody did. I don't mean just the quality that even my tin ear appreciated. Their make-up."

"On the women?"

"No. No. I don't see how you've pulled it off every Christmas; Catholic, United Church, Dutch Reform—brought them all together, in the loft as well as the pews. I'll bet there isn't another ecumenical choir like it in North America."

"Oh, I don't know about that, Matt."

"Damn rare anyway."

"Possibly."

"Mind you, Sadie's soprano still sounds shrill as a Skilsaw hitting a pine knot."

"Now and again." Midford stood up. "It's a little late, Matt." He looked over to the Christmas tree to the left of the dying fireplace. "Later for you than for me. Sarah won't be waking me up before daybreak."

"See you in church."

"It would—ah—be nice to see you there more often, Matt."

"Mmmmh . . ."

"I read your *Chinook* religiously."

"Okay. You know, something's been bothering me lately, Hersch, about your Christian God—about a few others, too."

"Which ones?"

"Oh, Mohammed, Buddha. Has to be taken seriously at all times, doesn't He. Yours."

"I suppose He does. Wouldn't be much of a God if He were taken lightly."

"Uh-uh. I don't mean that."

"Just what do you mean?"

"Wellll—what would be wrong or damaging if He were to loosen up and be funny now and again?"

"Where did you put my coat and scarf?"

"Closet—I'll get them for you. Some of the Greek boys had a sense of humour. And the aboriginals. There was a red trickster often."

"Are you going to get my coat?"

"Sure." He headed for the closet, Hersch behind him.

"Sometimes, Matt, I have a little trouble with you."

"Do you now."

"Deciding whether you're being totally serious or not. Thank you."

"Oh, I'm serious this time. I always take humour seriously."

"I have noticed that." He pulled on the toque, shrugged himself into his coat, bent down over his overshoes.

"No fun in Heaven at all," Matt said. "Hey, you don't suppose that may have been one of the reasons He kicked Satan off the Heavenly Council, do you?"

"I doubt it—very much."

"I'm not so sure. In a power struggle, wit, especially satire, can be a pretty handy weapon."

"It can." Canon Midford straightened up, tossed the end of his scarf over his shoulder. "God won that one."

"Again, I'm not so sure about that. The battle isn't over. Ever."

"I didn't say it was."

"Hitler and Mussolini reminded us of that. Not nearly."

"Good night, Matt."

"Which one's older, Hersch? Satan or God?"

"Which one's older . . .?"

"Close to senior-citizenship status. Probably the same age. There does seem to be a difference in hearing, though."

"Hearing?"

"Impairment. God doesn't seem to be hearing people as well as He used to."

"On the contrary. The hearing impairment is more likely ours." He turned away, opened the door, then turned back to Matt again. "Don't tell me you can't show up tomorrow morning in St. Aidan's because you're too busy doing an editorial on God's lack of a sense of humour, and His deafness."

"No."

"I'm glad to hear that. Matt, something that's been bothering me lately about you. More and more often your editorials and columns read like sermons. Leave them to me, and I promise you I'll keep clear of one-liners when I'm in the pulpit. Merry Christmas."

He did *not* tell June about a much earlier Shelby Christmas, one that Hersch and several others had told him about.

Well into the dirty thirties Canon Midford had taken over his Shelby parish. These were the desert years, when mid-America thirsted. Hot and constant winds siphoned wells and creeks and sloughs and hold-up ponds, blistered and cracked the prairie and the foothills skin, smoked up topsoil to smudge the sky, blot the sun. Light the lamp at noon.

Okie time had come. Grain elevators paid ten cents a bushel for wheat, three for oats and barley, but only if farmers were able to harvest a crop. No price offered for tumbleweed or Russian thistle or wild oats. Never, since Shelby's frontier birth or throughout her rural career, had there been hard times like these, when drifted land and blind homes must be abandoned. Dust to dust; dust to dust. Head north for the parklands and just possible rain in the Peace River country.

Canon Midford had come by Pullman coach to the new Sahara; many others travelled by freight, human flies on boxcars and flatcars and tenders, rolling East and rolling West. Most were looking for a chance to make a living, but some of the young were not seeking work: the scenery hogs, who had left the East to see the West, or the West to see the East. There was of course an older group, bindlestiffs or lump bums, the hobo professionals who long before any depression had been non-paying railway passengers. These had their own jungle jargon for the people you encountered: the hard tails, johns, harness bulls, gazoonas, gazeenas, gazoots, and gazats, or the canned-heat, vanilla, and after-shave-lotion artists, winos or McGoof hounds, wolves and their young proosians. The dinos were those who went into cafés and ordered four-course meals, said they were broke, hadn't eaten for three days, and were willing to wash dishes to pay for the meal. This dangerous stratagem could land them in the bucket for thirty days on charges of vagrancy and obtaining food under false pretences, though odds against that were much better if the restaurant were Greek or Chinese. When the snow flew, it was the Winter Christians, who hit for the nearest Sally Ann drum to promise the rest of their life to Jerusalem Slim so they could confess sin, sing hymns, and do Bible studies to get bed and three until the meadowlark would announce the spring. City downtown street corners had the dingbats, dinging passersby for the price of a cup of coffee or a night in the scratch-house.

In Shelby district as in most other Western rural communities Bennett buggies—cars pulled by real horsepower—
showed up, plagiarizing the Hoover buggies south of the
Forty-ninth, where teams were also being hitched up to car
bumpers. On both sides of the border, Thanksgiving and
Christmas were soon tainted with irony. Celebration by gift
was difficult on a twenty-five-dollar-a-month relief cheque.
His third Christmas in Shelby, Canon Midford decided to do
something about that.

He approached Mayor Oliver and the town council with
the suggestion that they have Santa Claus visit Shelby
Christmas morning with presents for every child in the
district. His Worship and a unanimous council approved.
The thing took off like prairie fire. A "Santa Visits Shelby
and Greater District Committee" was formed, to be chaired
by Canon Midford. Since the RCMP handed out the
monthly relief cheques and had a list of the vulnerable
needy, Corporal Broadfoot was named vice-chairman. Nettie Fitzgerald would perform her usual committee role: chief
shit-disturber.

First item on the agenda: toys. The *Chinook* would run
request ads: volunteers would gather in the fire hall at the
back of the community centre to accept and repair donated
gifts that had been outgrown: sleds and wagons, skates and
toboggans, dolls and teddy bears, doll houses and carriages,
doctor and nurse uniforms, cowboy and Indian suits, hoops,
tops and skipping-ropes, cap pistols, tricycles, and kiddy
cars.

Second item: Santa Claus. The choice was obvious: Art
Ulmer sober. He hadn't shaved for a decade, probably by
Christmas wouldn't have had a hair trim for two months.
With his rosy cheeks, cherry nose, and foot and a half white
beard he'd make a dandy Santa.

Item three: Santa's sleigh. Not too complicated. Rory
Napoleon's bobsled dray could handle the great gift cargo;
Hickory Brown could jigsaw plywood sides, paint them
Christmas red and green, and line their high arcs with tinsel.

Item four: the reindeer. Not so simple. Rory Napoleon's
dray team would not do, since your general run of reindeer
were not *black* or the size of Rory's Percherons. This
problem was solved when Rory explained that he had just

acquired a pair of two-year-old bays, and was sure he could
have them broken to harness in good time. Antlers for them
would be the twin set hung on the wall behind the Arlington
Arms reception counter. Elk. In his shoe and harness shop,
Willie MacCrimmon would design and fashion special
horn-holding bridles as well as harness so that the team
could be hitched up tandem style.

Item five: event location. No doubt about that: the town
square, opposite the Shelby Community Centre, where a
dignitary platform would be built, and a twenty-foot Christmas tree set up.

Very early in their meetings, Nettie Fitzgerald said they
must have a full choir in which she would sing lead
soprano, up on the platform with the mayor and councillors,
the school board chairmen, the head of the Western Stock
Growers Association, and the two Mounties in Boy Scout
hats and scarlet dress tunic. She was told that the platform
would not be big enough, but the committee agreed they
should not have left out the regent of the Crowfoot Chapter
of the IODE.

As regent of the Crowfoot Chapter of the IODE, Nettie
had accepted that, but insisted that they really must stage a
nativity play, which she was quite willing to direct, with a
real live donkey she had found out at the Bar P ranch.
Charlie Bolton said it wasn't a donkey; it was a mule. She
said it was practically the same thing. Charlie said the
difference was considerable: a mule was half horse, had a
mare for a mother, and, just like Nettie, was noted for its
goddam stubbornness. Nettie persisted, proving Charlie's
point; have it without the donkey then. Charlie said all right
he'd vote for that, but only if Arlington Agnes were cast as
Mother Mary and he as Joseph, and even though by the time
Santa made it to Shelby there would have been at least
fifteen nativity plays in church basements and schoolrooms.
Put to a vote, the nativity play—with or without donkey or
mule or Arlington Agnes or Charlie Bolton—lost deci-
sively.

Corporal Broadfoot had plotted out the strategy for
"Santa Visits Shelby and Greater Shelby District" in careful
detail. From his position up on the town square platform he
would be in charge of tactics. Santa must make his entrance

from the north, of course. In the sleigh loaded and hung
with toys he and his driver helper must take off well before
daybreak under cover of darkness, go up the hill slope north
of town, over and down as far as McNally's cottonwood
bluff at the bottom of the down slope, a distance of roughly
half a mile. They would take cover there, but keep a sharp
lookout at all times for wave signals to be given by Canon
Midford, who would take his position on *top* of the hill,
approximately halfway into town. It was a fitting coincidence that this very hill had been used by the first RCMP
under Colonel Macleod, as a lookout in the old Blackfoot
Crossing days, when they had put the run on the whiskey
traders in 1874, Corporal Broadfoot explained. Charlie
Bolton said that sounded like bullshit to him, but Corporal
Broadfoot said he could show it to him in a history of the
RCMP book. "Just proves it," Charlie said. "History books
is bullshit too."

From his vantage point Midford would have a clear
view of the Corporal on the platform, so he could receive
and relay signals to alert Rory. At twenty-minute intervals,
Walter Oliver, who had been cast as Santa's messenger,
would come out of the depot across the square, in Boy
Scout uniform with staff and blue knees, waving a yellow
telegram he would then hand up to his father. The following
year Walter at seventeen would make it to King Scout and
attend the Jamboree in England, then in 1939, at nineteen,
to Spitfire pilot in the RAF, and in 1941 to death in the
Battle of London.

It turned out to be a very white Christmas. And cold.
Twenty below. Rory had been over-optimistic about breaking the young team to tandem harness; even without the
elk-antler bridles in place they were difficult. It took four
hostellers to ear them down while Rory and Art in costume
got up and into the bobsleigh. Santa crouched to the rear
in a nest of his toys; Rory up front, with a firm grip on
the lines, his feet braced against the buckboard and the
team facing north, gave the signal. The hostellers released
the horses' ears and jumped free. Belly to the ground, the
whites of their eyeballs rolled up, the team lit out in the

direction of the North Pole. Because both had got the bit clamped between their teeth, it took Rory almost two miles to cool them down and get control. Only then was he able to turn them round and head back for McNally's bluff. The three-foot fall into the barrow pit gave him some trouble, but finally they made it into the shelter of the cottonwoods, where they uncorked a jug of Rory's Undiluted Best Number One Hard to fortify themselves against the chill as they waited for Canon Midford to give them the signal.

In spite of the weather, the turnout was great. The town square soon filled with young and old, behind the wide alley roped off along the front of the platform. Trucks and cars and rigs were parked outside the square for two blocks in every direction. The dignitaries came out of the community centre and took their positions on the platform. Mayor Oliver gave his welcoming address. Walter Oliver came out of the depot and handed the first telegram up to his father, who read it out:

> "Santa Claus left North Pole 12:06 A.M. Arctic Daylight Saving Time Stop With reindeer rig and sleigh load of toys Stop Just crossed Arctic Circle and entered Yukon Stop Headed for Shelby Stop Making good time Stop"

Walter Oliver's next telegram read:

> "Santa Claus again Stop Well into North-West Territories Stop Headed for Grand Prairie and Peace River Stop Merry Christmas Stop Ho Ho Ho Stop"

And the next one:

> "Still coming with Edmonton next stop Stop Blizzard conditions up here so speed reduced Stop After Edmonton Red Deer Stop Then Shelby Stop"

And the next:

> "Weather cleared Stop Red Deer behind Stop Shelby next stop Stop Coming fast Stop"

This would be the last telegram. Corporal Broadfoot waved to Canon Midford, who in turn signalled Rory, who began to fit the elk-horn bridles over the horses' heads. No problem; they were quite subdued by two hours of standing still in the biting cold. Rory climbed back up in the bobsleigh, loosed the lines, slapped them and yelled: "Hi-yahhhhh! Senator! Duke! Get your lazy arses out of it now!"

Both responded, and did well till they hit the barrow pit, where Senator, the lead horse, made a couple of rump bucks to get up and out onto the road. That caused the reindeer bridle Willie MacCrimmon had made for him to slide down and over Senator's nose to form an elk-horn necklace that bumped alarmingly against his chest. Duke's followed suit. That did it. Even Rory could not hold back the team urged on by the antlers rapping them into a full gallop. At least they were headed in the right direction, but much too fast for Canon Midford, who was to have hitched a ride to the edge of town, but who had to leap clear into a snowbank to get out of the way. Santa crouched, clinging to the sleigh side with both hands, his tasselled toque down over his rosy cheeks and cherry nose, his driver helper standing upright and leaning back with all his might against the lines to no avail, as they entered Shelby town limits.

Down Lafayette Avenue they flew, then Marmot Crescent, which would become Bison and in five blocks Main, which arrowed right through the town square. It was Rory's best option, if only he could keep the reindeer team on course. He succeeded. Never in his entire rodeo career had he ever faced a greater challenge. Wild-eyed, goitre antlers bouncing, manes and tails flying, harness bells ajingle, snort clouds of steam from their nostrils, bits welded between their teeth, they hit the town square of Shelby, Alberta, Canada. Not Pamplona. No amateur toreadors waiting for them here. As they passed the platform, Santa, now with tinsel and a hoop round his neck, forgot to deliver his ho-ho-ho lines, nor did his driver helper call out: "A merry, merry Christmas morn to one and all!" Instead: "Hold up goddamit! Whoa, you bay bastards! Whoaaaa-hup!"

They cleared the square, crossed the railway tracks, and kept right on out of town.

Back in the stunned square children were crying; parents were comforting. One tearful voice was heard: "Jesus Murphy! It looks like Santy ain't stoppin' in Shelby this Christmas!"

By following the toy spoor, Corporal Broadfoot and others were able to track down Santa and his helper. Both were trapped in drunken darkness beneath the upturned sleigh. The horses were gone. Three days later they were found ten miles south of town in an abandoned barn, where they had taken shelter from blizzard winds.

It could have been much worse; there had been no casualties. By the next Christmas, Rory had the bays well broken, and Santa's visit to Shelby went on to become an established annual event, ending the year after war was declared. The rains came; wheat and oats and barley and beef, eggs and milk and butter and chickens, went up. In or out of the army there were suddenly jobs for all. Canon Midford and Father McNulty, and all parsons, ministers, town clerks, and magistrates, were inundated with marriages that had been delayed till better times. No more flies on freight cars. Looked like war wasn't so bad after all. Happy days were here again.

Not for Rory Napoleon, though. The depression had hit him early, with his Livery Stable operation a dying enterprise kept alive only by the rummy room in the back and the manufacture of Rory's Undiluted Best Number One Hard. That income had ended when Corporal Broadfoot finally smelled out the still in the cave on the bank of the Spray River, so that Mayor Oliver as town magistrate reluctantly gave Rory a ninety-day sentence, during which time the Royal Bank closed down on him, and sold the Livery Stable property for a song to Ollie Pringle, Shelby's Licensed Embalmer and Funeral Director, who was buying up everything in sight, rural or urban. Dying had not flagged or faltered during the drought and depression years. Nor had the Maple Leaf Pool Hall, the Arlington Arms Beer Parlour, the Cameo Theatre, dentistry, medicine, or the practice of law suffered much.

The Royal Bank also came after Rory's quarter section,

leaving him with only the log shack on a gravelly strip of ten acres along the Spray River, capable of supporting only some chickens, one milk cow, and a growing herd of goats. Ollie Pringle took over the rest. In the following years Ollie and the goats would not be good neighbours.

The Napoleons and their children had survived—barely; the one-time World Bareback and Saddle Bucking Bronc Champion for three years running became a town employee, making garbage collection rounds, driving the honey-wagon through privy town down on the flats to pick up and empty the shit and piss cans, and pump out cesspools. The goats did well on salvaged garbage. The Napoleons just managed to get by, and with the declaration of war there came a brief ray of sunshine; Rory applied for enlistment. Hope blinked out when the army judged him an illiteracy and curling-rock liver reject. How often he yearned for the good old rodeo days, before the whole world had turned into a nuisance grounds with garbage-eating goats!

In the weeks that followed the Rotary luncheon, June was invited to speak to the IODE, the Willing Workers' W.A., and finally the Shelby Historical Landmarks, District Shrines, and Old Timers' Association.

"Well," Matt exclaimed when June told him she was to speak to the latter group, "that's fine!"

"What's so special about it?" June asked.

"In the first place, Nettie Fitzgerald's its president, and for the past eight years anyway they have been doing a history of Shelby and Shelby district."

"Why should that make it special?"

"If Nettie accepts you, it could help you a great deal. Also I think that the Shelby Historical Landmarks, District Shrines, et-cetera, have been looking on you with a certain amount of suspicion ever since you came to town . . ."

"Suspicion!"

He nodded.

"But why should they?"

"Rightly or wrongly they probably think you might be

about to poach on the natural territory of Shelby Historical Landmarks. . . ."

"But I'm not! Not at all!"

"And that's why it's special. You have a chance to convince them you're not. You should take extra care with them—and with Nettie Fitzgerald."

"I will," she said. "I certainly will!"

She did. Matt attended and covered her speech for the *Chinook*. June's talk lauded the group for their projected work; she told them that they would be preserving a precious record of the past, a task that became a little more difficult with the death of each old-timer, one that in a few years death and time might have placed quite out of reach. She ended with a generous offer to help them with any editorial advice they might need.

Matt kept his attention on Nettie Fitzgerald throughout June's talk; he saw the doctor's wife lean forward, her eyes flicking as she did. He could imagine her thinking of bureau drawers filled with the handwritten anarchy of eight years and thirty-seven contributors.

She was indisputably the grande dame of Shelby society. It would be only a matter of time till she accepted June's offer of help with the historical project.

CHAPTER 10

WITH THE FINAL GLACIAL RUN-OFF FROM DISTANT PEAKS LATE in May and an unseasonal four-inch snowstorm the night of her talk to the Shelby Historical Landmarks, District Shrines, and Old Timers' Association, June had an opportunity to observe Shelby's annual excited anticipation of flood. In the past, Matt explained to her, there had been extreme property damage as the swollen stream sought its ancient bed through the town from the CPR bridge, by Daddy Sherry's brown cottage, then down Main Street past the *Chinook* building and the Post Office. Now to the West there rose the earth and gravel breakwater within which the community lay as though in the shallow sweep of a protective arm. It was a twenty-year-old monument to the foresight of Mayors Fraser and Oliver, holding back the turgid urgency of floodwater, but not stemming the yearly lift of consternation within the hearts of the townspeople. It was just possible that the water *could* overcome Fraser dam; home basements might be awash once more; canoes and rowboats might be needed again on Main Street, as they were in 1934 when there had been thousands of dollars' damage to houses, stores, and stocks.

That year, the last that the Spray had poured disaster upon the town, train service had been disrupted, so that, with the North-South Highway also under water, mail and food deliveries had been impossible. Each spring the threat of such past disaster thrilled all together with a sort of shot in the community veins, at a time when feeling ran a little sluggishly through the civic body, convalescent after the fever of spring seeding had cooled and calving was over. The remote possibility of flood gave the town a welcome fillip of excitement.

This year the Spray rose to within an inch of sluicing over the railway bridge, but the muddy crest passed the town overnight, and people a little regretfully gave up their recall of 1934. They returned their business stocks and files to basement storage, and almost reluctantly stopped their evening visits to gauge the water line on the cement footings of the bridge.

It seemed now as though June had always been at her desk in the outer office. It bothered him a little that Millie seemed to have adopted a tight-mouthed and almost martyred air bordering sometimes upon sullenness, but there was little he could do about it. June seemed to go out of her way to be friendly. He did not know how many times she had invited Millie out to coffee with her, Millie each time declining with the excuse that she couldn't leave her filing or her paper-cutting or her accounts, and at the same time making the refusal a gesture of barely polite disapproval.

There had been more than disapproval on Millie's face when he had invited June to come with him to the HL branding. Because it was a Saturday, Joe Manley was able to come with them, and with picnic eagerness they had driven west into the lease country through fields royal with lupin and shooting star. They had watched the streams of cattle pour down the side hill trails and draws to the valley floor and the hold-up fields of all the ranches. Cowhand, storekeeper, cattle-buyer, and city oil executive stood under the mild spring sun; city eyes smarted from the bitter drift of willow smoke; burning hide and hair were distinct in urban nostrils as festive spectators watched the consummate deftness of calf heeling, branding, wattling, vaccination, castration.

With branding over, the community relaxed into the drowsing leisure of early summer, a time when Matt often found himself straining for news, forced to rely more and more upon such fillers as: "A five-year plan has been recommended for India to include birth control in an effort to cut down India's vast population increase." "The best cat gut comes from the intestines of lean, ill-fed sheep and goats and donkeys."

He had printed more of the dog obituaries as the poisoner, whoever he was, obliged with more deaths, the most tragic being that of Lucy Wagner's wire-haired bitch.

DIED Taffy Wagner, sole companion of Lucy Wagner, confined to the house by failing health. Taffy spent many years with Miss Wagner cheering her loneliness with her bright terrier spirit. A great many people will learn of her death with sadness.

This had come out the day that Nettie Fitzgerald had invited June to tea with her. Nettie's had not been an easy conquest, for Matt noticed that she had waited *until* June had brought some order and clarity to the historical material gathered by members of the Shelby Historical Landmarks, District Shrines, and Old Timers' Association. The invitation to tea was a reward.

It would be served on blue Crown Derby, Matt knew, not because Nettie was overly proud of her settings for eight in Crown Derby, but because using the blue was a gesture of bold grace and restraint. Besides ordinary Crown Derby, Nettie had settings for twelve in the rich plum, orange, and gold of Royal Crown Derby.

As she often said, Nettie loved lovely old things. Her living-room was proof of this love. Matt knew that tea would be served from a tilt-top table that was a lovely old thing and from a sideboard with ball-and-claw feet that was a lovely old thing. By the fireplace would be a fire screen that was a lovely old thing shaped like a shield that slid up and down a pole set in a rosewood base. The shield part itself framed bolting cloth worked in lovely old greens and pinks, which held a lovely old court lady with high white hair; only the very plump cherubs hovering tipped over in each of the four corners were young; ribbons, with a vee sliced out of the ends, curled over their legs and conveniently up and around their crotches.

He supposed that Harry did not spend a tenth of his waking hours in the living-room, but rather in his study with the stuffed green-wing teal and ring-necked pheasant flying radiantly down one wall over the five shotguns Harry had hung on brackets made of mountain-sheep feet. There were two paintings there, raw with orange and magenta and artery red; one, harsh and angular as hunger, showed Stony Indians in a prairie chicken dance; the other, sinuously wild, was of Blackfoot in their hoop dance. Matt wondered if June would see Harry's study at all.

He was still in the office when she returned from her audience with Nettie. She told him that Mrs. Fitzgerald had seemed quite pleased with her work on the history.

"I didn't have the heart to tell her that they were too optimistic about it," she said.

"In what way?"

"They anticipate all sorts of profits when it is published. To fit out a museum in the community centre—a museum of Shelby pioneer history. It's quite a worthwhile project."

"The history or the museum?"

"Both. They'll be lucky if they break even—something like that has a limited and local appeal."

"Unless they interest the brewery or one of the meat-packing companies."

"Oh, she knew about that but it didn't seem to interest her. She didn't seem to think they would get much co-operation in the museum itself—said there was a great deal of apathy toward cultural projects in Shelby."

"Well . . ." Matt considered a moment, "Nettie isn't the most fortunate champion Shelby could have for culture, you know."

"Perhaps not," June admitted. "But she should get points for trying, shouldn't she?"

"I guess she should," Matt agreed. "Depends a lot on what her reasons are for trying."

"What do you mean?"

"Nettie is a snob," he said flatly. Then, "That may put

it a little too simply and bluntly and Nettie's not a simple woman . . ."

"She is blunt enough."

"Oh yes. What I meant was that her values are snobbish values—always. She's terribly conscious in everything of social ascendancy. Her artistic appreciation is pretty shallow. She doesn't truly take cultural things seriously but as a means—they're tokens indicating position in society. Were you in Harry's study?"

"No."

"You might have found it interesting. Harry makes no pretence at being a patron of the arts, but in there with all his shotguns and stuffed game gathering dust he has a couple of paintings—they're Indian things—one of the prairie chicken dance, the other of the snake dance or the hoop dance. Harry likes them—as art he likes them almost as much as he likes his lovely engraved Greener shotgun. My point is that Harry hasn't gone out of his way to make himself more appreciative or sensitive to art, but he does have these paintings because he *likes* them and not because they're an embellishment of his social standing in Shelby society. Anything Nettie . . ."

"This still doesn't destroy her contention that Shelby people don't care about cultural things."

"I suppose it doesn't."

"Do you agree with her?"

"I don't know." He thought a moment. "What did she say to prove her point?"

"That the town's main interests were fishing, hunting, curling, hockey."

"I imagine she's right—but I don't think these interests are peculiar to Shelby. Couldn't you say the same for any Canadian city?"

"She said that the fifty-thousand-dollar subscription for a new curling rink was taken up right away last fall—the Celebrity Series failed here three years ago."

"Oh, that—well, we've hardly the population to support it. But in proportion we have as many people who would appreciate it as most cities do. There are a number who have a subscription to the city series—drive up each time. A number go to the Symphony in the winter . . ."

"But not many."

"No," he admitted, "not many."

"She seemed to think the library was inadequate—do you think it is?"

"Why, I don't know. In what way?"

"I don't know either," June said. "I thought you might."

"It's a library. Sadie Tracey handles it Saturday afternoons in the community centre. Look, I hope you're not taking everything Nettie says for gospel. There's a bias there and . . ."

"Credit me with a bias, too. You once asked if I liked everyone I interviewed and I told you it didn't make too much difference. I agree with you that Mrs. Fitzgerald isn't the best champion for culture—and her kind aren't limited to Shelby by any means."

"Thanks—for all of Shelby."

"Now, one more thing . . ."

"Yes, Doctor."

"You know the stories you've been running. The dog obituaries?"

"Yes?"

"What sort of response have you had to them?"

"Satisfying."

"It's an unusual way to handle them."

"I guess it is."

"Has anyone—has there been any unfavourable response to them?"

"Not so far."

"Mrs. Fitzgerald?"

"I see. Well, Nettie's suffered Harry's dogs for years—every one of them a Chesapeake over a hundred pounds, shedding hair tufts all year round all over her velvet . . ."

"That didn't seem to be exactly her point. She pointed the stories out to me in another way—as evidence of—well, of limited horizons in Shelby. That with all the exciting and wonderful things of importance happening all over the world . . ."

"The dogs were important to the children that lost them."

"She felt it was *over*-dignifying the death of a few dogs."

"I'm a weekly, in the business of personal neighbourhood news. Everyone here reads the city morning paper and afternoon paper, and has a radio—television set. I—she—I don't give a damn what she thinks!"

"I'm sorry, Matt. Perhaps I shouldn't have . . ."

"It's all right. There's no reason everyone should respond favourably, and whatever Nettie thinks, it *is* an important thing. The poison is in wieners, and they're a threat to the lives of the town's small children who might pick them up. There were four more this week."

"Do you think what you're doing is going to . . ."

"I don't know," he said. "I thought it might. I hoped it might. Of course, these new dogs could have got hold of old bait dropped out some time ago. I don't know."

He sat alone in his office after she had left, telling himself over again that he did not give a damn what Nettie Fitzgerald thought. He reminded himself of how tired Harry had been looking the past two weeks, fatigued from sitting up night after night with his Greener over his knees. But it had been no use. He leaned forward over his typewriter.

Died of strychnine poisoning Champion Prince Rufus of Shelby, son of Duke Homer Williams Field Trial Champion Empress Noreen Sweeney, in spite of fruitless use by his master, Dr. Fitzgerald, of stomach pump, emetic, and irrigation. Royal sire and gentleman.

He could not remember exactly how the matter had come up with Ruth that evening after supper. She had commented on the dog stories; his reply had been unenthusiastic; she had asked what was bothering him; he had said that nothing was bothering him.

"But it is, Matt."

"Prince got it this afternoon."

"Oh—I'm sorry." .

"But it isn't that, Ruth—it's about these dog obituaries. Ruth, I think I should have had some second thoughts before I ran them."

"Whatever for?"

"Well, I've been thinking about it—they're dogs. And you know the most terrible thing there is—is death, human death, the loss of someone you love. I haven't wanted to belittle people's grief . . ."

"I don't suppose you have."

"And if a person believes that a human is a very special thing, then it isn't right to, well, to demean death . . ."

"You can't—how can you demean death!"

"I have—by writing sentimental slop about dear old pets!"

"Matt, oh, Matt—you aren't, you haven't—it was a wonderful and beautiful thing you . . ."

"It was not."

"Yes, it was!"

"I don't know, Ruth. I don't know if it was. Suggesting an animal is worthy of—the death of an animal is to be compared with the death of a human. Human life is—damn it—it's a sacred thing!"

"Of course it is."

"All right then—I've been a smart alec."

"Matt, dear, are you suggesting there isn't room for compassion for humans *and* for animals?"

"No . . ."

"Matt, what's made you change? Who has said anything to you about it?"

"Nobody. No, that's not right. Nettie Fitzgerald."

"Nettie's told you she feels . . ."

"Indirectly."

"Nettie's feelings in the matter wouldn't bother you, Matt, would they?"

"Well, no . . ."

"You are what you are, Matt, and don't you let anyone . . . Hey, indirectly? How could she? Oh, I see, now we're to have death graduated on a sociological scale . . .?"

"Oh, Ruth . . ."

"Is that it?"

"No."

"It's not right, you know. One does subtract from the other. Adult humans at the top—and where does the death of a child fit in! Or an infant! Or Lucy Wagner's dog or Harry's Prince!"

"Take it easy, Ruth."

"You've got the wrong doctor—your Dr. Melquist! Joe Oliver and Jamie Saunders mourn rightfully and without any scale of life values. Who does she think she is!"

"That's not fair, Ruth. She didn't . . ."

"You tell your Dr. Melquist—you ask her just who the hell does she think she is! And ask her what she's going to do if life or death refuse to come into her scales and tables at all!"

In the few times that this had happened in their married life, he had felt helpless—and frightened. The near-hysteria did not frighten for itself, but for its wild exclusion. He left the house to walk without destination through the June evening with the foothills wind ticking through the leaves above him. He muttered a greeting as he passed Mr. Oliver behind his hedge.

Mr. Oliver was glad that May and part of June were over; on the twenty-fourth he had put his bedding plants in, and brought out Walter's cross to set it up between the gladioli section and the rose garden. It was particularly nice to get May over with, for May was a crucial month when chewing, sucking insects had tender leaves and shoots to work on. If you didn't get them in May, you fought a losing battle for the rest of the year. Now there were slugs to be salted and moles to be looked after. These careful spoonfuls of grey poison he was placing into the earthen limpets would take care of the moles.

One thing he had to be thankful for: in spite of killing late frosts he had managed to bring through one hybrid tea rose, thanks to trenching it last fall, covering it with two feet of earth, and soaking it down just before the first hard frosts of fall. At the base of the plant, last week, he had buried three little white plant pills, taking care not to disturb the delicate roots, and once a week from now on he would give it a good soaking with water and household ammonia. He'd better fill the red hand spray with nicotine sulphate;

spraying when the leaves were small he would get the undersides as well.

As he walked across the lawn toward the back porch where he kept his garden tools, he decided that on Saturday he must 2-4-D the grass; he would do that if it promised to be a good hot June day. At the corner of the house, he noticed a wasp inside the screen there. He went in for the hand spray in the porch.

Back with the wasp, he lifted the spray to exhale a cloud of mist. Caught in the expelled poison, the wasp ceased its attempts to crawl up the screen; its wings glistened, saucer eyes filmed over; the stuff clung to its Hallowe'en body, the working legs. It dropped down the screen, caught itself, then dropped again. There on the inside sill it lay with all its legs waving feebly aloft; they met; they tangled, separated to spread wide, then all legs caught and folded into the body. The long back legs had heen the last to die.

CHAPTER 11

"WHAT IS IT, MILLIE?"

"Those files, the back-copy ones."

"What about them?"

"I try to keep them in good order—way they should be."

"Indeed you do, Millie."

"Well, people shouldn't be going in there and taking stuff out of them. Isn't fair for them to get all pulled apart and put back any old way without the right dates in the right places in them."

Now he got it. He had suggested to June that she would be able to find a lot of useful material in the old issues of the *Chinook*, that she might find Uncle Ben's voice a very helpful and informative one.

"She's taking stuff out and taking them back home with—"

"That's right."

"If they get carted all over town . . ."

"Dr. Melquist is not carting them all over town, Millie." It was hard to keep the irritation out of his voice. "They're very important to her work. I doubt she'll mess up our files."

"Least she could do would be to do what you made the others do with them."

"What others?"

"Shelby History and Old Timers doing *their* book."

"What was that?"

"Sign for whatever she takes out of our files."

"No, Millie. Dr. Melquist will take good care of them and she'll put them back in proper order." He could tell from the corners of Millie's mouth that she did not share his optimism. "Millie, I've been thinking about something— your Saturday afternoons in here. I don't think it's been fair to you on your weekends." She'd asked for it, making such a fuss about June's using the files. "June is quite grateful that we've given her a corner in our office, and she'd like to do something in return for us to show her thanks. Especially to you."

"What?"

"She's offered to take over the Saturday afternoons. Answering the phone and—"

"But she couldn't! She wouldn't know how to . . ."

"She can take any ads that come in, any social notes. Put them on your desk for you on Monday. She can put the money or cheques for subscriptions in the petty cash . . ."

"Oh, no—no, Mr. Stanley!" Her face was stricken, and he saw that she had been dealt a mortal blow. He was suddenly quite ashamed of himself and would have softened and told her that if she didn't want it, they could stick with the old arrangement, but Millie had turned and fled from the office. His first impulse was to go after her, but he realized that June was out at her desk, and that the worst thing he could do would be to deepen Millie's mortification in front of her. God damn it anyway!

The compassion had diminished before he had an opportunity to speak to Millie alone, and he decided to let it go as a firm arrangement from now on. For the rest of the week Millie went about her work more subdued than usual. She said nothing more about the files that June was using. She did not show up at the office on Saturday afternoon.

Mame Napoleon did. She came in just after Matt had finished showing June the ritual of Saturday afternoons.

Mame's mission was to collect four dollars from Matt, since the Senator was without change to pay for clearing his backyard of the winter's collection of debris and the branches pruned from the backyard cottonwoods. Rory had dropped Mame off and gone on to the nuisance grounds with the load.

"You know," Matt heard her say as he went to the petty cash box, "I better call you Miss Melquist—Doc don't fit."

"That's all right," June said.

"She workin' for you now, Mr. Stanley?" she asked him as he handed her the four dollars.

"She's working here," Matt explained, "but not for me."

"How's that book of yours comin' along?"

"Just fine, Mrs. Napoleon."

"Senator's gonna see if he can help us out about our goats," she said to Matt. "Out again into Ollie Pringle's an' Ollie's threatenin' to get Oliver after us. Rory told the Senator and he's gonna do what he can. Senator's always ready to help a person if he can, but I guess I ain't tellin' you nothin', him bein' Ruth's daddy."

"I guess he is," agreed Matt.

"You know"—Mame turned to June again—"I was askin' him—after I explained about the goats—we got to talkin' about you. Well—not you exactly," she said quickly, "more about the sort of stuff you work at. Senator he explained some for me."

"Did he," June said.

"Yeah. He figgered it was . . . "—Mame leaned against the counter—"some of it was down our alley." She took a package of fine cut and papers from her blouse pocket. "The Napoleons." She put them back as Matt held out to her his package of tailor-made cigarettes. "He might have been right at that." She paused while she lit up. June waited. . . . "He said all about how people were all into classes. All over the world. I found that real interestin'. I knew there was top dogs. The lucky ones, but the Senator he explained how they were the ones that were polite and had good manners. Never struck me that way with the Shelby cream."

"How did it strike you?" June said.

"I always figgered they was just as sloppy an' mean when they got drunk—only them havin' more money to buy it with, they managed to get drunk oftener an' longer."

"Do you think they do?" June said.

"They might. I never give it too much attention. But I guess it's right they can afford to have better manners—be more polite—an' I guess that could be a good thing."

"Yes?" June encouraged her to go on.

"Way some of their good manners could rub off onto the other folks—us common folks." Mame looked at Matt. "What about the bottom of the heap?"

"What about it, Mame?" he said.

"Likes of us—Napoleons. I given that end of it a lotta thought."

"Have you," June said.

Mame nodded. "You would too. Way I see it, us Napoleons we're the only one of our kind in the district. I figger that gives us some kind of rights."

"What sort of rights?" Matt asked her.

Mame leaned forward confidentially on her elbows. "I ain't too sure what kind, but we must have 'em. You might say the Napoleons serve a purpose around Shelby, Miss Melquist."

"Oh—what sort of purpose do you mean?"

"Well, all the other folks can look at us an' they can say we had a bad year but, by Judas, we aren't in as bad shape as the Napoleons by a long shot. We're a lot of comfort to a lot of people. We're standin' by if they want somebody to give a hamper to at Christmas time. They got any old boots or suits or dresses, they can give 'em to the Napoleons instead of throwin' 'em into the garbage." Mame grinned at Matt. "That makes 'em feel good."

"How does it do that?" asked June.

"Any little kids won't finish up their porridge or their tapioca—leavin' crusts on their plate, their parents can say to them, eat up your tapioca, don't leave your crusts. Napoleon kids'd be glad to have 'em—lots of times they go to their bed hungry."

"Do they, Mrs. Napoleon?"

"Do they what?" Mame asked her.

"Often go to bed hungry."

"Hell no! An' I'll tell you another thing—I'm not gonna stick no tapioca in front of my kids. They hate it. Specially Byron. Nobody makes Byron eat anythin' he don't wanta eat."

"I guess they don't," Matt told her. "If you two will excuse me I have a date to take a little girl to a birthday party."

"You go ahead, Mr. Stanley," Mame called after him. "I'm just puttin' in time till Rory rolls back from the nuisance grounds."

She turned back to June. "Look, I don't want to hold you up with your work . . ."

"That's all right, Mrs. Napoleon."

"Mame."

"Mame. Come through and take a chair here. More comfortable." June pulled Millie Clocker's chair over by her own desk.

When Mame was settled with another cigarette, June said, "Byron—I've wondered, Mame—how he—the name is interesting—named after the poet."

"What poet?"

"Lord Byron, the great English poet."

"Never heard of him."

"But didn't you name him after . . ."

"I didn't. Rory did."

"Your husband named him after Lord Byron."

"No, he didn't. He got the name from a CNR section-hand he'd known years ago out in B.C."

"Well, there you are," June said, "the section-hand knew the English poet, and he mentioned the name to your husband and he named your son after Lord Byron, the poet." She saw that Mame was slowly shaking her head. "Isn't that right?"

"Nope. The section-hand didn't know any poet named Byron at all. He told Rory it was a nice name because he read it off one of the CNR Pullman coaches—Byron Manor. Artistic one in our family is Elvira. She can draw anything or paint anything you want, an' she gets that from me."

"I see."

"Freehand." Mame stubbed her cigarette in the ash-tray on June's desk.

"What I was sayin'. Maybe somebody gets hailed out or rusted out or the mortgage gets to leanin' on 'em a little too hard. Well, all they got to do is look at our ten acres rotten with wild oats an' sow thistle an' mustard—they get to feelin' better right away."

"That's how you . . ."

"I bet a hunderd folks has said to theirselves a hunderd times: there's lots worse can happen to us—look at the Napoleons."

"And do you feel bitter about . . ."

"Me. I ain't bitter. We got nothin', Miss Melquist, but we're happy. An' that's what most of us is here for, ain't it?"

June nodded.

"Some does it one way, some does it another. Look, I ain't got any automatic washin' machine—we see by coal-oil lamp. I got no vacuum cleaner like Mrs. Fitzgerald, Mrs. Pringle. We got no television set an' we walk out back in twenty-below. We got no floor polisher like Mrs. Oliver. Well, all right."

"How do you mean?"

"All right. I'm just as well off as any woman ever was fifty years ago. Matter of fact, I'm better off. Take Mrs. Fitzgerald's folks. Know what they was livin' in out here fifty years ago? Sod hut with a dirt floor. Me, I got a wood house. Such as it is. The Napoleons is happy most the time an' we serve our purpose. Cheap! At twice the price!" She stared for a moment at June. "Maybe that'll help you along."

"Maybe," agreed June.

"You go to Mrs. Fitzgerald if you want to find out all about the cream, anything you want about the skim, you come to me." She smiled suddenly. "One thing I can tell you about Byron, Miss Melquist—he's got all kinds of guts. Isn't anything he won't tackle. Prenatal influence—Byron, he's the only one my kids was born on top of a Ferris wheel."

The afternoon was such a nice one and the party at Tregillis's was only three blocks away. He had handled her as he always did when they adventured forth together, on the main principle of a hunter in the field training a young and high-strung bird dog, letting her go free ahead of himself, hoping that she would eventually deplete her astonishing reserve of undisciplined energy. For Sarah the freedom had to be illusory, Matt actually holding her on a sort of mental leash, always ready to dash after her, generously anticipating mercurial variation from the main course and into the road, hedges, flower beds, mud puddles, open stores. The child had a squirting tiptoe speed but no predictable trajectory.

Sooner or later a toe stubbed in a crack in the cement walk, then a head-long sprawl, put a period to these dazzling bursts; until he came to her she would lie on her stomach, back arched to hold her head up and away from the unfriendly ground. When he had placed her, crying, back on her feet she would stand with hands out and fingers extended, as though they had become two enemies of her soiled body. He would kiss her wet cheeks, assure her of his love, brush the dirt from her dress front. Her capitulation then was so complete as to sadden him, the warm little hand passive, stirring not in the slightest effort to escape from his.

After he had delivered her to the shrill and merry hell of the Tregillises' back garden, he had been undecided about returning home. Ruth would still be stiff and withdrawn, and that was unusual for her. She was Ruth. They had differences of opinion, quick squalls of impatience, annoyance, of anger with each other. He *had* been known to shout at her; she had cried when expression, expletive, or other communication failed, but the rough weather was soon over with her. It always had been.

And now he was remembering her pregnancy and the most wonderful of all springs.

"It's a good month to have a baby in," he'd said when she had told him.

"Any month's a poor month to have a baby in," she contradicted him. "Us women know."

"No, April's a good month. Not too hot, not too cold. You get the worst of it all over during the winter. You know—wear a big winter overcoat without people knowing you're wearing it to hide your condition. There's not so much stirring in the winter anyway, so it won't spoil anything."

"You mean like your fishing with Dad?"

"No, it's—I mean it, Ruth. Winter . . ."

"All right, Matt. You go ahead. You have the baby. It's okay with me."

"Don't you want to start a family?"

"Of course, dear. Joe Manley and Mrs. Nelligan are delighted. "

"Joe Manley!"

"He knows. I met him just as I was coming out of Harry's office and he took me into the Palm for a cup of coffee."

"But where does Mrs. Nelligan come in?"

"Well, Aunt Fan was having tea in the café. I told her. I guess she told Florence Nelligan. Harry warned me about her. He warns all his patients about her."

"So, I'm not the first to know. Second—after Harry."

"Third or fourth, Matt. Joe told me. He told me Flannel Mouth told him all about Maud Parlee's baby last spring and how Harry drowned it."

"What!"

"Before he got it out—quite. Then her sister back in Dah-koh-tah was walking along a board walk and the neighbour was killing a rooster and the sight made her faint. She fell off the board walk and the child had a birthmark— like a red rooster comb—on its buttocks."

"Jesus!"

After the second month she began to have trouble with her hips. They felt as though they were pulling apart. At night Matt rubbed them for her till he thought his arms would drop off. It took all his persuasion, and Joe's, to get her out for walks, tramping over the foothills with the snow squealing underfoot, his arm linked in hers. Joe had often accompanied them on their walks, insisted on it.

"Damn it, Matt, it isn't fair! You and Joe have twice my stride—and you spell each other off and I have to go the whole course. Yesterday it was thirty below and the drifts were at least three feet deep. Why don't you and Joe just go walking together and leave me at home with a good book."

"Because neither Joe nor I are—is going to have a baby."

"If you were, you'd both abort. The only reason I've held onto it this long is because I'm stubborn. I am *not* taking another five-mile cross-country paper chase with either of you till the end of the week!"

He watched for bulkiness, was a little disappointed as nothing dramatic showed immediately. Then, within weeks, it did—alarmingly. For the first time he could truly accept that she was pregnant; he was also positive that she must be carrying the baby in a horizontal position straight out.

They had talked a great deal of the baby, wondered at its sex, the chances of its being twins, and discarded that possibility as too remote and wonderful to happen to them. In the meantime they had settled upon calling it "he." Ruth, recognizing Matt's desire for a boy, had agreed in this.

He knew that she had hated herself for having such a conventional pregnancy, and that she was alarmed at what had happened to the flywheel of her emotions. The worst time had been when he had come home from the office at noon near the end of February. He had hardly hung up his coat and hat before she had, as Flannel Mouth Florence would put it, "taken him by the face."

"Why didn't you take your overshoes off! Look at the snow melting and puddling all over the linoleum!"

"I'm sorry."

"That doesn't clean the floor I just washed this morning, does it! All you had to do was take them off before you came out of the hallway!"

"All right, Ruth. I said I was sorry."

"Did you take the garbage out?"

He hadn't. Was he blind? She'd put it out by the door for him. Dammit, it wasn't much to ask. His hips weren't killing him! Hers were!

He hoped they were! Did she have to light into him as soon as he stepped inside the door! He'd been feeling pretty cheerful!

Well, she wasn't.

Nor was he now. That was no reason for throwing a wet blanket over him. He wished to God she'd be a little less touchy!

He slammed out of the house and went for ham and eggs at the Palm Café. When he came home after work he found her with the baked smell of freshly ironed clothes filling the kitchen.

"I've got Parker House rolls for you tonight, Matt. Nettie Fitzgerald told me to try this new yeast you don't have to let set overnight."

She'd stopped suddenly, staring at his bewildered face. He realized that she had completely forgotten. "I'm sorry, Matt—about—at dinner time."

"That's all right." He fell back upon the expression he often used when he had been hurt and he wasn't all right. Their evening had been an interminably long one with the walls listening. She seemed truly upset by the time they went to bed.

"Rub my hips, please, Matt?"

He did so perfunctorily.

When he stopped, she lay beside him, on her back, staring up to the ceiling. He could tell by the rigidity of her body that she was angry—probably not feeling so sorry now for what had happened at noon. Had she really expected him to eat her damned rolls made from a recipe of Nettie's and get delirious about them?

Of course he *had* messed up the kitchen floor. And she had asked him a couple of times not to forget to take off his overshoes . . .

"Matt! Matt!"

"Mmmmh?"

"Matt! The baby moved—twice. Matt, dear."

She had taken his hand so that he could feel it too; it had taken a long and uncooperative time for it to happen again, but when it did, it was glorious.

"See! It's—it's as though something slipped, Matt! It's as though something suddenly dropped inside me. It sort of stops your heart for a moment!"

"It stops mine!" said Matt.

The pains started a week before Harry had promised, while she had morning coffee with Aunt Fan, who had dropped over. She phoned Art's Taxi; Aunt Fan went with her to the hospital; they left a note on the kitchen table for Matt to see at noon. When he arrived at the hospital, out of breath, she met him in the hall; the pains had stopped. She told him that the baby wasn't coming for a few hours anyway; she knew for sure; he'd better get something to eat and go back to the office. He returned after five; she seemed to feel a little guilty in her bathrobe, walking up and down the halls with him. The pains hadn't come back again. "I feel a little as though I were leaning on the shovel handle when I had a job to do," she said. "Or like sleeping in and being late for school. Only this time there isn't anything I can do."

The third day with no results she told him that she felt foolish and ridiculous. That afternoon they stopped their wandering down the halls, and got Miss Hardy's permission to slip out through the service entrance at the rear of the hospital to talk with privacy under the trees there.

"Harry's promised results," she told Matt. "Tonight."

"The baby will be born tonight?"

"That's what *he* says, dear. Don't rely on me."

"But how can he—how can they . . ."

"I think they'll give me something to speed things up."

"Is that—do they do that . . .?"

"Matt, I'm all right. I'll be all right. It'll be a quite normal birth. It's not *me* that Harry's worried about. There's another confinement came in yesterday—kidney complications, I think. That was the door with the 'Do Not Disturb' sign on it. He doesn't think he'll be able to bring the mother . . . Oh, Matt—we're so damn lucky!"

"All right, dear."

"It's an Indian woman, from the reserve, Magdelene Powderface. I guess she's . . . Harry says it's bad enough when they bring them in. But this woman's—oh, Matt, my darling, hang around . . ."

"All right, Ruth."

"And don't worry!"

"All right, Ruth."

But Harry had sent him home, and he had fallen shamefully asleep on the living-room couch, to be awakened by Miss Hardy's phone call.

Through the April morning woven with birds' cries he had run past Oliver's store, Wing's Palm Café, all the stores with their blind windows, past the lumber yard, then to the hospital street cool with dew that lay upon the lawns, racing through the dawn's faint sounds and half-lights, up the hospital steps.

"Miss Hardy!"

"Oh, Mr. Stanley." She looked up from her desk.

"How is she!"

"She's fine. I was just phoning you."

"Is she—what is it?"

"If you'll go to the waiting-room . . ."

"But I want to . . ."

"You can't see her yet. Shouldn't for a while—she hasn't come out of the case . . ."

He turned at the sound of a door opening down the hall, saw that two nurses were wheeling out a patient.

"Matt."

He turned back to Harry, in white, rubbing his hands. "She's all right, Matt."

"Oh, Harry! What is it!"

"I think there's someone else would like to tell you that, Matt."

Harry nodded towards the stretcher coming down the hall toward them. As it came to him, Matt looked down upon Ruth's face, drawn, glistening with perspiration. Her eyes were closed; the white sheet moved, her body under it rippling with faint shudders.

"Ruth—Ruth! Oh, my darling Ruth!"

Still spasmodic under the sheet, she opened her eyes. "Matt?" He could barely hear her.

He bent down. "Yes, Ruth."

"She's—uh—girl . . ."

"Oh, darling!"

"Guh—goh-ing—grow—hup—buh-better—any—guh—goddam man . . .!"

It was hard now to recall with any sense of immediacy a time when she had not been. Almost as difficult to remember her as a baby. It was as though the present held its own child so vividly that the younger one must fade and withdraw further and further to her sad vanishing-point.

When a father had finally discovered this, he had discovered the fact of his own mortality.

He knew that he and Ruth had quarrelled over more than whether or not he had made an error of taste in doing the dog obituaries. They had quarrelled over a discontentment he had not admitted to himself, a yeasting sense of inadequacy that Ruth was quite unfairly blaming June for. What was it June had said in her talk to Rotary? Something about an individual's fixing himself in a satisfying relationship to his society? What a lovely and empty statement! How did you fix yourself in a satisfying relationship with masses of people? It was like love, wasn't it? One at a time. Someone you knew, someone near and dear. You could love your wife, but it was difficult to love the town council. You could like Harry Fitzgerald or Joe Manley but not the IODE or the Activarians or the . . . You could love your little girl, but a hell of a busy job you'd have getting amorous about all Shelby and Shelby district ranchers or farmers, or the congregation of St. Aidan's. His mission in life was to fix himself in a satisfying relationship with his wife and his daughter and his friends, and that, up to now, was what he had done.

He'd better get home to Ruth.

Mame Napoleon had left and it was late now for anyone to be dropping in to the office. She supposed she ought to leave for the suite, tidy up, and go to dinner at the Palm Café, but the processed records were building up rather alarmingly, and should be checked off as soon as possible before they lost their freshness.

Not that Mame Napoleon was likely to lose any freshness. Ferris wheel! Did the woman do it deliberately? Not deliver herself of children on Ferris wheels, of course, but present such a drily casual façade to the world. She had to admit that she had been startled.

"Prenatal influence. Byron, he's the only one of my kids was born on top of a Ferris wheel," Mame had said.

"What!"

"Byron was born Dominion Day—first of July, nineteen hunderd an' forty-six."

"On top of a Ferris wheel!"

"That's right."

"But how did—why . . .?"

"Britch presentation."

"But—on a Ferris wheel . . .?"

"All my kids but one was britch. Oh—it's my fault. Way Byron isn't scared of anything. I never been as strict with Byron as I been with the others—him bein' born that way on top of a Ferris wheel—about him bein' foolhardy the way he is. He'd naturally take more chances than a kid wasn't born on a Ferris wheel. Wouldn't he?"

"I suppose he would."

"He was an' he has been."

"But how did it happen?"

"What?"

"Byron's being born on a . . ."

"Oh, the Ferris wheel stopped."

"Yes?"

"Mechanical trouble. We never did get good Ferris wheels at our fairs. When this one stopped, me an' Rory was left swingin' on the top seat."

"Yes."

"For quite a while. When we paid our tickets an' went up, it was just Rory an' me. When they got her goin' again, an' we come down, it was Rory an' me an' Byron."

"I see."

"Mostly my fault," said Mame. "Fair was almost over an' I told Rory I wanted just one more ride before we went home. I guess it was just one ride too many." She stopped. "Ah, Miss Melquist, wouldn't that be a little too personal for your book?"

"Oh, yes," she said quickly. "I was just interested."

"You know," Mame said, "it gives a person a good feelin' in a way."

"What does?"

"Findin' out from you an' the Senator how there's—how a person, he's part of a whole herd. Knowing that there's proba'ly hunderds, thousands of folks just exac'ly like the Napoleons all over the world."

She had stared hard for a moment at Mame then, trying to discover whether the woman meant more than she had

said. But Mame had not, she knew now; the woman meant
only exactly what she said, and she said it with surprising
clarity most of the time, perhaps because so little personal
concern seemed to muddy her outlook—or inlook.

All the same—on a Ferris wheel! She must check on
Monday with Matt. She selected a card from the file box by
the typewriter, then paused. If her own mother had possessed some of Mame's insouciance, things might have
been easier—no emotions boiling all over like a kettle
unwatched on a stove. No demanding affection, insisting on
dutiful and distasteful embraces—the guilty feeling of
owing your mother love and knowing that you would
always welsh on the debt.

It was two weeks now and three letters unanswered.

She picked up the card again. Even Nettie Fitzgerald
would have been preferable—whatever she was, Nettie had
a hard strength. Mustn't let Nettie's strength fade. She took
up her typing.

> . . . between the rest and the select group of village
> aristocrats who, because of their common geographical
> situation in the community, are commonly referred to
> as the "North-siders." There is actually little cultural
> superiority in this group from which cultural and social
> leadership should come. The Foothills Sketch Society,
> the Shelby Annual and Perennial Society, the Shelby
> Historical Landmarks, District Shrines, and Old Timers'
> Association, may seem contradictory and tangential
> aspects, but are in fact of little cultural magnitude; they
> are important rather for the degree of prestige they
> confer and as evidence of membership in the elite.
>
> Most of those questioned have rather limited tastes
> in music, the visual arts, and in reading; they afford an
> education in lower-class tastes and values. It is an
> inevitable consequence that the majority are hardly
> conscious of good books, though a few may criticize
> themselves for not finding time to read them. Exami-
> nation of the basic pattern that emerges in this regard
> reveals that any correlation with class and status
> factors, or education for that matter, is quite illusory.
>
> Let us turn now from anomalies that may cut across

our convenient abstractions and consider briefly the model man—35.7 years of age, shop owner, renter in the retail trades, farm or ranch operator, with a wife 33.1 years of age, 1.5 children. He has a median education of 2.3 years of High School . . .

CHAPTER 12

RUTH HAD BEEN REASONABLE, JUST AS HE HAD KNOWN SHE would be; she had agreed that they had made too much of something that June had nothing to do with. He had been feeling low and should have had no uncertainties about his work—no self-doubts. He had a long way to go before he would be in Joe's state; *his* lamp would never burn low and smoke with tired discontent. For that matter, hadn't she noticed Joe lately; he had become more like the old Joe of their first acquaintance. And, look how the rest of the town had come to terms with June. She was an acquired taste they had learned in a surprisingly short time.

Actually, Matt told himself on his way to the office Monday morning, she was now a matter of offhand pride. After all, she had selected their town out of a whole province as a target for her survey. Wherever she went she was greeted by most with a nod, a comment on the weather, a solicitous inquiry on the progress of her work. You could trust the town; at least he liked to think you could trust the town.

June was not in the office when he arrived, but when he returned at noon she was at her desk.

"How did you make out with Mame?" he asked her.

"Fine. Oh, that was something I wanted to ask you about. She told me a rather startling thing after you left."

"Yes?"

"About Byron. It's probably true, but I thought I'd check with you . . ."

"Almost anything could be true about Byron."

"Was he really born on a Ferris wheel?"

"Oh." He had expected anything but that, and for the life of him he didn't know how he was going to answer her. When Harry had told him years ago, it had taken his breath away; he guessed it had taken Harry's breath away at the time. "She'd promised me, Matt—on her word of honour—no more, not another one. I knew it wasn't much good getting Rory fixed—not that I'm a cynical man—but I had a feeling, a strong one, that this time I was going to get her into that hospital. And then she comes to me and it's too late. Six months too late."

"Then it's not true," June said now.

"Mmmmh!" She had taken his silence for a negative answer.

"It isn't true that Byron was born on a Ferris wheel on Dominion Day."

"Does it really matter?" he said. "It isn't a very rich sociological plum, is it?"

"No, I'm just curious. I'd like to know why she should go out of her way—so far out—to tell me that, to lie . . ."

"Oh, she wasn't lying."

"Then Byron *was* born on a Ferris wheel."

"No—he wasn't."

"She didn't tell me the truth?"

"She did—in a way."

"Matt, you can't tell the truth 'in a way.' Either she was lying or she wasn't lying."

"No," he said. "Mame is not an easy liar . . ."

"Then why should she tell me . . .?"

"She was being considerate."

"How do you mean, considerate?"

"Considerate of you, really."

"By lying to me!" When he had some difficulty answering her, she said, "Was Byron even born on Dominion Day?"

"No," Matt said, "Byron was born . . ." He drew in his breath and released it. "Byron was born exactly nine months *after* Dominion Day."

"Oh."

He looked down to his desk top as he felt his face flushing. He could hear Harry's bewildered voice of years ago: " 'Mostly my fault this time, Doc. I always been fussy about the Ferris wheel,' " she said to me. 'Fair was almost over an' I told Rory I'd like one more ride before we went home. Ferris wheel broke down. We never did get a good-type Ferris wheel at our fairs, you know. An' there was Rory an' me with the motor broke down an' our seat swingin' from the top of midnight for a good hour. What else was there for us to . . .?' "

Matt heard his office door snick shut.

She knew of no more terrible feeling than that of being left out. With an uncontrollable sinking of her heart she could recall her first year at St. Catherine's, a great part of it spent in the infirmary, since the isolation of a ranch childhood had bequeathed her a Pandora's box of chicken pox, measles, mumps, scarletina, to be released as soon as she left home and associated with other children. In classroom and schoolyard that year of periodic isolation she had been simply an onlooker, the always uninvited one around whose waist no friendly arm circled, upon whose ear no delicious confidences fell.

In her own home now it was disconcerting to have the memory of that unhappy time return to her, which had happened to her several times recently. In some way inexplicable to her, it had to do with June Melquist. It was also, she told herself, unreasonable and silly and small of her to think so. Perhaps she envied the other woman her cool self-possession, and she shouldn't; a person should not indulge herself in such emotional unfairness.

She felt helpless to explain to herself why it was that June Melquist seemed to bring out the worst in her; unless it was the woman's unflagging yet unobtrusive reticence, there was nothing specifically she *disliked* about her. How could you dislike her; she gave nothing of herself to like or dislike. You knew nothing of her home, her parents, whether or not she had brothers or sisters. Had she taken piano lessons as a little girl? Gone to Sunday school— Methodist, Baptist, Presbyterian, Catholic? Did she consider baking bread basic? And Thurber and Emily Dickinson, Edna Millay? Whatever else was she or had she been besides a listener?

She was listening now to Joe Manley standing in his favourite place by their fireplace hearth, one knee kinked, an elbow resting on the mantel, his lean face intent, hair lifting slightly from the back of his head like the crest of some wading birds. It was what Ruth had long thought of as his "holding forth" pose, putting her in mind of a declamatory heron. He was speaking on the extremely intimate nature of small-town life:

"Everyone knows almost to the cent my monthly salary with allowances for pension deduction and Teachers' Association dues."

"Yes, Joe," she said, "and they would know if you were sick or in need of help."

"Or any exploits"—Joe turned toward her—"I might have along the river road."

"Look at how all the neighbours seeded the Parker section for them south of town," Ruth said stubbornly, "after the drill wheel fell on Mr. Parker's hip. They turned out to harvest his crop in the fall when he went to Rochester."

"They're probably the same people who are capable of raking up the thirty-year-old suicide of a father, the dementia praecox strain in a family, the manipulation of lumberyard funds . . ."

"Joe," she said angrily, "you're exaggerating!"

"No, I'm not. Friendly gossip isn't so interesting, Ruth."

"Perhaps it isn't, but it's not so vindictive as you're implying . . ."

"Maybe I am," Joe said negligently. "You would know better than I—being born here. I'm more fortunate that way."

She was wondering how the conversation had taken this

odd and menacing turn—for her out of all proportion to the words on the surface.

"Why are you, Joe?"

"My childhood's mercifully hidden in the past. Can't be dragged out and used against me. Living in a small town is just like taking up residence in the underwear section of the Hudson's Bay catalogue. I hate to have Mrs. Nelligan see me that way, but that's how she does. Just like one of those men with a foot up on a chair, wearing only reinforced-at-points-of-strain underwear, chin in hand, with that terribly determined air of carelessness—or perhaps with arms up and over one shoulder as though about to hit a golf ball. Or else we've got our arms clenched behind our backs in professional-strong-man poses. No, there's a whole group of us, and we've got that muted seriousness of pall-bearers—and we're quite ignorant that only our underwear stands between us and the eyes of the town. Lucky we got our underwear on."

Perhaps humans should be permitted to go about their living without the stealthy magic of gossip stripping them to their combinations. And perhaps Matt and Joe did sometimes feel as though they lived on glossy catalogue pages, but it was disloyal of them to make so much of it in front of Dr. Melquist. Conversations like this had become much too frequent, she felt. They made her feel helpless and inadequate, and reminded her that she was not nearly so clever as they were. But the way you felt about your town and neighbours wasn't a matter so much of intelligence, was it? It was a matter of familiarity and faith, as simple as breathing and waking each morning in the same house, and talking again and again with the same people.

Even though these conversations were light-hearted, Matt had been seduced into a careless attitude that bothered her; their amusement about the town had a ring of arrogance in which she couldn't indulge. Joe was more the sinner than Matt, yet she could forgive Joe sooner, since he was not her husband and since it was quite evident now to anyone that he was in love with June. The signs were countless: the way his face came to life when she entered the room, the extra care for his clothes, the extra attention for whatever June was saying.

Yes, she could forgive him more easily than she could Matt, but at the same time she could be impatient with his ingenuousness. There was really no excuse for mirroring feelings so clearly. He wasn't eighteen, and dignity was lost in letting the whole thing float transparently to the surface, especially when there was not a trace to indicate how June might feel. She had often hoped that Joe would find someone before it was too late. She couldn't help hoping that; she abhorred an unmarried man just as nature abhorred a vacuum, but better a bachelor vacuum than the hopeless and unrequited fondness this would most likely turn out to be.

So she did have more than a sentimental annoyance with the woman; Joe was an important person to her and to Matt; he mustn't be hurt. Perhaps, she argued with herself, she had too great an emotional stake in the town and in her friendship for Joe Manley. Her concern for both might be out of all reasonable proportion to the reality of the threat she imagined for them. And to be completely honest about it, why had she been so careful to hide her concern? She must have been a little ashamed of it or unsure of it, and that was what upset her most about it—that she had for almost the first time in their married life hidden something from Matt. Hidden was too strong—she had been mildly defensive and restrained.

Emotion never solved anything, she warned herself, even as the sail of her feeling spluttered with annoyance, snapped round, jibing and bellying full with anger. Damn the cold woman, anyway, with her horizontal and vertical groupings of people. At least, she supposed, the woman did group them horizontally and vertically, because if she didn't, then it had been a very dull evening wasted with the sociology text she'd managed to get from the town library three weeks ago. What an unfortunate terminology, as though people could be arranged end to end or stacked upon each other like cordwood, or simply thrown into impersonal heaps!

She'd take her Shelby people—the Fitzgeralds and the Tregillises, Canon Midford and Sam Barnes and Clem

Derrigan and Daddy Sherry—yes, and Mame and Rory Napoleon, she thought, with a rush of protective affection. On ranch and farm and village she'd take them all ahead of the vaguely homeless ones: the travelling salesmen lying on their narrow hotel beds in strange towns, staring up to alien ceilings and bare light bulbs; the coffee-counter lonely ones, the neon-light hermits, and the boarding-house dwellers and the apartment denizens. It had begun to sound in her mind like one of Hersch Midford's all-inclusive invocations as though to an only partly attentive God in church: the non-attenders, the ailing and the old, at home and abroad.

Even though she was pretty certain her judgment had only shallow, emotional roots, and was little more than inarticulate protest, she knew she was right.

So! She'd been right about Miss Melquist from the very first, while she'd been staying here at Aunt Fan's. It had been way last month past midnight when she'd heard the footsteps on the stairs, then past her door and down to the end of the hall. Two sets! And then the voices, and she knew the lighter one was Miss Melquist's right away, and soon after, that the deep one was Joe Manley's. And then she couldn't hear the voices for quite a while and she knew that Joe had gone right into the suite with her, because she didn't hear his footsteps coming back down the hall.

Then she'd heard just the male footsteps going past her door and then down the stairs. He hadn't been in there more than a few minutes. It took a lot longer than that. Never happened that fast in *Alluring Love* or *I Confess*, but he *had* been in there with her, and it was just the *first* time, but now they both had their suites at Mrs. Nelligan's there'd be another time and another and then another . . . And this was the kind of woman Matt had in his office, winding him around her finger and acting like she owned the place. And having all kinds of people in there when she was by herself on Saturday afternoon. Mame Napoleon lolling all over *her* chair! Even if she hadn't happened to walk by and look in through the glass door, she'd have known Mame had been in there on her chair. She'd have smelled it when she came to the office this morning!

And how come she was so chummy with the Napoleons! Fine kind of people for her that pretended to be so genteel and high-toned. Look at the way Matt was doing all he could about the dog-poisoning and all the time she was chatting away and having Mame in his office and there wasn't any doubt who was up and down back alleys all day long and who had to gather up all the garbage dogs dumped out of the garbage cans tipped over. It was easy for Rory to drop out poisoned meat as he went along behind people's homes as nice as you please doing his job. That way he could clean out a whole block of dogs and there wouldn't be as many dumped garbage cans any more. She'd known for a long time and she'd told Aunt Fan over a month back and Aunt Fan had asked her who it was and she hadn't told her then but she'd told her Sunday, the day after Miss Melquist had Mame Napoleon into the office sitting on her chair. Aunt Fan had been shocked and wanted to know how she knew it was Rory Napoleon so she'd told Aunt Fan about the dogs dumping over Rory's garbage cans and Aunt Fan said oh, she didn't think it could be Rory Napoleon, but it was, all the same.

A lot Aunt Fan knew about what went on in Shelby. She thought everybody and everything was so sweet and lovely. She wouldn't if she'd ever worked on a telephone switchboard—especially night shift. Then she'd know all about Willie Baker's conversation with Gracie Carlyle and about Taylor's straw stack! Gracie had gone away to the coast for a year, then come back pale and harried-looking; Gracie's married sister in New Westminster had adopted a baby daughter and Millie missed her guess if that baby didn't look a lot like Gracie or Willie.

There was just as much stuff went on in Shelby's Shady Motel as went on in *Alluring Love*. That city dry-goods salesman had a steady glowing flame in his dark eyes, she bet, as he swept Mrs. Laura Partridge into his arms out on the river road. She was pretty sure Mrs. Partridge didn't feel the tiniest stab of guilt as she was kissed hungrily, passionately, yet with warm tenderness underneath.

And here she was tapping away on that typewriter, looking so sweet and pure just like she hadn't done it with Joe the night before. But she wasn't going to put up with her

messing up files and running the paper and bossing people
around! Last week Mr. Sheppard had stopped her in front of
the Palm and asked her to come back to the telephone
office, where she belonged. They needed girls like her, he'd
said. Trained and experienced, he'd said. At pay twice as
much as she was getting with Matt. And no Miss Melquist
breathing down her neck. She'd said to Mr. Sheppard she'd
think about it.

Just let her pull anything more and she'd see; she didn't
have to take anything from her if she didn't want to.

Not that it was Matt's fault; it wasn't his fault at all. It
took a woman to see through Miss Melquist—right through.
It wouldn't be fair to go and leave Matt in the lurch just
because of her. He needed her in the office, and she'd stick
with him the way she had for three years, even if he did pay
her half what she could get from the telephone company.

But in a way it had been more exciting on the switchboard those years with all the voices from all over the
district.

She heard the typewriter over there begin to tap again.
She wondered how long it did take anyway.

CHAPTER 13

ACTUALLY, MATT EXPLAINED TO JUNE, THE SHELBY FAIR, Light Horse Show, and Little Britches Rodeo began for the town at least ten days before the most important day of its life: July 1.

"You've noticed the number of Indians in town the past few days?"

"Yes, but there always seem to be some on the streets."

"More than usual now. During the rest of the year they go in to Mable Ridge—it's ten miles nearer the reserve. Not that they're on the reserve much now. Camped with their families on the ranches, haying and fencing."

"They work for the ranchers?"

"Oh, yes—off and on, from branding to bringing cattle out of the forest reserve in the fall."

He explained to June that they were good cow and horse men. Only during the rodeo did they come into the town en masse, children spilling out of hay-wired buckboards and democrats, the women holding the lines, the men herding ponies behind.

"Most of them are at the Rodeo Grounds now," he said. "I'm going out there if you want to come along."

Just as they got into his car, a gold and royal blue trailer rolled by the office.

" 'Professor Noble Winesinger's Travelling Clinic and Academy of Scientific Education,' " Matt read from the trailer's side. "The fair spirit has entered the town."

"What do you mean?"

"With the Indians and Professor Winesinger . . ." He started the car up. "Oh—and the oldest old-timer. Daddy Sherry. He's part of the Shelby Fair spirit too, I think."

On their way to the grounds he explained that Daddy, with his Fenian Raid, Riel Rebellion, and Boer War ribbons, had this year been selected by the fair board for the honour of leading the parade behind a matched pinto team in the phaeton that stood by Malleable Jack Brown's blacksmith shop between fairs.

"He's claimed the distinction for the past fifteen years but it's always gone to Doug Hunter."

"Doug Hunter is older?"

"No. No doubt Daddy's been older—by about twelve years—but in the past Doug's had proof of his age in the birth date entered in his family Bible. Daddy hasn't."

As long as Matt had been in Shelby, Daddy had been unsuccessful in winning over the fair board by telling them how he had come West by shrieking Red River cart in '72, when the town had been simply a whiskey-runners' fort at the crossing where the CPR bridge now stood. Luckily, lobar pneumonia had taken Doug and his family Bible out of competition last winter—forever.

"Actually it should have been Daddy all along. But up till this year Oliver's been head of the fair board and he's a stickler for rules and regulations, and in the 'eye of the low' twelve years' more age means nothing without proof. This year Harry Fitzgerald runs things."

"What was Mr. Hunter's age?"

"Ninety-five."

"What!"

"Doug had just turned ninety-five when he died."

"But that would make Mr.—Daddy Sherry . . ."

"A hundred and seven."

"But he couldn't be."

"Here we are." He stopped the car inside the gates. "We'll have to walk the rest of the way. Always rains just before the fair and rodeo so the grounds are a swampy—"

"Matt—a hundred and seven . . ."

"He is, though. Come on."

Ahead of them they could see the five teepees spearing up beyond the stock pens and the rodeo judge's platform. At some distance from the Indian encampment, the sun glinted from a long yellow and blue trailer still hooked behind a red Cadillac. As they reached it, the tall, lean figure of Professor Winesinger emerged.

"Well, Professor. Nice to see you again another year."

"Good day," the Professor greeted him in a deeply beautiful voice. "Bless you, sir."

"Same to you, Professor. Professor, I'd like you to meet Dr. Melquist."

There was a brief hesitation before the Professor bowed to June. "How do you do, Doctor." He turned to Matt. "I'm afraid you have the advantage of me. We've met but . . ."

"Stanley, Matt Stanley. I have the newspaper here—my wife's father . . ."

"Oh, yes." The moustache and trim beard parted in a red little smile. "The Senator. I always look forward as I roll across the prairies to seeing the cowboy Senator once more. Means we're both still alive. He is?"

"Yes," Matt said.

"Fine, fine." He glanced sideways towards June. "Ah—you're a doctor . . ."

June smiled. "Social sciences."

"Indeed." The Professor's own smile widened. He turned to Matt. "The Senator wintered well?"

Matt nodded. "Pretty good year for him, I think. How's it been for you?"

The Professor shrugged. "Fair—fair. It hasn't varied much from year to year since the drought period. In the long trail from Manitoba I can always depend on a rich harvest of gall bladders. Across the border and into the Moosomin country of Saskatchewan, my goitre territory was not disappointing. Kidney stones held up this year, and there's always arthritis. I didn't do quite so well as other years in the post-nasal drip and bronchitis country of Arcola or on my annual side trip into the rheumatic district of Filmore, but around Crocus I found hemorrhoids, ruptures, and quinsy rampant. The Swift Current and Maple Creek line was wonderful for sinusitis, and in Foxhole, Medicine Hat, Grassy Lake, and Fort Macleod I had the highest slipped-disc incidence of my entire career."

As they left the Professor, Matt was thinking that Ruth's father had known the old charlatan for almost fifty years. "He must be about the last of his kind on the continent," he said to June as they walked toward the Indian tents.

"Which is one thing you can chalk up to progress," she said.

To Matt the Senator had justified his liking for the Professor by saying that he sold much more than the contents of his bottles of Lightning Penetration Oil and Tune-up Tonic as he cast the spell of his voice over the upturned faces of his listeners, peeling up the sheets like the layers of an onion from his chart of the human body.

"Well, there's this, June—his effect is limited to the range of his voice. Difference between a scallywag in a small puddle and the scallywag in the ocean of national radio and press and television."

She did not answer him as she stood by the rope corral with its herd of Indian ponies, all quite thin with hip bones poking. He saw her look beyond them to a group of Indians, extra-lean men in tight-legged blue Levi's that seemed to hold permanently the kink of their knees. He led June over to one of the tents, where three women sat upon the ground, legs straight out ahead of them. Just before they left, a woman he did not know came over and tried for a snapshot. The Indian women as one threw themselves forward, flipping their shawls over their heads. As in other years, the Leroy Studios would develop many fine studies of buck-skinned legs protruding from what had the appearance of heaps of old clothes. Only the very small children would stare out from photographs for the family album, Matt told June as they walked back to his car.

"What's the attitude of people toward the Indians?" she asked him.

"Oh, I don't know, not much of any attitude really."

"Ignore them?"

"No, not exactly. It's just that they don't enter into our life much—one way or the other . . ."

"But they must—to some extent."

"Shelby isn't their town really. Mable Ridge is—further west and closer to the reserve."

"How about Mable Ridge people?"

"They take them in their stride. I've heard a few complaints from a couple of Mable Ridge merchants that Stonys don't make good charge customers—but I think both stores still give them a certain amount of credit, afraid the other competitor will get the business if they don't."

"Mm-hmh."

"I'm pretty sure there are two prices for merchandise there—high one for Indians."

"That's a sort of discrimination, isn't it."

"Self-protection, I'd say. They are poor credit risks, and when the merchant computes his accounts with them, even with the mark-up he doesn't make much. I don't think they make an exorbitant amount from Indians."

"Have you ever seen any discrimination? You know—in conversation do you ever hear people make disparaging remarks about . . .?"

"Nope. You can't take the Indians and give us a colour problem."

"I'm not trying to."

"He's not the Negro, and Shelby isn't the Southern States or South Africa."

"I didn't say it was. But he is an underprivileged person. He has no vote, can't drink by law, has no self- determination. You say they work for the ranchers—surely you must have heard ranchers . . ."

"Sam Barnes has told me he couldn't have operated during the war years if it hadn't been for the Indians."

"I see. How does Sam feel about Hutterites?"

"Hutterites? I don't know."

"What's the feeling about Hutterites in Shelby? Surely they enter into community life."

"Well—it's a little different there, I guess. I imagine there's some feelings."

"Of intolerance?"

"I don't know whether you could call it intolerance or not."

"What would you call it?"

"Look, you can't have a bunch of people whose way of

life is so—so different—living in their colonies, speaking German, beards, caracul hats, shawls and polka dot aprons. They were pacifists during the war—they set themselves apart and they are apart from the rest."

"I know."

"But I don't think a person should accuse the rest of the community of intolerance."

"What about the discriminatory land-purchase law that keeps them from acquiring property the same as anyone else?"

"That's a provincial regulation. Shelby didn't do that to them."

"But Shelby's part of the province. Have you heard anyone speak against the provincial regulation in regard to Hutterite land purchase?"

"Yes. I have."

"Who?"

"My father-in-law. Canon Midford. Joe."

"But I imagine most of the people had no objections against it."

"Look, most of the people know the Hutterites about as well as they know the Stony Indians."

"Ignorance is frequently a good beginning for intolerance."

"And they probably go for months without once thinking about Hutterites. When I said there was some feeling, I meant the odd farmer envious of their land holdings, business men disgruntled because they deal directly with wholesale houses instead of the local stores."

"When the province put through the special legislation making it impossible for Hutterites to acquire more land for new colonies, did you do anything?"

"What do you mean?"

"Did you support it in your paper?"

"I didn't support it and I didn't attack it."

"Did you approve of it?"

"I did—I do and I don't. I can see that it's not good for them to live in their colonies isolated from the rest of us. At the same time I feel as Hersch and the Senator do about the land-purchase regulations. Perhaps I should have written something about it. I didn't. This was an omission on my part—but not to be taken as evidence of an intolerance toward the Hutterites by me or by the majority of Shelby."

"All right. All right, Matt. I believe you."

Now how had they got onto that track—all the way from Professor Winesinger and his Lightning Penetration Oil and Tune-up Tonic to whether or not he should have done something in the *Chinook* about community intolerance of Hutterites. He hadn't done anything because there hadn't been any—no, that wasn't quite true. There was intolerance in a few people—but only those he had mentioned to her.

The conversation was still disturbing him when he dropped into Harvey Hoshal's for a haircut after lunch. Like most of the other business men in town, Harvey was wearing a string tie and brilliant shirt, a radiant orange with black pearl buttons. Harvey clinked as he moved between the instrument counter and the chair. Harvey didn't do things by halves and would wear his spurs till the Shelby Fair, Light Horse Show, and Little Britches Rodeo was over.

"Harvey," Matt said as the barber was fitting the tissue strip around his neck, "what do you think of Hutterites?"

"Hooterites?" Harvey reached for the sheet and gave it a shake-out. "I'll tell you one thing. It isn't many shaves I sell the buggers." He tucked the sheet around Matt's shoulders. "Against their religion. 'Cordin' to them the Bible says it's a sin to put a razor to your face. Always meant to look it up for myself. Never did. An' I guess that's because maybe I'd hate to find out they were right. Knock the props right out from under my business, you might say."

He turned away from Matt; then the clippers took up their hum. "Some the fellows aren't too fussy about them—never buying anything locally. Well, that's their business, I say. I happen to know there's plenty our own business men drive up to the city once a week an' load up with their week's groc'ries. They buy their suits there, their kids' clothes—that's their privilege. I don't hold it against them an' I don't hold it against the Hooterites. Shade to the south, Matt."

And that pretty well summed up how most people in Shelby felt, Matt told himself, but somehow he had the feeling that it was not a fair answer to June's questions. She was right in wondering why he had not done a piece in the paper at the time of the land legislation. As he walked past the crude manger constructed on the street before the Arlington Arms, he was wondering why he hadn't. He brushed by the hitching-post that stood before Oliver's Trading Company Store. Was it possible there were all kinds of things he was overlooking, spending his energies on trivial issues like whether spring came first to Shelby or spring came first to Mable Ridge, investing the death of dogs with the dignity of human deaths?

The town had awakened to the almost immediate brilliance of a July morning bright with the song of birds, sparkling with the diamond and amber and ruby glint of dewdrop on blade and leaf and stem. It was the traditionally fine weather the town enjoyed for the Shelby Fair, Light Horse Show, and Little Britches Rodeo, the party of the year. Other parties were held annually: the church suppers, the Activarians' Winter Carnival, the Santa Claus Visits Shelby Party, the Foothills District Bonspiel of the Shelby Chapter of the Caledonian Society of Knock-out Curlers. But this was the main party of them all, when townspeople, farmers to the east, ranchers to the west, Stony Indians from Paradise Reserve, and tourists on their way to the city Stampede, would all for one day be distilled to the eight acres of the Rodeo Grounds.

"It should be right down your sociological alley," Matt said to June. "It's a sort of one-day-mushroom society." On the Rodeo Grounds, he told her, she would find *State*, pomp and provincial circumstance represented by Mayor Oliver and other political dignitaries; and *Church*, with the various Ladies' Auxiliary feeding-booths; while the Royal Canadian Mounted Police, in the canary and crimson of dress uniforms, with carnival brilliance would symbolize *Law* among the rides and games of chance. Almost all the usual hungers would be taken care of right on the grounds, with rest tents for the young and the old and the tired and the suckling.

Millie and June and Joe Manley and the Senator and Clem Derrigan on folding chairs on the walk before the

Chinook office watched the parade at ten in the morning, led by Daddy Sherry in the phaeton behind the matched pintos. For the first time since Matt had married his daughter, the Senator was not in the parade itself, his arthritis having settled in the small of his back, so that he couldn't climb on a horse, and if he couldn't get into a saddle, he said, he was damned if he was going to ride in a limousine with a bunch of people everybody knew to be too old and brittle to fork a horse. Ruth was missing from their party, for she had gone early to the Rodeo Grounds to prepare for the tea that would be served later by her Bridge, Flower, Book, and Discussion Club in the octagonal-shaped Grain Exhibits and Handicrafts Building. The little triangular sandwiches, cakes, cookies, brownies, and ladyfingers were a conscientious bonus to those who paid twenty-five cents for wandering past the tables of entries in the Annual Perennial and Annual Flower Show.

"Rowena's taking over Sarah, Matt," she'd told him. "The morning's your own. But after that you've got Sarah so that Rowena can go in the afternoon. And it would be nice if you could make sure Dad's settled with his friends in the Old Timers' tent, after he's taken in the quarter horses and judged the Flower Show. I'm worried about his back."

When the Indians and the cowgirls and cowboys and chuckwagons, the floats of the implement companies, of the Boy Scouts and Girl Guides, of the stores and garages, Four H Clubs, Activarians—when all had passed the *Chinook* building and wound through the rest of the business section, by the hospital so that the patients could see the parade from their opened windows, Matt's party went out to the Rodeo Grounds, where Mayor Oliver would open the thirty-ninth Shelby Fair, Light Horse Show, and Little Britches Rodeo. He opened it without disappointing or upsetting anyone, for all had heard before the same solemn clichés from their federal Member, from their Premier, from Mayor Oliver himself on many community occasions. He did not open the thirty-ninth Shelby Fair, Light Horse Show, and Little Britches Rodeo single-handed. He was assisted either by addresses from or simply by the presence on the platform of: the Deputy Minister of Economic Affairs and Co-ordinator of Provincial Culture, the President of the Rotary

Club, the President of the Activarians, the President of the
Loyal Order of Homesteaders, and the President of the
Shelby and Greater Shelby District Emergency and Disaster
Relief and Civil Defence Committee. Ranked with him
behind the public-address microphone were: the Quarter
Horse Association Inspector for Texas, California, Okla-
homa, Wyoming, and Montana, representatives from the
Bare-Back Riders of North America, the Stock Saddle
Riders of North America, the Steer Riders of North Amer-
ica, the Calf Ropers of North America, the Brahma Bull
Riders of North America, and the Steer Decorators of North
America. Behind these were delegates, secretaries, presi-
dents, or vice-presidents of: the Hereford Breeders, the
Shorthorn Breeders, the Appaloosa Breeders, the Palomino
Breeders, the Tennessee Walker Breeders, and Canon
Midford, no breeder but rather Scoutmaster for the Shelby
District Troop Nine of the Boy Scouts.

Joe and June came with Matt and the Senator to see the
quarter horses in the barns, passing and walking beside
cowboys wearing their rodeo numbers in their hats, or
pinned to the backs of their bright satin shirts. Joe pointed
out two of them picking their way bent-kneed over the
sawdust that had been churned into the mud.

"Men off the range," Joe said, "naive and unspoiled—
pitting their determination against the primitive will of the
elements and the cruel vagaries of nature. Simple but honest
and noble thoughts must be theirs—blown through with the
fresh chinooks of mountain draws—flowering like the carpets
of shooting stars and Indian paintbrush on the hills—fresh as
pine and pure as mountain stream . . ."

". . . fuckin' hammer head an' a ewe neck." The man
had crossed just in front of Matt and the Senator who
walked before June and Joe. "I drawn the son of a bitch but
I ain't gonna get any ride out of him. I swear he's mostly
Clyde. That's the trouble these half-assed stampedes." His
voice had a nasal twang alien to Canadian foothills.

"That fellow never saw a branding," the Senator said,
"or a round-up. Acrobats—they're just performing acrobats
traded their trapeze for a mean horse."

Joe left them at the barns; Matt heard him arrange to
meet June after lunch.

When the Senator was sated with horses, they left the barns and started towards the Old Timers' tent.

"Good day, Senator, Matt, Dr. Melquist."

It was Mr. Oliver. They did not stop to talk with him but continued towards the Old Timers' tent.

Meeting the Senator like that and knowing that he was probably on his way to judge the Flower Show made Mr. Oliver feel just a little sick. He had been wonderfully relieved when they had all hurried on their way. It would not have looked good for him to be seen talking with the Senator just before the judging. Not at all.

And he must *not* go near the Grain Exhibits and Handicrafts Building where the flowers would be judged, either. In many ways showing flowers was difficult. It had been a long day since he had got up and walked over his lawn to the flower beds and Walter's cross. He must make a careful selection before the sun had come up to fade their colour, wilt a petal, or carry a prize flower past the peak of its bloom. He had cut his gladioli two days before, just as a tip of colour was peeking through the green bud sheath; he had hung them down in the cool darkness of the basement; he was not worried about how his gladioli would do. They were sure.

Roses. It had been a good snapdragon year; he had six sprays of that lovely bronze variety—straight, close, fat crowding blossoms, the colour like shot silk. He picked six lavender sweet peas for the "Six—One Colour" section, and for the "Six—Mixed" he had half a dozen long-stemmed ones, each with five blossoms. No. Snapdragons and gladioli and sweet peas did not worry him. Roses. They did.

He looked out past Walter's cross and to the brilliant part beyond where the gladioli lifted, each with a lath stake to hold it from the distorting influence of the wind, dogs, small children, and the inexplicable, uncooperative will of nature, which insisted on directing them in every way but the right one: straight up. The stakes were marked in careful printing: Maiden Mist, Sir Wilfrid Laurier, Florence Nightingale, Queen Elizabeth. Then there was a gloriously

salmon flower tinting in its ruffled edges to pink; it had been
a sport three years ago from a common pink variety, and he
had nursed it through the bulblet stage to this climactic year.
Upon *its* lath stake was printed *Minnie*. It was Minnie
Oliver's favourite.

Roses had become more and more satisfying. They
challenged in this country. Actually gladioli were the easiest
to get results with, if one trenched and irrigated, keeping the
chill town water off the plants themselves. But for all their
flashy brilliance, they were not his favourite. Roses were.

He looked down now at the rosary part of the garden,
where among the coarser bush roses bloomed the Brahmin
of all the plants he'd grown, the first hybrid tea he had ever
been able to bring through a winter. He had trenched it,
mulched it, soaked and frozen it for the winter; he had
sprayed it, fed and fertilized it; he had pruned it, staked it,
dusted it, and now it had produced among the others one
superlative bloom which, cut at this precise moment, would
be excellently right by late this afternoon, when the judging
would take place. He bent over it, saw that it held still a
clear bead of dew that trembled as he clipped the stem. It
was a pity the drop would not be cradled there when the
judges looked at it in the Grain Exhibits and Handicrafts
Building. And he must steer clear of them for the rest of the
day. He must. It wouldn't do for him to run into Aunt Fan
as well.

In their special tent between the airplane swings and the
permanent dance pavilion, the old men reminisced on their
benches; apple boxes filled with sawdust had been strategically scattered about over grass unbelievably radiant
under canvas-filtered sunlight. As June and Matt and the
Senator entered the tent, Clem Derrigan and Dave Carter
and Scotty of the Anchor E were recalling the passing of Sid
Bovey half a century before.

Bovey had died quite suddenly in the old Arlington,
with no one near him as he staggered to the bar to celebrate
a spectacular five-under-for-double that had won him
eighty-nine dollars in one hand of Black Jack. He had made
it only to the floor—face down. The Senator had been there

when they lifted him tenderly to the bar top, where his head had come into inadvertent contact with the cash register and had rung up one hundred and ninety-eight dollars and twenty-one cents.

"We figured his heart quit," said Dan James, once foreman of the Turkey Track.

"That's generally what does it." That was Walter Thorpe of the Thorpe and Carberry Cattle Company, which had operated leases only slightly smaller in acreage than Wales.

"We was just rememberin' how Sid Bovey went, Senator," said Clem, his hard apple cheeks glistening in the blue drift of smoke from pipe and cigarette and cigar. "You was there."

The Senator nodded.

"August. Eleventh August nineteen an' three," said Dave Carter. In his pepper-and-salt tweed he could have been any urban octogenarian now retired from the responsibilities of directorate or board or bench or operating-room. Only the crimson kerchief knotted at the throat and the high-heeled boots told that for almost three-quarters of a century he had been a cowman. There was nothing in his ascetic face to show that he had trailed two hundred head of steers to the Klondike, that he had once finished off a wounded grizzly with a fence rail. "Hot. God, she was a hot day—too hot for a man to die in."

"Wouldn't keep long in that weather." There had been little need for Scotty's comment; all of them were remembering how there had been no caskets available in Shelby. Instant burial had been imperative, so they had got a banana crate from behind the Palm. With honest contrition and dead Sid they had started what was now Shelby's cemetery. Perhaps it was the shape of the banana crate, round with a top flaring out like a wastebasket, which had dictated the unorthodox manner of their friend's burial. They had lowered him upright into a seven-foot well, where he had stood the past fifty years in the embrace of earth and banana crate.

Now they recalled old round-ups, and the bad winter of nineteen six and seven that had changed ranching in the

West forever. They mentioned 'Knackers' Johnson and Soapy Smith and Kamoose.

"Remember 'Nigger John' Ware . . ."

"He could ride . . ."

"So could you if you learned as a slave boy—an' a whip for every time you rolled off . . ."

"Well, it was horse an' a gopher hole killed him . . ."

"Mind the time Johnny hokey-poked that remittance Englishman's horse . . ."

"What remittance man?"

"Harrow."

"Our way," said the Senator, "we didn't have a remittance man that wasn't an Oxford graduate and a morganatic cousin of King George."

"That's right," said Clem Derrigan. "One time we had a couple dozen titles ridin' up an' down Paradise Valley alone. We had earls ridin' for the Rockin' E, an' dukes brandin' an' cuttin' on the Diamond T, a duchess cookin' for the AL, second-class lords stackin' an' hayin' an' fencin' for the Bar N . . ."

"And a French count operating the mail route," said the Senator.

"Hell," said Clem, "there was so much purple blood around, winter of ought-two, the weasels all moved East to save their pelts from endin' up in ermine chaps!"

As soon as they had entered the tent, Matt had drawn June to one side and apart from the Senator and his old range friends. He knew that this was the one day in the entire year that she would have a chance to find them together, her only opportunity to listen to them reminiscing at their ease without their usual reticence.

Matt saw the Senator consult his watch. "I've got to get him over to the flowers," he said to June.

"It's a shame to take him away. Let him warm himself a little more with the past."

"Can't. He's half an hour overdue now. I'll leave you with Clem to look after you. For God's sake don't use a notebook on these boys."

"You think I'm crazy!"

"No." He should have guessed that she would know better. "Clem."

"Yeah, Matt?"

"Look after Dr. Melquist. I've got to take the Senator over to the Grain Exhibits and Handicrafts Building . . ."

"Sure—sure." Clem looked at June. "Ain't you feelin' well?"

"She's all right," Matt said. "But I'd like you to make sure she meets Daddy Sherry when he gets here."

"Sure, Matt, sure."

As soon as Matt and the Senator left, the conversation in the tent dampened. It was as though their presence had made them accept her, or at least ignore her. She understood now why Matt had spoken as he had to Clem.

Then there was a stirring near the tent opening and she was no longer worrying about the men and their now laconic quality. She was looking at the oldest human being she had ever seen. She stared at him quite openly as Clem guided him toward her. She was certain that he was the oldest human she would ever see.

Clem helped the old man lower himself to the bench beside her. "Daddy!" he shouted, "this is Dr. Melquist."

The thin shoulders were hunched under the afghan, the hands trembled over the crook of the cane. Daddy gave not the slightest indication that he had heard Clem's introduction.

"Has his good days an' he has his bad days," Clem explained to her. "Today's one of his bad days."

The milky eyes, sunken back into the small ball of a skull, looked straight ahead; their lids slowly hooded over, then slipped up, only to blink deliberately again. He was chinless and turtle-old.

"You ought to talk to him some time, though," Clem advised her. "He's got three wars an' two rebellions under his hide. Just look at them wrinkles, would you. Deep enough to hold a three-day rain."

Far down in Daddy's breast there was born a hoarse sigh; it was a distant, growing ventriloquial sound, arriving finally in a breathy whisper, "Eye-digh-yah-yah—she shouldn't—she shouldn't—loft was full—loft was full—tinder dry—tinder dry—hay." He looked slightly up toward June. "Why'd she do it! Why'd she do it!" It was a passionately frightened plea.

"All right, Daddy," soothed Clem. "It's all right."

"Wasn't!" Daddy lashed out at him. "Takin' a lighted lantern into a barn like that!" The eyes moved from side to side as though trying to escape. "Mary Jane—Mary Jane— why'd you ever—why—eye—digh-digh-digh . . ."—the thin voice trickled away weakly, to fade finally from hearing deep into the core of him again, like the cherry red of heat fainting from iron as it cooled.

"We can set here." Clem was indicating the bench next to Daddy's, slightly removed from the other men.

"How old is he, Mr. Derrigan?" she asked as they sat down.

"Well . . ." Clem looked up to the ridge of the tent. "Daddy claims a hundred an' seven." He sent a rusty stream to the apple box at his side. "I figger he's only about a hundred an' two. He's in the little brown cottage next the CPR bridge. Mrs. Johnston does for him. Daddy, he'll be able to tell you lots about the old days—stuff isn't in the hist'ry books—like General Middleton havin' a bobcat vest, an' Louis Riel when they kep' him in the tent he got the shiverin' shi . . . uh—yeah, you catch him right an' he'll be able to tell you lots."

"I will," she promised. "But how about you?"

"Me!" Clem's apple cheeks flushed even redder; his eyes flicked with embarrassment toward the other men. "Why, I wouldn't have nothin' to—wouldn't do you no good to talk to me—ah—Miss—Doctor . . ."

She smiled at him. "I think it might. When did you come to this country first, Mr. Derrigan?"

"Clem," he said.

"Clem." She waited a moment. "What year did you . . ."

"Ought-four."

"From?"

"Huh?"

"Where did you come from—Clem?"

"Oh—Texas."

When she realized that he had come to a full stop, she said, "What brought you North?"

Clem had crossed one knee over the other, was making

nervous little circles with the foot, head tilted on one side, eyes averted from June. "I just come."

"You came to Shelby district?"

"Nope. Pincher Creek. Then I rode in Maple Creek. Then I come to Shelby. Year the blue snow—ought-six an' -seven."

"Blue snow?"

Clem nodded.

"*Blue* snow."

He looked at her for the first time since the interview had begun. "That's right."

"The snow was *blue*?"

"It was . . . Swift Current an' Maple Creek country. I don't know about the foothills stuff, because I wasn't ridin' out here. I come in the spring. Hooked up with the Senator."

"And you live with him in town now."

"That's right." Clem had uncrossed his legs, leaned forward with elbows on his knees; he seemed more at ease.

"Retired."

Clem looked startled.

"You don't ride any more, Mr. Derrigan." She had done it deliberately. She knew that there had been much more to the blue snow business, that he had refused deliberately to go further into it; she had just as deliberately used the word "retired."

"Well, I . . ."

"You have no ranching interests yourself."

"No, I guess I don't, Miss Melquist. I never exactly thought of it that way though. Retired," he said with distaste.

"Many people retire at an earlier age than yours . . . seventy . . ."

The distaste had become apparent annoyance. "Well, I ain't retired all that much!"

"Of course you aren't." She knew that she had gone too far with him.

"I ride now an' again—keep my hand and my arse in. I can still rope a calf."

"Visit the ranch?"

"Brandin' time. I still got some juice in me. I get up in the hills time to time."

She nodded. He lifted his head slowly and stared at her with steady candour. "An' there's always a girl now and again." He said it so mildly that the effect of his words was delayed. After a surprised pause she matched his light tone:

"Oh, come, Mr. Derrigan, aren't you a little—isn't it a little late in life for you to have an—an *effective* interest in girls." Even before she was through, she knew that she had delivered herself into his hands, for he was grinning widely. It was a grin of recognition and of acceptance; whether it was in the old Arlington or the Klondike or a Sixth Avenue East crib or the Old Timers' tent, Clem knew the only type of woman who would talk with him so.

"Oh, I don't know, Miss Melquist. It might take me a little longer now to have what you call an *effective* interest in girls." His eyes held hers deliberately. "But I don't begrudge the time."

"Mary Jane, Mary Jane," came Daddy's ancient parrot croak, "an' Lucy an' Fannie an' Nettie an' May an' Millie an' Scatterpiss Annie an' then there was Sadie Rolling-in-the-Brown-Blanket—eye-yigh-yigh-dah-dah-dah . . ."

Matt and the Senator had hardly stepped away from the Old Timers' tent when they met Aunt Fan, straw-hatted and wearing an extra ribbon pinned at her bosom next to her hearing-aid; the ribbon said: "OFFICIAL."

"Oh, Senator, Mr. Stanley. So glad I'm not late. If the Senator hasn't got there yet, then I'm not late. Really," she said as she fell into step beside them, "I haven't the right—I shouldn't be a flower judge ahead of Mr. Tregillis, but I don't suppose the bank will let him. They like their managers to stay out of things, don't they?"

Matt agreed that perhaps it might be bank policy to keep branch managers from being judges at flower shows.

"Touchy for them," said Aunt Fan, "like being in politics. Mr. Tregillis is very close-mouthed about it. I don't suppose in all his years in Shelby he's given anyone a hint what he really is."

"I don't suppose," said Matt.

"Obviously not Social Credit or CCF—you don't find bankers who are Social Credit or Socialist."

"It does seem a contradiction in terms," the Senator said.

"So he is either Liberal or Conservative. I imagine Conservative, because he was so annoyed with the baby bonus and the old age pension. I imagine Conservative."

"He's Liberal," the Senator said.

"Really Mr. Oliver should be one of the flower judges," Aunt Fan said. "Bit awkward for him, though; growing flowers he enters flowers, so it would be hard for him to be one of the judges as well. It's all done very honestly. They're set out on the tables and they're quite anonymous. No one knows whose flowers they are at all, do they, Senator?"

"No."

"He always wins in spite of that. Last year it was nice having Mr. Singer to help judge. This year just you and I, Senator. It *is* a responsibility. I should have thought they would have picked *someone* to replace Mr. Singer. In case there was a difference of opinion, then the third would break it. Of course, Mr. Oliver always wins; his gladioli are far superior to the others—you can tell at a *glance* which are Mr. Oliver's gladioli. If he loses out on the sweet peas, he makes up on the snapdragons or the pansies or the mixed bouquet of nine annuals class. For quite a few years there's only been one entry in that—Mr. Oliver's—he's the only person who's managed to *grow* nine different annuals. Sweet peas *are* difficult."

"I guess they are," the Senator said.

"To judge. We must go by the length of the stem in sweet peas, Senator—as well as the brilliance of the blossom and how many blossoms there are. Five are unusual. Don't you think they should trust us to be impartial, and not hide the names the way they do? I believe it was Mr. Oliver's *own* idea. I'm always so worried Mr. Oliver's flowers won't win, because they're the finest and they *should* win. Except for gladioli and for roses, of course. I think the roses are the most important to Mr. Oliver now. It used to be gladioli, but now it's tea roses with him because they're so *difficult* to grow in this country."

They had reached the door of the Grain Exhibits and Handicrafts Building.

"Take it easy, Senator," Matt said. "You're on your own from here."

"They're lovely too," Aunt Fan said.

"Head back for the Old Timers' tent and Clem when you're through," Matt said to the Senator. "I have to go home for Sarah so Rowena will be free to . . ."

"It's only a crick in my back, goddamit," the Senator said. "I'm just going to judge some flowers, not enter a cutting-horse contest!" He turned into the Grain Exhibits and Handicrafts Building with Aunt Fan.

Rowena had not given Sarah her lunch by the time he got home, and the child was so excited about going back to the rodeo with him that he hadn't the heart to make her wait until he had prepared her something. "We'll eat at the rodeo," he promised, to her delight.

He would have thought that the prospect of eating away from home and riding on a merry-go-round would be of lasting brilliance for her, but obviously nothing could stay vivid long to a three-year-old. One block from the house they came upon a woodpecker industriously at work upon the Fitzgerald house. They heard the cobbler-knocking first, then both stood transfixed by the bird fast against the peak front. As it broke off its peremptory labour, Matt saw that Sarah's face was quite stilled, her lips slightly parted; only her head turned as the bird suddenly detached itself from the house and flew low down over the lawn and past them.

They walked on then toward the Rodeo Grounds; faintly borne to them on the breeze came the up-and-down tooting of the distant merry-go-round. Over the uneven cloud of trees that marked the edge of the town the slow Ferris wheel smoothly lifted its swinging seats high to the July sky, then lowered its passengers round and down from sight again.

When they had passed the gates, Sarah's hand went into his. It was as though they stepped together into a loud and gaudy trance. Orange, yellow, purple, green, all the primitive colours of cowboy and Indian and citizen shirts and kerchiefs and dresses were radiant about them. The hoarse and lilting calls of barkers assaulted them from every side, the growling surf of ride motors, the mechanical teeter-totter music of the merry-go-round, the rising roar and lambasting explosions from the motorcycles of the Wall of Death.

They were carried along in the desultory drift of the carnival crowd, stopping to buy a canary with wood-shaving tail for Sarah. They caught a glimpse of Mame Napoleon and Byron and Buster and Esther and Evelyn and Avalon and Elvira waiting to go on Byron's birthplace—or rather his place of origin.

He realized that he was tired, not with the physical weariness that he saw in some of the faces around him, but with an inner fatigue mildly shaded with melancholy. It was as though the carnival bombast had brought to him a long-delayed understanding of the quiet backwater life he was leading. He knew now that he had cut himself off from the mainstream of journalism. What had happened to him since his university days—what important thing had he done? Or what important thing was he likely to do in the rest of the one life that he had? Quite likely nothing, he told himself, and the sad conviction of this conclusion could not be denied.

"When we going on the merry-go-round, Daddy?"

"Pretty soon, dear."

The carnival air held the sour smell of mustard, candied with the syrup aroma of pink floss, rich with hamburgers and hot dogs frying.

"We'd better get you something to eat first, Baby."

Con, whom he had roomed with twenty years ago, was deputy minister of something or other in the federal government. Jim headed the buying department for Wood Gundy at the coast . . .

He stared down at the lime and lemon containers, looking infinitely cool with ice chunks and fruit rind floating on their surface. Not just getting to the top of the material heap, not just wealth, not just importance—these were all simply a pointless extension of the life he led now. Perhaps Con and Blair and Jim could be just as badly off as he was—might have no more sense of destination.

He saw the two Indian boys then. He judged them to be

about twelve. They stood with eyes steady upon the woman working before the spitting griddle. Silently they watched her shovel grease back on the iron plate with an offhand movement of her spatula, roll out three wieners, tuck them inside buns and hand them over the counter to waiting customers.

"Yes?" She was looking at the Indian boys.

They shook their heads barely perceptibly, but did not move away. The woman looked over to Matt.

"Two hamburgers and a lemon drink, please. Without mustard." His eyes wandered to the Indian boys again. Their shirts were open at the neck, showing almost white below a sun-darkened vee of skin; they did not seem to be aware that he was staring at them, their gaze still upon the woman in the booth.

"Make that four hamburgers—four drinks." He nodded towards the Indian boys. "For these boys."

When he and Sarah had their hamburgers, he found that he was not hungry. He dropped half of it to the ground before they went to the merry-go-round.

Later in the grandstand he was hardly aware of the rodeo violence below them. The chuckwagon horses rounded the barrels, their wild manes flying as they came pounding out to the dirt track. To marry and to beget and to provide were not enough at all.

Chute number three opened to squirt out a bucking, jolting horse in seeking, halting, pitching jumps, the rider with one hand clutching the rope surcingle between his thighs, head rag-doll loose—just off balance, just on—then cartwheeling off long before the blast of the judge's horn. He was picking himself up from the dirt, looking back over his shoulder at the horse that had thrown him and gone pitching on its way. He walked over toward the chutes, holding his side and limping.

"He ain't bin hurt, he ain't bin hurt," the man on Matt's left was shouting. "He ain't bin hurt. He didn't even try!"

"I ain't bin hurt, I ain't bin hurt," Matt echoed the words drily to himself. But he knew he had been, and he also knew what was bothering him—he had not even tried.

Now that the afternoon show was over, the Midway had achieved a pulsing roar that would abate only for the supper hour, then try for the final evening climax. It had a numbing and dazing effect, Matt thought, as though it were about to dissolve consciousness of one's self. He carried Sarah asleep in his arms on his way to the exit gate, then by a crown-and-anchor concession he saw Professor Winesinger with arms held wide as though in benediction over the attentive crowd before him.

". . . compounded from the herbs and flora of these boundless plains—Professor Winesinger's Lightning Penetration Oil and Tune-up Tonic. I may say that I have dedicated my life to travel—to unselfish and restless travel over this Western land solely for the purpose of bringing the salutary benefits of this ancient Blackfoot remedy to the suffering humanity of the prairies and foothills. I suffer with you. I have seen the tortured face that betokens the jagged kidney stone moving. I have seen upon the brow of my fellow man the agony of rupture pain, and the gnawing, unceasing, grinding ache of the peptic and duo-denal ulcer."

He *had*, Matt realized; at least the old cynic had been *aware*. You could say that for him. That was at least something.

"Now, today, I wish to take you with me down the alimentary canal to the major point where Professor Winesinger's Lightning Penetration Oil and Tune-up Tonic does its best work." He paused, and then with the reverent deference of one saying, "Gentlemen, the Queen," announced:

"The gastric glands . . ."

"Hurry, hurry, hurry!"

". . . which are of three varieties: cardiac . . ."

". . . everybody down now—we spin the wheel an' we find the lucky winners!"

". . . true gastric, or peptic and pyloric. Professor Winesinger's Lightning Penetration Oil and Tune-up Tonic hits all three of them instantly and at one and the same time."

". . . the more you put down—the more you pick up."

He had put very little down, Matt told himself sardonically, so it seemed that there had been very little for him to pick up here in Shelby.

"Hits them hard, stimulating the flow of pepsogen, and whipping up the flow of gastrin. When you stare upwards tonight at those fireworks—that display of pyrotechnical beauty will be nothing, nothing whatever to be compared to the beauty and the glory of the fireworks going on in your body, in the tissues and the cells and the nerves and the arteries of those who for two dollars and ninety-five cents wish to revivify themselves with the energizing Professor Winesinger's Lightning Penetration Oil and Tune-up Tonic."

He turned away with Sarah in his arms. God, if it were possible to set the fireworks off in one's self—if it were only possible!

As he carried Sarah through the gates, he saw the spare figure of Aunt Fan headed for the downtown district.

It had been trying, with just her and the Senator to do the judging. Right from the start she had been upset about the gladioli—until she had seen the salmon one with the pink edges all uneven, and she had been relieved when the Senator had agreed with her that it was the best. And this year there had been quite a few "Table-Centres—Nine Annuals," so *that* had confused her and she couldn't make up her mind between two of them that were much better than the others. Then she had recognized the silver pitcher with the grapevine design that Mr. Tregillis had won in the bonspiel three years ago, and that she had seen at Tregillis's many times. She knew then that one entry must be Sadie Tregillis's and the other Mr. Oliver's, so that made up her mind. It was the nicer bouquet of the two, anyway; Mr. Oliver hadn't had to rely on cornflowers to get his nine annuals. Cornflowers were almost weeds really, they grew and spread so.

And finally it had been the roses. Thank heavens there had been no difficulty there; most of them had been quite cabbagy, except for the tall red one, which was truly beautiful—but not nearly so lovely as the apricot-coloured one in the tomato soup tin. She had known as soon as she saw it that it must be Mr. Oliver's; it would be just like him to try to throw a person off by putting it into a can. And the Senator had agreed on the roses.

He had also suggested that as far as he was concerned the apricot rose was the pick of the show and that he would like to give it the Grand Championship cup. She had hesitated; it would be much *safer* to give it to the salmon and pink gladiola, which she *knew* to be Mr. Oliver's. Then her conscience pricked her; after all, she was pretty certain the apricot rose was Mr. Oliver's too, and she had already been swayed a little by her recognition of Sadie's silver pitcher in the "Table-Centres—Nine Annuals." This wasn't the time to be *safe;* it was the time to be a *little* impartial.

Upon the apricot-coloured rose in the soup tin they had hung the blue and gilt Grand Championship ribbon, and before it placed the silver cup that had been held five years in succession by Mr. Oliver.

The grandstand show was over for the evening; Harry Fitzgerald, president of the Shelby Fair, Light Horse Show, and Little Britches Rodeo, had made the presentations of cheques and cups for the stock-saddle riding, bareback riding, steer riding, decorating, calf roping, chuckwagon racing. The cooking and handicrafts awards came next, with the flower ribbons last. Until this year these had always been rather anti-climactic, following upon the conferring of money and honours for the lustier competitions. This thirty-ninth year was an exception.

In the afternoon's excitement there had not been time for the news to travel far, so that to most of the audience Harry's announcement came as a complete surprise.

"Winner of the Grand Championship ribbon of the twenty-third Annual Perennial and Annual Flower Show— Mrs. Mame Napoleon."

Mame, seated with Rory and the children in the front of the grandstand, was startled. When she had left Penny Novelty with the rosebush to take the kids to the picture show, she had left the thing behind and had to go back into the theatre. She would have forgotten it again on the bus seat if Byron hadn't picked it up and carried it home with him. There she dropped it by the door on the south side of

the house, intending to stick it into the ground somewhere
or other the next morning. For over a week it had lain
forgotten on the goat manure piled against that side of the
house for winter insulation. Had it not been so strategically
placed that it caught the thrown contents of the slop bucket
and the washbasin whenever she went to the back door, or
if it had not been by Elvira's play spot where she spent
engrossed mornings and afternoons digging with an old
tablespoon to fill and empty and fill again the rusty pot her
mother had given her, it might have perished for want of
moisture—or from the hunger of the goats that steered clear
of Elvira, always.

Even the young shoots that had sprouted in the sun had
weathered the nights of frost, for compassionate warmth
breathed up from the rotting goat manure on which it lay.
Then one morning on her way to the woodpile she noticed
it; at the same time she saw the tablespoon excavation
Elvira had made the afternoon before. The thing might as
well go in there. She tore the burlap from its roots and held
the plant upright in the hole while she filled in and patted
dirt and goat manure around it.

With its southern exposure, and the careless daily baths
of wash and slop water filtering down almost hundred-proof
liquid goat manure to the roots, the plant rallied. It had
already served the normal tea-rose span of life in a city
greenhouse, forced under glass and tropical steam heat to
contribute long-and slender-stemmed blooms to tea parties
and corsages, hospital rooms and wedding bouquets, bou-
tonnieres and funeral wreaths. Considered almost spent, it
had been uprooted and wrapped with others to be shipped
out and sold cheaply for whatever dregs of energy remained
in it.

Through June it had produced dark and leathery green
leaves. For a while Mame and the children had watched for
the appearance of buds, but they had soon tired of this, and
left the rose to sun, slop water, goat manure, and its own
devices. She could quite honestly say she hadn't given the
goddam thing another thought till this very morning. When
they had all left for the fair, she had glanced back and seen
the one rose from the gate, had told Rory to wait while she
ran into the house and got the tomato soup tin. In spite of

the goats, and Elvira, it had produced one yellow rose. She might as well enter it in the flower show.

Now, as she took the cup from Harry, Byron standing beside her, his pant laces dangling, the blue ribbon flowing down his shirt where he'd pinned it as soon as his mother had handed it to him, she looked out into the pale pond of upturned faces in the dusk before her. She supposed a person ought to say something; everybody did when they won something. She pulled her beret down more over her ears.

"It wasn't us," she said in her hoarse, carrying voice. "Jist luck, I guess. I got it at the Penny Novelty when I took the kids to the clinic last spring. So I guess it was just luck—an'—an' goat manoor." She made out the faces of Mrs. Tregillis and Mrs. Fitzgerald; the whole St. Aidan's Church Ladies' Auxiliary would be down there. "An' the Lord," she amended quickly. "I don't know what makes anything beautiful," she said almost helplessly, "unless it's luck, the Lord, an' goat manoor."

And Canon Midford, as shocked as anyone else when the award had been announced, thought that if the philosophy of salvation must rest upon basic simplicities, then luck and the Lord and goat manure would do as well as any. Mame Napoleon was right. She could have written Ecclesiastes with her wonderfully steady sense of the ways of the Universe and of prize-winning roses.

It had been a lonely day in the *Chinook* office. Matt could have shut the office, knowing that there wouldn't be anybody come in on rodeo day. And she hadn't dared even suggest it to him, because Miss Melquist was right there ready to jump and suggest *she'd* take over the way she was already doing on Saturdays. So all she'd seen had been the parade in the morning. It wasn't fair! And then there'd been the disappointment when she'd got the copy of *This Is True* at lunch time from the pocketbook and periodical rack in the Palm Café. She had known that there would be nothing there even before she bought the magazine, and she wondered now how she'd ever dreamed the editors would print the story she'd sent in to them. They probably hadn't even read it, just because it was written out in longhand, and it certainly wasn't something she could get someone to type for her. They would never print her true story ever.

"I was only nineteen. I was lonely and hurt at the time. He was a well-poised and sophisticated man. He could turn any girl's head. I always liked older men and he was the editor of our town newspaper."

They probably knew it wasn't true, and that Matt had never made fierce and savage love to her out along the river road. The true thing about it was that she was hungry for love just as she had written, and that he was the answer to all her prayers. His caresses would never become more and more desperate each time, and there was utterly nothing she could do to make them so. She would never have anyone for her own, someone who would worship her and adore her and be the father of her children.

If she ever did have a husband, she knew one thing: her marriage would be a wondrous and lasting thing. They would love and trust one another forever: he'd never cheat and two-time her the way other women's husbands did. Miss Melquist could try till she was blue in the face, and she'd never make a dint in their very special tender love for each other. She'd have to poach on some other woman's territory.

It wasn't the ten-thousand-dollar prize for the winning story she cared about. She didn't care about not getting that at all, she told herself as she turned out the light over her bed. What was ten thousand dollars compared to the deep and lasting love of a wonderful man! Like Matt!

. . . in part the community has a divided aspect so that there is a double contingency of the process of interaction. This is in spite of a symbolic system shared by the ranching patterns to the west and those of the farming totality to the east. While the cultural dichotomy may not seem great, it does engender a day-to-day communication problem of long standing, in the normality aspect of expectations, the "Hobbesian" problem of order.

Both farm and cattle communities share a laconic

quality in all verbal exchanges. "I guess" crops up frequently, as well as "Afraid that" and "Could be." Often the speakers studied tend to fall back upon the shrug, the grimace, the shake or nod of a head, which cannot be entered into the spoken record against them later. Great store is set by the humorous retort which is an easy avoidance of a responsible answer. Within their own socio-economic class and socio-cultural grouping, however, they are anything but laconic.

There is a crudity and coarseness to the quality of the inter-personal humour, which is not wit at all in the higher sense, but draws on exaggeration, the tall tale, the ludicrous lie for its communicative impact. Here again one cannot mistake the kinship with the range and the prairie; significantly, the principal strain of this humour is a mordant one. . . .

The community well recognizes it is not a classless one, that there is in fact a firmly drawn line between the select professional and business group and the lower limits of the middle classes. The class gratification-deprivation balance . . .

The fireworks had blossomed and died from the foothills sky. The stands were empty. Most of the concession booths had vanished. Only half-dismantled skeletons remained of the merry-go-round, the Ferris wheel, the Wall of Death, and the Airplane Swings, as busy men called to each other across the littered wasteland of the Midway. Through the darkness horses far from their home pasture whinnied to each other, or in the barns knocked a hoof against wood; bobbing lanterns here and there swept faint light through the chill foothills night.

The doorway of number one barn blazed; four men—the owner of the winning chuckwagon string, the winners of the stock-saddle riding and the roping money, and Professor Noble Winesinger—sat intently about a bale of straw, where silver and bills lay heaped. Professor Winesinger held by far the best hand: a tight of queens and tens.

CHAPTER 14

JUNE'S PERSISTENCE AND INDUSTRY IMPRESSED HIM; HE KNEW that throughout the day and in the evenings she carried on her interviews, and he was quite sure that she worked late most nights in her suite. She had called on Harvey Hoshal in his barber shop, all the store-keepers in turn. She visited Ollie Pringle, Canon Midford, and Father McNulty; on many afternoons she had tea with town wives. The woman seemed tireless as she accompanied him on many of his news calls: several council meetings, a calf sale, the Young Conservatives' Dinner, and the final play-off game of Little League Baseball between the Shelby Muskrats and the Mable Ridge Colts. He had driven her out into the country, where she questioned rancher and ranch hand as they wiped the sweat of haying from their foreheads, and talked to farmers just down from summer-fallowing tractors.

And God only knew the ore she was mining out of Florence Nelligan, her landlady ever since she'd left Aunt Fan's. He wished to hell he hadn't suggested she move in with Flannel Mouth Florence, the gossip mother lode of Shelby. One good thing about it, though, Joe was pretty steady up there on the wagon, which wasn't easy for him; he was at his most vulnerable during summer holidays. Evidently he and June were hitting it off pretty well together.

Just after the Shelby Fair, June had called on Nettie Fitzgerald again.

"Blue or Royal Crown Derby?" he asked her on her return to the office.

"Royal."

"Hmh—you're doing all right with her then. She recovered from her holiday?" He knew that Harry had taken two weeks off right after the rodeo and that Nettie had gone with him to the Paradise Guest Ranch up Paradise Valley. Harry had told him that the holiday was a complete flop, chill and damp under dripping eaves, the river a muddy torrent, the evenings before the roaring fireplace depressing with bridge.

"She said she didn't know when she'd had a nicer holiday," June was saying. "An interesting couple from Victoria and guests from Boston and Montreal. It rained quite a lot, she said, but seemed always to clear enough each day so that she could get out with her paints and brush."

"Poor Harry didn't get a chance to try his talent and technique with rod and reel. He's much better at angling than she is at painting, you know. She just barely manages to justify her position as secretary of the Foothills Sketch and Water Colour Society."

"But she *does* paint, doesn't she?"

"And Harry doesn't? Look, June—nothing would upset Nettie more than to have Harry suddenly take an interest in painting, or any of the things she considers cultured. For Nettie, culture's like religion—a woman's province . . ."

"Oh, I don't imagine she . . ."

"Yes, she does. Culture and religion are something nurtured mostly by women that men get into largely by mistake—or unavoidable necessity. Like making up the deficit when the Celebrity Series fails."

"Is that the way most Shelby men look at it?"

"I don't know." He considered a moment. "Now you mention it, I suppose it is. No. Harvey Hoshal is a hi-fidelity enthusiast and quite a linguist."

"Linguist!"

"Didn't that come up in your interview with him? I think over the past thirty-odd years he's learned—in a rather shallow fashion—five languages—French, German, Italian, Spanish . . ."

"What's the fifth?"

"He's working on that now. Cantonese—has his lesson from George Wing over coffee every morning. To come back to Nettie—she's had a rather hard blow this summer."

"Yes, I know."

"But not half so hard as Harry. He had hoped Willis would be going into premedical school this fall. If his boy became a doctor, then at least they'd have a profession in common."

"Mrs. Fitzgerald said something about his writing supplementaries."

"God—all five of them! Willis will never make medicine or any profession. Harry's accepted that now."

"Mrs. Fitzgerald feels it's her fault."

"How?" he asked her.

"Not sending him away much earlier than she did to boarding-school."

"What difference does she think that would have made?"

"She seems to feel that Shelby schools haven't had—well, her words were 'a climate for scholarship'."

"I see. How does she explain Roy Maclin? He went through Shelby schools. Perhaps he would have won a *couple* of Governor General's Medals if he'd gone to boarding-school."

"She didn't mention Roy Maclin." She looked at him for a silent moment. "You know, she could be partly right."

"How!"

"Well, the provincial average of passes for the Grade Twelve departmentals is sixty-two. Shelby's is twenty-nine this year."

"Have you told Joe about this?"

"I got it from Joe. He says that every once in a while a year like this comes along—a poor crop."

"There you are then."

"Matt."

"Yes?"

"Sarah likes to dance, doesn't she?"

"Mmm-hmmh. She'd rather dance than eat."

"Supposing—when she's a few years older—supposing it's evident she has talent . . ."

"Dancing!"

"Or painting, or acting, or music . . ."

"Oh."

"See what I mean? About Mrs. Fitzgerald's being partly right?"

"I don't know. I'll tell you in perhaps eight years."

"There are others who could tell me now."

"Perhaps," he said, "perhaps there are."

He found it a little difficult to get back to work after she'd left.

There was Mrs. Dodds for voice and piano; if she needed ballet when she was older, he could drive her up on Saturdays to the Arts Centre in the city, couldn't he? He wondered how the Shelby average had compared with the average of the province other years. Joe was damn good, but the board had experienced difficulty in replacing Mr. Duncan with Mr. Sparrow last winter, and he had heard that Shelby teachers' salaries were low. How did the schools measure up in the inspector's reports? Been years and years since Joe had gone away to summer school. For that matter, how long was it since Harry had been away for a refresher course?

He stared down at the paper in his typewriter:

Friends will be glad to know that Webb Bolton has returned home from hospital, having pretty well recovered from a painful and persistent siege of carbuncles from which he suffered for several weeks.

As June came out of Matt's office she saw that Millie was over by her desk. She could have been wrong, but she did sense the nervous completion of a quick turn towards the stationery shelves which now occupied Millie's attention. Surely the girl did not have to spend so much time in that part of the office. Not that it mattered, for she kept most of her material in the suite, and Millie was quite welcome to read anything she might find on the desk here or in the typewriter.

Neither of them said anything as June went over to her desk and sat down. Millie had disliked her from first sight, she knew; knowing that, perhaps she should never have taken Matt up on his offer of desk space here. She'd done her best to get along with her, and her best would never be good enough.

"How's your book coming along, Miss Melquist?"

The question surprised her; she could not remember when Millie had ever spoken to her first. "Fine—fine, Millie."

"You must be quite a ways along with it now, aren't you?"

"It's going well."

Millie was not looking at her but rather past the corner of the desk and toward the floor. "Won't be long till you're all through with it, I guess."

"It's not that far along, Millie. It's the sort of thing that takes time—quite a bit of time." So that was what had moved Millie to speak first: the hope that she was near the end of her work and would be getting out of the office. "I'm afraid I'm going to be around for quite some time longer, Millie."

"Oh." The disappointment was quite clear in her voice. "I just wondered."

Millie still hesitated by the desk. "I guess you've talked to quite a few Shelby folks."

"Yes."

"Mrs. Fitzgerald, Mrs. Beeton-Cross, Mrs. Nelligan . . ."

"Yes, I have."

"Jenny Pringle?"

"Jenny Pringle—is she any relation to Mr. Pringle?"

"That's her father."

"I've talked to *him*."

"Jenny's in the telephone office—I worked next to her—before I came here to work for Mr. Stanley."

"Did you."

"Jenny would be a good one for you to talk to—anybody ever worked on a switchboard, I'd think you'd want to talk with them."

"Would I."

"You might get something pretty interesting to go into

that book of yours—like people driving out on the river road."

Millie was still not looking at her directly, but there was a slight smile on her face. "But I guess that wouldn't be the sort of thing you'd *want* in your book." Now there was a conspiratorial quality in the way Millie was regarding her from the corner of her eye. It was a new and startling facet of Millie Clocker, and not an endearing one at all.

"Perhaps not," June said shortly. Somehow it was very important to her to do something rude to the girl. Slapping her would be too violently rude. If she had not been sitting at the desk, she could have turned her back on her and walked away, when the more usual thing would have been to exchange a few more words with her before taking leave. She did the next best thing. She began to type.

Though she did not look up from the typewriter, she knew that Millie had stayed for some time before returning to her own desk. How in the world had Millie known that she had driven out along the river road with Joe Sunday evening! There was no mistaking her knowledge: it had been the whole reason for her conversation. Pawing and peering over her notes as she'd caught her doing a couple of times was one thing. This *really* annoyed! This was insupportable! It was not the fact that Millie had been nibbling on her privacy that had angered her; not that in itself so much as discovering that she was not in complete command of her feelings. It had been many years since she had been this angry with anyone, and then of course it had been her mother. Well, she *was* a rational human; no wild horses were going to run away with her!

The day after her exchange with Millie, when the girl had left for her coffee break in the morning, June spoke to Matt.

"Matt, there haven't been any dog-poisonings for quite a while, have there?"

"No."

"Do you think your stories made an effective appeal?"

He shrugged. "Can't tell. Generally they slack off. Could pick up again in a month—next spring—they've been uneven in the past . . ."

"Rory Napoleon still makes his garbage pick-ups?"

"Mmm-hmh. Why?"

"Talking with Aunt Fan, she seemed to feel that . . ."

"Hey—hey—Aunt Fan didn't suggest that Rory Napoleon . . ."

"She asked me if I thought he might be . . ."

"Well, he isn't. That's strange. I'd never have thought Aunt Fan . . ."

"I don't think it was her idea in the first place."

"Probably Mrs. Nelligan—sounds like her."

"No, it wasn't."

"People you've been talking to—have you heard anyone suggest Rory? Other than Aunt Fan."

"Oh no."

"A person never can get to the start of things like that. I'd like to—for the Napoleons' sake. They're having it rather rough right now, you know."

"Yes, I know."

Matt referred to an item of local news he had not printed in the *Chinook:* the incident that had led to the interdiction of Rory Napoleon, forbidding him to drink alcohol. There had been an argument in front of the Arlington Beer Parlour, and Rory had terminated it by decking Ollie Pringle. It was true that Ollie had started the initial argument, but he'd had provocation in the fact that Rory's goats had just that afternoon got into his lush cover crop for the third time in one week.

After the fight Mr. Oliver held a long and hortatory conversation with Mame Napoleon in his store, as a magistrate and as a friend, asking Mame that she put her husband up for membership on the "Indian List." When Mame showed reluctance, Mr. Oliver said he was sure Mr. Pringle would not press charges against Rory either for assault or for trespass if Mr. Oliver advised him against it. This, Mr. Oliver said, he did not feel he could do unless he had the assurance that interdiction would make future violence unlikely. Otherwise he would have to let Mr. Pringle and the law take their course. Mame had unenthusiastically agreed; Mr. Oliver had thanked her for her co-operation, at the same time warning her the Napoleons were still vulnerable through their mobile livestock and had a continuing responsibility to see that there was no further goat trespass on Mr. Pringle's land. They had.

"June," Matt said, "find out from Aunt Fan who it was who said that Rory was poisoning dogs."

"I don't have to ask her—I know."

"Who?"

She was a little ashamed of herself now for having brought the matter up with him; she knew that pique had moved her to do so and that she could not go through with her original intention, no matter how much Millie had annoyed her the day before. "I can't say, Matt."

"That's funny . . ."

"It—it would be rather small of me to . . ."

"I know that if the thing keeps travelling it's going to be rough on the Napoleons. It should be stopped—right away."

"I know it should."

"All right then—why don't you . . ."

"It's up to me to stop it. I think I can—quite effectively."

"Thing like that, it could lose Rory his job—whoever it is should be told . . ."

"I'll tell her."

It was a distasteful thing she had to do, and awkward. She did not want to speak to Millie in front of Matt, and it was not until two days after she had spoken to Matt that she had an opportunity to bring it up with Millie at a time when he was out of the office. She was surprised that Millie made no attempt to deny she had told Aunt Fan that Rory was the poisoner.

"I'm sure it's Rory," she said, and again June was surprised at the positiveness in her voice—almost defiance.

"But you don't know."

"I know."

"You can't. You can think it is—wonder if it is—but you can't be . . ."

"He's the one all right."

"How do you know he's the one? Have you ever seen him doing it?"

"No, I haven't."

"Has anyone else ever seen him?"

"I don't know if they have. All I know is . . ."

"Then if you haven't seen him, you can't be sure. It's a terrible thing to cast suspicion on someone."

"It's not so nice for people to poison dogs either," Millie said.

"I agree with you. If there were any reason to believe that Rory Napoleon . . ."

"Dogs tipping over garbage cans and the Napoleons being what they are is plenty of reason."

"No, it isn't. You're just guessing about it and you're telling others about your guesses as though they were fact, and you could hurt the Napoleons a great deal by doing it. Rory could lose his job if . . ."

"He ought to if he's poisoning dogs."

"*If* he were poisoning dogs—you don't know—you're simply *assuming* it without any reason to assume it. You can't do that, Millie." She looked at Millie, saw a tightening of her mouth, an unusual directness in the girl's gaze. "Can you?" She had underestimated Millie's stubbornness. "Can you, Millie?" Still the girl did not answer her, nor did she turn her eyes away. "Millie—I—it wasn't my idea to bring this up with you, but I've promised I would. So that it wouldn't go any further—and hurt the Napoleons. I'm going to have to speak to Aunt Fan too. I don't enjoy it."

"Don't you though!"

She had not thought the girl capable of such fierceness, or herself of such immediate emotional response. For a moment she could not trust her voice to reply evenly. "Millie, I'm telling you for your own good. Slander is a nasty thing and this is a particularly nasty slander. There are laws and there are punishments . . . you cannot go on saying that the Napoleons . . ."

"It's none of your business!"

"But it is. Already I've been involved in unpleasantness because of it, and I won't be through with it until I know it's finished. I promised Mr. Stanley." She had scored then; she could tell from the way that Millie's pale face crumpled.

"You went and told him!"

"No—I didn't . . ."

"You did!"

"I didn't, Millie. I simply promised him that I'd do my best to stop it by speaking to you . . ."

"Then you must have . . ."

"I tell you I didn't—but if you don't stop it I'll have to."

"You won't have to."

Both turned to see Matt at the counter; neither had heard him enter the office. "She didn't tell me, Millie, and she's right—you'll have to stop it."

For several long moments Millie's eyes were on Matt; she opened her mouth as though to protest but there was no protest, simply a choking sound. She did not move as Matt came through the door to them. "It's a terrible thing, Millie, when people are . . ."

Past June, past Matt, past her desk, past the counter, Millie fled. She was accompanied by a muted keening sound; it lingered on the air like the after-quiver of a chime even when the street door had closed behind her.

"Damn it," Matt said.

"I handled that badly," June said.

"Wasn't your fault."

"Yes it was. I let myself get annoyed—it would have been better if I'd told you and let you speak to her. This was the worst possible way."

"Not too much harm done. She'll get over it."

"I don't think she will—been quite a bit of harm done," June said. "If only it hadn't happened in front of me."

"In front of you? You're just an innocent bystander."

"I'm more than that—Millie doesn't like me."

"What if she doesn't?"

"And if it had been anyone else but you . . ."

"Me! I don't understand. Why do you . . ."

"She hates me, Matt. And even though you haven't noticed it—she loves you."

"Are you crazy!"

"No—her mortification is . . ."

The office door had opened again. This time it was a stooped and elderly man unfamiliar to June. Matt went to the counter.

"Mr. Stanley." Joe Bunch placed several folded newspapers on the counter top. "I came about this."

"What, Joe?"

"Them stories." He pointed to the folded newspapers. "About them dogs. I'd come sooner only I gener'lly get my magazines an' papers off of Rory after he's finished with 'em. I didn't get these till yesterday."

"What about them, Joe?"

"I'm the one."

"The one what?"

"Doin' it. Been doin' it all along. I come in to tell you. Guess you didn't figger it would be me."

"No," Matt said, "I didn't. It's still a little hard to believe you . . ."

"It's me all right."

"But why did you . . ."

"Cod-liver oil."

"Cod-liver oil?" June said.

"Folks in this town—lots of 'em—gives their dogs cod-liver oil. An' in Oliver's Tradin' Company Store there's shelves piled high with tins of dog food. Two for thirty-one cents—for food, like for a dog. An' cod-liver oil. Did you know that?"

"No, I didn't," June said.

"You just look at Doc Fitzgerald payin' board for his dog at a fancy kennels up in the city. Nine months outa the year, thirty dollars a month, sendin' him to school. What they got for dogs there—inner-spring mattresses! Look at all the dogs in this town, all the food they can eat, warm bed—they got everything without even tryin'. What I got—scratchin', an' I'm hungry all the time. I got no coal most the time to warm my shack in thirty-below. What right they got to go on livin' easy when I can't!

"You know what I could do with that four hundred dollars Doc paid every year for that dog? I could be a human! Live like a human instead of a pack rat! I could get underwear. An' I could get myself a decent coat! I could get a dress-up suit. Fifteen years I can't get enough ahead for a dress-up suit! How'd you like that? How'd you like scratchin' for a livin' any one them dogs would turn his

CHAPTER 15

AFTER THE FIRST SHOCK OF DISCOVERY, THE TOWN HAD settled back, without too much bitterness toward Joe Bunch, the poverty-stricken recluse who lived in a tar-paper shack out on the river road. Relieved actually, Matt thought, that he had not been sent away to penitentiary, but rather to the Provincial Mental Hospital, there to spend the rest of his days wandering the dogless grounds. Matt knew that Harry Fitzgerald's recommendation had been important to his commitment.

He felt that of all the people in Shelby, including those who had lost dogs, he had been most shaken by Joe's confession of guilt, or rather by his self-justification. It was as though Joe had been accusing him. For if it were possible for people like Joe to be in want in Shelby while love and care were lavished upon pets, then he *had* been rightfully accused for the way he had handled the dog-poisoning stories, and in a sense he *had* given dogs equality with humans—in death. He could find no excuse for his lack of compassionate attention, his dormant social conscience.

Nor was he reassured by his chance meeting with Mame Napoleon in front of Finlay's Vulcanizing a week later. Her eyes were redder than usual, her beret pulled even further down around her ears.

"Why, Mame," he greeted her, "I haven't seen you in weeks.".

"Oh"—Mame's gaze slid past him—"I been away, up in the city. We go up every month—get checked over. Keep their mouths shut. Except for that I been stickin' pretty close to home."

"I see."

"They say I'm A-one—up there. Only my nerves is all unstrung. They say I got to quit worryin' so much. It's them goats, you know."

"Is it? What are they . . .?"

"Now don't tell me you ain't heard all about our goats an' Ollie Pringle's cover crop an' Rory bein' put onto the Indian List," she added sadly. "By me."

"Well, yes, Mame."

"Rory and me we appreciate you not puttin' anythin' into your paper about it—Rory givin' it to Ollie Pringle in front of the Arlington for him takin' Rory by the face an' sayin' our goats was all over his land."

"Were they?"

"Just over the cover crop he was savin' for his yearlin's out of the hills. Mr. Oliver had to get into it with both of his flat English feet too."

"Did he?"

"Hell, yes. Still spinnin' in the wind like a button on a backhouse door from our rose winnin' the Champion cup."

"Oh, I don't think so, Mame."

"Well, I do. He wanted to get even, he went about it the right way. Talkin' me into puttin' Rory on the Indian List. That way both of us suffers. Rory without his beer—me feelin' just awful for doin' a thing like that to Rory. Oliver, he's like that."

"Like what, Mame?"

"Never quittin' till he evened her up. Stubborn. He was to drownd they'd find his body upstream."

"Mame, I don't think you're being fair about Mr. Oliver. I think he went out of his way to help."

"However it was, don't make too much difference. If it wasn't Oliver, it'd be the rest of them."

"The rest of them?"

"Hell, yes. Pick, pick, pick. That's all they ever

do—pick, pick, pick till I'm beside myself. First it's the kids, then it's the goats. Everybody talkin'—goin' at it pick, pick, pick. Sayin' I ain't really Rory's wife, sayin' we ain't really married. Pick, pick, pick till my nerves has just got me so's I can't har'ly sleep nights. Everybody—why I was just sayin' to Rory last night—I was sayin' there's nobody in this town's friends of ours unless it's that nice Mr. Stanley an' his wife. Pick, pick, pick—that's all they ever do."

"I'm sorry, Mame."

" 'But they got a heart,' I says to Rory, 'them, they're the only ones in this town that has. Rest can't keep their mouths shut.' Rory says, 'Let 'em. Let 'em.' Well, it bothers him just as much as me. His nerves is awful from them goin' on behind his back, talkin'! He can't sleep, he can't eat. Or maybe it's from missin' his beer. Adds up to the same thing. We're both jumpier'n cut calves."

"Don't pay any attention to them, as Rory says," he advised her.

"I can't help it. I try, but it don't work. We got all the goats penned up now an' Byron put brush over the top so's they can't jump out, so that means we got to haul feed to 'em, an' soonerer later they're gonna come up outa there like a fountain an' Rory had his last warnin' from Oliver an' Ollie Pringle, he'll have Rory up before Oliver again, an' Oliver said he'd fine him next time an' we ain't got the money for no goddam fine an' he won't be able to pay an' he'll go down for a month an' I don't know what I'll do with all them kids to feed . . ." Her voice broke; her pale, reddened eyes, which had been glistening, welled up, and from each a clear tear rolled down her wrinkled cheeks.

"Please," said Matt. "It'll work out all right, Mame." Without regard for the passersby he put his arm around the woman's shoulders. The act destroyed the last of her control. The tears streamed as she cried with her hands to her mouth and then with her fists pushing into her eyes like a crying child.

"What you need is a cup of tea," he said. "Come into the Palm Café."

"If it's all the same to you, what I need is a bottle of beer," said Mame.

In the Ladies and Escorts room of the Arlington Arms she quieted down. "I'm sorry, Mr. Stanley. I didn't mean to, but I couldn't help it. I feel better now." She picked up her glass, swallowed, set it down again. "I guess they got to talk about somebody an' we're the ones. But Rory an' me been livin' together for thirteen years now—you'd think they'd get used to it. We never got married. We could of—but we didn't. Rory said we would, an' then Avalon come along an' I was so busy with her, an' then when we might of I was bigger'n Dolly's rump with Evelyn an' it didn't seem the right time for it then. An' after Byron come—well, it seemed kind of silly." She emptied her glass. "I love Rory an' he loves me an' if them goddam goats would only stay in their goddam pen an' off of Ollie Pringle's goddam cover crop, I'd be the happiest woman in this here goddam country." She came to a full stop. "Here I been goin' on without even askin' how all you folks is doin'."

"We're just fine, Mame."

"Little Sarah, cute as ever."

"And spoiled."

"You go right ahead an' spoil her, Mr. Stanley. What are they for if they ain't to spoil, I always say—specially girls."

"Ruth doesn't seem to agree with you."

"She would," Mame said with conviction, "if it was a boy."

"While I think of it," he said, "I was wondering if Rory could find the time—I want some ploughing and grading done before it's too late."

"Sure, sure. What for?"

"Part of the garden back of the house—the south half. We'd like to put it into lawn."

"Lawn—new lawn. Then you'll need goat manoor!"

"Well, I don't know that . . ."

"Sure you will. I'll tell Rory to haul you a load-dollar seventy-five a yard. You'll want it for your new lawn."

"Mame, I think commercial fertilizer or cow manure well rotted . . ."

"Don't worry, this stuff is well rotted. I'll tell you somethin' . . ." She leaned confidentially across the table.

"Rory can just as well haul you goat manoor as cow manoor. It stinks, I agree with you there, but it'll sure put the life into your lawn. You can't beat goat manoor! Stuff grows that high. We had pigweed out there that high! I'll tell him to bring you goat manoor."

"Well, I don't think it would be so good here in town . . ."

"An' on your garden next year, you'd really have cucumbers—radishes the size a turnips with that goat manoor."

"He'd better make it cow, Mame," said Matt firmly. "I'm afraid the neighbours would object."

"Oh . . ." She sat back in defeat. Her face had lost its excitement. "Sure they would. Sure they would. I'll tell him to haul you cow manoor. Ord'nary cow manoor. After he's ploughed an' graded her for you. Of course they wouldn't let you have goat manoor on your new lawn." She was silent a moment. "It's goat manoor that's really got the poop to her though. I wonder why." Her face held an absent look as she contemplated the mystic strength of goat manure. "I'll tell him to haul you plain cow manoor," she said sadly.

After he had left her, he realized he could not honestly accept the generous way in which she had excluded him from "they." It was true that he had felt warmth toward the Napoleons, but it had been only the warmth of amusement; with them he had always been the careless spectator and listener. And if this were true of the Napoleons, how much more of Millie Clocker!

June's startling revelation that afternoon in the office had filled him with distaste. Only the most reluctant feeling of guilt for his part in Millie's mortification had taken him to see her. He had put it off for almost a week and then called on her at Aunt Fan's to ask her the last thing in the world that he wanted—to come back to work for him. And when she had told him that she had already promised Mr. Sheppard she would go back to the telephone office, he had been inordinately relieved. She had been a meek and mild and contrite Millie, very sorry that she couldn't come back. But not quite sorry enough, he felt, as he saw faint indecision slip over her face. He had left abruptly before there was real danger of her making a wonderful sacrifice for him.

It was hard for Millie to know whether she hated Miss Melquist or loved Matt more. If it hadn't been for her they'd still be together in the office. She'd given her something to think about anyway; she could tell by that startled look on her face after that hint about the river road. Something had been going on all right; people couldn't hide that kind of thing.

She bet Miss Melquist felt a warning pulse-beat in her constricted throat and her heart pounded out beware, beware, beware because Millie Clocker is suspicious. Millie Clocker's seen the signs. The signs were always there for the ones that could see them. They'd been there when Claudine's husband, Kent Stanhope, had gone away to South America on his three-months business trip and Claudine had her affair with Gregory. Viola had seen the signs and known all along what was going on. Ever since grammar school Viola had known that Claudine reached out greedily into life for just the material things that money could buy. Claudine, with her blonde striking loveliness, hadn't got away with a thing. And it was to Viola that Claudine came and said, "I'm pregnant. I'm in terrible trouble. While Kent was in South America I got pregnant." But Miss Melquist probably wouldn't get into terrible trouble at all, because she'd know what to do and wasn't taking any chances at all, out there on the river road night after night under the trees . . .

Oh God, she'd never wanted anything more in her life than for her to get pregnant and be disgraced and shamed the way she'd disgraced and shamed her in front of Matt!

He had wanted her to come back with him; he'd come to her and pleaded with her to come back, and when he had seen it was no use he had slowly and sadly left. Just like with Viola. "When he tried to kiss me, I twisted my lips away from his. He turned and strode wordlessly away. I wanted to call him back. As his tall, distinguished form faded into the dusk I recalled that night three years before when I had cowered in the bedroom corner, when I had

CHAPTER 16

MATT HAD NEVER QUITE MADE UP HIS MIND WHETHER SPRING or fall was his favourite season. More and more of late years fall had recommended itself to him; certainly it demanded a deeper and subtler appreciation of its charms. There was no doubt in Ruth's mind, he knew; for her the gold and blue days of September had always meant harvest and round-up, the wild hoot and bark of men spooking cattle out of mountain draws that spilled the yellow of autumn cotton-wood into the valleys, another year's release from high urgency.

Over the swathed fields spreading out from Shelby, devouring combines rolled with their wide mouths low before themselves. The men did not harvest alone, for sharp-tailed grouse lifted over them in chittering flight, occasional partridge coveys fluttered and planed, and crimson-eyed pheasant cocks, with bronze breasts dis-tended, moved up out of the coulees and the river banks to strut through the ripe grain. From potholes, reedy sloughs, and river backwaters came the ticket-ticket confidences, the fully derisive quack of whole communities of ducks; on sibilant wings they launched their punctual assault against the dawn and sunset skies. Daily they welcomed the splashing arrival of each new contingent of pintail, mallard,

and canvas-back from the North. Thread after thread of
snow geese unravelled from the far horizon, grew loud and
shrill as they circled over Cooper's Lake, broke formation,
then, still calling, fell like snowflakes through the sun.
There came a late September night when the two-note plaint
of Canada honkers drifted down to ordinary mortals far
below. Their high, wild call lifted Matt from sleep; in his
pyjamas, and barefooted, he rushed outside the kitchen door
to stand in the chill fall night, and to stare upward with
pounding heart. The next morning they would be riding the
far centre of Cooper's Lake, magnificent as Nelson's fleet
before Trafalgar.

The next morning, Nettie Fitzgerald looked across the
breakfast table to her husband.

"I heard them too, but I didn't jump out of bed." The
statement had the sharpness of accusation.

"Good," said Harry without lifting his attention from
his grapefruit.

"Time to get out your gun," she said to the top of his
forehead.

"That's right, Nettie."

"You'll be spotting them this evening."

"No."

"Tomorrow at dawn then."

"No."

"I notice the field glasses are in the car."

"They've been there since last fall." He looked up at
her. "I won't be spotting or pitting in this week. They'll be
feeding on Albert Douglas's barley swaths. Two miles south
and a quarter west on the . . . ."

"I know where the Douglas farm is."

"Willis down yet?"

"No, he isn't. There isn't anything for him to come
down for."

"If you'd let him take that job with the seismic crew
he'd be . . ."

"He doesn't have to do work with a labour gang."

"Better than sleeping till noon every day—haring
around in that car all night."

"Perhaps he wouldn't be," she said, "if things had been different. If he'd grown up where there were a few cultural advantages—where people thought of something besides curling and goose-hunting!"

"Willis has never curled."

"I didn't say he had!"

"And he couldn't hit a goose at twelve feet with a ten-gauge unimproved cylinder. If he'd been permitted like other boys in this town to have his own gun when he was fourteen . . ."

"I've never had any intention Willis should be like other boys in this town!"

"Nettie, I know what you have against hunting. You equate it with living in Shelby! You've never forgiven me for sticking here when I could have specialled in Vancouver or Montreal or Toronto—when I turned down the Association at the Edmonton convention . . ."

"That's not right!"

"Isn't it! Well, this is right. I like this way of life—I love this town!" He turned from her abruptly, then back to her again. "And I am not spotting geese this evening, but if I manage to finish at the office in time this afternoon, I will walk along MacDougall's coulee, where I will do my damnedest to knock hell out of as many Chinese ring-necked pheasants as I can!"

Only the slight tightening of her mouth showed that he had scored; he started again for the door.

"I don't see how you can manage it," she said after him. "I don't see how you can get away in time and get back from MacDougall's coulee in time."

"In time for what?" He asked it almost calmly, for now as always after an emotional outburst had taken out the dike of his patience, mild self-disgust was spreading through him.

"The supper."

"What supper?"

"The St. Aidan's church supper."

So of course she had won again, he told himself as he drove to the hospital. He would attend the church supper; he certainly wouldn't miss Hersch Midford's event.

When and how had he gone wrong with Willis? He

should have known that he was right and that she was wrong years ago. They should have crouched together under morning and evening flights of ducks; their hearts should have stumbled together at the jack-in-the-box surprise of a rocketing pheasant cock. He had never watched his son's face the first time he felt the tug of a kite line, known when he had slopped in the self-pity of Black Beauty, rejoiced in the conceit of Toad.

He knew that all over the world there must be men who had found it easy to be good fathers to their sons, and he knew now that he had not been one of them, and that he had discovered it much too late. As he had done many times he remembered the October dawn years ago when he had walked over stubble white with frost, with Hugh Cameron and his son, Ian, by his side. They had dug no pits, for their spotting had shown them that the geese were feeding on the green-sprigged margin of summer fallow next to a hailed field where tangled and broken barley stalks afforded excellent cover. Barely after they had got the decoys set and themselves hidden, the high and shrill disorder of the nearing flight thrilled the eastern sky. Their unrelenting advance, inevitable as growth, climactic as death itself, urged the pulse and tightened the throat.

He looked over to Hugh Cameron crouched on his knees beside his son. His gun lay on the ground before him; his hands were gripped tight upon each other and his eyes were closed. His face was tilted upwards, limned in the pale dawn light.

His attention was taken from Hugh's fervent face and up to honking anarchy, the tipping and tilting grey blizzard of wings over their decoys. Already the accordion feet of some were lowered. As captain of the hunt he leaped up; yelled the signal to shoot.

Neither he nor Hugh had fired till they heard the light, flat burst of Ian's single-shot, and saw the boy's very first goose drop to earth.

For him there had never come such a first and ritualistic morning with his own Willis at his side when he might have prayed for his son's success. And such a morning never would come.

He would forget MacDougall's coulee, he told himself

as he opened the office door. Tonight—Hersch Midford's church supper.

"The ladies of Cottonwood Rebekah Lodge cleared about $25.00 at their bake sale held in Oliver's Trading Company Store last Saturday." And that finally did it, Matt told himself; he had just time to make it home, to change for the supper. The whole week had been rushed. Every auctioneer in the district seemed to have been favoured by last-minute instructions from someone or other to sell machinery, cattle, household effects, and other articles too numerous to mention—seven of them to set up, and then Colonel Stettler had to rush in at the last possible moment with his half-page Harvest Auction Sale copy. Also, seventeen Cards of Thanks were probably some sort of record.

He wouldn't have time now even to correct the opening of the upland game season story:

> Guns were banging all over the countryside last Saturday as hunters took advantage of the fine weather which marked the opening of the hunting season on upland game. Good bags of pheasant and sharp-tailed grouse were brought back by many, the pheasants seeming to be more numerous. And the hunters were more numerous than either the grouse or the pheasants.
>
> There was an increase in the No Shooting signs posted, probably because of the number of livestock in the country—although it is reported that in many cases the signs meant little to the would-be hunters.

The report on the Shelby Chapter of the Caledonian Society of Knock-out Curlers' meeting to discuss the progress of their artificial-ice subscription campaign would have to be pushed ahead to next week. It looked as though he would be busy till dawn, and God help him if he had trouble with static electricity and the paper again!

He had to admit that he missed Millie and that he was going to miss her more, even though June had taken over most of her duties. It wasn't fair to her, he'd told her when she'd made her offer, but June had insisted, saying that it was little enough penance for having been the cause of the trouble in the first place. He had disagreed with that.

"Let's say partly, anyway," June said.

"All right."

"I'll do what I can to help—it won't interfere now with my own work too much—and it will be only till you can get someone else."

He knew that she had done most of her interviews and was at her desk more and more, checking off and collating her records. Until he had found someone else then, he'd agreed.

She was just leaving as he came out of his office.

"Going to the supper tonight?"

"Yes," she said. "I've just time to get to the suite and get ready."

"I've cut it fine, too. Joe taking you?"

"No."

"Alone?"

She nodded as she shut up her briefcase.

"Better come with us. I'll pick you up on our way down."

At home he found Ruth looking grim. They would miss the first sitting! There was always a second and a third, he called to her as he headed for the bedroom where she had laid out his shirt and tie and suit and clean underwear. She followed him to the bedroom door. The second or third sitting meant they would get home long past Sarah's bedtime! The child was already tired and keyed up, had been a perfect hellion ever since she had come in with her hair a matted tangle from an afternoon in the sand pile, and he could forget taking a bath, just shave and get changed!

"I'm not taking a bath. Her hair looked all right to me."

"You didn't have to brush at a kicking, pulling, screaming head for half an hour!"

"I guess not. We're picking June up on our way down."

"Oh, no! We won't make it at . . ."

"It'll just take a second. Where are my socks?"

"Why didn't you tell me she was coming with us?"

"I didn't know till I was leaving the office. Where are my socks?"

"On top of the dresser. Isn't she going with Joe?"

"No."

"Why not?"

"I don't know. She just said she was going alone and I asked her to come along with us."

"Oh, Matt . . ."

"There's a hole in this . . ."

"Why did you have to ask her when you were already late! This is one night, Matt, you could have come home on time!"

"I couldn't. And I'll have to go back to the office after the supper."

"Oh, no!"

"One of these has a hole in the toe."

"It's Book Club night!"

"I can't wear these—one of them has a hole in the . . ."

"I said it's Book Club tonight!"

He came to the bedroom door, brandished the socks at her. "I said I can't wear these things with a hole in the . . ."

"What do you want me to do? Darn it now when we're already twenty minutes late?"

"No, I don't want you to darn it now. I want you to darn it a week ago. I want a pair of socks *without* a hole!"

"The rest are down in the wash."

"Look, you knew—you must have known. I don't keep holes in socks a secret from you."

"You'll just have to wear them. I meant to darn them this afternoon but I hadn't figured I'd have so much trouble with Sarah. Matt, I told you I have Book Club tonight."

"Get Rowena then."

"I can't get a sitter this late! They're all CGIT and they'll be cleaning dishes till after ten!"

"All right then, I'll wear these socks. You'll have to miss your Book—"

"How can I! It's at Betty's. I missed the last time at her place and she's so sensitive and she'll take it personally and it's *her* turn! It's the Kenya chapter and that's an important . . ."

"Good God, don't tell me you're still—ever since last Easter you've been *Inside Africa*."

"Oh, Matt, what am I going to do!"

He was stuffing in his shirt as he came out of the bedroom. "Never mind. I'll come home. I'll go down to the office *after* you come home from the goddam Book Club."

"That's white of you."

"Call me *bwana* when you say that. See that Sarah hasn't rumpled herself up while I shave. We might make the third sitting."

But they had made the first after all, to find the waist between the anteroom and the main Sunday school part of the church basement crowded with waiting people: town and country fathers tight of collar with weight on one foot and hands in pockets stood beside hair-slicked sons with weight on one foot and hands in pockets. Mothers, vaguely distracted in their best, tried to keep an eye on small children playing informal tag through the forest of adult legs. Older daughters in tartan skirts and nylon, woollen, or cashmere sweaters now and again touched fingers tenderly to precise waves from the Shelby Beauty Parlour or home-permanent kits.

After they had lined up past Harvey Hoshal seated behind his little square table where he received payment, they entered the banquet room. They walked down one side by the kitchen opening where Mr. Tregillis and Charlie Tait could be seen carving turkey, then turned off between two rows of tables constructed of long boards laid over trestles and stretching the full width of the basement. Just beyond Malleable Jack Brown they found a gap and sat down across from Harry and Nettie Fitzgerald. Too late to do anything gracefully about it, Matt saw that Millie Clocker sat on Nettie Fitzgerald's right.

He looked away from her and down to the table with its settings of silverware tied with identifying bits of coloured string or ribbon or yarn, the water glasses, cream pitchers, sugar and salad bowls each bearing inked strips of adhesive tape for their owners' later recognition. Down the aisles came Canadian Girls in Training in full uniform of pleated skirt and middy and lanyard, each holding steaming plates, tea or coffee pots high above the heads of expectant diners.

From his chair placed strategically at the corner of the table nearest the kitchen serving opening, Canon Midford stood up and stepped slightly back. Heads turned in his direction; several CGIT were stilled in the act of lowering plates before diners; the conversational hum faltered, softened, died finally. It was as though a kinaesthetic breeze stirred out from Hersch, bending forward those heads nearest him, travelling the length of the room to bow those of people still standing in the hall doorway, and, as the last lowered, he began the saying of grace.

"Amen."

All heads rose in concert; conversation resumed; the arrested CGIT girls again took up their drifting and plate-setting-down and pouring; buns were buttered, salad bowls passed, knives and forks picked up. Chewing started; the shallow and angry champ of Malleable Jack Brown, the slow and shyly circular movement of Millie Clocker's compressed lips, the nervous swallowing by Nettie Fitzgerald, who now and again gave a quick ta-ta rub to thumb and fingertips as though to rid them of non-existent crumbs. Whenever Nettie picked up a piece of bread or muffin or bun, Matt thought, she held it lightly as a magician would his wand.

As usual Ruth had managed to shuffle the seating so that he was between her and Sarah; the child would be his entire responsibility through dinner, but he did not mind tonight. As he tucked in the corner of her serviette for her, he saw the eyes of people across and down the table stray to his daughter. They ought to, for she was perfectly dainty in her crisp dress of dotted Swiss blooming over starched crinoline—bluebells and snowflakes, and a poignant ribbon of narrow black velvet circling her neck, where a gold heart locket lay. Her fragility in the blue dress laid a finger on his heart.

He had hoped for an outside seat so that when she sprayed mashed potatoes, gravy, and indiscriminate food bits, they would land harmlessly on the open floor, or at least be kept in the family—on his own or Ruth's lap. But tonight she chose to be the chatelaine, sitting decorously straight with her face grave, her chin just achieving the board table top. She handled her spoon and her cup of cocoa with the grace of twenty years' experience, deftly and without overloading, with none of the extravagant silliness that often descended upon her at mealtimes.

He looked beyond Sarah to her mother leaning slightly across the table to speak to Nettie. Still dark with summer tan, her face presented its fine profile—vitally black hair curling tight and close to her head. Oddly he thought of a Dartmoor pony. Ruth might not appreciate the comparison, but both possessed the same neat grace. He had been so damn lucky! She was the most important thing that had ever happened to him—and Sarah, of course. So far it had been a good life they'd had together—and with these people. Perhaps it was a quiet backwater here, but it had its compensations and he must not lose sight of them.

When they had finished, he took Sarah by the hand to the cloakroom, where June joined them for the ride back. Ruth stayed behind for a moment to speak to Sadie Tregillis. When she caught up with them she carried a dish covered with a serviette.

"You people go on without me. I'm late for Betty's now and it's quicker for me to go out the back way and walk across." She held out the covered dish to June. "This is for Aunt Fan. Drop it off for her. Sarah should go to bed right away, Matt. I'll get back as soon as I can without hurting Betty's feelings, and then you can go down to the office. I'm sorry."

"That's all right."

"I'll darn every one you own tomorrow. Good night," she said to June.

"Good night."

CHAPTER 17

BESIDE MATT IN THE FRONT SEAT OF HIS CAR, JUNE HELD
Sarah in her arms. When the car came to a stop before the
Cayley building, she realized for the first time that the child
was asleep.

"Let me have her." Matt held out his arms.

She handed Sarah to him, but she did not turn back to
open the door immediately; instead she stared at the man
beside her with the little girl sleeping in his arms. Over one
cradling arm Sarah's legs hung limply down, her slight
body caved in utter repose, her cheek resting on Matt's
other hand, her head against his far shoulder.

She leaned toward them to kiss the child; she felt the
scratch of tweed on her cheek. For a moment the face of
the child lay against one shoulder and her own face against
the other. She was suddenly and fearfully sad. When
Matt turned so that the light of the street fell full upon his
face, she kissed him.

"Please, don't try to understand that," she said. "It was
for Sarah really."

"All right," Matt said.

"Another Sarah."

She got out of the car. She took several steps across the
walk, then came back and opened the back door to take out

Aunt Fan's tray from the back seat. She walked to the street door and entered.

As Matt started up the car and drove off, Millie Clocker entered the Cayley building.

It had been quite some time since she had left Matt and Sarah in the car, taken Aunt Fan's tray in to her, then gone home to Mrs. Nelligan's; yet she had simply sat in front of the typewriter, still inexplicably sad. Through her partly opened window came the faint yet distinctive drift of smoke from leaf heaps which must be smouldering near by. Now and again the lights of a passing car blanched the faces of buildings across the street and brightened her own window with a momentary pulse of light.

With luck she might never have to go into a church again; she had that in common with her mother anyway, hating church, though not trying to hide it in the deeply steeped piety and sweetness so patently false. As a girl she had wondered which was worse for her mother—the Sundays themselves, or the Saturday nights when at last her mother must accept the fact of yet another Sunday. The house would be a mess as usual, demanding that it be made presentable for the next day, her father busy with his sermon in the den, the only ordered place in the house.

For a moment her heart hurt as she thought of her father's straight, clear gaze, the hair-splitting honesty of his clean and logical mind. Her father's strength—her mother's weakness. Such undignified and debasing weakness—and with it a frightening and contradictory wilfulness that won cheap trophies every day, won them with tantrums and tears and coquetry.

Idle promises gaily and easily made to a child, and almost never kept. They were always at cross-purposes, and when she was older there were the appeals to her father to iron things out. Her mother had always exaggerated or omitted or pretended confusion and he had never questioned the distortions, so that it seemed that he had always taken her mother's part.

She had watched her mother for all the signs of weakness and self-indulgence, and had schooled herself

quite deliberately to be the opposite. She had not listened—
she would not listen to her mother. She did not believe
her—she would not believe her mother. She was not
interested in acute advice about what a young girl should
know about young men. Young men did not like young girls
who were smarter than they. Young men liked young girls
to talk to them about *themselves*. Young men talked about
young girls who let them get fresh with them—too fresh
with them.

The questions—the questions! Why did she spend so
much time with books? There were other things, weren't
there? What was wrong with tennis? Didn't girls her age go
to parties any more? Didn't they have dates any more?
Didn't they go to movies with boys any more?

Had it been worse before her father's death—or had it
been worse after her father's death? "We've just got each
other now. It's just the two of us against the world now,
dear. We've got to help each other." How intolerable to be
leaned upon, till life became like a dream of pursuit in
which she could only move her arms and legs so slowly—
oh, so slowly. She knew how her father must have felt
during all these years with her mother. "I don't know how
I would have done without you, June. You're the best
daughter in the world. No one could ask for a better
daughter than you are. I'm so lonely without Daddy I don't
know how I can stand it!"

Then there were the sweet fictions her mother built out
of her dead father, gelding him of anger, of humour, of
impatience, of character.

She had waited a decent year after her father's death
before she told her mother they would not live together any
more. At first her mother had not believed her. Then she
had forbidden her to leave. She had stormed. She had cried.
She had even attempted to be practical, pointing out that
keeping two ménages was out of the question. "You have
your work. It would be too much of a drain on you to study
and do research and keep house and get meals. We can be
happy together and I can cook for you and do the housework
for you."

Her mother had literally asked for mercy. She could not

stand the loneliness of living alone. "You'll simply have to, Mother."

"Couldn't we put it off for a little while—until I get used to the idea. Give me some time."

This was when she might have weakened and, generous in victory, might have given her mother some ground, but she had steeled herself. "This weekend, Mother." For the very first time in her life she had won a contest with her mother.

Tonight the harshness of tweed at her cheek, little Sarah in Matt's arms, some sleight of light on his face, had compelled her. He would understand. Her father would have understood.

She sighed. She picked up a sheet from beside the typewriter:

The tables attached (Census of Canada Tables 19, 20, 21, 23, Vol. III) provide data relative to Shelby's and Greater Shelby Municipality's religious stratification system. The largest religious groups are those of the United Church of Canada created from the union of the Methodist and Presbyterian churches (41 per cent) and the Church of England in Canada (21 per cent). The Roman Catholics, Salvation Army, Baptist, and Mormon are the only other groups of any size, accounting respectively for 7 per cent, 6 per cent, 5 per cent, and 5 per cent. This excepts, of course, the two communal colonies of the Hutterian Brotherhood. The Church of the Burning Nazareth, Christian Science, Lutheran, Adventist, British Israelite, Ukrainian (Greek) Catholic, and Confucian comprise the balance. (See Table 23: Population by Specified Religious Denominations for Census Subdivisions—also Table 21: Population by Religious Denomination and Sex.)

From this it may be hypothesized that a Protestant hegemony is real in the community. Indeed, the continuum of religious status holds high catoptricality to the Puritanical affect-action patterns indicated by many of the interviewees, and, if not isomorphic, has definite linkage with the generally conventional sanction-disapproval patterns of the community. Conformity is

rigidly directional: religious intolerance, intense jeal-
ousies, and interdenominational contention are close to
the surface daily. This somewhat intangible socio-
religious atmosphere is a maximal factor in the community.

So it had been him! It had been him all along! Right from
the start! Before she had even moved into the office! That
was why she'd moved into the office! And she'd been all
wrong about Matt; they'd worked it together. He hadn't
really wanted to hire her back that day he'd come to the
suite; why would he want her back when they'd got rid of
her so easily and they could be alone in the office all day
long! The dirty things! Oh, the dirty, filthy things!

Now she knew why Joe Manley hadn't been at the
church supper. He'd just been a blind they had to hide what
was going on! Both of them had used him for a blind.
Sitting there so cool and so smart and so smug, and smiling
that slow smile that was hardly a smile at all. It had been all
she could do to keep from crying it out then, right into her
pure face that hid how false she was underneath. People
should just know how she was carrying on all over the
place, and even smirking about it in the church basement at
a public church supper with the little red Sunday school
kindergarten chairs piled up against the wall behind her.
And Mrs. Fitzgerald sitting right there and not even
dreaming what she was really like!

It was just at dessert that she had known she would be
sick if she had to sit there any longer and look across the
table at her, and if she hadn't left early, then she wouldn't
have come down the street and seen her kiss him in the car
and known it wasn't Joe Manley at all but Matt! Right under
the street light and his baby in the car! If people only knew!
If Mrs. Fitzgerald knew what kind of a woman ate across
from her! Well, she was going to know, all right. Mrs.
Fitzgerald was going to get told about Miss June Melquist
and about Mr. Matt Stanley!

But of course she couldn't do that. She couldn't *tell*
Mrs. Fitzgerald; you couldn't tell anyone to their face
something so shameful and so dirty. She would have to do

it some other way, and it wouldn't be just Mrs. Fitzgerald either. She'd phone Florence Nelligan! But that wouldn't do either—they might recognize her voice. And Mr. Oliver, the way he was the Mayor and he was almost a judge, and the Senator being in the government, and there would be others, she thought excitedly. Aunt Fan! No, not Aunt Fan, it wouldn't be good for her with her bad heart. Why, it was just like making up a list for a party—when you were a girl and you had a birthday party!

It would be some party! Mrs. Nelligan and Mr. Oliver and the Senator and Mrs. Fitzgerald—oh, and Canon Midford. But if she couldn't tell them, and she couldn't phone them, then she must write them without letting them know who had written—a letter to each of them telling them all about what was going on right under their noses!

She had already gone to her dresser and pulled out the top drawer and two boxes of lavender stationery with deckle edges. Actually there weren't two full boxes left, for she had used half of one for the true story she'd sent to *This Is True*, but there'd be plenty for what she was going to do. Nobody would suspect it was her paper, for she had never used it to write anyone a letter ever since she had bought it three years ago at the fall one-cent sale in the Drug Store—fifty-five cents for the first one and fifty-six cents with the extra one thrown in.

"Dear Mrs. Nelligan:
    I think that you should know . . ."

It was frightening but right at the same time; the letter took her and ran with her; there was no conscious summoning of words to unmask the real filth of the woman, the boys-in-the-schoolyard words, the scrawled-on-windows-at-Hallowe'en words. She could feel her face flushed and her heart pounding at her throat. She had stepped completely outside herself, averting her attention from what she was doing, just as she had often turned her gaze from the obscenities written on the toilet walls of the Bus Depot.

"Dear Canon Midford:
    I think that you should know . . ."

Light-headed and breathless as though she were realizing those hopeless dreams of early childhood, and now soared from wonderfully delightful cloud to cloud!

"Dear Mrs. Dr. Fitzgerald:

I think that you should know . . ."

Only the opening was the same for each letter, but Mrs. Fitzgerald's flowed on two closely written pages longer, and was perhaps richer than the others in anatomical detail, particularly after the part that started: "You think everything is lovely and beautiful and sweet all the time, but you ought to get wise to what they are really like . . ."

"Dear Senator:

I think that you should know . . ."

The ringing excitement had already begun to subside before the end of the Senator's letter, and as she addressed the envelopes, the clarity of ordinary feeling had returned her completely to herself. It was over. She knew that she had given of herself as she had never done before, as she would never be able to do again. Now she was filled with peaceful satisfaction; her cheeks were wet; the taste of salt was at the corners of her mouth. But it had been a non-hurting crying, as though a storm of cyclonic violence had been followed by the surprise of soft, warm rain.

She fell into deep and instant sleep. When she awoke in the morning it was almost regretfully, and for several moments she lingered in shallow languor, warm with such complete contentment that waking grazed true drowsing. When she saw the face of the alarm clock on the chair by her bed, however, she was startled quite awake; never before had she slept so soundly that it had failed to call her. Now it was half an hour past the time when she usually got up.

Just as she threw back the covers she saw the narrow stack of lavender envelopes on the dresser top. They frightened her. They drew her across the room. They filled her with despair as they held her before them, bare-footed on the chill floor, reluctant to pick them up, even to touch them. She could not possibly mail them. She could not go through with it. Like everything else with her, it could not come to anything finally successful. It was surprising even that she had written them, for now she could hardly recall what she had written in them. She picked up the top one, then dropped it quickly as she saw that its flap was sealed; all of them were addressed and stamped and ready to go.

And she must go; there was not time to make her breakfast, not time enough even to drop into the Palm Café for a cup of coffee, barely time to dress and to make it to the telephone office. She dressed in panic, slipped the letters into the heart of the current *This Is True*, then buried the magazine deep in her lingerie drawer just before she went out.

CHAPTER 18

IN LATE AFTERNOON, SEVERAL DAYS AFTER THE CHURCH supper, Matt turned away from parking his car and saw the blocky figure of Sam Barnes.

"Sam, haven't seen you in months."

"Haven't been in for months," Sam said, "not since spring." Sam's trips into Shelby had become more and more infrequent with the passage of years. If he worked it properly he could get by with only six a year, buying two months' supplies each time, making the six coincide with beef shipments, income-tax returns, machinery repairs, the bull and calf sales. Usually he managed to have a visit with his old friends, the Senator, Clem Derrigan, Billy Thompson.

"I told your girl in there," Sam turned a thumb toward the office. "Fifty No Shootin' signs."

"Posting your land, Sam?"

"I am now. One bull shot an' . . ."

"But it's a month till big-game hunting . . ."

"The bull died just the same," Sam said flatly.

"I'm sorry to hear that. You been in touch with the Mounties?"

"They can't do nothin' about it. Nobody can do nothin' about it. I might of done somethin' about it twenty years ago—if I'd got out of this country, to hell an' gone North to the Peace River or Yukon."

"Oh, it's not all that bad, Sam."

"Right from early spring it is. Pilin' up Paradise Valley, trampin' over my lease. Leavin' gates open, scatterin' their garbage an' their tin cans an' their bottles. My brush an' grass is like tinder now. Just take the sun through one them bottles, just right, like a magnifyin' glass an' a steady strong chinook an' they can burn me right out."

"Let's hope you don't get burnt out."

"Yeah. How's Ruth?"

"Fine."

"Sarah, the Senator."

"They're fine," Matt said.

"That's nice." He stared speculatively at Matt for a moment. He indicated the office with a jerk of his head. "She workin' for you?"

"She's helping," Matt said.

"An' doin' her book."

"That's right."

"She knows how to ask questions." He turned away. "See you next spring."

"You finally caught up with Sam Barnes," Matt said to June as he entered the office.

"I did."

"He says you know how to ask questions."

"And he knows how to answer them," June said. "No doubt about how Sam feels."

"Don't forget he's just had a seven-hundred-and-fifty-dollar bull shot."

"Yes. But bull or no bull it's pretty clear how Sam feels about the town."

"Oh, Sam says things a little more strongly than he really means to."

"But he is a good example of the country's antipathy for the town."

"Does the country have antipathy for the town?"

"Do you think it does?"

"Not noticeably. Most farmers and ranchers think town

business men have it pretty soft—don't really work for their money, don't *produce* or *grow* anything—and I suppose in a way they're right. But don't depend too much on Sam. He's a lone wolf, always has been, would be whether he lived in town or country. He doesn't mind coming into town half so much as he pretends."

Poor old Billy, Sam Barnes thought, as he drove his truck away from the hospital; not very likely they'd heal that broken hip for him—not at seventy-eight, they wouldn't.

It was a wonder that more of them didn't have bones broken, the way they lived all scrunched together flank to flank, nose to tail, barely spitting-distance from each other. Every man to his taste, but he had always preferred the range to the stall, and wasn't fussy about dung on his hips. He was just as well satisfied that none of his cronies were handy this trip, for with harvest over and good weather holding, more people than ever were milling along the streets, in and out of the Cameo Theatre, the Arlington, the Palm Café, all the stores. Their cars and trucks crowded the curbs so that there was no parking place for him. He drove past the Salvation Army Band playing on the Marshall, Anglin, and Battersby Real Estate corner. He found an opening before the Hardware, squeezed in and killed the motor, then saw the No Trucks sign. With difficulty he backed out, drove twice around the block fruitlessly and slowly, then turned up the Post Office street and had gone almost a quarter of the block before he realized that he was pointing the wrong direction on a one-way street. It had not been so marked last spring: this was just a sneaking sort of surprise in the campaign they waged against a man when he came in off his place. The only reason he wanted to park was to buy their goddam merchandise as quickly as he could and get to hell out of their town!

He was successful finally in a side street that ran down from the Cameo Theatre corner. As he walked toward Oliver's Trading Company Store he felt himself jogged and jostled anonymously by the drift of people on either side of him. Within Oliver's he waited for half an hour till he could give Bob Thompson his list.

"Fill it out. I'll be back when it's ready." He turned away from the counter to bump into some woman who had been breathing down the back of his neck; when he stepped aside she did so too; when he corrected, she skipped in the same direction, until he felt as though he were astride a cutting horse facing a stubborn cow.

On the crowded street again he walked back toward the Arlington. He'd have a quick beer, pick up his groceries, and get out. Just before the Arlington he ran into Rory Napoleon.

"Rory—c'mon in the Arlington."

Rory just looked at him and silently shook his head. Sam pushed into the Arlington Beer Parlour. First time he'd ever known Rory to refuse a free drink.

First time in his life he'd ever refused a free drink, Rory Napoleon was telling himself sadly. He stood in the doorway of the Hardware Store, watching the slow flow of shoppers lured to town by the incredibly mild weather. A whole pay cheque in his pocket and it didn't mean a thing. Couldn't do a thing for him—not a goddam thing!

His eyes idled over the aimless passersby. Wasn't a one of them couldn't go into the Arlington if he felt like it. A man in denim overalls and smock with the flat shoes of a farmer stopped at the window to Rory's right; the boy at his side, wearing a fedora much too large for his small child face, pointed out the twenty-two rifle leaning against the wheel of a red bicycle in the window display. They brushed past Rory and entered the store.

Hell, wouldn't he like to get Byron a twenty-two. Byron could use a twenty-two—or a bicycle. Probably the only kid in the district didn't have a twenty-two or a bicycle, or a twenty-two *and* a bicycle. He couldn't buy a glass of beer with the pay cheque, but he could go buy Byron a twenty-two. Mame could still go into the beer parlour. All of them. Everyone but Rory Napoleon!

The door up the street, Oliver's Trading Company, opened and Bob Thompson emerged, knees half bent, arms clasped around a carton of groceries. He wrestled it into the back of a ton truck at the curb, then leaned on his elbows at the opened window, talking with someone inside the cab. Lucky, lucky, all of them. Always had the money for grub and stuff for the kids—and for beer!

From far down the street came a thin but vigorous assault upon the early evening air. The Sally Ann. Started already by the Royal Bank corner. Beer. He listened to gauge the distance from the muted brass pulse, dim but exuberant. Beer. Four town girls, uncertain on their high heels, walked by. Beer. Must be about in front of Marshall, Anglin, and Battersby Real Estate; Captain Leppard and Mrs. Leppard all set for harvesting Shelby souls. Beer.

The brave and distant sound of the Salvation Army band, the wildness of the fall chinook smelling of mountain draws and jack pine and melting snow, slipped him back to his boyhood days. There was the difference! How you were born was what did it! You either got born a horse or a dog or a fool-hen or a goat or a human. He had to go and get dropped in the corner of a reservation bull field, get laced into a moss-packed yo-kay-bo, get weaned on an elk bone, and grow up to haul their garbage!

Anyway, they sure threw the religion at you in the church tent—real Methodisty stuff. And he had more fun when he was a kid, by God! Tag around the tents, eat beans and bannock when it was there, roll in or roll out when you felt like it, grabbing hold of girls. That gave the missionary the heartburn. Onward Christian soldiers washed in the blood. Jesus wants me for a sunbeam. Throw out the lifeline. He'd wondered some about that one, until Billy Sheepskin had said it was just like colt roping.

God, he could use a beer! It was rough, the way a man's tongue stuck to the roof of his mouth and his throat got stiff for the tickle of beer and the earth taste of beer. And now the bastards had said God Save the Queen to it and that was all there was to it. He couldn't do a thing about it. Couldn't go in the place even; law said he couldn't even smell beer. Well, send the goddam law victorious—didn't know beer was glorious. Beer never hurt him, never hurt anybody. Let everyone suck beer down and not a drop for him!

They held a man down right from the start; then they tied his arms to his sides to make sure. He wasn't any different from the rest of them; anyone needed a beer he did.

Right now if a fellow walked up to him, offered him a drink of beer, he'd give anything. Anything! Ten years for one beer, twenty, rest of his life! Dear Jesus, for the salt coolness of beer sliding down his hot throat!

With his shoulders he pushed himself away from the Hardware Store window. The door opened and out came the farmer and his son with the hat swallowing his face. The boy was holding the twenty-two rifle with both hands.

"Give them gophers hell, boy," Rory said and turned down the street. He'd had just about enough, more than enough! He walked with his shoulders swinging, loped two blocks south, then crossed the railway track and turned west. He stopped before a flat-roofed building of faded yellow. The sign over the door said "Art's Taxi."

He went in. Artie Buller, seated in a wooden chair by a desk under the window, looked up.

"Artie," said Rory, reaching for his pay cheque, "you got a customer."

"Where to, Rory?"

"Not where to—how much?"

"Huh?"

Rory laid the cheque on the desk. "Thirty-one dollars and sixty-five cents. I could go in the liquor vendors, she'd buy me ten—eleven jugs."

"Hey, I can't sell you no . . ."

"Off you I should get five jugs."

"You're on the Indian List."

"Uh-huh—an' so's the fellows from Paradise Reserve. I want four jugs wine an' you drive us to my place."

"But, Rory, that's pretty serious, sellin' liquor to a fella's been interdicted—two-hundred-dollar fine."

"Pretty serious sellin' liquor to Indians," Rory countered. "I still got connections out at Paradise, Artie. Wouldn't be too much trouble to get somebody out there to tell Corporal McCready you been sellin' 'em liquor. I'll just wait here whilst you . . ."

"They won't take cheques at the vendors'."

"Didn't say they would. I'll sign the back of her. You can cash her anywhere—it's a town cheque."

"Just liquor store wine," suggested Artie hopefully.

"Nope—dee-looxe." He referred to Artie's presentation

grade improved by the addition of grain alcohol to the mother catawba. Rory took one of the pens from his jacket pocket, bent over the desk, and printed his name on the cheque in large block capitals. He did it with painful slowness and great satisfaction.

Just like everywhere else the goddam Arlington Beer Parlour was jammed. Sam finished his beer and made his way to the Men's. Every urinal occupied! He made his way out and then through the back door to the alleyway, moved over and faced the brick wall, unzipped his fly. Just in time!

He was down to the last drop when he heard somebody behind him: Corporal McCready of the Royal Canadian Mounted Police.

"Sam, I'm sorry—you'll have to come with me."

"Yeah—I want to report the hunter shot my bull."

"That too, perhaps. I'm going to have to charge you . . ."

"What the hell for!"

"Indecent exposure."

Though he had promised Ruth he would try to make it home on time for once, Matt hadn't been able to get away. Colonel Stettler had come in at the last possible moment with another sale ad. He couldn't recall when there had been a full column of In Memoriams. Those were what had eaten most of his afternoon actually, for the remembering bereaved were always reluctant to make their decision from the book of selections he kept under the front counter. Number nineteen seemed still ahead of all the others:

> A day of remembrance we recall,
> Without farewell you left us all.
> But your memory lingers fond and true;
> There's not a day, (First Personal Name),
>   that we do not think of you.

And number thirty-two, which would appear in this issue three times, was a close runner-up:

Deep in the heart lies a picture
Of a dear one laid to rest:
In memory's frame we shall hold it
Because he (or she or Mother or Father or Sister or
    Brother) was one of His blest.

He wished he'd been able to keep his promise to Ruth
about being home to dinner on time. After their talk at lunch
it had been especially important. She had asked him how
June's survey was coming along and he had said he
supposed it was coming along all right.

"How soon will she be finished with it?"

"Pretty soon," he said, "a month or so, I imagine."

"What conclusions has she drawn about us?"

"I don't know, Ruth."

"Don't you think you should?"

"If she thought I should, she'd have told me."

"And she hasn't."

"No," he said, "she hasn't."

"I wonder why not."

"Oh, Ruth."

"Because, Matt—you've had a great deal to do with it."

"Not such a great . . ."

"Yes, you have."

"I've helped her."

"Why?"

"I don't know why. I just have."

"A person might almost say you'd collaborated with
her."

"I have not," he protested.

"And yet you haven't any idea of what conclusions she
may have drawn about us—none at all."

"No, I haven't," he said.

"Has she been afraid to tell you?"

"Ruth, I'm sure she hasn't been afraid to tell me
anything. I haven't asked her and she hasn't offered to."

"She should have. Haven't you wondered why she
hasn't said anything to you about it?" When he didn't
answer her she said, "You must have, Matt. You've
introduced her to people, opened the doors of Shelby homes

to her, got them to accept her, confide in her. She's used the *Chinook* office to work in—pushed Millie out . . ."

"Now hold on—that wasn't her fault!"

"No, that's not fair," Ruth said. "All the time she worked for you Millie was a cross to bear. But all the same, Matt, I'm right and you know I'm right." When he made no comment, she said, "What about Joe?"

"Well, what about him?"

"Is she all through with Joe?"

"What a hell of a way to put it. Maybe Joe's through with her. However it is, it's Joe's business and it's her business—it's not my business!"

"You seemed to think it was. When she first came here, you were all for . . ."

"Joe's private affairs are . . ."

"Having them get together. They aren't now. I wonder what's happened there."

"I'm sure I don't know."

"Don't you want to know? He's your friend, Matt. Do you realize he hasn't been to the house—we haven't seen him in over a month!"

"Whose fault is that?"

"Oh, it's nobody's fault. It's just that he hasn't . . ."

"But you're implying it's June's fault."

"No, I'm not. I'm not interested in June Melquist, not interested in her at all. I'm interested in you and Joe, and my friends. She's no more important to me than the wind over my hand! But you are! Oh, Matt—you've changed. You've . . ."

He had tried to reassure her, to convince her he had not changed, but he knew he had not been successful. And perhaps the reason for that was that he had not been too sure himself that she was not right.

He was going to be almost an hour late for dinner. As he drove home past the Mounted Police Barracks, he saw Sam Barnes's truck there. Sam was just coming out of the police building. Decided to report the shooting of his bull after all, Matt told himself.

CHAPTER 19

THERE WAS ONE THING TO BE SAID ABOUT BEING INTERDICTED for over three months, Rory Napoleon decided: when a man did get hold of the stuff it had gained in muzzle velocity, increased its range, and improved its penetration power. This was no quiet little wine in the four jugs Artie had bought and spiked for him; it was as quiet as the lightning charge of an upright grizzly. Artie had told him the advertisements claimed that its vigorous bouquet hinted fragrantly of "Dance, Provençal song, and sun-burnt mirth!"; its smell reminded Rory of dark alleyways, scratch houses, and railway jungles, where it was more familiarly known as McGoof. Many in town called it Artie's Own; among epicureans of the Paradise Valley Indian Reserve it went under the name of Old Wolverine; all were agreed that the year that mattered most was the year in which it was drunk. Fortified as it was with grain alcohol, esters, ethers, and ketones, it bewildered the sinuses and antrums first, in time numbed the taste buds, and by the half-gallon mark had bruised the palate and stunned the stomach, liver, gizzard, lights, and higher nervous centres. At the end of a gallon Rory could generally expect locomotor ataxia, clarified now and again by vertigo. Or, as he put it, two gallons got him as drunk as he wanted to be.

By dawn of the next day he had achieved this holiday state of total anaesthesia, reclining on sweet-clover hay in a corner of the pole shed south of the goat pen. Eight hours later he awoke chilled and sobered in dusk musty with the smell of mould, aslant with dust-vibrant bars of sunlight. He reached for the half-filled jug at his side.

A gallon and some eighteen hours later he teetered out of the shed and across the yard to the goat pen. He made a place for himself by pushing aside the brush that Byron had piled on top to keep the goats from leaping to freedom and Ollie Pringle's land, then climbed up and hooked his heels on a lower pole. He stared down upon the forty-seven goats below. Though some humans in their looks might suggest animals ursine, porcine, or piscine, bovine or equine, vulpine, lupine, canine, or feline, all people for Rory Napoleon, drunk or sober, always resembled goats.

It might have been a matter only of common clues in eye and jaw and nostril. Rory was not interested in the perceptual why; he only knew that now he looked down upon the Daughters of the IODE, the members of Shelby Rotary, the Activarians, the Knights of the Loyal Order of Homesteaders, the town council, and the North Siders—in goat form.

"You—Mrs. Fitzgerald," he addressed the white nanny with the full bag, just beneath him, "can go piss up a rope, for I ain't emptyin' another can for you till you get your cesspool down past hardpan."

Matter of fact he wasn't hauling any of their stinking garbage. Just why in hell should he have to do the dirty work anyway, forever? Ought to be somebody else's turn for a change. He shouldn't have to do it all the time, just because he was Rory Napoleon and that was an awful thing to be. It was the worst thing there was! He was ignorant and he was smoked and there was nothing he could do about it. They didn't have to get their dollars out of their back and out of their wind and out of their shoulders like he did because he didn't have any education. That didn't make them any better than him.

"I'm a human same as anybody else, ain't I? Don't that mean something, Oliver?" He appealed to the billy behind Nettie Fitzgerald, the one-horned roan with the glassy wall-eye fixed upon him. "Don't it mean something if a person's a human? Ain't it more important to be a human than to be a horse or a dog or a goat? It's a head start, Oliver. I got the selfsame guts you got. I got Mame. I got kids. I got human blood in me! Jesus, I'm only a *quarter* smoked!"

He had almost lost his balance on his precarious seat, and when he had regained it, he spoke to Mr. Oliver in a more reasonable tone. "I really don't get no kick out of garbage, Oliver. I never got used to it yet, no more'n the fellow wore the elk turd under his cap for thirty years."

But Mr. Oliver had turned and was making his slow way through the herd to the opposite side of the pen. Rory was suddenly filled with uncontrollable anger against Mr. Oliver, against all of them. He could not remember when he had felt so violent a feeling toward anyone before in his life. He wanted to hurt them for making him do their maggot work. He half rose from his perch.

"I was born human!" he shouted after Mr. Oliver. "I'll die human! I eat human! I drink human! I am human! I'm me! I'm Rory Napoleon!"

All the assembly had turned their attention up to him, but they were just goats now. Forty-seven plain goats. "I'm a human," he explained carefully to them. "What's more, I am the only human on this whole earth which *is* Rory Napoleon."

He could clean himself by hurting them. He had that coming to him, and they had it coming to them. If he could only clean himself like a maggot, the way they did when you put them into sawdust or oatmeal or bran and they wiggled and squirmed and twisted the filth from themselves—cleaned themselves!

He grabbed the butt end of willow brush by his thigh and wrenched it loose from the pile blocking the pen; he attacked the rest furiously, flushed with wine, elation, and exertion. It was only a matter of minutes till he had the top of the pen cleared.

"All right! All right now!" he yelled at them. "You can come up outa there. Nothin' to stop you now! High-yuh!" he shrilled as they huddled together at the far side of the pen, blinking up at him in the astonishing sunlight.

"Get your lazy arses out of it! Move, you shaganappi,

spring-heeled, china-eyed English bastard, Oliver! Hough-hough-hah-hup-yaaaah, Mrs. Tregillis! Hell's about to go out for recess, Mrs. Wilton—yah!"

The black Nubian Mayor Oliver made a bound from the ragged edge of the herd, then a nervous dash across the clear space before him. He was overtaken by a white nanny.

"That's the way," encouraged Rory as she sailed with teats swinging over the top rail of the pen. "You first, Mrs. Fitzgerald, an' the rest is sure to follow!"

In three minutes the goat eruption was complete.

The herd undulated as though he were shaking out a huge and ragged blanket before himself. Except for the delicate hail of hoof tips upon the CPR traffic bridge it was a singularly discreet procession. Now and again some would straggle behind the main column, then move up to join it, but in the lead always was Nettie Fitzgerald, with the noses of Sadie Tregillis, Minnie Oliver, and Florence Nelligan at her flank, Mrs. Wilton and Mr. Oliver crowding close upon them.

After the bridge came the railway right-of-way, and beyond that the north end of Main Street. There was no gradual introduction to the business section, simply the lumber yard on one side and the Catholic church on the other, so that Rory and the forty-seven goats burst upon the street with the clean surprise of an ambush.

It was Saturday night. He couldn't have selected a better Saturday night. No other Saturday was the climactic night of the Foothill Stock Growers' Convention which had swelled the town's population with over two hundred delegates. It was that Saturday night of the month on which the Shelby and Greater Shelby District Emergency and Disaster Relief and Civil Defence Committee held their first and only meeting in the Ranchmen's Club over the Palm Café, since the Stock Growers had hooked the Civic Centre for the three days of their convention. It was also the night that the Cameo Theatre was exhibiting to its only packed house since the advent of television to Shelby a VistaVision religious spectacular that showed the slaughter of five thousand Christian extras and nine thousand animals in the

Coliseum, as well as the Crucifixion, and the sack of Rome. The Russians had just shocked the world with the announcement of their successful satellite; ten days before, a two-hundred-yard section of the new Trans-Canada Pipeline had exploded twenty-nine miles east of Shelby. The previous June the Liberal government had been defeated by the Conservatives after fifteen unbroken years in power; Canada had lost the world hockey championship to Sweden; the Milwaukee Braves had taken the World Series; and the Northern Lights had the night before tented the entire sky with frightening brilliance.

The day, the week, the month, the year were unique in a chain of chance fragile with coincidence which might have parted at any link short of the final anarchy. It could have been broken if Millie Clocker had kept her head at the switchboard, if the Ranchmen's Club, where the Shelby and Greater Shelby District Emergency and Disaster Relief and Civil Defence Committee were meeting, had not been above Main Street, if Dick Moon had not stepped out of the Hardware Store for coffee when he did, if Morton Moon, staying behind till his dad got back had not been a passionate twelve-year devotee of television western serials, and had left the ten-gauge double-barrel in its place on the Hardware Store gun rack.

At the head of the brightly lit and teeming Main Street to which Rory had herded his goats, Nettie Fitzgerald (goat) stopped, facing Howie Northcote and Alfie Barnes (humans), who had just rounded the corner. Pressured from behind by Rory, the goats crowded and jammed together. Nettie turned toward the solid line of cars and trucks along the curb to her left. Then she turned to the brick veneer wall of the Royal Bank building to her right. She turned back toward Howie and Alfie, backed up a couple of preparatory paces and lowered her head. Howie and Alfie turned. Nettie (goat) took Alfie (human). Mrs. Nelligan (goat) took Howie (human). Both boys were sent sprawling and wide-armed to the sidewalk. The herd lifted and flowed over their prone bodies. People dived for store doors and the openings between cars, clearing the street ahead. The goats might have charged the full length of Main Street, except that Nettie veered through an empty parking space halfway down the block, taking her followers into the centre of the road.

There, with complaining brakes, the Saturday-night traffic came to a halt and quickly bottled up the street back in both directions to the ends of the block, so that the goats were hemmed in. This was only for a moment. They turned off at an alley opening, but could go no farther, finding it blocked by the Shelby Transport van unloading there. They trotted up the sidewalk as far as Oliver's Trading Company Store, where Mr. Tregillis (goat), window-shopping, caught sight of the fresh vegetable display and led a splinter group of seven through the open door. Eleven others of faltering faith in Nettie's leadership followed Mr. Oliver (goat) to the front of the Arlington Beer Parlour, where one of the outgoing patrons obligingly held open the door. To any of the Napoleon goats any opening was a familiar phenomenon, and now in their frightened bewilderment they automatically sought the security of the confinement they had known for three months. The offer of sanctuary in the beer parlour was accepted by all but one.

Nettie Fitzgerald (goat), meanwhile, had taken her diminished retinue of twenty-nine as far as the Cameo Theatre, where the double doors stood wide in readiness for the changing of shows. They entered the darkened interior just as Alaric's Visigothic hordes breached the outer gates of Rome.

The dissenter from Mr. Oliver's (goat) group had been Father McNulty (goat), who turned away from the Arlington Beer Parlour, trotted to the corner, and went up a side street and out of the business section entirely. Three blocks away he came to the shelter of a vague cluster of buildings and stopped to clip the dry grass there.

Mr. Oliver (human) had tried with ineffectual pokes of the store broom to dislodge Mr. Tregillis (goat) and his browsing colleagues from the fresh vegetable and fruit counter. He admitted failure finally and phoned Millie Clocker, asking her to ring for the police and to have Fire Chief Alsop also turn out a couple of available men. In his excitement he did not explain to Millie that there was no fire, and that the men were needed for extraordinary duties.

Millie set off the fire siren first, then plugged in for the
Mounted Police.

Within the Arlington Beer Parlour the banter and laughter and friendly argument had changed to curses, grunts,
shouts, and roars as beer-inflamed men and sober goats
mixed together in bleating, butting, kicking, struggling
nihilism over a floor awash with spilled beer, broken glass,
and overturned chairs and tables. The concussion of the fray
vibrated the common wall the beer parlour shared with
Moon's Hardware next door, and Morton, looking after the
store during his father's coffee break, took down the
double-barrel ten-gauge from the gun shelf and slipped in
two number four magnum shells.

On the Cameo screen torches had been touched to the
Palatine Hill. While gladiator and Goth battled against the
leaping Technicolor flames, people in outside seats became
uneasily aware of numerous rustling, moving shapes tapping along the darkened aisles.

Father McNulty (goat) was quietly grazing his own
business when the siren on the fire hall beside him set up its
scooping wail. He catapulted to the roof, bounded the
length of the eave, then superbly leaped the dark gap to the
building beyond, went up the slope, and picked his way
along the ridge. When he came to the end of that he could
discern a towering skeletal structure; his hoofs clanged as he
soared upwards and came to brief rest on a cross-rail before
climbing to the top high over the town buildings.

On hearing the fire siren, Harvey Hoshal (Rescue and
First Aid), Malleable Jack Brown (Flat Bottom Boats and
Flood Control), and Charlie Tait (Shelter and Alarm) went
to the Main Street window of the Ranchmen's Club smoking-
room where they were holding their meeting of the Shelby
and Greater Shelby District Emergency and Disaster Relief
and Civil Defence Committee. They saw the Mounted
Police cruiser wheel round the Royal Bank corner with red
light flashing, sensed the confusion in the street below, and
heard the rioting uproar from the Arlington Beer Parlour.
Charlie Tait ran to the phone and gave Millie Clocker the
blue alert. She signalled the red, however, which would
sound the siren again, ring St. Aidan's Church bell, warn
the hospital staff, summon Dr. Fitzgerald with stretcher-

bearers, and flush out Ollie Pringle with ambulance and pulmotor.

Morton Moon stood before the Arlington Beer Parlour with the loaded ten-gauge in his hands. He had no intention of using it as he had seen sheriffs and their deputies do on CBC. He was simply waiting to hand it to someone older and much braver than he. The fury within the Arlington had abated, for waiters and patrons at the bar end of the parlour had formed into a slowly advancing line facing a slowly retreating line of goats. Pete Bruner stood to one side of the door, ready to throw it open at the strategic moment that the goats were close enough to recognize the triangular *gestalt* of themselves—the door—freedom.

Now on the street before the Arlington, Morton heard the sounds of two new sirens: the one on the fire engine racing south on First Street, the other on Ollie Pringle's ambulance racing north on First Street. St. Aidan's bell began to tongue the night. The fire siren gave three preparatory whoops before it took up the sustained ululation of the red alert.

The church bell penetrated the stirring darkness of the Cameo Theatre, where furry barbarians were garotting fine old Senators with their own togas and carrying shrieking Roman matrons through falling marble columns and burning rubble. The strange scrambling in the aisles and the hysteria of three sirens instantly convinced all the patrons that the theatre was ablaze.

It was as though the downtown section of Shelby had become the toy of some idiot giant child and was now activated by a great hopper trickling alarm that filled each heart with a cargo of dread till it ran downhill, was tripped and spilled, only to be refilled again, this time with grains of consternation, the next with fright, then terror, and finally panic. As panic-stricken Cameo patrons erupted from the theatre they thought was burning, the panic-stricken herd burst out of the Arlington Beer Parlour. Ollie Pringle's ambulance reached Main and First streets at the same moment as the fire engine. Father McNulty (goat), perched high above the Shelby power plant, put out a moist and inquisitive nose to the thing of gleaming glass and metal and cable on the roof before him. Morton Moon went down in a smother of goats. His hand convulsed on the trigger of the ten-gauge goose gun, discharged both barrels at a distance of eighteen inches from the twenty-six-foot plate window of his father's store. The shotgun blast coincided with the superb head-on collision of the ambulance and the fire engine, as well as with the crackling detonation that signalled the electrocution of Father McNulty (goat), who had grounded the Shelby power plant transformer with a Queen's Birthday fountain of sparks and a sheet of violet that lit up the town and the district as far as the correction line. Citizens of Mable Ridge heard the explosion; those of Khartoum said they had.

In the pitch of sudden darkness on Main Street there were too many people and too many goats. People stampeded blindly toward the Royal Bank corner and were brought up against the barricade formed by the fire engine and the ambulance. They swept back through the lightless night, driving goats before them, until the goats came up against an obstacle and returned, heads lowered angrily in the dark. Some people sought safety in cars, others in stores. Those in cars and trucks turned on their headlights, so that a grotesque magic-lantern show of goats and humans was projected against the flat faces of the stores; it was neither VistaVision nor Technicolor, but the sack of Rome had been pale by comparison.

Within the stores, kerosene and mantle lamps, flashlights, and candles were brought out, but they had hardly been lit before full light came on from the town's auxiliary power plant. Some order was reasserting itself, for many now knew that there had been no fire, invasion, earthquake, pipe-line explosion, or falling Russian satellite—just the Napoleon goats. Except for the Arlington Beer Parlour cuts and bruises now being treated by Harry Fitzgerald there had miraculously been no serious injuries. None of the stretchers were needed. Charlie Tait started to phone Millie Clocker to give the all-clear signal, but was persuaded by the other members of the Shelby Emergency and Disaster Relief and Civil Defence Committee that another sounding of the siren might be unfortunate.

In his doorway Willie MacCrimmon was handing out stiff new blond lassoes to Foothills Stock Grower delegates, ranchers, and ranch hands, and to farmers and townspeople who wished that they were ranchers or ranch hands. From the tops of truck cabs and cars and the Post Office War Monument they roped goats; they spooked them out of the Cameo Theatre, heeled them in Oliver's Trading Company Store, cut them out, looped them, dragged them and herded them into the railway loading-pens, where they stood reflectively.

Right after he had turned the goats into the top of Main Street and given the wild whoop that had precipitated them upon Howie Northcote and Alfie Barnes, Rory went back through the lumber yard, retraced his steps over the CPR bridge, and made straight for home and the feed shed. There he fell upon the hay and reached down for the last of his jugs of wine. He finished it.

Slightly after midnight Constables Dove and Clarkson entered the shed. One took Rory by the legs, the other by the armpits. They carried him out, a snoring hammock between them, to the cruiser, and headed for town and the barracks.

The following Wednesday afternoon his case was heard before Mr. Oliver.

CHAPTER 20

IT WAS A WEEK AFTER THE TERRIBLE NIGHT THE NAPOLEONS'
goats were loosed upon the town that Millie knew she must
post the letters she had slipped inside *This Is True* and
placed in her lingerie drawer. In the first place she sensed
that Miss Melquist must be coming to the end of her stay in
Shelby and the letters should be mailed while she was still
in town. Secondly, she had seen June and Matt having
coffee together in the Palm Café, and when they had left
they had gone right past her and hadn't even spoken to her,
just like she was dirt that wasn't worthwhile their noticing.
The next morning during her coffee break she slipped into
the Post Office but failed, for it was mail time and the place
was crowded with people. That afternoon she came off
duty, went up to her room, put the letters into her purse,
walked straight to the Post Office, and found it deserted.
They were too thick to slip into the slot all at once, but went
through in three batches. She could hear them slap as they
fell into the bin.

Nettie Fitzgerald turned away from her mailbox in the Post
Office, took the four steps to the table under the window.
There she separated what was obviously Harry's office mail

from what was household. Mostly bills, since it was the beginning of the month. She held a square lavender envelope in her hand for a moment.

It was addressed in neat, round handwriting, and was evidently a town letter, and that was unusual; except for Christmas cards, wedding invitations, funeral thank-yous, and monthly store bills, people did not usually write letters to people in Shelby. They phoned. They dropped in. They met in the street.

She opened the letter.

"Dear Mrs. Dr. Fitzgerald:
   I think that you should know . . ."

It was as though partial aphasia had robbed her of reading comprehension. Her eyes no longer travelled properly along the closely written lines, for the obscene words were very distracting. Each called attention to itself; one shocked glance could take them all in at once. So it was with the next page and with the next. Dazed, she lowered the letter, automatically returning Mr. Oliver's greetings as he passed by her.

Who—who could possibly have done it! Who hated her this much—enough to send a letter like this to her!

Mr. Oliver customarily picked up his mail on the way home from the store for lunch. He would save the letters until after he had eaten and gone to his armchair in the living-room. There, under Cousin Rupert's picture and Walter's, he would open and read them.

Because it was the only personal-looking letter of them all, he picked up the lavender envelope first.

"Dear Mr. Oliver:
   I think that you should know . . ."

Once he had accidentally dropped a lighted match into a deep drift of cottonwood fluff along the back fence; the running flame then had been no more instantaneous or fierce than the flame of his anger now. And then just as

suddenly the anger was not so much savage as it was
distressing, a deep and helpless anger. Never, he knew,
would the writer of this letter be discovered and brought to
justice. Even if faint chance brought the writer under the
eye of the law, the penalty could not possibly be a just one.

He looked down to the letter again and it was of such
primitive obscenity that his mind held back from examining
it. The only thing he could be clear about, *wanted* to be
clear about, was that he must turn it over to the authorities,
even though he was certain the police would be unable to do
anything about it.

He knew now that he would not have his usual hour nap
before going back to the store, and he felt suddenly very
tired, so tired that he was not in command of his thoughts at
all. He was thinking numbly that it wasn't exact to call them
four-letter words. "Whore," for instance, had five letters;
the one used in suggesting the camouflaged inadequacy of
Dr. Melquist's secondary sex features possessed only three
letters. Since the rest was out of the question, he supposed
he must get the letter to the local detachment office of the
RCMP. He stood up. Of course, they came generally in
pairs, so that with an "s" they could be considered a
four-letter word. They could be.

A thin cloud of gnats passed over the grass at his feet, lifted
in clutching, circling flight. The Senator felt a crawling
tickle at the bridge of his nose, over and down one cheek;
he lifted one hand, but it had left him, then returned. The
hell with it—the hell with it! And he knew that he was
dismissing more than the irritant fly. At any moment his
mind would be busy again with the hurt that had bothered
him ever since Clem had come home with the mail. Forget
it—forget it!

It seemed colder now; some of the Indian-summer
warmth must have faded from the afternoon. He must have
mercifully dozed, and while he'd slept, the climate within
his own body had imperceptibly changed. No way of telling
what time it was, with the sun obscure now behind haze. It
wouldn't be four o'clock anyway, because children passing
the far side of the hedge usually marked that hour for him.

A woman had written the thing; he was sure of that. But why! Why! There could be no truth whatever in it; he had known that as he read it. Nothing could possibly shake that instant conviction, but at the same time he could find no assurance that this was just the beginning of the thing. He had no way of telling where or how it would end, and how much damage might be done. This was just the same old confusing ground that he had been over and over again.

He lifted a hand and brought it down several times on the chair arm—solidly. Fruitlessly he had been seeking the faintest scent to give him direction, and no way had opened for him. He felt a water drop chill against his cheek, looked up; it had come from the sprinkler, and what was Clem doing, watering the lawn in October? There was no use in keeping the grass green a few more days. The monkey faces of the pansies had been long shrivelled, the tall delphinium were dry and broken stalks along the fence; this year was dead now, the Indian summer simply a brief illusion.

Never before in his long life had he felt so helpless.

Canon Midford had picked up his mail late, after his hospital rounds of visitation. Mrs. Charlie Tait's gall-bladder attack the night before had been the herald for a church basement crisis, for while Mrs. Rita Dalgliesh could handle the Junior Choir practice competently, musically speaking, she was hopelessly untalented in the art of discipline. The nineteen members of the Junior Choir, ranging in age from eight to seventeen, attended practices reluctantly, and gave their attention grudgingly to what they considered an essentially unjust adult project making new demands upon their out-of-school time. His tall male presence at the back of the basement had been necessary from four to five-thirty.

He had been able just to look in on the Mission Band monthly meeting before hurrying to a few moments with Daddy Sherry recovering at home from a bronchial attack, then on to Aunt Fan, and finally to an appointment with Roy Tregillis for a final polishing of the Church Building Financial Statement before its presentation to the board of stewards.

He returned to the rectory and made himself tea, which he took into his study. How long, he wondered a little selfishly, was a person incapacitated by a gall-bladder attack? When he had finished his tea, he pushed aside the papers on his desk, opened the left top drawer, and took out a narrow slant-nosed vise. From the right drawer he drew a plastic bag of feathers, thread, wax, and scissors. After a day like this, often on a Saturday night when he found himself badly blocked in a sermon, he found release in tying dry flies, for himself, for Harry, Matt. It was a solitary and mesmerizing occupation that somehow freed his mind and imagination.

He had finished twelve flies when he noticed the mail he'd laid on the desk top. He picked up the square lavender envelope. He opened it.

"Dear Canon Midford:
    I think that you should know . . ."

He let the letter drop to the desk, and the breath of its descent drifted three of the grey flies along the varnished surface. Fly patterns—God's patterns. Fragile! Oh, so terribly fragile.

"Of course something ought to be done about it!" It was difficult enough for Harry Fitzgerald to keep his impatience under control without standing in her bedroom in a striped flannelette nightshirt knowing he must present a ludicrous figure, annoyed with himself that it still could make any difference to him. "I didn't say something shouldn't be done about it." He knew now that the matter was too serious to be ignored, that she hadn't, as he had thought at first, deliberately timed her summoning to put him at comic disadvantage. "But I hardly think it's for you to do it."

"If it's what's going on I think I should."

"It isn't going on!" She was not the picture of grace herself with her hair in that net and grease all over her face, but at least her bathrobe spared both of them. "Isn't a bit of truth in it!"

She was sitting on the stool before her vanity; she held

up the lavender letter he had given back to her after she had called him in to read it. "If somebody writes a letter like this there must be . . ."

"None of her damn business!" That had been jarred out of him, and this was too deadly important a matter to let his restraint go so easily. He had caught himself just before he said it was none of Nettie's damn business either; for once in their life together he must have her on his side. "Nettie, it's none of—our business."

"But it is, Harry. If I can do something to stop it—if I were to tell . . ."

"You're not to tell anyone!" It was not impatience now, it was fright that stirred him. "My God, Nettie, if you did that, do you realize it would make you almost as—as culpable as whoever wrote that letter!"

"So nothing should be done about it." He recognized the flat tone of her voice; she used it whenever she was convinced that there would be no assistance or co-operation from him, that she had been foolish to expect it to begin with.

"Yes, yes—something should be done about it—about the person who wrote the letter," he amended quickly.

"I don't mean about who wrote the letter. I mean about what the letter says. We'll probably never know who wrote the letter—I mean about that young Melquist woman and . . ."

"Nettie—Nettie, the letter's accusations are false. The writer, whoever she is—is a sick woman!"

"I'm not so sure."

"Not so sure she's a sick woman? You don't know what you're talking about!"

"That isn't what I'm talking about. I'm talking about the letter itself. I'm not so sure that what the letter says isn't . . ." She stopped. For the first time she was looking up at him; and for the first time in years he saw an expression of uncertainty on her face. It was replaced almost instantaneously by unmistakable annoyance, and it had been a long time since she had ever permitted him to see that. "Harry! You don't have to—I'm not one of your women patients who—who's . . ." She did not finish. He continued to stare at her. She dropped her gaze.

"It doesn't matter, Nettie, what you *want* to believe about that letter—about what it says . . ."

"It isn't what I *wanted* to believe at all!" she protested. "Why, I hadn't even wanted to discuss it at all! A letter—that letter—words like that—you were the only person I *could* show it to!"

"It isn't what you *want* to believe about what that letter says," he repeated. "It is unlikely that Dr. Melquist . . ."

"I have no way of knowing what she is like. You haven't—you don't know her."

"But I know Matt." It was difficult to tell whether forcefulness was needed now, or whether it might not push her out of the brief indecision he had surprised on her face. "Isn't it nice to think the best of people until the facts prove us wrong, Nettie? You shouldn't . . ."—but he must rephrase that—"none of us should be ready to think the worst!"

"I am not ready to think the worst of people!"

"You are now—right now with literally nothing to go on. A poison-pen letter from an obviously maladjusted and frustrated woman . . ."

"Who could quite easily know what she's talking about all the same!"

"Who sent an obscene and anonymous letter to you! Who hopes that you will help her to hurt someone else as badly as she is hurt herself. To cause suffering as great as she is . . ."

"You're not always right. You know you can't always be right about everything!"

"I'm not," he admitted. "I don't want to be. Forget it—burn it."

"I suppose . . ."

"And let's hope that's an end of it." He picked up the letter from the vanity table. "It could be, you know. It might go no further than this—you have a wonderful chance to be charitable. Just think . . ."

"But if it were true . . ."

"It isn't."

"How do you—how can you be so sure?"

"I am."

He could see that she was quite carefully considering. If

only it had been anyone else but him to persuade her to see the thing properly.

"If it were true," she said slowly and as though to herself, "I might be doing more harm by not . . ."

"Nettie." He might have known that she would come up with an answer to his plea for charitableness, the old, old argument, familiar as ritual. "No one does anyone any good by telling things like this—true or untrue. They become evident to the people they concern soon enough."

"Oh—and let them go on and on?"

"You're assuming they *are* going on and on."

"Sometimes we have to tell people. We have to tell them unpleasant things because we are their friends and we owe it to them."

"Please—let's not delude ourselves! We often tell our friends unpleasant things about themselves in the name of friendship, when actually we enjoy inflicting . . ."

"Perhaps I should speak to Canon Midford. It's the sort of thing he'd . . ."

"You're not listening to me, are you! It's none of his damn business—or yours—or mine—even if it were true! It isn't! God damn it—you drop it!"

"You don't have to shout and swear at me!"

"I couldn't shout at you and swear at you enough! I haven't shouted and sworn at you nearly enough when you've needed it! You need it right now! I've never been more serious about anything in my whole life! You are not to spread this—this . . ."— he held up the letter—"infection any further!" He ripped it across, then again and again. "That's the end of it!"

CHAPTER 21

THE SENATOR'S LEAVING FOR THE FALL SESSION IN OTTAWA had been delayed by a bout of flu. Matt knew that Ruth was worried about her father, that she wasn't sure he was well enough to go.

"I don't like to persuade him to stay any longer, Matt. For all his complaints about drafts and the Parliament cafeteria beef, the prospect of going East means a lot to him."

"I know. Just thinking of entering the parliamentary arena does something adrenal to him."

"It always has in the past. I'm not so sure now. He's lost his old sparkle."

She made one last attempt to persuade him to put off his departure for a week.

"You aren't looking too well, Dad."

"I'm fine."

"I don't think you are. You don't look it."

"How could a person after this flu?"

"But it doesn't usually hit you so hard, does it? Think you might get Dr. Fitzgerald to check . . .?"

"No. Another week I'll be all right. You leave me alone and Clem can leave me alone. Poor young man always makes a good old man."

"You weren't a poor young man."

"You have no way of knowing. I'm a long way from joining Bovey, Ruthie."

"I hope so."

But she was not so sure the evening before her father was to leave them. They always had dinner with him the day before his departure, and this time he had invited Aunt Fan, now almost a month past her heart attack. The Senator and Aunt Fan had been singularly silent through dinner; both had the same tired look of vague distraction. Seeing it on Aunt Fan's face as well as her father's disturbed Ruth even more; surely there wasn't a characteristic expression for all people with heart trouble!

After the rather glum meal, she made Aunt Fan go into the living-room with Matt and the Senator and Sarah. She stayed with Clem and the dishes.

"Clem," she said as she set the last dish on the rack.

"Yeah?"

"What's wrong with Dad?"

"Huh?" He wasn't fooling her; drying a platter did not require that much concern.

"Is Dad all right, Clem?"

"How do you mean?"

"How would I mean? His health . . ."

"Oh—that." It was almost as though Clem had been granted a reprieve. "Sure, he's all right. He . . ."

"Don't hold back on me, Clem."

"I ain't, Ruthie. Honest. Not a thing wrong with his health. Oh, he's feelin' peakid, sure. But he's—his health's just fine. Will be." He was looking steadily at her now, and she knew he meant what he was saying.

"Clem—Clem!" Sarah had run in from the living-room, her voice passionately high with urgency. "Now, Clem!"

Clem bent down and scooped her up. "All right." He turned to Ruth. "I promised her a story. Me and Sarah, we'll stay here in the kitchen. You go out with them in the livin'-room. Senator's last night."

She paused to look back as she went through the doorway; Sarah was already up on Clem's lap. He was seated in the oak-runged rocker that had been in the ranch kitchen of her own childhood.

"Drought," Clem was saying, "girl, you never seen drought like that an' you'll never see her again. Lickin' up the topsoil, pilin' it agin the fences an' the houses an' barns an' granaries. First thing we knew there wasn't a specka dust left on them poor frogs' sloughs. Kind of tragical way they died—lacka dust."

She sat down by Matt on the couch and looked across to her father anxiously. Some distance from the rooms source of light, the floor lamp at Aunt Fan's elbow, the Senator did not look a poor old man now with his slippered feet on the buffalo robe before him. The robe with its saw-toothed margin of green felt was an old familiar of hers too, she thought, and her skin tightened against the recall of its wire harshness. As a child she had been unable to decide which was blacker, which prickled more: the buffalo hair or her father's moustache. And he still did possess some of the majesty of an old and bearded buffalo knee-deep in foothills grass, magnificent of shoulder, a virile old bull.

She was suddenly reassured. Clem had told her the truth; it was just the after-weakness of flu. Her attention strayed to Aunt Fan in the full light of the lamp, and there was no denying the strained greyness of features there. Poor Aunt Fan. She must get over to see her more often. Poor lonely Aunt Fan, almost as desperate as Clem's drought frogs with their "lacka dust." It wouldn't hurt to put in an order for Christmas cards early with her; this year they'd have her come for Christmas Eve and stay overnight and share Sarah's tree with them.

The day had not started at all well for Aunt Fan. As usual she had awakened not instantly but as though she were walking across uncertain ice that held her, gave a little, broke here, supported again—then gave way completely and finally. She did not welcome waking up in the mornings as she had when she had been ill and Dr. Fitzgerald had kept her in bed; sometimes she wished almost *wistfully* for another heart attack to give her a quiet holiday again.

It wouldn't be so bad perhaps if Mrs. Nelligan hadn't told her the week before about the letter. She had felt just sick. Utter helplessness had risen in her such as she had not felt since her brother, Hubert, had died. Why in the world did such things have to happen! And what could *she* do! Everyone in town must know if she did; she was always the last to *hear* about such things. How hopeless it was if a thing like this could happen to people you loved. Without the slightest warning something like this sprang on one with claws and fangs, and it was terrifying.

And in a way she had been partly responsible; you could say she had, for Dr. Melquist *had* stayed in her suite before she'd moved to Mrs. Nelligan's. Of course, there wasn't a shred of truth in all the talk. Sometimes she wondered whether the truth of it really *mattered*. The talk was the worst part; it had been the talk that had hurt most with an alcoholic brother who cheated at cards if he could, and hadn't a captaincy in the Royal Horse Guards at all.

She stared at the enamel beads under the rail at the foot of her bed. By turning her head she could see a patch of bright sunlight just beyond the door to the kitchen, then by turning a little further, the dresser and its drawers with their serpentine bulge, as though each drawer were identically pregnant. Perhaps the talk would die down before too much damage had been done, perhaps even before Matt and Ruth had heard about it. They might never hear about it. That was one thing about being deaf: she might not even know about it *now* if the last battery had given out a little sooner; she might have just smiled and nodded while Mrs. Nelligan told her and she had *pretended* to hear and had not heard at all. Oh, she wished the battery had not lasted!

Ever since Mrs. Nelligan had told her, she had moved through a soundless world, carrying her own hush with her wherever she went; it was as though she quietly unrolled before herself a deadening felt carpet. Last evening she had sat by her opened window, looking down upon the town's Saturday night. She had seen farmers throw back their heads and laugh in uproarious silence. For a while the Salvation Army had held its street service just across the street in front of Ollie Pringle's, with Captain Leppard tilting and winding no sound from his dumb trumpet while Charles Adams thudded stillness with stillness against the drum and Mrs. Leppard held the hymn book just at the climax of her bosom, head slightly back so that the bonnet ribbon showed under her full cheeks, and went through an exaggerated pantomime of song.

It might be a good thing if the whole community could be struck deaf from time to time, so that vicious talk could have a chance to die out and everyone could start *clean* again.

The floor felt chill and shreddy to the soles of her bare feet as she crossed to the cardboard closet where she had hung her clothes. She sat on the edge of the bed and began the long and laborious task of lacing her shoes. There came a slight giddiness as she straightened up. That always faded. It was her blood vessels—the small ones that had got hard.

She shrank from the prospect of another two days of silence, till the end of the month when she would receive her rents and have the money for new batteries. *Unless*, of course, she should sell a magazine subscription, and that wasn't likely, for she had to hear to sell and it was unlikely anyone would be *coming* to her and asking her for a subscription. She hated selling subscriptions anyway; she was supposed to *force* them to buy, and that was next door to begging almost. It wasn't like seeds at all, which people needed *seasonally* and for which they came to her as a matter of *course*. Nor was it like Christmas cards, which were a great deal like seeds, weren't they? You didn't *force* Christmas cards on people any more than you did seeds. No one bought them out of a sense of charity. She'd better have a cup of tea. Things always looked better after a cup of tea.

First the gas ring, then fill the kettle and wait to add a pinch of tea—or rather wait to pour it over the old leaves from last night. That made it taste like iron. Why should tea taste like iron with those little oily spots floating? It must be the oily spots that tasted like iron. One thing—without the aid working she couldn't hear the little bursting sound that frightened her when the gas caught from the match. There was that.

In a way it was better when she hadn't batteries, for it gave her a rest from the sound storm. She had never got used to the crackling penny thunder in her ears. The pelleting static tired her, and people's voices always came out at her with the raucous hoarseness of pheasants squawking. Then she had to smile and hold out her hand as though she were warding them off, glance apologetically down at her bosom and try to adjust the thing. And of course then she couldn't hear her stomach rumble. It did often, but how badly she could never be sure, because of the aid's proximity to the source of the disturbance. She liked to tell herself that the thing amplified her stomach as it did everything else, but she couldn't be sure—particularly when she caught the startled glances of others.

Being constantly hungry made her stomach constantly complain—just a nagging and nesting hunger that very seldom swooped forth in full flight, always stirring uneasily with beak open so that she was never without that vague and undefined hollowness that sometimes nudged her thoughts off balance to send them fluttering. At such times, she was not quite sure what she was saying, and there was the attendant giddiness. Then she would swallow quickly, and that would sometimes bring the fledglings of hunger back to their proper places.

She saw that the kettle was trembling so it must be ticking now, would sing in a moment. She must save the butter for tonight—oh, Sunday, last night had been Saturday. Then it was dinner tonight at the Senator's and Matt and Ruth would be there, and you couldn't close your mind to terrible things no matter how hard you tried. Even if the battery *hadn't* held out she would have *had* to hear sooner or later the nasty things people were all saying about Matt Stanley and Miss Melquist.

It was nice the Senator was leaving for Ottawa; the talk would probably be all over by the time he came back. And she wouldn't have to worry about the butter at all—or the bitter tea with the oily spots.

Clem had come in from the kitchen. Sarah was asleep on the Senator's bed, he told Ruth. He had put the puff over her; she'd be fine. The Senator and Matt were in the goose pits again with sad reminiscence now that the game season was over for another year. They had just referred to Dr. Fitzgerald's passion for geese.

"Can't hold a candle to a fellow I knew in Empress district back in ought-eight," Clem was saying. "Gandy

Powelly—had a sort of round eye anyways, long in the neck, spraddly way he had of walkin'. Made a lot of money in flax an' he used to migrate south to California every winter, come back north to put his crop in. You'd swear he been born in a goose pit—grey honker."

Now Ruth was feeling a return of her concern for her father. Why had Clem seemed so relieved earlier in the kitchen when she had been asking him about the Senator? As a matter of fact, Clem himself had not been particularly festive this evening.

"That hoarse voice of his, with a sort of a break in her. Never used a caller. No, sir. Throw back his head, kind of arch that long neck of his—big Adam's apple, used to bob up an' down when he'd call. Come out clear an' true. Draw a goose lookin' for her mate, four, five miles."

Clem did not have the Senator's full attention; Ruth could tell. Something *was* worrying her father.

"Claimed there was no other human kids in the district when he was a kid, so he played with wild geese instead. Kind of got to know their language that way. Understand every single word they said, till he begun to notice a word drop out here an' a word drop out there. Time he had his ninth birthday he kind of lost the knack. Mind you, he could still get the drift of what *they* was talkin' about."

It took more than flu to make a person look that way; it took more than being tired; it took much more.

"If he was still alive, I s'pose he could still understand honker language, in a general sort of way. Tell if a flock was mad at another bunch hornin' in on their barley field. Tell if they was pleased with their grub, when they was all excited—upset excited if a kiyoot was headin' their way— pleased excited when they was talkin' over the comin' trip to Mexico. I know he could understand *that* way. An' he swore hisself till he was nine he could understand every single word. Maybe he could."

She was trying to recall any clue that might mean he'd been to Harry Fitzgerald for a check-up. If he had, and if there were something seriously wrong—it would be just like him to conceal it from them, and that might explain the way he was looking—almost haggard!

"Geese was Gandy Powelly's life, you might say. You

take when most fellows gets to an age—well, when they find out there's women around. The girls wasn't for Gandy Powelly. He didn't have no time for 'em. He'd be out along the Red Deer River, layin' "—Clem let go at the spittoon—"on his belly or in a stubble field behind a stook, watchin' them big grey honkers—all day long, night time, light the moon. Course in time he turned *queer*."

That must explain it. She would have to talk with Harry Fitzgerald; whatever her father had pledged him to, the doctor had no right to keep anything from them.

"You'd see Gandy in the beer parlour, pool hall, barber shop. He'd just set an' never say anythin'. Didn't seem interested in what other humans had to say at all. Like he was—well, like a fellow in another country an' he was homesick. Somebody'd mention geese though, and Gandy'd pick up his ears, that beak of his'd kind of twitch. Any other time he just faded back from folks . . ."

That was it—as though her father had faded back from them. He *was* withholding from her.

". . . homesick, lonesome, in a foreign country. Lost his—this special sort of goose citizenship he had right till he was eight years old."

"Nine, Clem," Matt corrected him.

"Yeah, nine—nine."

"Ruth." Matt turned to her. "I think we'd better start . . ."

"All right, Matt. You might drive Aunt Fan home, then come back for me and Sarah. I have to put her snowsuit and overshoes on. You go ahead with Aunt Fan. That'll give the car a chance to warm up, too. That cough of hers . . ."

"Okay." He got up, stopped before Aunt Fan and raised his voice. "I'll take you home now!"

She smiled and nodded to him and continued to sit.

"While Ruth's getting Sarah ready!" he shouted. "I'll drive you home!" He gestured toward the front door. Aunt Fan smiled brilliantly and this time got up from her chair.

When they had left, Ruth did not go in to Sarah immediately; she waited until Clem had gone out to the kitchen, then spoke to her father.

"Dad, what are you holding back on me?"

The question obviously startled him. "Holding back on you?"

"You're not taking off for Ottawa tomorrow without telling me. Have you been to see Dr. Fitzgerald lately?"

"Oh, no. No."

"Then has something happened that you *should* have called on him?"

"No—no, it's not that."

"Then what is it?"

"All right, Ruth—I guess I'd better tell you."

CHAPTER 22

MATT HAD ALWAYS DISLIKED WINTER, LOOKING UPON IT AS A season only to be endured, and it was hard for him to recall a winter he had faced with more distaste than this one. It should not have been so, for the weather was more like spring, with the night temperatures seldom reaching freezing. People congratulated each other on the wonderfully soft days they were having, as though the benign chinooks were a community accomplishment. In spite of this he felt the constraint he associated with winter. The days were short and frost would not leave the earth for five months. It was the season of disenchantment, unless a man were a member of the Shelby Caledonian Society of Knock-out Curlers.

For reasons he did not clearly understand, the prospect of a confining winter seemed much more depressing than it ever had before; he had not known himself capable of such unrelieved ennui. It was as though he had put the final stamp to a long-delayed emotional conclusion: Shelby and Shelby ways and Shelby people bored him. He was tired of Webb Bolton's boils and carbuncles; he was not enthusiastic about doing an editorial exhorting the Department of Agriculture to review the Bang's disease regulations; he was not appreciative of Olga Wolochow doing the Highland

Fling, Cora Swengle singing "Hanging Apples on the Lilac Tree," or Stanley Tregillis reciting "The Fool" at the Home and School Amateur Night.

Something had happened; he had lost his talent for empathy with people dropping in to the office. He had the intuitive suspicion that people themselves did not feel so warm toward him, or that they had never been so warm toward him as he'd thought they were. He was not a Nettie Fitzgerald fan, since it was difficult to like Harry as much as he did and be one, and her usual reserve was easy enough for him to accept. Of late it had seemed cooler than usual. But why had he not noticed before that Harry was a very brittle man, abrupt to the point of rudeness? Why should he find himself having to *make* conversation with Hersch Midford? Why had he ever been undecided whether to direct his attention to *both* Mr. Oliver's eyes or just to the one that wasn't false? For the first time he had realized that Mr. Oliver seldom looked directly at a person at all, which meant that the man was not so judiciously pompous as he had thought. Though that was an improvement, it was startling to discover that Mr. Oliver was ill at ease with him.

But the truly disturbing one was Ruth. God, Ruth was Ruth! Never before had he heard this persistent off-key note in their marital harmony. It was an indefinable drawing apart from each other, and it seemed to have been noticeable ever since the Senator's departure for Ottawa. For all its vagueness it was real. He knew that it existed, though he could not recall a spoken word or a look or a gesture as specific evidence of it. To be excluded from her fondness was the saddest thing he could think of for himself. And there was nothing he could do about it, for it seemed to him that mention could only magnify it.

As far as the town was concerned, he supposed that he had fallen out of friendship with it, that all he could do was to hope that it was a brief lapse.

As far as Ruth was concerned, perhaps she'd straighten out now that June was leaving. Another week. Surely it wasn't June that Ruth was bothered about!

Couldn't be, he reassured himself, as he went up the Post Office steps.

"Mr. Stanley."

"Mame. Haven't seen you for quite a while."

"Not since Rory turned the goats loose."

"I guess not."

"They're all back in their pen now," she told him, "except for one of 'em. He got fried on top the transformer, you know."

He found her cheerfulness hard to understand, for on the interdiction charge alone Rory had been liable to a two-hundred-dollar fine or three months in jail.

"Oliver really threw everything he had at Rory—six months or three hundred dollars. Then there was all that damage. Them clear windows like in the Hardware Store, they come high."

"I guess they do." He could only guess at the extent of civil damages Rory would be responsible for.

"Five hundred dollars for the window alone. An' the Arlington Beer Parlour—wrecked the Arlington."

"I know, Mame."

"Inside. I was sorry about the light plant an' the fire engine an' Ollie's ambulance. Over eighteen hundred dollars—far as they know. Then with the three-hundred-dollar fine, that's over two thousand dollars. Oliver figure Rory's got that kind of money in his hip pocket?"

If that was all, Matt thought, it looked as though Mr. Oliver had fallen over backwards to be just with Rory.

"Kind of perked the town up a bit," Mame said.

"It did do that, Mame."

"But it was kind of unfair, blaming it all onto Rory that way. When it was Oliver's fault to begin with."

"Oliver!"

"Sure."

"Now, look, Mame . . ."

"Him makin' me put Rory onto the Indian List. He hadn't done that, then Rory would of been drinkin' his beer peaceful in the Arlington. Instead of that he goes on a hard toot with Artie's stuff, an' there's what happened. What's he expect?"

"He certainly didn't expect what happened."

"Oh well, look on the bright side."

She was almost laughing as she said it, and he was beginning to think he had overestimated her concern for

Rory in the past. "Is there any bright side—with Rory serving six months?"

"Oh, Rory ain't in jail."

"He isn't!"

"We just got that cleared up this mornin'."

"But how did . . .?"

"Fine's all paid. We're squared away with the Hardware Store—power plant an' Arlington too."

"How did you manage . . .?"

"Come by mail—cheque for three thousand dollars. An' what's more she was good too."

"Someone sent you a cheque for three thousand dollars!"

Mame nodded. "Yeah. Ain't that funny!"

"Well, yes . . ."

"Just like that. Must of been lyin' in the Post Office two, three days. Rory didn't even need to put all that time in the cage if I'd of gone for the mail."

"But who sent you a cheque for three thousand dollars!"

"Note with it," she explained. " 'Reward Money for Rory Napoleon.' It was Sam Barnes signed it. Hell, we har'ly know Sam Barnes, though Rory rode for Scotty in the old days, an' Scotty's is next Sam Barnes. Now, why would Sam Barnes send Rory alla that money?"

"If anybody were going to," Matt assured her, "Sam would."

"It sure come in handy, I can tell you. I guess he won't miss it too much, for Rory says he's got a capital herd over twelve hunderd head, so what he give us maybe was a dozen beef, an' what's a dozen beef out of twelve hunderd. He could lose more'n that in one day's calvin' in a bad spring."

"I think you can bank on it that Sam got his money's worth, Mame." Matt put his hand on the Post Office door and pulled it open.

Mame grabbed a handful of Buster's sweater neck and stepped down to the walk. "We got to meet Rory now at Marshall, Anglin an' . . ." She stopped, looked away from Matt. "That's somethin' we're not makin' public yet."

"Okay, Mame. Glad to hear Rory isn't going to the penitentiary."

"Oh, he ain't out the woods yet," she said. "Oliver's warned him—second time they find him with liquor it ain't any fine—three months. Ah, Mr. Stanley, like I say—we all got our troubles. Rory and me, we, well, we're all for you."

"Thanks, Mame."

"With yours. Come on, Buster."

Matt turned back from the door. "With my what?"

"Trouble. Takes them with trouble to sympathize with them that's got trouble, an' that's one thing the Napoleons can do," she said as he came back down the Post Office steps. "We're the folks can sure understand how it is with people goin' pick, pick, pick all the time."

"Hold on, Mame—what are you driving at?"

"All the talk—me an' Rory, we don't believe a word of it."

"A word of what?"

"The talk."

"What talk?" He felt his patience snap. "What talk, Mame!"

"The talk about you an' that Miss Melquist."

"About me and Dr. Melquist!"

"An' them letters sayin' about you two lyin' out along the river road, an' you an' your pretty little wife gettin' a divorce."

"Mame, for God's sakes what are you talking . . ."

"What everybody else is. You'd think they'd shut up—but nothin' shuts them up. I tell you, nothin' ever shuts the mouths up in this town. Pick, pick, pick—that's all they do, an' the less truth there is in it the more they go at it, pick . . ." She stopped with mouth ajar, looked up at him from under the beret, her reddened eyes filled with new concern. "It ain't the truth," she said on a rising note. "You aren't—you wouldn't? You got more sense than to go goatin' around after that woman!"

"Yes," he said, "I have."

"What we thought. Same as it always is. Less they got to go on, more they go at it—pick . . ."

He had turned away from her.

"Pick, pick."

The first shock had been quite mild, actually; the information she had dropped so carelessly was such an outrageous surprise that it stunned attention, sealing emotional response instantly. Even when it came, the release of feeling was slowed by incredulity. It was ridiculous; people wouldn't say or think such things of him—they couldn't! It was ridiculous! It was impossible—and if there had been such talk he would have known it. They couldn't have concealed it from him—from *them*—it involved Ruth, too. But even as he reassured himself he could feel an undercurrent of uncertainty pulling at his heart. Unwillingly he was remembering, and as his memory went back over the past weeks, he could feel his confidence thinning.

Now he told himself with only frail conviction that it was ridiculous; there had been too many oblique references and glances, too many unexplained silences and hesitancies. He knew now that he had mistakenly blamed himself before—that the change had not been so much in himself as in the townspeople. He could only guess at how widespread the talk was now. And how had he been so insensitive as not to have seen it in their faces, vague with deliberate impersonality put on to hide their thoughts, sharp with inner relish, or cold with downright unfriendliness. However had he missed the countless signs, the thousand flicks of an eye, the compression of lips, the inexplicable flush of embarrassment.

If nothing else had told him, he should have guessed it after his conversation with Nettie Fitzgerald the day she had brought him the notice for the Home and School Amateur Show. He remembered that he had felt that she was meaning much more than her words revealed on their surface; it had been as though they had some subterranean intent that was not quite visible to him, and that the significance was quite menacing.

And Harry; he had noticed the change there. Now that he looked back, it had not been rude abruptness so much as something else: as though Harry had been busy secretly within himself, trying to gain a sureness about something he believed about Matt, or knew about him, or suspected about him, all the while deliberately veiling it from him. God damn it! His closest friend! All his friends!

Joe Manley! It hadn't just been the rough summer Joe had put in and his unrequited love for June, as Ruth had suggested! No wonder he hadn't run into Joe in weeks! Hersch Midford and Oliver! Even Aunt Fan! All of them had known, had whispered and licked over it, imputing unfaithfulness to him. No, no—that wasn't right—most of the town did that, but not his friends. They knew him well enough to refuse to accept that about him. But what they had done was to keep it from him. They had not come to him—not one of them—and told him what was being said about him behind his back. For three months—at least! Not one of them! Why should they keep it from him!

Now it was the terribly frustrating anger of helplessness, the bound anger that cannot reach or see its binding ropes, the pent-up, walking-the-room anger. It was the inarticulate anger he had forgotten he was capable of. It was a demeaning anger, and knowing that it demeaned him only made him angrier. To be so senselessly ambushed by someone who meant no more to him than the wind over his hand!

He came right to the point with Clem Derrigan.

"Square with me, Clem."

"What about, Matt?"

"What everyone has been saying about me the past three months."

"Oh—that."

"Then you've heard it."

"Yeah, I heard it."

"Well?"

"Nothin' to it. I know you, know Ruthie, an' I known Melquist an' the likes her in my time. Nothin' to it."

"That's nice."

"I sized you up hell of a long time ago. When you first started runnin' with Ruthie. Kind of interested in the fellow she'd marry."

"Were you."

"One thing I knew about you. You was straight—an' you'd play it straight with Ruthie."

"Then why didn't you tell me what was going on?"

"Nothin' to it. Why the hell should I?"

"Because it concerned me and Ruth."

"That's right," Clem agreed. "You an' Ruthie."

"What about the Senator?"

"Felt the same as me, I guess. I figger he did—from what he said."

"When?"

"After he got that letter."

"The Senator got a letter!"

"One hell of a letter. You know, you hear them words every day of your life an' they roll right off. Then you see 'em wrote out an' they're—I never knew a woman would be able to use them kind of words—but it was a woman wrote 'em. Well, now I did know a woman, in the Klondike. She could swear in four languages—English, French, Dogrib, an' then she was livin' with this Finn . . ."

"How long have you and the Senator known?"

"Must be right from the beginnin'. I'd say it was that letter started the whole—whoever wrote that letter must of started the whole thing. I don't know how many letters there were. Enough, I guess—like somebody startin' up another newspaper in opposition to the *Chinook*!"

"There's always been an opposition to the *Chinook*," Matt said shortly. "So the Senator got one, and he didn't say anything to me about it."

"He didn't believe it."

"But why didn't he tell me about it? Why didn't he . . ."

"No point in hurtin' you."

"Damn it, Clem—it's worse, knowing your friends have known all along, haven't said a word to you. Because they're afraid it might be true? There might be something in it after all?"

"I can't speak for the others. Senator an' me didn't say nothin' to you because we knew there was nothin' to it at all."

"You did. How did you know, Clem?"

"I already told you. We know you. Hell, the Senator's like me—he wouldn't hire a two-faced man to haul guts to a bear, let alone marry his daughter."

"But if you knew it wasn't true and if the Senator knew it wasn't, I don't see why he wouldn't say something to me about it. Why did he have to keep silent about it?"

"Because he didn't want to hurt you."

"You said that before."

"I know I did, an' I'll say it again. I know how I felt an' I s'pose the Senator felt the same way an' Ruthie she must of . . ."

"Ruth!"

"After the Senator talked it over with her. Night before he left for Ottawa."

"Ruth! Ruth has known all along!"

"No, not all along—three weeks or so after the Senator got the letter. He took it hard, when he had that flu . . ."

"She hasn't—he didn't . . ."

"Sure he did. She's his daughter an' they're pretty close."

"And she's my wife and we're *not* close!"

"I didn't say that. I said . . ."

"She didn't choose to tell me! Why not!"

"Goddamit! She's your wife! Maybe you should know the answer to that." Almost instantly his voice softened. "You'll get over it, son."

"I don't know, Clem, I don't know!"

"What's botherin' you mainly is pride."

"No, it isn't pride. It's—it's . . ." But he couldn't tell Clem what it was. It was so terrible that he couldn't admit it even to himself. Ruth had known almost as long as all the others. She had said nothing to him. It wasn't pride at all!

He had not thought that she would ever want to keep anything from him. To think that she might want to was frightening, but that she could, and had, was destroying. This was a mortal wound.

It took him hours to bring himself to speak to her about it.

"Ruth. I know now."

It was all he had to say. Her face suddenly stilled.

"Oh, Matt!"

"I still can't believe. I can't understand why—how you could . . ."

"Matt dear, is that what's been bothering you?"

"I can't understand why . . ."

"I'd hoped you'd never know about it. I knew it would hit you hard."

"That isn't what I mean—that isn't the bad thing about it now. I can't understand why you didn't tell me!"

"For the same reason Dad wouldn't have told me if I hadn't forced it out of him. We both know you. We both love you."

"Isn't that all the more reason to tell me!"

"Dad didn't think so. I don't think so."

"Not telling me has made it much worse!"

"Hold on, hold on. I'm the poor wife in the thing—not you. I'm the one that's supposed to get all the sympathy."

"It's not funny, Ruth!"

"No, it hasn't been. Oh, darling, I'm sorry. I'm sorry it had to happen—and when it had happened I was only trying to save you . . ."

"From being hurt. Your father and maybe others and—and you. It's bad enough your closest friends keeping it from you, but for you to—Ruth—I don't see how you could—for a whole month!"

"Only for you, Matt! I couldn't have done it for anyone else but you! It would have been easier to tell you—anything would have been easier than what I've done! I've waited and waited for it to die down . . ."

"And I'd be none the wiser."

"Yes. Yes. If it had been the other way around—if it had been me instead of you—I would have wanted you to do it for me."

"No. Believe me you wouldn't, Ruth!"

"I think I would. Anyway—I thought it would be. If it wasn't, then I'm sorry I was wrong—*if* I was wrong!"

"You were! You were!".

"What do you think this last two months has been like for me!" she said. "Do you think it's been a picnic for me!"

"No. What I think is—keeping it from me is the most terrible thing about the whole thing!"

"Matt!"

"It's—the result is the same as though I *had* been unfaithful to you!"

"Matt, it isn't . . ."

"Or as though you had been to me!"

"All right, Matt . . ."

"Because if you had—then you would have to keep it from *me*. You'd have to make sure I didn't know about it! Smile to me when you didn't feel like smiling to me! Choose every word, every expression, carefully so it wouldn't give you away. That's what really counts with someone you love. Not the roll in the hay, but keeping them from seeing the straw on your back. Keeping them from knowing about it, hiding behind a false face and false answers, withholding from them because you've done a disloyal . . ."

"But that isn't why, Matt—it's because I love you!"

"All right—because you love me. Because you love me you lie to me . . ."

"I have never lied to you!"

"Not literally!"

"Not any way!"

"All right, all right. For the very best reasons you did something I thought would be impossible—for you, or for me—and I feel just sick!"

"*You* feel just sick! After what I've been through for you, for two months, and now all you can do is tell me I might as well have been unfaithful to *you*. Well, just name me three candidates, mister! I think this is the most noble attitude I've ever seen you take in anything! *I* feel just sick!"

He was filled with instant contrition as he saw her tears. "Look, Ruth . . ."

"Don't you say another thing!"

"Ruth, I'm—I was trying to . . ."

"I don't care what you were trying! Go away—leave me alone!"

"Ruth!"

"Get out! Get out! Get the hell out! Fuck you!"

Dr. Fitzgerald's receptionist, Kathy Warden, told Matt to go into Harry's office when he told her that he wanted only a minute with the doctor on a personal matter. Before the stares of the waiting patients on their chairs along the wall, he walked across the reception room to the office door.

Harry, just slipping on his white jacket, turned to him. "Matt."

"Harry." He did not give himself time to think of the best way to open the matter. "I've just heard about—about what's being said around town—about me and June. I want—tell me what you know about it. You have known?"

"Yes."

"For long?"

"Quite a while, Matt."

"What I don't—what I want to understand is why you didn't say anything to me."

"Because I knew it wasn't true."

"Whether you thought it was true or not—don't you think you ought to have told me? Damn it, Harry, you're my friend. I would have told you. How come—why . . ."

"I've told you, Matt—because you're . . ."

"Who'd you hear it from?"

"I—that sort of thing. It's hard to say where you heard it first . . ."

"No, it isn't, Harry."

"Nettie."

"Where did she . . ."

"Matt, what are you trying to do? Trace it back? Find out who started it?"

"I don't know what I'm trying to do! I just want to know why this should happen to Ruth and me! I want to know why our friends should . . ."

"Not one of your friends has believed it. We've all known it wasn't true."

"And discussed it among yourselves—not said a word to us."

"Because we haven't wanted to hurt you."

"You have."

"I'm sorry, Matt. It's hard to know what to . . ."

"Where did Nettie hear about it?"

The doctor stared at him without answering.

"Where, Harry?"

"She got a letter."

"From whom?"

"Anonymous."

"You and Nettie talked it over."

"Yes."

"Decided not to say anything about it to us . . ."

"Or to anybody else, Matt. Nettie wanted me—wanted to. I wouldn't let her."

"Why?"

"Because I didn't—because I knew it wasn't true—because I'm your friend . . ."

"I think a true friend would . . ."

"I don't. Why hurt a friend unnecessarily?"

"What do you think it's like now!"

"I thought it would blow over, Matt."

"But it didn't. And you knew it didn't. Then why haven't you told me—after you knew it hadn't blown over. Why, Harry?" When the doctor did not answer him, he said, "You must have had some other reason. Didn't you? Other than being my friend. What was your reason, Harry?"

"I had a reason."

"What was it?"

"I can't tell you." The doctor was not looking at him now. "It would be easier for me to tell you, Matt, than not to tell you."

"But you can't."

Harry shook his head.

"Is it an ethical—professional one?"

The doctor shook his head again.

After Matt had left him, Harry sat long and still in the chair behind his desk. Why? Why had she done it! Up until now she had at least been an honourable opponent. What kind of loyalty was it that made a man shield a woman like Nettie and hurt a man like Matt Stanley even more!

"Doctor."

He looked up at Kathy Warden's head round the door jamb.

"Miss Clocker has to go on duty."

"All right. All right."

It was a wrench to tear his mind from Matt's visit. The X-rays were back—nothing, as he had suspected, so it had to be functional. The girl had been brittle enough before her night of horror at the switchboard when the Napoleon goats had been loosed on the town. It was going to be ticklish, telling her that psychotherapy would be needed before it was too late.

"I'm more concerned about the attitude my friends have taken," Matt was saying to Herschell Midford.

"What do you mean, Matt?"

"Keeping it from us. If they were my friends, why would they . . ."

"Because they were your friends."

"That's what Harry said. But once the thing was all over town—I can't accept that. It seems to me if you heard something like this, Hersch—as soon as you'd heard you'd come to me. Right?"

"Well, Matt, I've—known about it for some time."

"How long?"

"Late this fall."

"And you didn't come to me either."

"I didn't, Matt. You see, I got a letter—an anonymous letter—an obscene one. I seriously considered coming to you, at first—but my second thought was to let it drop. I have had some experience in this sort of thing."

"Then at first—right away . . ."

"I hoped it would die right there, go no further. You see, I thought mine was the only letter. I thought that for three weeks, since I hadn't heard any more about it. Then Mrs. Nelligan came to me. She told me she had got a letter. She didn't bring it with her, show it to me, naturally—but I could tell from what she said that it must be a copy of mine or very close to it."

"That was three weeks—a month after you got your letter."

Hersch nodded.

"But you didn't come to me even though you knew it had not—died down."

"No."

"I can't understand why you wouldn't."

"Well, Matt—in the first place I wasn't too sure you didn't already know. That—that if you did—my mentioning it to you might suggest to you that I took it seriously. No, that isn't what I mean—that I placed any credence in it. And, Matt—I know now I should have. I didn't. I'm terribly sorry I didn't."

"I see."

"That's all I can say."

It was a week later that he discovered Mr. Oliver had received one of the letters.

"I intended going to the police," Mr. Oliver said almost apologetically, "but I didn't. I didn't think they'd get anywhere. They wouldn't. Not that it's any reflection on them, you know. But it would be just like the dog-poisoning—sort of thing it's difficult to trace. I think it is."

He showed Matt his letter, the only one of them all that Matt actually had read. It was like the reopening of a wound after it had begun to heal, so that there was pain and surprise that it could still be acute. His anger was refreshed. He went to Johnston's Drug Store in an attempt to find out whether or not the stationery had been bought there. It had been, Mr. Johnston assured him; the paper was distinctive, so distinctive that he had been forced to carry it in stock for almost twelve years, then finally disposed of it only through two one-cent sales a year apart. He recalled that Mrs. Tregillis and Mrs. Fitzgerald had each bought several boxes of it, that both women had told him it would make nice Christmas gifts, and that for all he knew they had given it away to many of their friends.

Matt knew now that he was no longer very interested in discovering the unknown who had sent the letters. That one person should want to do this to him was not nearly so important as the fact that an entire community had given the vicious act wide life. He could perhaps forgive one—he could not forgive all of them. How had he stood their boring intimacy as long as he had, their sententious dullness, their unassailable complacency with the small world of Shelby! Every single one of them—parochial as hibernating gophers with no more arousing goal than to eat and sleep and mate and beget, and to climb to the top of such a very, very small heap!

"It's not right, Matt!" Ruth protested. "You're making too much of it."

"I don't think I am."

"You are. The thing doesn't bother me nearly so much—as your response to it. It isn't—what happened isn't what's the matter, Matt!"

"What do you mean?"

"I don't think you . . . For a long time—before this— you haven't been happy."

"Haven't I?"

"I don't think you have. I think you've been discontented. It hasn't worked out for you—either this sort of life—or this sort of work! Somehow June Melquist—her work—your—friendship with her has done it. Not the talk, the gossip, the letters—they've simply brought it to a conclusion sooner!"

"So I should be grateful for the letters."

"If that's right—yes."

"I don't think it's right."

"But something's been bothering you, Matt—before we ever knew her."

"Has it?"

"If it hasn't—then it's me . . ."

"Don't be ridiculous!"

"Then—it's us."

"Good God, Ruth, it isn't us!"

"Then—why have you shut me out!"

"I haven't! I haven't!"

"With the rest!"

"Ruth—Ruth! I haven't!"

"I hope you haven't! Oh, Matt, I hope you haven't!"

CHAPTER 23

NIGHTLY NOW THE LONG CURLING-RINK BUILDING GLOWED with light, whispered with the ardent swish of brooms as men slid crab-wise down the narrow rinks ahead of slowly spinning rocks. It was as though the male lifestream of Shelby had suddenly constricted itself to flow with hooting excitement, the roar of granite on ice, the trock-caw of striking rocks, through the booming tunnel of the rink. Although it had been a snowless Christmas, the weather had tightened and the bluely pebbled ice was fast for the Shelby Caledonian Society of Knock-out Curlers' January Bonspiel, won again this year by Skip Willie MacCrimmon and his rink of Malleable Jack Brown, Charlie Tait, and Harvey Hoshal, all men with exquisitely co-ordinated curling arms, nerves of steel, and deadly eyes, who asked and gave no quarter. This year they curled with all the compassion of Covenanters, and the consistent precision of the guillotine. They would quite likely make the provincial finals, and might conceivably go on to win the Macdonald Brier Play-Offs for the championship of Canada and therefore of the world.

Matt did not renew his membership in the curling society; Roy Tregillis took his position as second on Hugh Cameron's rink. Late in January he let his Rotary member-

ship automatically lapse through non-attendance. He was
not sure when he had first entertained the idea of leaving
Shelby, wondered about the possibility of finding a buyer
for the *Chinook*, and considered the opportunities the city
might afford in the way of public relations work with one of
the utility companies or perhaps the larger independent oil
firms.

Although he had not spoken of it to Ruth, he knew that
he had come to a firm decision. He was grateful for the
relief it gave him, like that of the one sober man at a party
who waits only till he can speak to his host and free himself
from the strain of being polite to tipsy guests. It disturbed
him that he had not confided in Ruth, but he would have till
spring to do that, or perhaps earlier, when the Senator was
home for the Easter recess. Once he had made it, his
decision saddened him; he dreaded the time when he must
tell Ruth, and he would not let himself think of what her
response might be.

Now that June Melquist had left, Ruth thought that the most
striking thing about the woman's visit had been its unobtrusive nature, with no clear-cut beginning or ending. No,
that was not right, for she would never forget the ending.
Seven months of deftly practised sleight-of-hand to direct
their attention from herself had been unsuccessful in the
end!

Her stay among them had been unfortunate for Joe
Manley. There could be no uncertainty about that; she
supposed she would never know how unfortunate, but it
was quite evident that Joe had loved and lost, that he had
loved inarticulately, and the losing had been the most
desperate of all: unnoticed defeat.

And for Matt it had been disastrous. For both of them it
had been disastrous! How disastrous she had not really
known until the day before June left, when she came to visit
Ruth at home. Ruth did not know how long before the visit
June had known about the letter. June said that she had
come to say goodbye, but before leaving she brought up the
matter of the letters.

"I know about them," Ruth said.

"Oh." There was no surprise in June's voice. It was as though she had been aware before she came that Ruth knew about the letters.

"This must be a different experience for you," Ruth said.

"I've never been the target of small-town slander before—if that's what you mean."

"Not entirely. What I mean is, I don't think you're— you aren't emotionally engaged in this way—often."

"No."

"It happens to many people quite often, doesn't it?"

"I suppose so."

"But not so often with you as it does with others."

"I don't know," June said.

"You should."

"Why should I?"

"Because I think you make a practice—quite deliberately," Ruth said, "of making sure that it doesn't happen to you. And because I think you're successful at it, and you know you're successful at it." It was the first time that Ruth had ever seen her face flush. She was quite beautiful, actually; it hurt to admit it, but she was.

"Why do you dislike me?" June asked.

It was a question Ruth had asked herself many times in the past seven months, and had been surprised to find that she was not sure that she did dislike her. "I don't know whether I do."

"You do."

"I don't think so. How could I? This is the longest and the most I've ever talked with you. There may have been longer times, but you've never given me anything to build like or dislike out of."

"These letters about Matt and me . . ."

"They're nothing to me," Ruth said.

"Aren't they?"

"No."

"Why aren't they?"

"Because I know Matt." She stared at June. "And I know you."

"You've just said that you didn't know anything about me."

"I don't know anything to like or dislike. That's true. But I do know that if it's difficult for me to know anything about you, then it's difficult for Matt, too. After all, what's the legal term—having carnal knowledge. It would be difficult for a man to have carnal knowledge or even a carnal feeling about you." She could feel the heat rising in her cheeks; she was quite ashamed of herself. "I'm sorry."

June had risen to her feet, her coffee cup left untouched by the couch. "I agree with you. You don't dislike me. You hate me. I can tell you why. My coming to Shelby has upset your husband and you're not clear why it should. I must tell you that it would have happened sooner or later—whether I'd come or I hadn't come. You're a discerning woman and you should have known it long ago. Maybe you have known."

"Known what?"

"That Matt has sold his talents and abilities cheaply here."

"He has not!"

"I don't know why he has, but he . . ."

"He hasn't!"

". . . a lack of iron, perhaps. Circumstances which made him weaken and falter and accept a small audience, small challenges. I feel sorry for him . . ."

"Don't!"

"And for Dr. Fitzgerald and Canon Midford—any of Shelby's professionals. Hostages to fortune."

"All right!" Ruth said. "All right! You've given me something now! If that's what you came here to prove, you have given me something now!"

Now, three months later, with June Melquist two thousand miles away, she knew that she could never forgive her. And she knew that she was not alone in the matter. Not by a long shot!

CHAPTER 24

THERE HAD BEEN LITTLE WARNING AS THERE USUALLY WAS with most foothills storms: the sensed change in atmospheric pressure, the dark curtain that meant hail, the far thunder against the mountains. Yet late in March a storm loosed itself upon Shelby and the surrounding district that was to take its place in community memory along with the flood of 1934, the blue-snow winter of 1906–07, and the Paradise Valley fire of 1923, which had run the length of the eastern slopes and into Montana. This storm, which brought neither flood nor fire nor blizzard, did not ravage lease or farm or town property; no lives were lost. It was an emotional hurricane that spun destructively through heart and mind, laying waste self-esteem and pride and respect.

It began with a Canadian Press item. Carried on an inside page, it was of conventional obituary length under the heading: DEATH OF A FOOTHILLS TOWN.

But the next day all had read the editorial in the local city newspaper that received wide distribution each day across the province. Entitled "Under the Microscope," it told them that a serious sociological study had been completed by Dr. J. L. Melquist for the Chandler Foundation Bureau of Social-Science Research. The survey had already attracted the attention of a national magazine as the latest in

a number of such surveys of small-town communities, all
failing to protect the anonymity of the towns or people or
areas under study.

The Shelby report was particularly brutal in its criti-
cism, a most flagrant invasion of their privacy. The city
editorial questioned Dr. Melquist's conclusion that the town
lacked an encompassing and integrated life in family,
church, or school, or responsible professional and municipal leadership. The editor of the city paper was sure that
citizens of Shelby and district would be surprised to
discover that they lived in a dying community unaware that
it had long ceased to fulfill its function as a market town,
and was in fact the casualty of an agricultural revolution
evidenced by the flight of its youth from furrow to city, and
the swallowing up of many of its smaller farms into larger
mechanized holdings, which foreshadowed the imminent
decease of the foothills ranch economically dependent on
government leasing of public parklands.

The front-page news story the next day singled out
much more hurtful detail. Shelby's treatment of Paradise
Valley Reserve Indians was unforgivably racist. The Hutterites in their colony west of Shelby were the target of
ridicule and contempt comparable to the treatment of Jews
in Nazi Germany. Throughout Shelby district, the illiteracy
rate was higher than that of the North-West Territories.
Child abuse, both physical and sexual, in or out of the
home, was endemic. Though the town crime rate was low,
rustling in the lease area was high. Alcoholism in town and
country probably would set a *Guinness Book of World
Records* all-time record. The Shelby town council had never
heard of social welfare.

Within hours after the city paper had reached Shelby,
the survey had become the main topic of conversation in
homes, on street corners, and on party lines. Feelings ran
high in the forums of Malleable Jack Brown's blacksmith
shop, Harvey Hoshal's barber shop, Willie MacCrimmon's
Shoe and Harness, the Post Office, the Palm Café, the pool
hall, and the Arlington Beer Parlour. It was Rotary night, so
that current club business was pushed aside for discussion
of the survey. Later in the evening Mayor Oliver called a

special meeting of the town council, to which Matt Stanley was invited.

When the meeting broke up well after midnight, Matt knew that he had little to report beyond bewildered hurt. He promised that he would obtain a copy of the survey for them as soon as he could. Before going home he stopped at the office to phone the managing editor of the city paper that had printed the editorial. Driving home he realized that his confusion must be almost as great as anybody's in Shelby, but he was too tired to sort out his feelings and to discuss the survey even with Ruth. He did not go in to her but instead slipped into bed in the spare room. As with many others in the town, sleep came reluctantly to him that night.

The survey arrived the next day. It was not a survey paper intended only for pedagogic eyes. To his horror he saw that it was a fat paperback, published evidently for public consumption by Eastern University Press. He took it back to the office. His eye ran over the island of acknowl-edgements in the centre of one of the front pages and the sight of his own name startled him.

"With special thanks for the generous and helpful co-operation of Matthew B. Stanley, publisher and editor of the *Shelby Chinook.*"

He turned the page. It was not, he soon realized, going to be easy reading with the eye stuttering between paragraph and footnote, progressing as it must like Eliza with her baby over the sociological stream from statistical cake to statis-tical cake of tabled data.

"Households By Number Of Persons And Average Number Of Persons Per Household, Rural Farm, Rural Ranch, Urban."

It was wonderfully impersonal and cold to be so inflammatory. The sociological prose was dedicated always to the use of the Latin- or Greek-derived word, to hyphen-ated diad and triad terms, to intransitive and copulative verbs, or, if unavoidably transitive, hamstrung by the passive voice, rendered quite mindless by the absence of personal pronouns. Academic pig Latin!

"Occupied Dwellings By Tenure, Showing Water Sup-ply, Bath, And Toilet Facilities."

Yet it was possible to discern, through the abstracting

mist, the community beneath. Now and again he glimpsed the town as one might fleetingly catch a familiar face in swirling fog, often his ear heard or thought it heard known voices. They were clearly the voices of Sam Barnes, Nettie Fitzgerald, Clem Derrigan, once or twice Joe Manley. More often than he cared to guess the voice was his own. Most often of all: Flannel Mouth Florence.

The survey's conclusions were hard and unmistakable, not only the more measurable economic ones mentioned by the city editorial, but those summing up fragile community traits of manners and custom and spirit. For ten years Shelby's population had remained almost constant in a cultural wasteland; the close association of its people caused any eccentricity to be quickly noted, and the mass were quite ready to show their disapproval. Religious tensions in the town were strong, and conflict between town and country was close to the surface. Though the civic leaders enjoyed prestige, they were not in any customary sense an upper class, for the true elite of Shelby were the North Siders, who showed little interest in conducting municipal affairs. Many of these socially privileged were members of the professions, who had come to Shelby and stayed in its shelter rather than face the more demanding competition of urban practice. This group paid only lip service to the puritanical and conventional standards of the rest of the community. Shelby contradicted the myth of Western warmth and hospitality, for its people were slow to accept the outsider. When not downright disagreeable with each other, Shelby people were earnestly dull, their humour a primitive and mordant one erecting its amusement always upon a foundation of exaggeration and sarcasm.

He was not sure whose idea the community indignation meeting was, but two days after Matt had turned the book over to him, Mayor Oliver brought into the *Chinook* office the notice alerting all Shelby and district residents for 7:30 P.M., March 30, at the Civic Centre. Three days later, because excitement about the forthcoming meeting was so strong in the town, Aunt Fan's death went almost unnoticed. She had simply not wakened on the morning of March 27. No one had known until noon of March 28, for Millie Clocker had taken leave of absence from her switchboard on advice from Dr. Fitzgerald; it was pretty generally believed in Shelby that Millie had suffered a nervous breakdown, and that it would be a long time before she had completed her treatment at the provincial mental hospital. So it had been Chuck Fowler, on his meter rounds for the gas company, who had noticed that a light still burned in the room beyond the kitchen of Aunt Fan's suite. He assumed that she must have gone out without turning it off, and stepped inside the door to do it for her, to discover the bedclothes trailing half on the floor and Aunt Fan with head and arms pendant.

Dr. Fitzgerald had been called. Aunt Fan was moved across the street and up to the second floor of Ollie Pringle's Funeral Parlour. Her funeral was held the day of the evening indignation meeting, in St. Aidan's church, almost half filled and with Hersch Midford officiating. Matt Stanley, Mr. Oliver, Dr. Fitzgerald, and the Senator, home from Ottawa for two weeks, were her pall-bearers. Mr. Oliver had been much more than that, actually, for he had made all the arrangements which would have been handled by relatives, had there been any. He confided in Matt that with the disposal of her building and the payment to the town of tax arrears, there would be just enough to take care of Ollie Pringle, the plot, and a modest headstone.

Although Ruth tried to dissuade him, the Senator insisted on going out to the graveside service in the cemetery, which he had visited for the first time half a century before, when Sid Bovey had been stood to rest. He would see Aunt Fan through to the completing handful of thrown dirt, and he would take a nap before the meeting.

The Senator was not optimistic about the indignation meeting. It seemed somehow wrong that shame should be made a public matter; that sort of talk could not diminish mortification, and accomplished so little. Now that he looked back upon the men with whom he'd ridden, beside whom he'd squatted before a branding fire or hooked heels on corral poles—they had not been all that prodigal with words. Contemplation seemed to have fallen into disrepute; there was no time for it now—just talk in Senates, and

Houses of Commons, and board meetings, and all the
conventions of plumbers and florists and manufacturers and
teachers and doctors and accountants and stock growers—
they all had their talking conventions. Over the whole
nation the sky hummed and strummed to the talk of the
vigorous young male and female shills of radio and television. The atmosphere must be stunned with their *en masse*
talking, like the rabble yammer of a nocturnal pack of
coyotes around a lump-jaw steer carcass! He was so damned
tired of talk.

The book on Shelby had disturbed him terribly. His
response to it had upset him even more; no lusty sense of
outrage, only a feeling of hopelessness, and the discovery
that his faith had flagged and his vision languished. It was
upsetting to admit to himself that he had truly entered the
dry and windless doldrums of final old age, that he was tired
of the shortcomings and weaknesses and pettinesses of
human creatures and their penny-ante games and toy rituals.
The midnight hour had come for Aunt Fan. It was near for
him, too, and soon the desire to live would falter and
weaken a hair too much. Pall-bearer this afternoon. Pall-
bearers' burden next year or next month or next week. His
role was a matter of little concern to him now. Little at all.

Ruth had managed to get Rowena to stay with Sarah for the
funeral and for the evening as well; the Senator drove with
them to the Civic Centre. Matt had to let Ruth and her father
out at the entrance, since the streets were lined with trucks
and cars for two blocks in every direction. When he
returned from parking, he found the hall filled; rows of
extra chairs had been brought in and lined along the back;
all were occupied; men stood and leaned against the walls.
Bob Thompson met him, told him that the Senator had gone
backstage and that there was a place at the front for him
with Ruth. As he walked after Bob down the side aisle he
could feel the dry breath of concert hall heat against his
cheek, smell the lemon pungency of sweeping-compound,
the bitterness of countless shoes and boots polished for just
this occasion. He saw that a long row of empty chairs stood

on the stage. The table waiting at their centre held a glass and a water pitcher.

In his seat next to Ruth, he sat with waiting eyes patiently to the front. He watched a little girl of Sarah's age with starched skirt holding out stiffly from her bare legs run to the edge of the space between the front row and the stage. She stood hesitant, the tie ribbons dangling from her bonnet, discovered the audience, then with face stricken rushed back to her mother's knee. Nettie Fitzgerald rose from her place near the steps and went up to the piano at the left of the stage. As she spun the stool it shrieked; there came a preparatory shuffling of feet, a coughing and clearing of throats. She raised her hands warningly over the keys; the hall filled with the concerted creak and scrape and knock of people rising. Her hands fell unerringly upon the opening chords of "O Canada!"

The audience had hardly settled back into their seats when Mayor Oliver strode out from the wings. He was followed by the Senator, Mr. Spafford and Mr. Buller from the school board, Dr. Fitzgerald in his role as president of the Activarians, Canon Midford, Father McNulty, Roy Tregillis from the bank, and Macey Bowdry, president of the Farmers' Union. After a preliminary shuffle rather like an abortive game of musical chairs, they were seated. Mayor Oliver stood up behind the table.

In his usual solemn style Oliver opened the meeting. He outlined the charges that had been made against their town. They were not true, he assured them; after forty-eight years in Shelby, thirty of them in public life, he knew that they simply were not true.

This was the same statement made again and again throughout the evening. There was little else that could be said, Matt thought, and not a great deal was being accomplished by the reiteration—now solemn, now hurt, now angry, now bewildered, always earnest. There was a desperate quality to their earnestness, he thought, as though they all had their backs to the wall, yet each helpless one of them seemed to face a private and invisible enemy of his own, sharing only a common darkness as they had the night the town had been invaded by the Napoleon goats.

Matt felt that Hersch's address was not one of his best;

intended as a tribute, it seemed to have stolen some of its sad flavour from the eulogy he had given in the afternoon for Aunt Fan. When the Canon's precise British voice had finished, Mayor Oliver invited comment from the audience; for long and embarrassing moments there was none, then a small commotion boiled at the back of the hall. People seemed to sense the diversion through the backs of their necks, and heads turned round toward the source.

Hand tips tucked into the front pockets of his faded Levi's, negligently loose and smooth-gaited, Rory Napoleon came down the aisle. All eyes followed his progress. At the front he did not pause; he turned and went along to the open space below the stage. He mounted the steps. He walked to the platform centre. He stopped before Mayor Oliver and the other town dignitaries there. The light caught all the pens and pencils in his jacket breast pockets. Chin to his shoulder he turned his body slightly, weight on one foot, the toe of one riding boot lifting and turning on the pivot of the worn high heel.

"Mr. Chairman."

He turned back to the audience. "Citizens of Shelby." He pursed his lips while his eyes roved across the people below him, the light glistening from the film of sweat that lay over his ridged cheeks. "I seen by the papers what's happened to this town an' I listened here tonight. I got somethin' to say on this, an' it's this. Maybe you got a lot more than what's comin' to you—maybe a lot of what you got *was* comin' to you. An' maybe us Napoleons know that better'n anyone else here tonight.

"We're leavin' you—tomorrow—for the Yukon. Maybe it ain't gonna be all razzberries an' honey there, but she can't be any worse there than she's been for us here."

He raised his hand at the mutter of protest that rose in front of him. "All right, all right. A lot of you figger it ain't any skin off your—knuckles—where the Napoleons go. Well, it will for a while, I promise you, right until you get somebody else to haul your goddam garbage an' empty your goddam cans and pump your goddam cesspools. Just you look on the bright side as they say. It'll give you somethin' to talk about at Rot'ry an' over your bridge tables an' church suppers. Them that ain't on the sewer can visit them that is—an' there's always the side roads."

He turned away, then back again. "We ain't holdin' anything against you. We'll keep in touch through the pages the *Shelby Chinook*. Be glad to have you visit me an' Mame an' the kids if you're ever up Yukon way. That goes for almost all of you, an' I won't mention no names."

He hesitated a moment, then said, "That's all."

As he passed their place near the back of the hall, Mame and the children rose and fell in behind him; the pride of Napoleons left the hall.

CHAPTER 25

IT DISTURBED HIM THAT HE WAS NOT THINKING CLEARLY AND effectively; any sort of disciplined consideration had persistently eluded him since he had come home from the meeting. Only rabbit thoughts bolted from cover and into erratic flight, startled now in one direction, then another, circling back upon themselves without goal.

He wondered how many others lay awake in Shelby homes, trying to reassure themselves, unable to forget in sleep. He had known he would not be able to sleep. As though by earlier agreement he and Ruth had not discussed the town meeting, just as they might not mention a mutually embarrassing matter out of kindness to each other. She seemed to have stayed away longer than the checking of Sarah's covers required. He had undressed more quickly than usual and was in bed when she returned from the baby's room.

It had been some time before her breathing had become the even, regular sigh of sleep; momentarily he envied her, wished that he had talked with her about the meeting. About the meeting and about themselves and about their future. The night chinook grieved along the house eave, finding new and deeper sorrow as it thrummed the metal edge of the bedroom window weather-stripping. From outside came distant percussion—decisive—rhythmic—concerto for un-latched back gate.

The persistent ticking of Ruth's alarm clock was not going to permit him sleep. He rolled over gingerly away from her, carefully lowered his feet to the floor, and found his way to the end of the bed. His hand discovered the bathrobe there; he slipped it on and tiptoed from the room. Under the bland light of the lamp by the chesterfield he lit a cigarette. He had escaped the alarm clock and the banging back gate but not the wind. Here in the living-room it was a tactile rather than an audibly sensed force. The house stirred perceptibly, forgetting night-time patience and show-ing just a little concern for the well-being of its sleeping occupants.

From doorway to fireplace his eye wandered along Sarah's evening spoor: the tattered spine of a home and garden journal, the remains of one of his fishing and hunting magazines, the stubby scissors with which she had chewed them, doll's dishes, scattered cards, her pink plastic brush and comb and mirror, crayons, a sieve, and a wooden potato-masher. At his feet a top canted on its side, striped gold and royal blue and mallard green and red. Raggedy Ann with her improbably orange yarn hair lay beside him on the chesterfield.

He nudged the stem of the top with a toe; it rolled away from him in a brief arc around its point. Looking back now he couldn't for the life of him understand why he had never felt concern, or any need for caution with June Melquist. He should have. Oh God, how he should have! It was no excuse that she had been a good operator. She sure as hell had been. She listened well, knew how to wait those extra few seconds to elicit more, never interrupted or contra-dicted. What skilled sleight-of-tongue she'd pulled off, with wanted answers hidden up her sleeve the whole six months she'd been with them in Shelby.

It was significant that not a person at the meeting had seemed to blame him for what had been done to them and to their town. Certainly none of those whose opinion mattered most to him. Yet he had introduced June to them, helped her into their confidence, their homes, their clubs, their parties. In a sense he, too, had judged and found Harry Fitzgerald incompetent in his profession, and Canon Midford and Joe Manley. Just as much as June he had publicly declared their community a dying one, an inhospitable one, a bickering and intolerant town of people without cultural taste, without social tradition or economic future, leading dull and petty lives of unimaginative conformity.

He was guilty. Had June not come to Shelby he would still have been guilty. Sooner or later he would have turned from them and left them as he now planned to leave them. And as the Napoleons planned to leave them. He could only guess at what had compelled the man to display and express himself so forcefully before the whole assembled town tonight; perhaps the Napoleon hurt had much in common with his own.

He leaned forward, picked up the top. It had been a glorious present from Nettie Fitzgerald, the first thing under the tree to catch Sarah's Christmas morning attention. When he had pumped it vigorously, the lozenge-shaped holes around its equator had whined out a fainting, strengthening musical moan, which had first fascinated Sarah, then saddened her, and finally frightened her. She would not let anyone spin it for her, yet next to her Raggedy Ann it was her most precious possession.

Ironically the score had been evened; he had no reason to be distressed. They had collectively slandered him and June. In turn, he and June had held them up to contempt and ridicule and blame. Who was to say which was worse: the slander of one—or rather two—by three thousand; or the slander of three thousand by two.

There was no honesty in that, and no comfort. The survey was not true of them; perhaps it stated some truths, but it did not mirror Shelby. Even when angry disenchantment had distorted his vision most, he would have known the falseness of the reflection. .

He stared at the glittering top and the gothic lettering in gilt around the stem: GLORIA CHORAL. He set the point on the floor, and pumped it idly. As colours melted and ran together it borrowed a soft hum from some celestial hive. He pumped it strongly into louder, more solemn harmony. He punched it savagely till the goddam thing hooted.

He knew that Shelby could never be captured in a coarse net. Too much life minnowed through the statistical mesh; the individuality of people, the first gopher or crocus of spring, the combing of a calf-club entry, the wonderful comfort of a little sleeping girl's buttocks cupped in the hand, the death of a family pet, Webb Bolton's boils, and Mrs. Charlie Tait's gall bladder, all the terribly brilliant sensuous fragments that built the poetry of earth and the poetry of man. Millie Clocker and Aunt Fan's virgin loneliness, Nettie Fitzgerald's North Side snobbery and Harry's angry impatience, Sam Barnes's misanthropy, Joe Manley's tired and uncertain cynicism, the Napoleons' anarchy, Mr. Oliver's sterile equations of law and decree—all must spin together, must blend and blur and whirl to balance. Each unique Shelby soul must give its special gift of momentum. But they had not really been asked to spin in a living balance in the abstract world of Dr. Melquist, for she had propped it too skillfully with trend and generality, supported it with statistic and scale and modality. It stood. It was held upon its point. Dead.

Sarah's top had been gradually dying. Its song dissolved to low mourning. It fell, ran on its side along the rug, stopped.

Why must a person ignore individual men and women and be satisfied with the dimming vision of the herd and their "commonalities"? Consider the magnificence of one boil on Webb Bolton's neck; admire the immortality of Daddy Sherry and his sinewy old heart still pumping after one hundred and seven years. How unsatisfying the unhearable music of the spheres was when compared to the Jew's-harp melody twanging through the cave where man touched man, heard man, saw man, smelled man, loved man, and hurt man!

He was holding the Raggedy Ann doll he had picked up from beside himself on the chesterfield. He stared down at the button eyes and the triangle nose; the peppermint-striped tube legs flopped loosely as he turned it over and back again. If he lifted the apron, the skirt, and the petticoat, he knew he would find the valentine heart drawn in red on the flat bosom. The scrawl within the heart would say as it did to Sarah fifty times a day: "I love you."

He did not love all of them; he loved some of them; he respected or disrespected some of them; he suffered some of them; he trusted or he distrusted some of them; he admired some of them; he pitied some of them; he had never, as he had not so long ago thought, hated all of them. But one thing that neither he nor anybody else could do successfully in Shelby was to *ignore* any of them.

He had betrayed *all* of them. The survey denied individual life to each of them. It did what not one of them familiar with the others could validly do—damn them one and all. It damned them to themselves. It damned them to their nation. It allowed them no defence, gave them no day in court. Indeed, they had no court to hear them. To whom could they address their defence? What judicial panel could they argue before? With what voice could they plead? What collective voice?

He knew now of course, for the masthead of the *Shelby Chinook* had been announcing itself as "The Voice of the Foothills" ever since his Uncle Ben had come West in 1902. The people of Shelby had been held up to national blame, ridicule, contempt, and humiliation. The important shame was the one they felt before each other, in the eyes of their friends, their own.

He could just do it! He would have to go down to the office now, work right through till dawn! Even as he went back to the bedroom for his clothes he was mentally doing the editorial:

It seems high time that someone from our foothills went to an Eastern city to study the manners and mores of the social life there. If, from an academic perspective, *their* customs and ways of thinking did not conform with our comportment here, then of course *they* would be in the wrong.

Our town has been the target for such an investigation. . . .

It had come from his typewriter hot and rough and artesian, yellow sheets growing on the desk beside him. He had gone far beyond the projected editorial now. He pushed back his chair, got up and began to pace the office, pausing at the filing cabinet, swinging around, back to look over what he had already written, then round the room again, running a hand through his hair. He took out a package of cigarettes, struck a match, threw himself into the chair.

While the doctor was gathering material for her survey we wonder if she saw the St. Aidan's women taking turns doing Aunt Fan's washing for her during the illness that preceded her death. Or, speaking of death, did she see Mrs. Nelligan walking across town with pies, Mrs. Thompson with a baked ham, Mrs. Leppard with chicken, or Mrs. Oliver with flowers to the home of the Jess Richardsons where all the near and distant relatives had gathered two days before the funeral. This is custom in Shelby when a loved one has died.

We wonder if she saw the neighbours south of town seeding Melvin Parker's farm for him when he lay helpless in hospital. Did she see those same neighbours doing his summer fallowing? Did she see their combines threshing his crop at harvest time?

He knew now that it would be a special edition—without classifieds and the Chinook Round-up if necessary.

We know the learned doctor visited the St. Aidan's Thanksgiving Supper given in the basement October 19, but did she notice the bits of coloured string tied to the knives and forks and spoons of the people who'd lent them? Did she know that the yarned knives and forks and spoons were not all Anglican knives and forks and spoons, that some were Baptist, others Continuing Presbyterian, a few Catholic? The occasion was not nearly so ecumenical as Canon Midford's Christmas choir made up of the foregoing faiths as well as Mormon, Dutch Reformed, and members of the

Church of the Burning Nazareth. How possibly can she say that religious tensions and conflict are strong in our town? Shelby does *not* have an Orangemen's Lodge or a branch of the KKK.

If our professional men are here in Shelby, it is because they like the way of life in this small foothills community, not because they are unable to face the competition of larger centres, too uncertain in their training and skill for metropolitan practice. We know that our doctor is respected by other doctors throughout the province as a surgeon and diagnostician. We respect him for other reasons as well; he is a fine human and a deadly wing shot. We feel the same about Canon Midford, Father McNulty, and Captain Leppard. Our teachers will do, too, for they have turned out their share of Governor General's Medal winners, and in the past twenty years two Rhodes Scholars.

Of course we have no social structure. The hired man or the hired girl eats with the rest of the family.

Dr. Melquist was here during our August hailstorm. She must have seen the piling white clouds that trailed their streaks over Shelby district. She must have known that the crops were in and up and ripening, and an entire year's income was at the mercy of the skies. Surely she must have seen the upward glances given by people as they entered the Palm Café for a soda, the Arlington Beer Parlour for a beer, the Post Office. And when they came out of these places, she must have seen their eyes turn skywards again. It was a five- to ten-thousand-dollar concern to them.

After the first rolling crack of thunder came, the storm that battered and smashed Arnolds' let Hargraves' across the road go scot-free. It destroyed Milton Williamson and missed his neighbour, Tom Saunders. MacDonalds were ruined and Coopers. Those who were hit threshed nothing. But there was no whining. They had lost a whole year's income. Had they lived in a city, it would have been as though the family's wage earner had been laid off for the entire year. No money for groceries, for birthday presents, for a son or daughter's year at university, for a new tractor, for Christmas, a new stove, wallpaper for the living-room. And they simply said that it was *their* turn this year. That now—in August—they had ice to make a freezer of ice cream. They joked about it. They laughed at it. Ruefully. What might be called a dry joke or a dry laugh. They can be sardonic. We think you missed that in many of us, Dr. Melquist.

In the matter of our wit—we are quite sure that humour cannot be measured or calibrated or correlated. But we do recognize that much of ours is exaggeration. We live in a country of exaggerations, of drought and hail and blizzard and, often, loneliness. We have so much horizon and so much sky that a man sometimes feels a little like a fly on a platter. He knows his vulnerability, and perhaps his humour has become utilitarian in that he laughs at things that can hurt him most. At winters and how cold they are—at summers and how hot they are. We truly have the world's deepest snow, Dr. Melquist, the worst dust storms, the biggest hailstones, the most agile grasshoppers. Rust and dust and smut and hail and sawfly and cutworm are terrible things, but not half so frightening if they are made ridiculous. If we can laugh at them, we have won half the battle. Perhaps our humour is a defence. Perhaps. You also find it mordant. All right. Any man who laughs at death, laughs at his own mortality, and that is not so much evidence of wit as it is of magnificent bravery.

We are all right, Dr. Melquist.

The world's greatest known election of dinosaur skeletons exists along the banks of the Red Deer River, near Drumheller, Alberta.

He looked up to the framed masthead of the *Chinook* and the Pulitzer Prize beside it.

"How am I doing, Uncle Ben?"

"Not bad, boy. Not bad at all. *This* piece. But that dinosaur tag won't do."

"Yes, Uncle Ben."

"Never close anything off just for deadline reasons. Another thing. Always double-check your sources. You do, of course. She doesn't know what I'm talking about. Protect people's privacy. Better than I did. Aim true every time. No shooting from the hip. 'Those up, shoot up. Those down, down.' Excepting politicians. Once they go public, they're issued bullet-proof vests."

"I know, Uncle Ben."

"Another thing. The foothills needs voices like yours and mine. So does the rest of the world. I want you to hang in there and forget about . . ."

"Wait a minute . . ."

"Just because you're in Shelby doesn't mean you can't reach a wider audience. I did. You can, too. I have a suggestion for you. Right now you can be heard outside Shelby district. Do a paperback. You've got the presses for it."

"I'll think about it."

"No! Do it! And by the way—that Anglican priest— Midford—he isn't loose in the wrist with those young boys the way she implies, is he?"

"Hell, no!"

"All right. Do it for him and all the others. Thirty."

He saw that it was now full daylight. He switched off the desk lamp, stood up and stretched. He walked to the door and took down his coat. He wouldn't wait to run the issue before he told Ruth.

On the step just outside the office door he stopped. The eaves were dripping, the air was alive with moisture. What a wonderful and warm and compassionate thing a chinook was, thawing snow and earth and man!

He turned back into the office and took off his coat. He ran a sheet of paper into the typewriter. There would be room for just one Chinook Round-up item. Perfect tag.

The many friends of the Rory Napoleons will be sorry
to hear that they have left Shelby and we wish them
well in their new home in the Yukon. Mrs. Mame

Napoleon will be best remembered as the winner last year of the Champion Cup in the Shelby Annual Perennial and Annual Flower Show. This was for a perfect hybrid apricot tea rose, and growing it was a supreme achievement, for roses are difficult here.

ABOUT THE AUTHOR

W. O. MITCHELL, the only Canadian author recognizable by initials alone, was born in Weyburn, Saskatchewan in 1914. Educated at the University of Manitoba, he has lived most of his life in Saskatchewan, Ontario, and Alberta. For many years he lived in High River, where he gained a deep understanding of small-town life in the foothills. He and his wife, Merna, now live in Calgary.

During a very varied career Bill Mitchell has travelled widely (originally as an uninvited guest on CPR freight trains) and has been everything from a deckhand to the fiction editor of *Maclean's*. A gifted teacher, he was a visiting professor at the University of Windsor for several years, and a creative writing instructor at the Banff Centre for many summers. He is also a legendary performer reading from his own works.

Of these, his best-loved book is *Who Has Seen the Wind*. Since its publication in 1947, it has sold over half a million copies in Canada alone, and is hailed as the great Canadian classic of boyhood. Complementing that book is his 1981 best-seller *How I Spent My Summer Holidays*, hailed by some critics as his finest novel, although *Since Daisy Creek* (1984) and the haunting *Ladybug, Ladybug . . .* (1988) were also best-sellers. Besides *The Kite* (1962) and *The Vanishing Point* (1973) he is also noted for his two collections of short stories, *Jake and the Kid* (1962) and *According to Jake and the Kid* (1989). Based on the legendary CBC radio series, which ran from 1950 to 1956 and delighted audiences around the world from here to Australia, both classic story collections won the Stephen Leacock Award for Humour.

Our novelist and script-writer is also a successful playwright whose five plays are included in the collection entitled *Dramatic W. O. Mitchell*. He was made an Officer of the Order of Canada in 1973 and has been the subject of a National Film Board documentary. He is, in Pierre Berton's words, "an original".